DOGOD

works by Bill Reed

The Pipwink Papers\
Me, the Old Man
Stigmata
Ihe
Dogod
Crooks
Tusk
Throw her back
Are You Human?
Tasker Tusker Tasker
Awash
1001 Lankan Nights book 1
1001 Lankan Nights book 2

(Nonfiction)
Water Workout

plays
Burke's Company
Truganinni
The Pecking Order
Mr Siggie Morrison with his Comb and Paper*
The Old Pig Rat
Jack Charles is Up and Fighting
Just Out of Your Ground
You Want It, Don't You, Billy?
I Don't Know What to Do with You!
Paddlesteamer
Cass Butcher Bunting
Bullsh
More Bullsh
Talking to a Mirror
Auntie and the Girl

award-winning short stories *(see title 'Passing Strange')*
Messman on the C.E. Altar
English Expression
The 200-year Old Feet
The Case Inside
Blind Freddie Among the Pickle Jars
The Old Ex-serviceman
Mahood on the Thin Beach
The Shades of You my Dandenong

Bill Reed

DOGOD

a novel

3

This reprint published in all formats independently by Reed Independent, 2015, Melbourne, Australia

First published under ISBN 0170051463 by Thomas Nelson (Australia) Ltd in 1977

Printed by CreateSpace, an Amazon.com company

Available from Amazon.com, CreateSpace.com, and other major retail outlets around the world. Ebook formats are available from all major online ebook retailers.
paperback: ISBN13-9780994280527
ebook: ISBN13-9780994280534

National Library of Australia Cataloguing-in-Publication entry
Creator: Reed, Bill, 1939-author.
Title: Dogod / Bill Reed.
ISBN: 9780994280527 (paperback)
Subject: fiction
Dewey Number: A823.3

National Library of Australia Cataloguing-in-Publication entry
Creator: Reed, Bill, 1939-author.
Title: Dogod / Bill Reed.
ISBN: 9780994280534 (ebook)
Subject: fiction
Dewey Number: A823.3

To Bruce and his speaking Dogod-like personality

AMOS

Meseemingly a whole anno has turned as quick as a page pass. A prestigious year palmed on us in less time than it takes to toss up and wrist a flick. Generations of termites have come and gone; we lumber, aye. We bare remember whence we came, came we why, whycame betides, springing neaply from soar to sure. Save that Nora the Knob Gnawer has some of us in her graspy, while the sickleman ripes on upon. In troth.

(It must be a Dogod's life, since the Lord is our Shepherd.)

We are now up in Sydney, where we have a clear case of misplaced dogs' turds or cynical cynorrhoea, however you will have it. All the lottery kiosks in that metropolis and a growing groaning, both, number of State runey lottery ticket vendors don't have much choice how they will have it. They are getting it right on their doorsteps right in the middle of their footways right in broad daylight in the morning right when they are coming to work. Left right full and centre spread. Some dog's calling cad, it is, too!

By the left hand screw sausage pile it does seem the workings out of one poopy pooch. By the olfactory offence given and taken, there can be few such skunks in the dog community. And who could have thought that a bow wow doing his Bigs could produce enough produce for all the lottery vendoffices all over Sydneytown and even on the Opera House itself last night which, to give the awakeddity of the local police a wide berth, was the final blast, the end. Though, to admit it, the police did consider that, compared to the compered artyficial shit going on inside Opera Shouse, the real shit dog-deponed on the steps outside is positively flatulentti afflatus. Except for a one Constable Wilkinson, that is.

(dog knocks off man in two seconds flatus)

He, Constable Wilkinson, Sydney CID, in a moment of laxation, was the simple cause for a dire redirection of the search-section. He was spatulating one of these stinking piles into an exhibit envelope one night, during the dog watch, when he observed amongst the dogs worms, stirring it up in there, a gold filling. He did. At first he thought it to be a lighted lantern around which eels played and frolicked, as in Yorick. But then the good Constable thought, deeply thwarting his mind, dogs are not normally partial towards the consumption of gold fillings. Not alone, without there being other human remains. Nor had any dogs that he ever knew to live by the human scale have gold fillings for the upgrade tearing of human flesh. So what Constable Wilkinson idea'd, even though it caused a flash in his pan, was to send his specimen to Forensic, and they or it, in turn,

(hunting hound finds man with no meat on his bones just a drag)

discovered it to be neither bow-wow Bigs nor Fido faeces but the squittery shards of an unknown human hotdog, alias, alas!, a Mr. Fido Bigs. A trumped up turd nonetheless! Yes, and. It was then that the hunt turned to flushing out the infamous dog-shitter Fiedoe Bigs (real name Mr X) from amongst the city's three million pop. This mongrel amongst men! What mite he be? And, this is where we are at now, now that we have chronicled a caught up. Aye, and, as for Constable Wilkinson? He is around, around. Off course, but per rimming round, round. Rmm, rrrmmm.

(madly impetuous dog goes crazy over a woman)

Now we have Scotty, man not dog, despite a same blessed semblance. Scotty, as he swalks on and on in onanistic paces, has some else semblance to something familiar in his face. Alias? Yes, but

(five loafers and two dogfishes; Christ!)

2

for the moment we will let this pass as willy-nillingly as most of the women Fannies who pass him are unwilling to see him go by without a willing noddy at them. And those who do not care about his passing must be either geriatric, or jerryacting nonchalance. Or chugging along with the aid of walkie-talkies to add their sightless blinds. One or two transistorised, too, of course.

Anyway, Scotty is passing blithely along the street, although this is no ordinary street, nuh huh, for this is a Sydney street. And no maestro of the smiting word has ever attempted as yet to describble how wordinary a Sydney street can be. Though it is a bondage duty to mention that this street is a shade or two above the ordinary other Sydney streets, owing to the presence of Scotty trawling for trolls along a trillalee-lovelee-dayee down it. Concrete concourse, of course, and lunch houris' time.

(tombstoned His Master's Voice, Got Carried Away)

Scotty in wool-laned checked strides strides along this street, as we say, to the fluttering of butterfly eyes hiswaywise. Common c'mon reactions to which our Scotty great deigns a lipcurl or two. Aye, and a day of given grace it is generally too. A brilliant sparkling skyling vaults the up-there unbrushed by the cotton wads on meteoro-instrumental downturns, ah yes, and. Scotty in dazzle'o'daz, to match. His hair gleams, set to sheen. His pearlies are pure patina. His limpid pools clear blue i do azure you. Mien hardly of a mean man; the whole Olympian of him oozes like a Donis to a Red Cross blood bank. It is and he strolls. Scotty thrills. He stalls dollops of trollops. A troll here, a Molly Coddles there; hie a fern, hoc an ale. What a trawling trail, by trawl and error! Here at last is a human man that we can write on who is about to be woman kind. If you dare, personally. But,

(make a contented dog your target for today)

soft, what piaculars? A strong and stony stongo that is gathering moss? For is not that old man, known as Amos, umbilical and unbiblical, following Scotty? Openly and in public, not caring which. True! Trousseau much it hurts! Amos, the ancient, new in

3

our chronicle, yes. Old Amos, crone plated to our Scotty, doing that Mandarin two-step shiff-shoofph of his, and causing the only two phonemes he can remember to keep time, going: 'Bloody bloody bloody...' and not at all disgeared if Scotty up-revs, or if Scotty de-celeries. No. Unloseable.

(Tombstone inscription: Hear Told He Was A Dogs Body)

He, the Amos, is so old that nobody could even guess at his stupefaction for skin and boneossify. Beneath that skthin covering there is now only a mangled mass of what was once divine precision engineering. 'Strue; Amos is so old that it is said he is adzeless. So, it is

(dog catches on to what dog-trainer is all about)

Amos atuggingly following our Scotty flagship in line-astern along Castlereagh Street on a midday prom. When Scotty has to stop at a corner where a red light is refusing to change until all who wait to cross this Sydney road have signed next-of-kin forms. Having the bland inanimate impertinence to make even Scotty wait. When Amos takes the opportunity of the portside to align his ancient creepitude into an auraawful snuggle with the inner snug of Scotty's armpit. And crooning, like the crone he is, up at Sc.:

'Watcha bloody doin' whereya bloody goin'...?'

A case of bum over bounce. Arse longa. Especially when all those people there, tippy by toey, try to gain access to pieces of public asphalt as wells fargo as posse away from the pong of Scotty stuck with Amos. Nevertheless, our

(dog hanging around the river bank after scum)

zoetic Scotty maintains blithe blinkers in blinking well, and merely smiles handsomely. Amos is cooing like a turtle. He doves so to. And clucking hen-talk, a pecking disorder, into the handpicked follicles under Scotty's armpits, frizzed earlier by packed folicurlers. Nor can pinpointed side kicks fracture the old bugger's body huggers. Nor likely to prise open his growing purchase on the Scotty merchandise, never before been known to be handed out free. Leaving only one course open. So, like a

(head dog only wants to pick your brains)

shoot off by a shogun, Scotty does a 007 stroke and dash in double quick time acriss the crossroad, cross against the red lights. Just as, inevitably, Constable Wilkinson is cruising around, around nearby in his craven cruiser. Yet as it happens, the good Constable was then, in that rare fledge of moment, not seeing, and did not redhanded catch the Scooting in his anti-red selfpropulsion. Never mind. That doesn't mean Constable Wilkinson isn't still around, around. Alert as ether. A rest assured, too. Going to be needed.

(rifle through a dog's rib cage)

Now, there are a number of ways of crossing a busy intersection against the red lights in Sydney town on a trading midday, none of which are biotically fructifying on how to defy double crossing thyself or Thy Maker. But this time Scotty is the me in phenomenon. He is. The mi in miracle, too. Last seen in the disappearing trick, it and he.

And when Amos tries to follow quick-marx too, he is immediately run down by a debble of a double page spread of a wind-swept newspaper whipped up into a coup d'oily eye image of a runaway risqué car. Causing confusion, and. Women gasped, did lurk out and lurch, did they shout. Some screamed, some creamed, some crying shame. Cops on pointer duty are encompassed coming passed, aye. Even cars confuse contuse. Meanwhile,

(Ma Kettle, it's okay now; the dog's satisfied with your boil)

Scotty is already a hundred metres, give or tyke, further onforward. And right turns pronto at the first shopping maul, through which he flies glissando. Leather to gloss tiles. Yes. Then

5

doubles back in on himself, being, too, a master of contortion with figures and also well aware that. One double back does not a hunch make. No. Bolting, as he does, into hide skelter-pelter in Servicea Bull's leather gods shop, slips his ring through Maceperson's jewellers, hightails it freely through Marryo's formal higher wear, moves his butt thrup Brendum Dum's gun shop, short cuts back and side to cheering in Baldex the barber, slips into Mamma Twain's Lingerie Lingerer, and finally trouves himself inside out of Cockloft's Trouser Emporium panting. Then onto Castlereagh Street again. Having performed a backtrek of superb convulsions. Off his own back, too. And no Amos in object or image plane. Which just goes to show, booty over beasty is like covering a bitch. Meaning that the success of the operation is in direction of the quickocity of the slip-up the back street. Truism, trudy. And *ohm*.

(Belle, give Tinky a ring; the dog's gone and toll'd her Nell)

Zarathustra in rethrust, Scotty is now resuming a billowed fiacring down the women-lined street of inner Sydney where female fealty has one major drawback to it. Scotty's foreskin. But that is an Assumption. Or is it? Why, for hex ample, on Scotty's return to the footpath of rose petals, did three octogenarian jennies sporting shockingly short mirror-minis bought for their art ritis jaunts, drop their bundles in his osteopath and send him telepathic waves of 'what does astrology say about your anatomy, lover?' Or forwhy did three self-insinuated virgins throw themselves bodily upon the partho of genesis, that they would birth wherever he lived Not mentioning the general chaos amongst all charley horses in hosieries along the bourse. Or why the unaccosted number of essensual menses maid-to-measures that gave up their lifeblood then and there in haemogobblin' despair of evermore being pass'd over when our preambling Scotty swags on past Parsifal bullishly byebye without as much as a sideglance long? Amenorrhoeic questions, regularly, hard to prevent!

And if all this wasn't enough by way of attempting to luff him or leave him, now he finds Amos back in on his hammer. He does and is, both. That damn shoffle shoof sallying articule by articule behind once more. May Dogod sick him!

(heavy smoker smoked out by pack, got caught by galloping consumption)

Well, furybund Scotty! He swings into the nearest men swear shop, and assumes a posture of a totem of Bushido Bungho About To Armbosch Lord Amos, that white old devil now nearing and nearly now. Almost abreast to be. Gavelled! Given a Scotty galosh that draws gallic streams of blood-cuddling gallimanfry out of him, no crud! And,

(Tulip, the dog can't forget your mint condition)

Amos Well, no sooner do those Scotty scratching and manacling fingrrrs grip his scrawny crane for greater purchase, than the Amos gyrastunts geotactical to the earth there in ultra sones of ow! ow! ow! ylike asif he were being mortarized by a tunny of bricks, and. Causing a straggle, if not millions, of the public people to descend to rescue the old codger from the clutches of this film star maniac. Whereupon our Scotty, not so much cowardly as Custer, ducks around a swinging shopping bag from the hip of a hep female dingbat (first slugger for The Wombs) and

slips greasewise into that worn meanswear shop behind him. Wildly taking in the Wild West homily range. Where he finds himself surrounded by Texan arses drooping jeans from posters posteriori photoglyphed presumingly. Posterns! Enough to turn a poetaster into a Levi-tated past muster, when all he should be doing is to try to engage in an uninterrupted fly passage to the rear exit without being taken by the balls. By ladies' lamp-ontos for an unpronto Tonto. Ought to be outlawed. While,

(Lily, come out; the dog's deflowering elsewhere)

outside on the parquetry of human airs, Amos has been rerighted into upstand and is in quail of assault and battery at the other end of an awful cry-hueful finger going at Scotty. Who tries to pump his legs for the rear escarpa but oh a torchturous unlighted way, this. Too much decor decoy of destraction, e.g. the cats o' nine tails and Longfellow the Ketchup Hangman's noose size 15 sameas the Scotty neck, so perfect for the scrawnies of shawnees or for a very prurifact personal community aid. Like they want outside to use. Against the Scottyself, aye.

And all the time that this is going on, there is a got-up Annie Oakley (real panhandle Miss Caley Lainy, telfonica 266901 for fornications a.h. a.m. o.r. p.m.) who is looking down on him from the top of her curly lip to the lip of the top curling step of a steepish caricole there, and. Making herself known with, 'They ever going to have yours for a necktie, pardner'. Whenceupon Scotty reins in to bumblefum, all innocent fums and no thingers, around a counterfull of Wild Bill Hicory's nicked neck scarves, going in's sivan syllables carouso to her caricole there, 'Scarves bandannas bandits bomboro or bananas skintly how much, eh?...'

'Oh, pull the other one.' Annie Oakley. In her western outfit, she really is a cow-poke. Annie Ole Oakley'll do.

(Noah, you silly bugger; it's only Dogod pissing Itself laughing that you fell for it)

Meanwhile, Amos is reeling off a re-construction before an assembled, as he is large, police officer who could resemble Constable Wilkinson, but who mightn't be Constable Wilkinson. Yes and yelp! Scotty's eyes soar in Scotty spasmodic oscillatories, to say the least, just a panic-striked moment before he galls up a gallop off. Like a galoot outa the calaboose across tha' Rio Grande disguised as a Western back door marked 'Prairie'. And, oh yes, behind him, Annie Oakley cannot refrain from waving him off with 'Get Ah Long, Little Doggie, Get Ah Long', and does refrain it.

(aged man been around too long, gone sour to his dog)

Finally in suave again not long arfter, Scotty climbs the steps to the bank with as much style and grace as you would expect from someone Everest on the lookout. Isn't he ever Hilaryous; knowing it, too.

And just to demmo how full of protean the human meatball is, a one and elderly Mrs. Ylace Mislainy, a wee doe of woeman, craggy but not insurmountable and with enough money to make her a whee-dowager, choses that synchromoment to emerge from the bank that Scotty is about to render himself unto. At the sight of him she storps up stubbed before turning man-madic to get her flacker cloacing in time to let him passear on through it, the door or hers hopefully. But Scotty choses the door, leaving Mrs. Ylace Mislainy to sigh money isn't everything. She did and died soon after.

(dog about town would like to meet a Vital Sal, re morning reviver)

However, Scotty is now inside, bringing financial visions into focus. With all the gulls and buoys in there watching him sail in as they click and cluck, tch and tuck, ahem and ah him! Oh, there are smiles, indeeds. Smirkins, indeedo. Gigs and glees in diddlios. There are whisper-things indeedio. From all ages, fromages all, *give's a cheesie Scotty...* save from one lilted tittle tit appelling herself Miss Lacey Lainy who, nu to new mismatics, nota if not naif, has the ignorance to continue to

(Bill, the dog left the tip of you for the waiter)

count overcounter'd while ignorant of Scotty before her worthy of note. And it is only when Scotty performs a whiff to get her fumes and fuming, both, that li'l tit Miss Lacey Lainy, pot off her cuunt by Scotty's looking down her scopulacurvy scalp, upbrows her eyes to him from under a prim quim and, worse, primrosen arch. While all the other Gulls and Bills around her make with brays

9

guffaws snorts chortles neighs bours and moosings one and all. Like it's either a piggy bank or MacDonald's farm. Yes, until even Li'l Tit twigs on the bow, 'Oh! Is this *him*?!'

'*Him* she asks!' From back of the hall, somewhere a worn wit.

'Hey, his wife says if he wants his monthly checkie-weckies, he's got to go down to her place and earn again! Hee hee. Or no more checkie-weckies!' Ho ho! What a thrumming wickle throttle this little Miss Lacey Lainy could have as the necklace of her lost life! Seeming, though, to care little for the survival of her species or species, coined, as she beckons for Scotty to close in nearer before laughter makes her spill her beans on the floor before she can spill the beans on him. Reeling the poor man in by his newly-pressed tie, now pressured by splutter liquating from her drivelling lips, going:

'Is it true... what your wife said and and and', but Tit is unable to speechiloquy and gets ventriloquised by some comedico from backo banco.

'... there's fanny all you wouldn't do for her coin'

'Right, you're all roperted!' Scotty. Yes, always the misspell when saying it, and tending up to them on his own and marching towards the door marxed 'Manager'! No sweat! When you're after heads as a valuable and irreplaceable customer, go straight to the heads man. Bog Sitting Bull with fucked tongue, him. And doing an elegant Scotty bulldoze into the mahogany manager manger, saying as he opens the sanctorum, 'Scyou oozy me for barging in, burgled staff bungled but...'

What more can be said? With that selfsame managrrr caught curling around the laughing toe region and groping sightlessly to switch off the intercom intercourse (flick off when having same) hickless and stitchwith in haha glee and only capable of nogging shakenhod at our Scotty, going: 'Y'killem everytime'. High funance! A positive furnace of bank erupted. Even Miss Lacey Lainy, that little tit twit of a fuckwit, is now afloored

10

flabbergushing twitterflit to roll herself, rolling so as to flaw herself, and flapping a railway ticket at Scottyself in toccata of, 'Ya wife... here... ya railway ticket...'

(Nude lady given the ultimate sixty-niner by a Heinz-variety)

Oh, tis clairly clear now. Since each and every uncouthed there is either couched or crouched or clutching their crotchets on the wallow-to-wallow carpet at his/her feet. That they are all quite beneath him. So Scotty elegants the ticket from Li'l Tit's shakey dyke-pullers, going: 'A hey a nonny ho. My wife's a donkey too', whereupon he beau brummels off to a background with a swagger plainly indicating, going: 'O ratchet i am a pawled.' And part, takes. Bies and girls.

(little pug hits below the belt)

Still around, around,
Constable Wilkinson is working himself up to a potch thinking of the still-free rotten cur, ruttish to the core, that foulfoot peter patter, that human houndrel of a mong who has made things so unpleasant subsole outside so many downtrodden lottery ticket vendories. Namely he who uses the alias of Mr Fido Bigs. The mere thinking of his existence somewhere gnaws Constable W's mind right down to its hone, and. Producing in perspex the sharp inspiro-thought of:

'Dogs don't think like us. Grr, it makes you savage'.

Even his rock-like setting beginning to chin. Then dies down. He has been too long in the force to let sleeping lies dog him. It's just that the whole doings of these doggy dungs stink to high heaven. Especially in his book where he keeps a specimen for instantaneous comparison. Without comparison, that, too, and. Really the whole affart is enough to give him the squirts. It is. Squinting his peepers stickily pass the glass of his cruise car at all those squirts pedistraining along Castlereagh Street all quiet and nice for a non-naughty non-Sundae desert. Momentarily. Though he feels like he's concentrated for a year. Before he turns his mind back to Mr Fido Bigs and how to catch him red-faced. Clues cloy clawing. As he continues his rounds, still around, around. Body and mind as one.

(patriotic dog carries out its Judy)

But hark. For lookye. There is as wide a grin as one could conceive in a dental plate embedded in Scotty's lower hock-quarter. Having got no further than down the bank steps and having got no higher up the legs yet, Scotty and the teeth. Belonging to

(drill a dog through and through)

the gums that have stuck to Amos through sweet things turned sour. As well as that breath. But now abusing, openingly on the King's Hiway, the privatoria of Scotty's left kneecap, just above. And a most indigestible hunk it is. In suck now, marrow within that old-yesterday's mealy mouth. And not even the gathered crowd unto caring a cashew about the carryings on of carrion chewing livelegs. If he knew that, Scotty wouldn't be weeping aloud with frustration of peels and appeals on it. No. Going between mouthfuls of himself:

'Silly old codger only trying to prevent me from visiting my estranged wife. Strange, isn't it? Ha ha. Somebody help me. Reward offered.'

Turning nobody's head with enboundened civic duty, unless that too is a joke. One of them even offering Amos extra paste of dental fixture. Can only cement present attitudes. To be broken by Constable Wilkinson coming around, around to stop this rowdy, with a bad mind for such occasions of impromptu street theatre. And who be quiddity itself closing in fast in fact in Scotty vision of holy hell and framed.

12

(starving dog worked fingers to the bone)

So that Scotty frankly tries again to unclutter the Amos mouth off his leg with such a tearing hurry that he stumbles on his fallen back beneath the astrides of an opportunistic poodle with hairpins just happening to be the haemosucker to end all him-o-slurpers in all the dog's world. It mounting his other scutter without further ado but definitely thinking of one more, and proceeding to pelvis the Scotty inviolable doing its beast to the rhythm of *make-a-babe, labi-a-baby*. Not even Amos now trying to kick it bloodybloody getorf getorf will prevent this beast from besting a downed man good. No. With Constable W. drawing nearer with curtains for them all. Until

(jaw of the dog, end of the tether)

Scotty so shudders with the possibility of life dishing out even further abuse, that he actually sheds teeth and pelvis, both. Consummated anyway. With one convulsion of the corpus that suddenly achieves him a breakthrough. The crowded ranks about included, and is up and off, off and flying on two legs. One that had been caniballed. The other that had been canine balled. And outstripping all that embarrassment at last, providing we don't count Amos and his mandarin shoo-footshuffle within the Scotty bear tracks scudding. Once inevitably again, and. No sweat at all.

(dog carries around lost look of an explorer)

There is something *en train* at the pharlap end of the plat that the next train is almost in leaving form from. Yes. Some Mad Moolah must be going loco. Obscenic phonetic, probably got from a gutter, now guttural, with just a touch of the caca-phoney. And do we or do we not catch a glimpse of Scotty up there at the top carriage, trying to caste himself b'body or b'buggery at the carriage door with one leg within and with one leg without, with one arm therein and one arm there without, and with a skylent scream kakaulling out for the Rod Crest or St. Jonz or the Poll Isce

to comeon help quick. No lie. Tis he, making the umpteenth odd
scene of himself for that day, and

(murderous dog, a damnable bounder)

by all that's stunning by eye catchitude, there is also a glimpse to
be caught, out, of some of Amos' soma attached onto Scotty's tie
presumably performing in a pantomime as Little Toot Toot the
Tug and. Yfere there, caacaalling out for Blood E. Toecaps,
blacken blueser of gooliestones, and Bloody Mary, begetter of the
Dogod worm It is. He and he. Both of them. Inseparable, except
that Amos is the one trying to stop the Scotty getting on. Or is it
Scotty who is making boot impressions on the leatherhide of the
other trying to stop the Amos getting on The suspense is killing
the timetable.

(cold shoulder disagrees with the dog)

Departing now the train at last. Even the fracas at the far form of
the platter seems to have boiled over, covered in steam now
anyway and that. Is no mean feat since dieselectric is the word.
But then this is NSW Railways and anything can happen. No
fracas is but a fricasse of a fractional moment ago, and:

Perish the thought is a Traveller's Aid warning to all railway
passengers. Aye, tis.

(noli me tonguere, you dog!)

Nor to be seen to be sure a Scotty in the skedaddles, no, nor Amos
in a gony. Only Scotty's cravat creviced in the door and assuredly
waving on its own knotty accord to nobody in particular. Or in
general. Though perhaps in its own inarticulate way trying to draw
attention to the dark gap between the now kinetic parts of the train
and the platform just sizeable enough for the downseizing of a
psycho-ridden body of a skinny person. Or, most likely, an august-

14

born Aged. The train going, too: *amo amos amat amos amate amourn*. Foreboding, goodnight! Amos!

(dog leaving the table bears out what was speaking about it)

But getting back to being sirius:
The gun dog was slowed down by a slipped cartridge. Though its kennel mate returned with its muzzle loaded by its own master. Heard, too, that the music mad dog slipped a disc. The jockey's. And the joke-loving dog didn't spare the ribbing. Then again, a really green dog only barks up the family tree. Then the wise man puts a muzzle on the snout of the dog. Then pulls the trigger. Just as the sloping dog inclined towards skiers.

Y'Know, more than one tourist has left his heart in dog-town. They didn't see the two dogs of a mind picking master's brains. Nor the Baltic dog Baiting down his food. Not even the shaggy dog on a rocker. But they did um and ah over the dog that had the haggard face of an old lady. And the blind dog with the 20/20 visionary. Then there was the distressed dog craving a warm-hearted woman. In the dog-town cemetery was tombstoned: Hermit, Scavenged For His Life.

And this: Human Husk, His Dog Sucked Him Dry. (Rabies dog has got a real poisonous nature.) A shocking sight, though, was the black dog with white trash. Competing with the red setter making the bloody son go down. And again, as one dog to another: roll over, red rover; this toff's lost all his topping. Then again: U and the dog; now non-U. Though their tourist guide was a gregarious dog about to use its mouth to good effect. A mountain dog asked them if they wanted to share a tramp over the hill. They saw, too, the grossly over-fed dog that could hardly drag itself, after a man. Even on the field, the fallen soldier was just canine fodder. So

Gloria in X celsius to Dogod, One within the body of any man. O, *Ohm*.

15

SCOTTY

In this training compartment, Scotty seated, having sited by and
been sighted by, both, a primely unprimmed Virginia named Cleya
Mislainy who is predestined to come to a tacky end with her
unskimm'd creamator. Virgyne also. How can he tell? Well, do
just quiff the quism, quaff the qualms, squizz those quizzlings,
quipe the quoinsnivelling vellum-quivering quoit. Wafting by to
all men, and. A quietus coitus it would be. Any quests? Yes.
Sidelong tracks making at Scotty. Plus, too, th'fact that all virgins
giggle tipsily on account they have hefty skinful under their belts.
Yes, in troth, but is this sufficient

(come home, Cherry; the dog wants a second bite of the)

reason for Scotty to be crying large boohoos at her, bringing red
rims to the circums of his eye sockets? For Amos, perhaps? With
poor purrly Cleya M. turning her winsome lampers inonupon him.
Scotty going: 'Upheavement bereaval in the family way, sweet
child. Pardon, but i swoon swansong'.

'Oh,' Cleya, clamming up; and mouth shutting, too.

'Please... no need for words of sympathy. Tis enough that you
should feel free enough to come over here to hold me duke. Meet
duke'.

(friendly dog in-mate)

Imagine everything going wateryfall over the edge and toppling
before him as this young innocent comes webbing into his
spider's. But that was in *this* compartment. Whilst this following
was in *that* compartment:

(dogging the human frame: gay dog had a ball; old dog stuck on
gum; pup coming out foetus first)

down the corridor third left, there are three people, twoscore of
whom are Mr Headly Ferst and his char min of a wife, Mrs

Prymaria Ferst. A houseband to the wife and a wife to the hushband, yes, and duly together for all the dies of their live-us-alone. Both celebrating twenty-five years in the Pubic Service together with a cheap return daytrip to anywhere so long as it's back home to safety that night.

(dog ma says: average man in the street, fair game, but nothing to lairize about)

Mr Ferst is a man in the middleday of the time of his extentcy sitting there more than less nervous and really quite suspending of breath. With his eyes on the Third Person there. And poor prissy Prymaria, too, just as chokeful and chocked up as she looks across her specs expectently at that same Third Person and ponders how

(dog creche, master mind)

could she have vented the idea to her dear and dreary Mister H. that a daytrip might be a bit daring for their time of dayin and dayout to celestral those twenty-five years weno-where, but oh gee ogee let's do it wowee anyhow, hanging the expanse and be damned (pardon) to any dagos or drongoes probably just waiting for human exposures beyond the front fence. But, the poor dear never thinking that even those premonitions might manifester themselves so much rolled into the essence of this Third Person sitting opsite them, and. Who just has to be the re-incarnation of everything unimaginable. No carnation certainly. Were he not, thus making him so, Amos. Yes! The old boy being still, even if it is stretching anthropology to call him alive, and. Stinking well as if dead. But vitally alive within the nostrils of MrMrs Ferst quivering, them and them. With his

(dining dog finds unpleasant taskmaster sets its teeth on edge)

parade ground bashers off and one of his beetle crushers cochineal to the breeze in front of the affronted MrMrs affronting up and to the Fersts primarily holding onto each other tightly in case one of

17

them drifts off and away forever more. For in twentyfather years as Public Serbs never have they had to come nose to nose with a situation of lifessence that has footrot still attached to life by the living fact of putrescence. Not only that, but the very vehicle of its embodymint is above it leering at them caries, going: 'just taka bloody Captain's bloody Cook at them bloody spuds in there willya go on.'

And sure enough between the boneous protrubers that must clinically at least be class-ossified as toes are whole fields of black saltpeat or ignaceous vulcanised topsoil, which? The Fersts couldn't imagine! Especially now that

(dog finds vintner a full-bodied flavour)

they are suddenly not there anymore, and. Running on the spot, both, outside in the corridor facing the way of their own home. Never were, as people, very nosey. But a stun gathers no Amos. No. Nor a shun any attenshun. Amos smirks a sneer. Then stretches himself to the luxury of being left alone with the convivial company of the bogeymen in his nasal slots. Pleasant to jaw on with, yes, while chewing up the ash tray butt by butt. Make no tonal diff to his

chompers anyway. Colourchartic. Firkin hell, the bottom of the barrel

(a stitch in side saves canine time)

That was in *this* part of the comment. Meanwhile, back in *that* compartment, from which window outer suburban houses are giving way to gnatty Nature. And here

our now clearly clitorious Cleya Mislainy has become quite skittish by skirt and clitterish by Scotty, going: 'I don't get off for an hour'. Coquette by the sauce in it! And her fingers feeling their way touring those swardy and vast hirsute hectares contouring the

18

Scotty chest. A treasure troved, indeed, where lurks rare and tangible privilege, prithees and all. Going: Scotty, 'Feminales; may Gob bless'em'.

Cleya M. croakquettish, unquenchionably inquandary, 'Pardon?' before she realizes she has interrupted a precious about to say something gemmy and clomps his hand to her mouth; him ongoing edgily: 'all talk. Talc talk torque. Women. All the time, talis all about it. Well then, listen...'

(Dogod, It say: two heads go further than one)

(What is it Scotty initiates Cleya into that she can, and does, lose control of herself to babble and writher to withers accompanied by mountain moaneds, belabouring her labias so in flowjuice that one leg is aslipping upon th'other, not to mention her mouth becoming a revampired job? Well, this, of women:)

(you let a bitch tamper with your unders and its breath comes in pants)

'... of women and woeman, the thirstday childs of her and hers and higher herseraphims, of her succubus suckity, of her all all of her, of her succunymph of her succulolls of her succullimes of her succulibertina of her succucubby of her culmulust of her foldreams around the reamanna folds of her men, of her genestyrenes jeanstrippings, of her nomen; she the fonomen, her the culture nurchant, her the biofloss, the biod, the biotide of the man-aliveoes aloes;

'... and of her the carricot of succuman's stimulants of we the mam-maemen the seedlayers, of her the carricreche of romulus and remus of sempersumping simperman, yes; of she the bifurc conjunctive with commonman in and outrout,

'... and of her the nest, of her the nidus, of her the furrydown of her the intoxicunt, yes, of

19

her cord, her lass-up of lacelife, yes, her withinnings and of her our carry coleen, her, viant's exuviael collander seething, yes, her, the ectoplasmama of Mancoming. and me possibly? Get it?'

(It might as well be the Devil you know than the mongrel not yet named)

And that was only for starters. Cleya M. mightn't be the best listener in the world, but she is not listening. Anymore. As Scotty drives his drone on, homing in on her with cascades of dolcetry that have cast her in squelch. Showing herself of a pretty common mound, though, by either digging out the wax of her ears or waxing deaf, which?, through the fingers in each ear, if not. Her pretty little tongue trying to tippl her touching little snoz through a yawn she cannot hold back, if not. Her two eyes doing callisthemes in the top of her head and saying something about gawd. Gawd? Must be on the other side of the net from Scotty.

(bombastic dog dropped onto man-sized target)

But now a grrrotesquely grrrowing grrring and a grrrizzly neck-prickling brrr. Enough to make our man sit up bolted, firing his cat's eyes uppend away, giving to him a victim's eye-view of a Great Dane. If that is what you want to call something more like a sphinx. With its beadies on him from out in the corridor and its massive sneakers upon the wafer thin yielding (he yell'd!) glass of the compartment door. And if that wasn't enough to make him go all to pieces, there are its massif mastive bonepicking jaws. In full working order. Demonstrably. And eager, if not jawsting itself, to get into a position where it could muck up a bit of his Scotty mishmash. Husky enough for any husks left, too. Even Scotty's soundless screams go unnoticed. Nice doggy ha ha what a laugh.

When, in the nack of time, a hero of a ticket inspector arrives on the seen there with a where-the-fucu-u-been, and delivers unto that slavering Grrt Dane a wide and quite striking right across its chaffing chops, like as if to say, okay, Noland from Friezeland, fido follow me. Which it does. After it has dog paddled to shore from that lake of drool it left behind under its Scotty intention.

(moulting dog after Long Haired)

And so, away man and prodogious Dane, he with his back up, it with its tail down, leaving our Scotty saliving for yet another day, settling back into Cleya M. Who, in point of fact, had got off half an hour ago, but she had just forgot herself. Boredom can do that.

(the wise man shoots the dog Through)

'O', Scotty ohs oatily, 'for a healthy covering of smog'.

Distrained, our Scotty is alone now, and feeling more purlornly forloin than at any thyme in his surloin, aye. On's tot without there being one tit out, except a million or so crows going off their craaakkers. Indeed, Scotty is stranded on such a deserted railway station that, when it had no option but to stop, even the train shuddered to a halt. Not halting in leaving him there, though. Oh, no.

(city dog can't stomach a countryman's life)

He recces his redrims around the rim of that world there. A horror horizon! Even down to clean air. Even as a country view it is an ughly intake. Here dislandia of Oz is a whole empire of unvamped vapourings which rise not higher than the kneecaps. Could be mist or might be one of his wife's melodramatic effects, type of artificial shit she'd go in for. If there is a tree left as far as he can see, there's not much of a tree left. Probably drowned to death under the slimey of untold numbers of slugs. Or lost their foliages under the stares of a trillion snakes' eyes withering towards a wit's end, and. No wonder Scotty is at his. Dogod grief, even the engine driver had never heard of this place and was obliged to do a U-turn to droop our Scotty off. Scotty now going:

(chow to meet chinaman for Tang)

i bet this place isn't even sanitised by a Tourist Bureau brochure. A bloody Wuthering Higate of holy Horrorwood; and mist if i must; and drizzles on me if i grizzle; must go on or else i'll get in tango with a ghoul or two; gnawed at by a jehovah witness crawling out of the innate would-be, o true. If this be for reel i'd better get going like the clappers. Keep a healthy image of the de-beasted city in mind to ward off rottings under wetleaves. Put on a disjointed smile.

(Lassie takes its leading man for a late supper)

But nothing, nobody, thin or thingish, not even a safe niche like nix there, only flat and ferny-marsh, true. Only flatty-fern marshes reeking of a singularly flattish ferny and marshy air mellow in the limicolous atmosphere there, which makes everything seem a bit as though Emily Bronte had wiped her romantic streak all over herethere witherwuther to give it a fine Heathcoating. 'Strue.

(upstart mongrel hung up on its cross)

But tis necessary, by Dogod, to heresay that our Scotty was not the only critter to get off the train, no. The other was nunother than our old organzasm itself, august auragusting and orgiast Amos. Centipeding himself behind Scotty's broad-and-ripply in a rush to the reverse and fairly obtuse side of the station house, more like the outside dunny to a one room shepherd's shack. Where he huddles hisoldself into a hidey old hole, sneaky as all frig. Immediately setting up a fug that few could really overlook. Yet our Scotty unbeknownst there still faces that Baron wasteland afront him with a Scotty jaw set that could turn into a set piece from the film 'Biggies in the Land of Mongrel of Mongolia', or, 'Gonna Gobbi You Up and Spit Y'gristle Out'. Stultified or bung ho'd, which? or both? While,

(deserted dog would like to meet a cowardy custard, wants to give full desserts)

22

a huge thing, that was once a big black luminous limousine which recently had undergone a convertible to become a huge black limousine with converted door hinges, whoas slowly to a halter before coming to a standstall by the Amos-person right on cue. It does. All silence, too, since it is on the other side of the station from our Bigglesy Scott. Whenhappens that the Amosessence sidles its tang agency to enter itself within the bigblack limousine which, nturn and giving not a whiflf to Scotty that it was ever there, motives back along that bleak and Blake-like tricky bushtrack. From whence it had come like a top Holliewoode rental job. Is mum the word for it?

(dogs hospital fixes them up to sick them on again)

Meanwhile, our Scotty pauses for the action to ketchup, then turns left through a full fulcrum circle to listen for scythes or sighs. Which? And waits. Until, right on Kew, comes the garden faint (pass-outs available at door) baying of a wolf pack, or so it seems. Anyway quite enuff ruflruff to make your Gaul rise to bile, or your Biggies image to change to Hawk up, just to listen to this canine heresy. O poor and Scotty lorn figure; nowhere to go and already a pack on his back. Again. It happens every time his wife insists he comes. He leaves in cysts, too. But now he is

(mountie's dog always gets his bit of the man)

watching for the car that was once a dirty great black limousine and is now a bigblack limousine that is always sent to fetch him. When does his eye fall upon the note there that is hanging upside winded upon the station wall. And only for a miniminute wondering whether wall-eye or won't he read even an ious of its facet, knowing it is some more of his wife's lymphetic lingo, typed and typical upon a used and scraped-down fly-paper, going:

THERE IS NO CAR TODAY. DO TAKE A CAR RIDE.

Right on the hooter! His. Ha ha. Wife is still a wit, eye wash.

(dogs don't cry over spilt bulk)

23

Hero, though, to the lust, Scotty takes his luff in his hands and motors his peds to padding along the brackish track, backbreakishly, muttering defiance in single file to all or sundry, or both, who might be within two kms radiatus of him. Nobody is. Nor pinus either. Only those hounds in the distance that howl even louder to hear again that Scottysound which sends a cold blood sweat of anticipation running updown the spindle of anything Scottivorous. Must be doggy neurotics. Fresh flesh frenetics. Y'know? And what a dirty trek to play on a man. Indecently exposed to things that might lay a charge on him at any moment. Up to his neck. Going beyond the Beyond. Whoever the

(the dog loves you for yourself not your money)

smutt joker his wife is, she ought to be carded off down the laine. Got all the warp needed for a good dressing down. Aye.

(ambitious dog leaves home to get a head)

As the big buck'n'black limousine sweeps through scroll handwrot iron gates that head up a driveway going towards a country mansion and. Only the car is really moving; all else is allusion or all elision. It is. Even the house itself looks like an original boris karloff who has been made to look like a Victorian monstrosity by whoever the crazy Victorian architect was who built the back door around the front to confuse the most uppetty of the airborne bats. Plenty of them, too. Teeth and all.

(chipped on a tombstone: Remaindered From Bottom Of The Dog Heap)

Scotty preparing himself, as he trudges, for the sight of the Fang, knowing that he is so far out from anywhere that twould not even be a dogoodcr about to bring out the dogcart for to carry him off.

Morgueways. Starting to feel dogged now, how can he stay dogged?

(bloodhound on entrail of escaped con)

And, by all that is minimumly humanly possible in a dog's world, if those two Dobermann Pinchers waiting for him at that mansion are typical, then all is rejuicing at the news. Of his impending render. The dogs sort of going: hallelujah, I've a bum! and wineing hurry-hurry hungers we are. How presumptively freebooting can you get? Want a man's meat a mile off.

(stoned dogs quarry chunks of man)

Now, the mansion itself houses an unusual garden. Were this not a country mansion, it would be a country mansion. And the garden? Guilden with gourdes and other gorgonic garrulities too grouse for mere praising wordy worths or organic wurlitzers. Aye, but even as it is, chance allows a few things to backchat a bit. Like the rusticated old gardener with gardenia waisting low over some two or so lowly flowers overlawn. And like the dozen or so dozy cows meadowing it up on the grassy verge (vergin soil, too) with that hifi quaddling fiddly-dees and fidelity-dums syncopating rather loudly to the moo-mooings of the loud speaker tweeters omniabout there. (There, the tweeters; three guesses where the woofers are.) And it isn't until your double take apprehends you by the gardyloo that all things in the garden are not at all rosey, but rosin really. Or, lettuce be more explicit, nothing there semens to be what it seems tuber. No. For closer inspection reveals, by all the calves on calvary, that the gardener, the flooming bowers bowls bulbs gladdy glazes the mowcows the groundunder muzac the mardi grasy verges are nothing but cardboard cutouts in figured figurines. Really. Stuck up as you can get. Except

(forensic scientist found, with traces of the hair of the dog that bit him)

25

when Scotty looms upon the garden gates, when do the two Dobermann Pincers spring into life from their cutouts within one idyllic cardboard scene, and. Enthrust themselves to their instincts. Forgetting their mannas, too. As they pitch themselves, pinching themselves, is this for real? bodicely, the bitches, behind their in-flight fangs as if perfectly willing to bend their wills to breaking point if necessary into a Scotty savaging. Like, the last one there is a scavenger. They do, and a difficult task for four sets of such tusks or two death-dealing doggies like these against a rawbone like him. Still, they will try. Like all warheads will.

(love-starved dog seeks sexpot in the flesh)

Not long after Scotty is but a form asquat and frankly aswing-ing from the top ligna of the friendliest gum he has ever leapt upon and looking for all intended purposes like Christ cruxed crying for chrissake stop these houndinis dogging me heels me shoes pincer alruddy, yes, and. With his cobblers still being clobbered by our two snappy slobberers, there comes a tweet sound to the ears across the grassy graceland. When they ear it, SS inspired, SOS inspiring, the doggies just bound happily back to the front door through which

(dogs like livering it up)

they slip insidewards with two tongues wagging that will be rested with a well-rewarded Ern. No doubt, and the door shutting after them. O grand slam!

(chosey bitch says her man has to be well hung to get tenderness)

Descended from that tree, now, with so much trusset to his own trestle work that he looks like a troglodyte caved-in, Scotty affronts the front door there really scotched as to what more could lip against his stiff upper. Now swings open it and the door; how easy the door and it yields to his fingertips! Ten agencies of entry, ageing fast. And enters within, where

(dog trick captures cardsharp's hand)

the hallway is dancing with a flood of shafty sunluce flash as if to ask who the fuck did it up. In in-persia latex latest. Expugning a decor that dekkos as if the myrrh had got to someone's frankinsense, frankly, and made Asif All 'Ell Ben broken loose. Djin with tonic here; make your own bedouin you lie in. Absolute bedlam, too; even the arras arranged arrantly, and.

Obviously the work of some shocking roadsider Occident staking out a sheik-down for an Arabelasian night for Al-Bel-Ben-and-Me. Going, Baalies to the expense and hang the cash-bar! Here we all go round the myrrhberry bush. Aye. And bombarding the Scotty retinals all screwed wincing and trying to hindi the admission of anything like it to their sensitives.

(fey dog like to encounter a Fay front up)

When, suddenly and in a most actual way, runs a nude near nymph near him going across the hallway. With an omphalos of a mostmoist phallic nature, and frosty little feeties patently covered by black leather high heels. Then stopping full of strapping potential, demonstrating her capacity to take him in. Eyes opening, too, and:

'Say...'

'No i didn't, Miss. I'm speechless.'

Now this yoni, Eclya Mislainy by name and maddenly maiden, approaches. To spread her good news a few labiarinths apart and showing a surprising amount of delight. Of and at him. Her thighs and his sighs. Labia love to part, and. Thrusting her twatnot furwad forward with her oboyoboy flam going flimsily: 'But you've just got tobe It! Wow! You are It. Golly. I mean, your wife, she doesn't make with the shit, does she, gosh'

27

(game dog hunting for a game dame)

Scotty wistful about becoming just crazy over her baby mounding service, and breaking out in a sweat witli the enthusiasm. When, in this unguarded moment, she stoops to conker his chestnuts to see if he's for really. His scream was. Groping backwards, and her groping forwards, going:

'Boy, and i thought nothing, but nothing, would ever happen to au lit tool me. Mean, well, fucit all, here's you, It itself, in the flesh just like your wife tells it. C'arn, why won't you show me watcha really like, meanreally, in there behind all those clothes, uh? Gimme sneak preview. Please oh gosh, uh?' The biggest thrill she's had since she last wore panties. Which just goes to show how long it's been, and Scotty: 'Miss...'

'Eclya Mislainy. I'm a yoni. That's a virginal Hindu symbolic representation for an expressionistic cunt, did you know?'

'No.'

'You really all that uneducated, too'

'A degree or two.'

'Ho ho. Pull this one.'

'May i?'

'Sure go ahead.'

'It's certainly a yoneur to make your acquaintance, Misslainy.'

'Gee, they tell a girl, and you think to yerself, hell nobody, but nobody, could be a lose-out as all that. Oh fuck, now i'm all embarrassed.'

She should talk. Scotty hardly can. Too busy fighting off what he is feeling. At its most maniac, and going:

28

'Please, Miss, don't be. Generally i'm in favour of nudity.'

Which stops yoni Eclya M. right in her tracks. Nudity? She recalls this as a word she giggled over once at Sunday School regarding a strip-tease job up on some place called Calvary; and, spurred on in such an infantile mammory, prods her veinus mound disapprovingly:

'Y'mean this? What's this compared? You could pick up this old shape on any street corner. But you... mean, underneath it all... listen...' And presents our man with another breathtaking jolt by stiff arm and shock, hers and his, towards his roughcuts, '... can i get your touch quotient' And does. Hanging on with a very cold hand.

'AAAGGHH!'

Scotty crotched, now croaking, while yoni Eclya M. nodly sads her head, going:

'Sure, i understand. Real sad, huh? Hey, hows about trying to stretch it with a three hundred kilogram weight?'

Then drawing closer to shield the top of his fishmouthing head with the centre of her universe, lullabying like she did see a mammy do in an old film repeated on TV, before:

'Listen, we want you to know we all sneaka sorty, well, admire you. 'Kay?'

Kay? What say? Who is dekaying with his thronged-upon forked after all?

(business dog wishes to trade personnel with another)

But Scotty asks not how he is supposed to relax with his thropple nearly thronged and his marbles nearly tombowlered. He does not. Only nodding at her, our yoniest of all yoni symbolics, as she hup-hups in bobbledebum and boobybob all the way back from where she so unashamedly chrysalised from. That door over there. Opening it now with her front portents parting enough to cause Scotty's eyes to gulp from their glue on the small of her downy back down there, and speaking into that other room with such body in her voice, going:

'Hey, i've seen It with my own eyes!' Then to go back side in. O, cruel life that allows Eve's two apples in thy eye and then have them peeled off.

(police dog got very hard over the sex crime victim)

This is 'Art' Munro
who, obesely otiosely and obtruncatedly large and all latticed with lacey largesse, rolls himself dearboy dearboy towards our Scotty besotted and spotted. There is nowhere to hide except within the fun folds of 'Art' Munro himself as he trolls trawling all lesser fishies in the sea tow'ards Scotty to reach him, net him in and now digest him by blubber external, blubbering: 'Dear boy dear boy dear boy,' by way of a deep humanised rubble far off in the jelly of nerves jangling and tricklets trinklinking down like blaa mange, as if, summitwhere far off, faraway up by the far adios Faraday Layer there is a small pippy pipe of a voice box in neuro-vibes. Yes. Scotty now enfolded by 'Art' M., resembling a teeny embryo olio'd in a large jar of multicolourous fairy jelly, shaking Scotty kaleid collide i love all thy shaken to pieces. Then stopping pardon, with a peck to the forehead but not so much as a further to do, before he doth turn out our Scotty from beneath an unnamed part of his corporation to push him towards a cupboard door. Which hinges on being a cupboard, and:

(dogs' hospital, sick idea)

'O, aren't i a naughty nanny nuncle, dear boy? But do ingress, go ingrow. Thou be just bare timely the hither. Within the class, thy newest disciples, impatient in wait for thee. Aye, those that be befeatured b'Nature with drabness compared to thee now await to accord thee thy due 'omage. So urry, dearest boy!' Then slams to shut the door to send Scotty within that broom cupboard doing what?, and stationing his roily-polymorphous phform into an MC waiting by the door through which our yoni Eclya Misslainy had previously stumbled her cloven bum cleverly into against all our desires. Aye. 'Art' M's watch on the wait, too, ticking away, for our Scotty to get ready. Really?

(dog grate, fireside full of dead ashes)

Motioning towards the innards of that yoni room, 'Art' Munro erapts for a few and erupts for a few with jumpish gestures of viboscillations that in a lumpish elephant would be considered an eruption of raptures. But which in him is a sharp move for silence. Whereupon, a silence which does make you (doesn't it, Dozey?) want to up'n'ask just who is there in that room there? Well...

Variegates, each of apart of the other, all newtered newts twould seem, say, some dozen or so. Satiated and situated, all, in front of drawing easels easing drawers and oodling of doodles of charcoal on white. Aye, an arstudio. Containing a baker's dozen yonis and yonkers, mostly masculine and fenomen, or vice versa and not vice adversa, and. All yrapt in what the ymage 'Art' Munro promises to produce by his waited abated door. Breathes in marathons. And there's not

(Charity, the dog didn't ask you to throw your whole being into it)

one of them there who still has his estimators on the nearest propinquous pubes. Or her sights set on a lengthy engagement. No. For now all yonis and yonkers are perfectly still, where just a short ago they were all either stiff and patting, if not loosened and parting. Even in imminent danger of creating an educational environment. Will they never learn?

(dogs' hospital x-ray unit, lost person's bureau)

Five minutes later,
'Art' Munro munifactures a smile with a grin that is so wide that it almost reaches to the far ends of his whale's mouth. He does, and. Again jestures for silence with an expansion of such measure that it almost reaches to the outstretched flappers of his sea-cucumber hands, going:

'Mes enfants charmants, be bold behold. Now, before thee, aye, the Essence of It all, that which does now freak out to enshow thee that Nature Itself be the primest freakiest of us totems all. So humble-humble, aye and eye...!'

Whereupon: they clap are clap't, whistle are whist, stamp are stumped; they tumble; they acrobat; they cry, they gaarkle, they clear their throe'ts; they dance they roll they rock a minuet to a minute hand; they are in bliss, nirvana or nothing; nothingness and all. For the moment has come they have all been waiting for. Yes, and even 'Art' Munro himself has taken two paces back in order to keep the castle keep freep and clairthru. He motions comein c'mon. This is It. Each there braces for the wondora of It to manifest Itself. Upon them alight afflatus. Flatulence can wait and 'Art' M. going now, yes, now:

'Maestro enter entero enteritis O Maestro...'

(pup got milk teeth, now baby's gone)

Appears. It does, and. Even the silence declenchs its teeth. If It isn't a crowd stopper, It must be world beater. Standing stunning before them now. The Itbeing in Itflush allovergosh and all gee jabber and jorricks the Itessence ItstufT Itthyle Itgoods Itflesh-and-blood It-mould Ittype Itproto Itplast Itzoon Itarcane Itdroop Italive Itspook Itphysic Itnoos Itorror Itform Itmodular Itsistence Itno-joke Ittiness It-is-it Itsufferingself Itstanding there with all revealed unto all there of Its nuddied factuality. And Its

(chiselled on tombstone: Cur'd Awhey)

32

head like an astral dome baldly sparkling Kodak on a bright blue day Its. Spectacle lens as spectacular as opti-sensors at the terminals of an extrastellar teleoscope scoping in on infirmaments of worlds as yet unrealised in optometric circles Its. Teeth like tooths of a great golden gearwheel Its. Quasimodo hunch like nothing on the face of the monde unless you count burial mounds Its. Enbonpaunch like a She-Kangaroo carrying twice her own weight at the bottom of a pouch with hernia Its. Dick, even, would make a two-day-old buck kangaroo want to enter the Olympics against all negro comers by comparison Its.

Flatfeet, too, Its Knockness of Knee Its bottom half of legs like a geisha'd duck's. Plucked, Its. Whole own thing a sight not to be relieved, and. Thrust upon those young girls and boys unseemingly so that there were screams. Males included. Yoni and yonkers of such yongth could never have dreamt of seeing any suchThing before, even though

(dog coats are out on top more than ever before this year)

we have. We have! Scotty, yes, but not as the Scotty we know as Scotty, oh no. Open your eyes and bravely look closer. For tis Quilty. Aye, our Quilty in the First Part and from the First Part of this book which you have not seen asyet but be coming up nowsoon as the Third Part flashback in the flesh. Gob damn the man's dog-gone missing parts! Yep,

Quilty, who is explained in the next chapter by way of a flax flashback why he should really have been the Chapter One of this whole biodography, and who is now the one, oyes, unmasked unwigged uncovered unstrapped unhoistedup uncorneallens'd uncosmeticed unadvertis'd; in fact unbecomingly, all unstuck. Quite. As Scotty come up Quilty, aquiver and aquaver like a high strung guitar pretending to be a plucked goose. And falling short everywhere. With all the lacquer, still just the lacker. Aye, forsooth.

(gay dog fancy lady killer)

33

Getting sirius again:

Sherlock Holmes's last words: nom de chien! And talking about the body... top dog got brains. Bottom dog got sole. Oh yes, sporting dog fetched on the balls. And the bum dog got the arse. The pompous dog got the parson's nose. The persistent dog got the guts. The brave dog got the heart. Rover, though, got tangled all up in its mind. Then again: the rude dog got shouldered out. Little mutt only knee high, too. But the humble dog touched forelock. Greyhound finally got a true racing heart. Mountain dog fell off the shingles. Farm dog took in the corn. While the sneaky dog got inside the leg. At the same time, dirty dog tongueing inside thigh. Then again: outward bounder got good foothold. And the second top dog was recognised with the highbrow. As usual, the scruffy looking dog hung around the rear door for human relief to come soon. When it got caught up, too, the reforming dog made a clean breast of it. Giving the premature dog an arm jolt. It might have been the sorry dog seen with a fist in its face. Naughty dog got the tongue lashing. Blind dog claimed the eyes. Tough dog muscled in. Bag-of-bones dog all covered in sinews. Yappy dog getting on the nerves. Old sea dog sailing through the vessels. Game dog got a lot of stomach. And cocker was happy too. Lonely Hearts was left with: 'Poised dog would like to meet meaty lady for lessons in snappy dressing'.

O, most high Dogod, spare us Thy wreath. There is sheer guts in all thy missions. *Ohm.*

QUILTY FLASHBACK

Quilty was and is now asleep is our man Quilty. Is he ever a damnside dreaming, numbwise and dumbside down. And was since we have arrowed back to this fiecheback. And soppled with more and ever morphus fitfalls of the pitfull, even more than even yesterday's nachtfare of nightmare. Which nachtkered him out as it was. These are not nachtural nocturnal niggles, oh never!, but flights of fangs flung from horror hounds stuck to them by maneating gums going straight to the throat, his, attached to dogsbodies about to pack down on his last personal scream. Middle of nowhere. Only static crowds applauding fromst under an appreciative sign of the Dogstar, and not even a dogcatcher aroundaround to cluck shame over that pretorn gurgle about to be ripped from our man's throat by a skyfull of droolies about to lecher on his naked jugular. Only one miry custard thought: o where have all their leads gone if there's lead in me legs

Might as well say that the bowwow pilots the wake of the ship of life. Wake up, Quilty! Zzz zsawlogs zzz zzsawlogs zzzz

(charity's dog brimming with humanity)

It's a dogod's life, and our Quilty obviously no more capable of manipulating events than maggots are of maggotipulating a blue bottle. Just pix him as He Is.

Slight and just leaning beyond thirty years; so bald he must have lost the last trichk. Quite hairless bald. In fact, skeineless skulled. Where once divicut central, hairly curls now de-parted. And so missed out by a hair's breadth of head that he does not even have a pilus to lay his head on, no. Quilty Sewell is so bald that he is still balding when he has already gone and done it. So much so that even his follicules are going alo to pecias. Nor can we even stop there. Just take an eyefool of those videos, those dopplers, those scanners, those cornyballs, normly called eyes. They are prisoned behind glassy prisms so magnificently optical that they are able to chandelier out the blurred world with a myopia that can't even see itself. That's a fact that is.

(snobbish dog snubnoses fruity bird ojf the street)

This one, our Quilty S., not only needs opticose correction, he needs telescopic adjustment. His own children, numbering three or four, have even thrown away their kaleidopretties because they have got the real thing sparkle in Pop on tap. Aye. Quilty's goggles look more like observation windows for a lowlife onefish twoeyed aqueerium. They do. Nor can we even stop there; just, too, cop the

molars. They are pure plugged gold. It's true. He doesn't bite on; he stakes a claim with each chomp. Golden ambitions? Bright prospects! Even when he was young, he had so many gold fillings that his own mother used to keep on going all the time, 'You stop fossicking around with that grub, y'slug'. She did. Not only her, even the headmaster at Qu's old primary school threatened expulsion if the infant Quilty didn't wear a wig'n'gasmask for the good name of the school. Once, even, did his teacher write 'V. gourd' on the top of his unblessed head of nonpilus, and

(hangdog hooked on Lofty Hemp)

neither need we tarry longer on his hunchback flatfeet pot-paunch hooknose pijintoes knocknees or the other divers attribulations sameas various. No. After all, there is nothing wrong with his shrunken genitals that a bigger pudendum couldn't fix. Nor anything so wrong with his body that couldn't be explained away by one single gene alone. The first. It's just that

no one has even taken a shine to our Quilty Sewell. Unless you tote up the ever so few dozen eugenicists who have chased him with flaming big torches chaffing to char off our Qu's thin pencil line. Would you?

(take on a dog taken off some other body)

36

On the day we here put in question, now, our Quilty Sewell opens his optics, but not his optihods in the lid of them. No, but. The man persieves once more. The dawn of a start thou-art thought, thwart of this day or any other, the crack of a fat dawning. Oo.

Now Quilty strops up the leakhole in his mind mudcrabbing to gethru, thinking that even the thought of the world outhere is enough to give you the clivvers, yes, and. Now considering himself to be sveltenoughly prepared to give awakeness a go. D'we perceive behind his sleeping mask an allusion to a yawn awning? (Quilty alludes to a yawn behind his faece which we may say gives the illusion of an uncured hide hiding the allusion of Quilty Sewell's incurable yawn having illusions on itself.)

Now does he allow the delicatessen release of tibbly cerebrums bubbly. They come in dainty dancing atwee. Give awakeness a go. Give a go awakeness. Go give awake ago. Going, too: if it's a slice of life i am waking up for, it's not worth the cake. Who jugged me hair? Want to feel jiggered around the hareline. Here a mnenome (remember 'M'?) for my tombstone: Let Me RIP. Oh, yes?

Then rolls his vyers planetarily round his head. O lookee here it be morn already. Another mourning turned onover. Reminding himself to wear black for every day is a daily discovery ou-air the pain has moved to. Too. And then moves. He does,

(bloody dogs always at your throat to get a spurt on)

not. Cannot. For, above and around him are the various essences of: Alyce, wife, one of gone off, with arm flossed acrop his neck; dog, one up, zizzing sassily across his footroots, dog-toed dogtoad dogtiered dogtied, dogod damn it!; and six-year-oldest daughter riding, crop and all, on his chest. Aye, our beaut Quilty pinned neck chest pins torn-so torso, in fact, allover. Looking like he has just landho'd recently upon a Lilliputean shore f'sore. Wherdupon,

he deigns an uplook. What does he spy? He speyes the s-eyes of it all. There in meet-hook and hung-up lock-on are his daughter's dopplers throwing a Clothe light (from weaver to worn) upon her

37

Dad in an admirable unwaving contempt. Healthy sign of heal thyself in one so Jung, ya. Quilty's thinking going: if these be the winders of my child's soul, they need smashing with a brick. Listen, kid, i might be only one of those gangarened parentswine who dashed if they know, but behind these me anchovy eyes lies a real man. Me. Could cold you but realize, spermfall, the magnitude of the universe behind these, me star-pryers. So go take thy brother, thy two cysters, thy suffocating mother and thy dog and enter all with the all night heater. Bye.

Certainly, were it not for his kiddy's klinging klaws giving no quarter, except of the precious Quilty blood by the old quart, our Qu. Sewell might have succeeded in sun-arising hellothere up by now. Instead, he groans angsts in agonistik anglosaxophones:

'For fuck's sake.' He please.

'For fusk's cake.' He plets upon goodie Dogod.

'For suck's fuckit.' He comes plete choke circle.

But the world continues to buy and sell mercenaries, turns no hair, unearths few lairs;

(Lairising dogs, all flash-harry caninebals)

only where Quilty has shunk his shaft once or twice does the worm round on the shovel (stop shoving). E.g., without egging, his dog rolls up one eye at him grrristly; his kiddykins begins galloping all over his personal, meaning i'm queen of the cast-ofF; and wife Alyce hoves in his side with a kick towards the chilly out-of-bed, a symbolism with grunts to mean get out and go earn at work otherwise i cannot afford to sleep in. Before she pads up the sleepy river again for another dreamboat. And all this, just because our

Quilty has spoken (o, i am the broken spoken of the wheel of life) for the first time today. Silly man. Should have let them think you were dead.

(get caught in a dog's jaws and all is foreshaken)

Now Quilty is jammed up at the bustop. What's a bustop without buses? He ungloops his eye-leads and runs his scan around the life's atmospheric about him. But, before they can even see how oleacious in glob the globe is, Quilty's i-lids reblurr a quivering countdown to stickdown. He's seen it all anyway. Except his bus meantime blunderbussing on past; as he was rethinking that if you let the dog get at your dirty shirts, it will take you by the scuff of your neck. And leaving our Quilty S. absolutely in fury and irated. It does. In a nuthouse, he is shell mad. He yawns so hard that his jaw bones crack. With his

(where a police dog, there a Shep in wolf's clothing)

tongue twisting in an arabesque snook at the tilting world to clearly demonstrate that the human tongue, while atrophied from that of a dog, is still something of a wag, yes. Not to vox about the breath that he has released onto an earth that can barely cope with photochemicals. From cleaner exhausts, too. But even now, Ratshit Griffley,

aye, Kenny (Ratshit) Griffley

has parked his Leisure Rolls opposite Quilty and is beaconing him to beckon with that Griffley smudgily smirked dial outwards. With Quilt, going: O Dogod, give us this day our daily dread and forgrief all the coming trespasses, specially not Ratshit (Kenny) Griffley before coffee time today of all toadys; pull on my leash; i feel doggo already.

For this is none other than Kenny Ratshit (Griffley), author, lit git of write rodentship (the rat), host for some slackyak muse. Coiffured in a distinguished tincture of grey when he should be distincturely coffined up. Griffley, lionised where our man Quilty has been mauled. Griffley. The same job. But higher up. The same species. But higher upscale, the. Same daily acquaintances. But higher up in, aye. That bugger bugging Griffley. Publically smiling at our Quilty S. He is and does. Smiles. Slimes. Lurching

39

his lugger, hairdo and all. Up his boot with sprigs on, and. Stopping the through traffic as he does so. Our Quilty prays. Ratty Kenny (G) stays. If there be a moral in this, let this be amoral. Whereupon does our

(don't burn your bridges; the dog can swim anyway)

Quilty quickly throw out of his tongue to the end of his nose, pretending he is actually only a Sepik mask hanging around the door of the chemist there. In answer to which, Ratshit (K.G.) freezes in masqueraid of a leering deathmask of a theatre critic wrought in the death throes of a recondite rare moment, as in death mask. So that, there, Quilty to K. Griffley, sepik mask to

(gay dog like to rendezvous with a Romeo to roue-the-day-when)

death mask, a very curio-us impasse making a pass impossible for the car-tiers behind the (Ratshit) automobile and manu-automatically moving their optional human arms onto their hooters to blow their motorist noses. Very honkytonkily and rudely, both. Warning enough. Melbourne, that can wear a writer like Ratshit (Griffley) has got to be all warned down to the barest of threads anyway. So Rat shit K.G. performs a distinguished promptcue leave off of his rude attempt to cohearse our hero into a rude ride into work. It worked!

(fastidious dog prefers man of taste)

Now Quilty stands on his own bandies in the chemist doorway waiting for a bus to routine him to work, doodlebrooding that something over that bloody hill must eat bloody buses. Mentally adding, too, going: Gotta get me to work or the Great Gotcha'll proface me. They will come and hang a tag round my wristy and thrust a road accident onto me parts. Skidding you not, no. Life is one knee'd after another. Who need free exposure care curtsy of the local Outpatients Dieppe They might even come and forcefeed me with a fast growing cancer culture coated with my favorite hundreds and thousands. Do noway want to have to yummy off like that, oo no; i dessert a butter fate than to have the world desire the express expire of the esse of me, and i hate Ratshit Griffley, despite the fact that i've got a fearful coronary coming on and should love all. A nervous flush starting to rise up from my instep already and it's going to have a devastating effect on my corpus christi, when everybud must know that

all i ask in life is a busz, not a hive off.

(the quick brown fox slipped up on the dozen dog)

The bus, rare as gold, Quilty finally at last ingot, near flaking. On which he read on page thirteen, where else but?, that Kenny (Ratshit) Griffley has another raving grovel novel published. Photo there of him, too, etched right down to his last pimple dot. By acid, too, proving that etchers have all the main chances. Proving, too, that a man cannot read his legitimately-bought wastepaper without having that Ratshit Smirk smirching out at Quilty smoted. It does. And also being pressed upon by a fat bag asquat next to him, nudging him further off and over; all women might be sharp but they are mean jabs, and. Her clicking her reptilean wagger at being interrupted at a time when she was thinking about the time she once bagged a fat. She really was a fat bag. Nor will,

(dyspeptic dog bellyaches over sour master)

at the coffee shop for a quick coughy stlopover, the force of that painful memory gather coffee unto his breast. A man can be unswerving ofintent but the coffee can still remain unpoured if the female robots behind a counter turn out to be real cunts. Quilty is not complaining, only comehither plainting. At the coffee pot itself. Through which, if it will only jump up and transact with him, he's got the best chance of being served. It is a very cooling coffee pot, too, that all his meta is diabolically in dry dire of. Seems the whole trouble is that our Quilty must wait and wilt

41

while the seven Cunnies behind there hop to (Kenny) Ratshit Griffley's order for a chickenshit sarny to be promptly sent up via duds all dropped and a delivery upstairs. Barely tolerating

(the dog's picknick ; poor Nick)

Quilty to extrude his growing thyroid while they do so. Their eyes like long lashes. And it is not until Number Seven Cunny dims one of her iris lamps onto our Quilty that coffee swims contention briefly before it all being thrown in his face with: 'Y'see that our Mr. Kenny Griffley got a rave about his new book in this morning's paper? And Mr. Griffley also said for you to uptake his chicken sarnie when you finally get to work. And he said for you to hurry, too, because he doesn't want his dandy sandywich to get all mushy and because you're going to be fired today. Ha ha. No joke.'

O almitey Dogod, how can i carry the banner when i am already beginning to flag? Life's just one gay procession. Quilty is a-float.

(try not to be bloodcur'd awhey)

Fired? You little sizzler! Sacked? In the bag! Dismissed? Demisted! They can all go and get yukt, specially Ratshit Griffley who now is the stool i now leave behind in the dunny. Beneath me squat, aye. And tomorrow, all you pimplenicks, i alone able to uprise body p.m. or a.m., i a.m. and ever shall be, a.m. en all that. My tomorrow comes for you but once a yearn. And where will yr old Quilty be? Flat on his small wallowing in his hammock wafting sneaky little nimbus phews of Xtian high-piety out to thee. Post toast abed, and. Singing to himself Sweet Charon Coming Forto Carry U. No more ergo on; ego i x ist.

Letting his last day of work dwindle to ashes. All fired, up, and. Sitting, after all else have gone, as though he was the last survivor of the Great Reign of Terrier, the tastiest remorsel left until at-last. And now,

42

(hunting pack out on a man-size job)

just about to pack his sack up and go, when suddenly the cleaners are in swarm about him. And so darkfold last-century midEuropean that they work right on through him, with wrangles on their fingers and buhls on their toes. They do. They empty they scrubruburnish they featherdustmust they takeupputdown. Scourges of the scour, true. Quilty has seen it all before, but, tis not until one of them

(St Bernard to give you the dental treatment)

onehandedly lifts our Quilty above her shoulder to polish his bum, blow his hooter and then dewax his wan that he realizes, after ten years working there, how little he has been noticed around this wrenchouse. No matter, at all.

(the more terrier, the less jirma)

Bus'd again
our Quilty, and being bussed about. This is not the end of public transport; it really is the end. Crowded with rush houris. And Quilty's arms so pinioned alongside that he dare not fling out his flexers in case he grabs flesh and gets grebed out as a flasher. (The Word made fleche; arrow in here!)

Hardly daring to breathe for fear it will come out too regular and heavy. What's more, he is thrust beadie to beadie, snoz to snout, iris to highrisk, with a Pekingese pooch unblinking, only a dog's breath away from a beastly end. And the owner of this Peckingpug,

(vegetarian dog like to meet human vegetable)

obviously cares like nix that our Quilty is being pug nosed from pollar to pisst by a pug pest in unblink and snarl from stop to stop unstoppingly. She doesn't and he and it both know it. Quilty even

43

tries smiling at it, but finds no room for anything but an expression which translates pretty much as: show me a dog beneath me boot and i'll show you a lot of yipe-ee. It is not only that, though, but that darling Pikingese answers by taking Qu's coat button in its munchers like as if to say, which it dogly is, 'smine 'smine 'smine. As Quilty tries to ease his personal possession out of its maneaters with all the cherubic forgiveme dear animal for having part of my person under the roof of your doggie mouth. Knowing full well that

(the dog leaves, the human remains)

his stop is coming up fast with just as much steam as the bus has got going for it. He lurches for the relief door, climbing from one lacklustre to another, hand over fists, his and theirs respectively. And thrashing a flesh-threshing way towards that ordinary door that has changed into matter of life or suffocating death. Finally to make it to the roadise paraside, where he begins to wave byebye to all the charmingnice persils you meet on pube transport. Except that

cries of hue come from inside that bus. Cease this bustle! By which the bus brakes so hard that it nearly breaks the bus nearly busting a broken spring. What goes? and what the hell anyway And is about to Quilty walk away when suddenly a posse piles outskee of the bus with pudgy pugowner bearing down on him to pluck her tootsiepie Pekingese off our hero's coatfront. Hangdog look and everything, inclusive of accusing glances. Plus a dental bill to come later from some hopeful vet. But now the bus has worked itself up to a pitch that can carry it a bit further on at least. With Quilty's briefcase left on it and one matchless coat button muxmg up the mouth of a mutthead pesky Pekingese. Too damn easy. Too.

(dogs just love doing the fang-dango)

44

How can you win the race unless you're a bitch on heat? But at least by now, Quilty has dedrudged the trudgery back to his own front gate after what a day of falling in it, and. Is now where his own personic castle begins to make the moat of his existessence. Yes, and pausing now before that drawbridge

(show a leg and a bitch gets heat under her collar)

giving to the Outrealm a cameo of proprietrous piety and desme de mine in de gloaming surveye. Is our Quilty. And were it not for the othickacity of his goggles we might be able to see the tears in his eyes, were it not for the rend in his weepers. His nibblers giving golden inlays to a guilden sunlight setting over his baldwondrous and cupreous cupola without the lightning rod that should somewhere be mounted on such a domed structure. As his is. Moving

(man in the morgue in the dog house once and for all)

like it tis now to front up at his own front door. Where a note has been notched upon, not very houseproudly either. For is it not his beloved and dear wife's (Alyce) own writ large in scrawl on her knees with knobs on each letter and going to wit: 'Lechers, you bet, but no LACKERS, no dice.'

Ha ha. Alyce, the wit. Hee hee, Alyce, what mean? Obvious to wit to woo nothing. My wife has as much humour in her as inner hymen. Like nix. My wifee who whiffs a bit has as much grace as Greasy Joan killing the pot. Me own dear wyffe, who was a waif of the gutter, is ex-waaf, with as much bounce as a scrunched-up squashball staring at a brick wall. My wharfish fishwife, that poor dud mackerel, now wafting, has her toiletry as her only getup'n'go. It's true, thank dogod. She's such a poor mullet of muliebrity, that hear tell even the midwife wanted to throw her back. And when she first whaaa'd with the miracle of being born, the midwife thought that was the sickest joke she ever heard. Still, my Alyce's the ghillie and i'm The Boy, so lessgo in through the haven hatch to let a li'l light leitmotiv back into her poor dull biostyle. Which he

45

(dog catcher hoisted on his own pelt'd)

does. Our Quilty Sewell. Hatches open the haven to let his lovelife into Alyce's sorbent issue of life soggy dull. And runs eddylong into

coils and curlicules and churlycomes and other anti-Quilty whisperings in his own hallway. Before meeting an unpromised and unpromising, both, tall dark stranger. And if this is fortune-toll'd, 'tis nothing to ring bells about for bloody sure. For this t-dk-strngr is a real hobo of an abo from Dubbo dubbed Bob on a stack of good luck up in the Big Smoke, like girth the girls and make them gigolo. Yes, Bob, all bum and gumboiling chewygum, casually swanking down the Quilty passagesway with two buck marbles testily annexed on either side of his crutch seam. Bit seamy. And now grinding his pelvis to a halt alonside of a rather shucked Quilty, screed-ing:

'Hey, yube The Boss, huh?'

'Bey gours?' Quilty.

'The hubby, bub. Aggrieved party.'

What can the Quilt quip but quidproquo but?, 'Do forgive me for asking but have you ever considered a cod for a foundation piece, sir?'

'Bub, you've got yuself one face-bust of a missus. She so ugly, i hadtuh go'n wash me hands before could i button up me bodyshirt again. Phew both ways, bub.'

'Gleep gee gemini crickey, sorry, sir, come back here...'

Our Qu., but this Bob is so much an abo that he waves off our Quilt's hastened chastener and bumswooshes himself out into the white flesh world of fresh dog fur. He does, leaving Quilty in a pig's eye, in troth, slurping away in a mental trough of: Mau Mau and mau poor Alyce and mau innocent littling swaddens! as he

46

charges down to wheel his blancwhite wreaking revenge into his once knew, now reeking bedroom where

(one-armed man must've handed it out to the dog)

Alyce, stitchless and quite tactless, sprawls a lay on her back atop the marital rut pit. Akimbo acutely and licking her lip below a leer.

'Alyce!'

With that, yes!, Kenny Ratshit Griffley from the ball of the bed to the legs of her herby body shooting up with a box camera trained accurately to admit only snaps in snatches.

'Mr. Griffley!'

Snap.

'Mr. Kenny Griffley!'

Snap.

'You Ratshit!'

Snap dragon fotograft alyce same plant.

'Gracias, o gracess Alyce. Very contruelectable, my dear!' This being Ratshit Griffley, yes, and packing up without having been upset, nor obviously his aim. Whatever it is. And overfamiliarly patting our stunned Quilty on the shoulder by manna of a tomtom beat:

'Hello and goodbye; do watch for future fruity photodevelopments.'

Leaving behind Alyce as she waves ta ta with her leathery ridden crop:

47

'Don't forget, Kenny. Alyce with a Y in your next book. Y'm a I. Bye.'

(seen on a tombstone: Camped With A Dog-eared Outward Bounder)

Now Quilty is alone at last with alaska alyce. The air is chilly. She, who has made his conjugated bed the instant drop-off each night that it comfortably is. He wipes his weaty windscreens. He cannot read right his radarscreens: 'Alyce, i don't believe my own eyes.' He is electrode in wire hook-up. 'Alyce, i am shocked.' Waved. But she only tumbling her own admiring eyeballs along her own aweful, now awesome, femmiform forking a forty-five degrangle at her now public pubics and frizzling them and her, going:

'Gee, i even look like a cap Y, don't i? You can untie my ankles, lacker.'

'Alyce!'

'Untie me, cuckold, whatever that means.' Stretches, too, to waft unmentionable manfuls, and, 'You just couldn't know the depths some people can go to, lacker.'

(the dog is a man's best fiend)

Well, this is toffee enough stuffing to make our Quilty now dig his toes in. At last and yes. He fists his clenchers; for Alyce with lust, a bunch of fives. Can we blame him? After all, what strange semenars have menu'd upon this his hammock? What slip inon up the hairy parts of his spousie's pussy, Alyce in alley oops? How come, whoever did? He has trod bloody mills to keep his family in oats and his kiddykins in treadlies. So who has sown here? Going: 'Alyce, tell me that that low rodent ratshit of a Griffley has not cucked on me, Alyce. Also that that ferret-crossed mongrel dog of yours there sniffing khyber trails along devious roots on my sheets

48

ain't your ferret-crossed mongrel dog and that bed ain't my workpit and you ain't you, Alyce. Because if you don't you'll be dead for your dental appointment tomorrow, Alyce!'

(small dog tucked into the helping hand)

But Alyce has danced beyond the pale and is now bouncing up down up down, yes, and trampoulining girltones of 'slip my catch and you can bobble me' in the midst of what was once their sanctibed of silt. Waving some sort of paper, too. Dup-down whee-whoops, both her boobs bouncing bleeblupp-bleeblupp and her slack guts in such a slishsloshsloosh bellyfall of rise and sheen that to believe is to materially see, no shit. 'Y'know, lacker?' Alyce the yo-yo stringing together her words, 'You lack job i hear and you lack means of support lack hair lack 20/20 vision lack success intelligence fame and fucking fortune. You lack length too. Yalack the shellack. And yaknow what? Me, i don't lack for nothing, cos i've got a telegram for me, telegrim for you!'

'That's not a telegram, Alyce; that's a Kleenex with adulterous stains which your mongrel dog wants to chew.' Quilty, telegrim, you can tell.

So deft Alyce corrects the inconsequential foepar so that nduecourse both she and her shaggingdog are arapt arantly, which?, with it drooling upon the Kleenex and she drooling upon the telegram, and only our Quilty not got the message. Yet. But he does brave a grabfer, just as Alyce broadcasts her seedy Olympiscroll, going:

'Telegram read out, lacker, and herewego --"Congrats, you have won the $200,000 Opera House Lottery" ' and has just enough time to offtoss it at Quilty's feet before he explodes with a humblast of thanksgiving to a god almost human: 'YAHOO MEET ME MITTS ON THAT MINE MONEY QUICKMATE!'

(Bluey, we're sorry; the dog's always getting into a Blue)

49

And now bouncing himself, counterwise to her cuntwise, on the spring mattress foaming. For all that Alyce has got back on the boards and is standing muttly by the bedroom door watching him with her blank silli-supurous squint cartridges like a gelding that knows it isn't. But who gives a pig's root for Alyce? Face like a busted pastie. Never blamed her for it like i might have. Now that the heavens have opened i can jgig i can giggle i can become what i've always wanted to. A meglamaniac. I shall syph up four times ere i count the cost. Of plural mistresses. And instal gas chambers in every dog pound and one in Ratshit Griffley's bedroom so that when he switches on the light just before he dies he has visions of even illiterates booing.

Yet how stormy the C is between A-birth and B-buggered. The Moving Finger having writ damages. Q. Sewell was away, alfwayup and executing a starwards pirouette imaginably on Griffley's brain pickled in an unidentified flying oyster mour-nay, when he bifocals that Alyce has remained in coldhard glaze from the doorway. His furrow brows over his heel, as he ploughs up in the air towards an impending prang between the pain and the counterpane. Hearing tumbletones of:

(Hope, the dog's still waiting with its legs crossed)

'You No way known, lacker.' Alyce.

'Watcha mean, not me?' Quilty.

'Name on ticket is Alyce S. That's me, Tojo, not you.'

'I bought that ticket for you, Alyce!'

'Just shows how much you're a lacker, lacker.' Waving goodbye.

'Alyce!'

'Oh, and I nearly forgot. Your children were going to say bysies before they left on their world trip, but then they remembered you needed a mouthwash gargle something bad.' Alyce, pausing only

50

to extricate a black curly Bob pube from out of her meat-nibblers, before dredging up something else called Pity the Poor Sap deeper inside a cavity opening within her. She lowers her gravox a few thousand coarse grains and tones in almost the Alyce He Knows, going:

'You really do lack all round, don't you, lacker?'

'I bars second go all round, Alyce.' Quilty rolling off bed onto the grovel. 'Slips, Alyce. I bars slips.' Quilty, crawling back up the passage towards the front door with pooch trying to take liberties now that the Quiltyform has been brought to its sinking knees. Fast. Going off and out, which? and both, going again but gone right off: 'I bars another resay replay rerun alyce.'

Quilty, yes, scratching his way to catch hold of the front door knob. Impossible with a quiver like he's got and his ex-faithful hound trying to catch hold of his. To nibble or to nobble, either or.

(dogs cheek each other)

Now, the garden front lawn is he ex cursing so cruciatedly. On his knee-caps. And doing commonal garden goblin gutturals; his weepers wet and unwiped; quite exploded, a shell of a man, with each and every nerve azither. A zymotic lump of wheatgerm. Mounted by a mutt, just a mount. Yes, our Quilty S. The same one, yet changed in only ten minutes.

From being a loser to being a total lacker. Proving: when you hesitate, the dog ruminates. There is no pity in The Fang if you can't get up off the bottom rung, no, for Dogod is after your bottom ring. Just look

at our Quilty again. What was once a man is now a man-serving ex-pet, exposed to all the pussy-chasing elements of fact'n'fictence. Seeing nothing but a big fat zero making up his life. On his bank balance. No job no parentage nomore active no

51

wife no home no where to go. Televisionless nights stretched blackly before him. A lone figure confronted by a world out there full of normal-looking people who. Just might throw stones at him as he walks down thoroughfares, in case what he's got to make him look like that rubs off. A body who might blow up all bubo. A disadvantaged person like him got no right to be trying to make it on his own. When he was lucky to have been allowed to get through birth. Terrorful days of kids catcalling at his heels. Empty nights. Dear Dogod, he might be home now, but he wants to go home. He does. Stopping, turning his lugger, ligging his

(fast greyhound makes meatball of horse and rider)

christfallen look onto his Iouseyrich wife there at the window getting niggled at the tag that won't come off her new gold lame shockershorts with inbuilt trap door, and not getting from her nary a twat twitch of a response. Going by way of shoutback, 'You're being unfair, Alyce. I haven't even got a job anymore, Alyce. I am no dog, Alyce, even though our dog thinks i am some bitch on heat. Alyce? You answer, Alyce! *Alyce*? I am as vegetable in your soiled hands, Alyce. You don't have to dig me, just fork out. Try pitching.'

(if the dog sniffs you, start to smell a ratter)

But Alyce has sloped off to soap down her newly-adorned temple and. Quilty stuns alone, his vox creoling in the sub urban wilderness. It seems a long time before he realizes even his once dogpet has now given him up for being a poor cozen of a dog however ragg'd. Grrrr.

(dog in a manger; men a la carte)

The rush of nouveau-riche water echoes to Quilt from inside his ex-bin, no doubt showering hot-aqua spuma over Alyce's spermed body, o whale of a time. Lapping at her lapping it up. She always did like it hot, the lashing the better. And, lo, the innocent toctic tock of the water meter at his feet. Fancy. If this is not fate, then it is fit. That he reaches down to turn off the cold water main, but not so the hot water heater inside would know. No no. Upshotting that, at the same time as he closes his front gate for the lastlife time behind him, there rings out from within Alyce's scream of empathy with all lobsters suffering the boils...

Willyu wontu willyu wontyu, wontyu come and join the chasse

And that's how Quilty left his own plot and got onto the Scotty plot. Dogod isn't a blind dog to it all, just a graphfter.

(bull dog! Cover your calves!)

Siriusly though:
a good vet knows that all dogs need a good sleep. Then again, you should take good kaolin of your dog; it might help it let you settle down. Even though your dog will probably try to make a slob of you. It's no help that the better-trained dog at the table is a great goremaniser, a convivial host and makes a perfect man-savant. Most dogs try to stay with their set men-us. Then they get all het up and start picking bones with you. Mind you, if you've got one foot in the grave and slipping fast, you can rely on your dog not to let go until it's beaten. And when the dog starts pulling your leg, it's no joke. Don't worry, though, even if you're gone, if the dog wants relief it just empties its blooder. And if it plays with the children it must have just already eaten. You show me a human butcher and I'll show you a dog. Then again, the dog Spot on never misses. So beware; you've even got two canines in your mouth going bad on you. If you start feeling beastly, just paws for refreshment. Remember, Toby or not Toby, that is the Punch line. Then again, growing up is just boneing up for the dog. So never tryst a dog. They won't be love bites but sample tastings. And also, remember that tombstone inscription:

'Dog Gone'. And the ones next door to it: 'Dog Tired And Run Down, RIPed' and 'He Was Ignawed Too Munch'. So let's bow wow

down to the one Dogod, that Grrreat Gurrru. For the Son of Dogod has been scent down amongrrrel us. *Ohm*.

JELF

And how ever so very clevery-clive of you to have noticed the similarity of the 'y' at the end of each mon's moniker, leaving, as you also must have perceived, that rhymey give-away of Quilt and Kilt, if you took into account Scotty's probable nationality. Which you must've. So, with Quilty being Scotty and Scotty being Quilty, it hardly needs re-saying that with wig, con contact lens, knapsacked out with nipperfalsecaps back brace built-up shoes atall et al and all (add a hie ad hocly, too, of knockknees or hoc-nose), he is a real specimen. And if this does not raise a hmmm of confusion it will certainly raise a humph on somebody's back up. Since then, both Quilty's and Scotty's real name(s) is/are Jelf, then we will call him or them, which and both, Jelf. Jelf. Whose

(fast dog cuts out a dashing figure)

name now can hapfully fit eponymic epon the stage of this story. Yes. Jelf, thank you very much, standing in once-Scotty's place raising belie'ing hums dinging there and a few humdinging bellies here from themtherethose yonis and yonkers absolutely stunned into gawkitude at the sight of Itself. We being agen back at

the arstudio in a certain wife's mansion, remember? Or, for another hearing, you could go back to the dog-ear'd last few pages of Chapter Two, where fully is demonstrated that the must in the mutt be directly related to the ogod! in the nature d'ogod. Yes?

(give the dog fresh meat, and you give it fresh ideas)

Jclf, yes. To repeat:
Tis he who was born under the sign of the Dog-Star, super-siriusly; and ever since been going from one set of chops to another chop coming down. Dog-days? Dog-years of them! Dogod collar'd ever since he was but pup fatty. Now a dog's-dinner to boot out of burp of some mere whining hound's winewind. Nothing more than a poor tyke for the paw take. A mangruel cur under whey; a crumbly off a dog's biscuit; sheer grrr-ist to the maul. Yes, Jelf. None other. On whose dogsbody even the hair has

55

given up all of a piece; and hair's supposed to last alive years after the savaged body's bin savaloid laid, yes. Jelf. Protagoner, ist. He is.

Not only that but, if his ahah alias is Quilty, then his wife we know. She with the mooshed mush like a husky that's been gnawed over by a molar bear, aye. She with the striding gate between her legs and owner of all this mansion, this House That Jerk Bilked. She who is referred to on the breast-pleats of all of those so whale-built yonis there, wearing atit their tops manogrammed 'ALYCE'S BRASSERIE' right smackeroo on the brassieres. (Talk about circumspect inspection; don't talk, just torque.) Yes, you have gassed it. Tis Alyce! And this is Alyce's lousey 'ouse and Alyce is the 'wife', whiffly mention'd in the bank back there, and Alyce is the 'she' with the chequie-weckies, and

who else but Alyce could have engineered all these humiliations on the humus being of Quilty/Scotty/Jelf?

Alycealycealyce bloody Alyce (still) alyve still a lyce.

(too many cockers spoiled the broth-er)

Jelf, now that the applause from all the spanking good yonis and yonkers there has been died dwindlised, uperies epically (beowulf, you, and not a devil!) into the airthair, 'This be the lastimc, Alyce!' before, before the rezounding laughter, dragging his pathetic body pathetically up the central dias. O, that he should live to see the dias when! Seven dias make one weak. Our Jelf now mounted and regrooming himself into the gloom of his famous poses as Everyman Weed, doing

(dog with biting humour takes the mouth out of comedian's words)

his primal tableau of 'Quasimodo at a Tentacle Age'. See-quelled by the 'Necrophiliac Nature Buggering Itself Up'. Both with base and low relief on his part. Alyce is the genius; where does she unearth Its like this? And aren't ever those charcoals hot upon the canvasses! All yoni'n'yonker strainiums begin craning furrow-wards: uplook downstroke downluft upstrake loftstrike leftstreak downup laughstruck heads poor bastard hee hee. While 'Art' Munro wanders about their circle tutoring here or uttering hier tut or tuttutting thither and hither, ether higher and hier. Then voicing his appreci-applause at Jelf when he, as he does now, appends his im-provisual cameo of 'Phantasmagorical III'.

(Dogsteeth! life is just a grind)

'Bravo, dear boy,' goes 'Art' Munificent, 'Spendiferous in the execution as oos-swal, incredibous in the unveiling thereof. Snare, mes enfants, snare, nary stare. Wunderlines! Straffing strokes! This he be rare essence. So praise thy provendor of this thaumaturg, thy Alyce. Wondrous Alyce!' planting his two twin lickspitters onto the liptop of Jelf's polished agate nude noodle (so that, hold it!, two of his quicker students might capture on paper 'Baby Joe Sus, new shaven on account of ringworm, going goo goo gad eyes up at fat Mamma Margy upstairs', yes) while still spouting carryon of, 'Bear graphic witness what we puny normortals canst but marvel at... This man Thing. Nature's end of all freak-out'.

(a dog tongue-lashing cuts you to the very quick)

Now our tention is atturned to another part of the manse, namely the banquet room where there is a luscious banquetable set full. Down in the middle of. In long perspective, NNE but with very few other good points, is sat, suckling off his second fiddler and now burping flatus out over the Louie Cartoars silverservice, Amos. Yes! He of the vanced adze-years, and having recent reveiled a raving revelling for what was once laid and is now spread all over the table, flora and all. Amos purrs over his sticky

57

fanny-lingerer for a while, and then has at the Napoleon brandy, as he pip-squeaks to whoever could still conceivably be in that room let alone still watching how he packs it away, *'Who's got the bloody fags? where's the bloody fags? bloody...'*

Need to relate on, prelate? Toolate, so tootlebye. A meal fit for a king should ne'er be provianded on a thing unfit for a meal. He is too much of a mealy mouth to regurgitate dis-passiopeptically on. Quite. And long gone a bit deipnosophftist in the head, too.

(dog at the left foot on your bed)

Coincidentedly, Jelf is b'hooing and shedding unshelled tears in the called duty that is culled for in the execution of his 'The Concircumvenient Cuckold' diorama, with just that right amound of soupcjon sippisip of pathos (that which they use for lining pathments) gleaning from out of an evoked sadsack whose wife is just too easily fuckable by anyone to be for rill. Providing you used the sack over her head before you entered the sack with her. Yes. Nfact he is so pathos in need of a bathos that one yonker

presumes himself to be so weird, like comparative, that he is eyeing Jelf off from his canvas and winking his lashers. It's true; just how weird can you ghetto? Pure case, surely, of rape rapping on the dour of the unthinkable.

(man who level with dog end six feet under)

But there it is. All nearing completion of the utmost perversions, shown e.g. on cach'n'every canvass there through line distorted and line emaciated and line parabola'd and line parabola'ss and Harry Lyme (The Third Dimansion) and line outfreaking anything previous charcoaled from A to B straightway. And, weird to depict, each one of those canvasses contains drawings that have some part of Jelf's anatomy being consumed within the jaws of various types of dog. When,

(Tombstone Inscribed: Had His Trunk Packed)

just then the door opens and, jesus! judas!, Alyce indeems herself in all her full retch glory, her voice no less a foghorn for the brightness of the day:

'Boy oh boy, what told? Like, does It ever *lack*?'

'Art' adamant earnest and floutish floor-to-knees: 'Alyce, angel patron, provendor, power put pits, Mamma Maecenas of Man-depicts...' And Jelf al Quilty ias Scotty unposing for wind-up whine of:

'Wanna twalk twoo yoo Alyce.'

'Is that there man a peewee or is he a peewee? Would they hang a carcas like that from a hook or would they try to cure it? For old boot leather, ha ha.'

'Alyce, i want to taylk...' But unheard over 'Art' Munro who has his kisser kitsch full of Alyce toes, bumpious and all. Unheard of. And she shaking her medusa and her monthly chequered outpour for himjelf at Jelfhim:

'Chequie weckie, lacker. Do carry on!' Nor even waiting to take note of how limited our Jelf thinks her dial-a-log really is, before she frizzs out thrrrummm from the arstudio waving to all cherio wish ewe luck as i weave you goodbye. Yes, Alyce levant and taking off.

'Alyce!' Jelf lashing out with his tongue caught in his throat. And only getting gingle belles from all those giggling girls and tintinbulating Bills, who think he is only adding some touches of vocal awfulthenticity to his current tableau of 'Leper Going For Allah or Nothing'. With 'Art' M. rolling his polly and gurgling enough to tickle his thriggle at the Funstuff Jelfing,

'Oh, be he not a scream for such an arch bounding lacking loser...?'

(man-eating dog bound over to keep the piece)

O, yes, you may laff, World, but beneeth that outer Jelf shell lies a fictafact shell of a man with sensabubbles, aye, and a bleeding heart half-hearted beatingly borne on prosit, aye, living on peanuts, aye, and ne'er has any man sulphured so much for such a hell of a shellacking. A force-fed martyr, all right, but this is the last raw straw. Tis, believe it or not. Well, anyway and apart from what you think,

(solicitor's dog fed up to the teeth with being sued on)

Jelf suddenly leaps down from that dias turning a pose into a posse after Alyce, only pausing once between it and her exit door to vitely view one of the canvas amuckly charcold with an interpretation of what he might have looked like if Nature had been a little more kind and Dogod a little less open in its jaw intent. Its artist going:

'Hey, man lover, waddya think?'

'Slander.' Jelf outstretching even his own screech. Which so delights its artist that she (though a yoni) is abslootly styonkered. She is, going have-begun-squeal-travel: 'Hey, ain't that right!' and positively thrusting out her annal'd ring for Jelf to smackeroo lysol on, you choccy lips u if you wishywash. But even this cannot stop our hero now. Already he is in breakaway from 'Art' Munro's class and out thru the door through which Alyce axled her greasy head, before you can say, 'Look, lacker is up and out after Alyce and has just called us all rhodent rats; red what?' Which none did.

(homeless dog makes your heart bleed)

That Jelf vs. Alyce chase:
by way of where the Jelf emerges back into hallway and casts around loudly for Alyce to come back here for to have a few cutting wordsounds with him or alternatively a few cuts around

60

her larynx region, assuring her she won't feel a thing except a soaring pain. What a trip. Then

(manshy dog got no guts)

plungoes after her shouting come back here you femme futile you, launching himself to land up on the stares landing stepping and stairing two at a time, yes, and. Confronted with not only a corridor leading to doorsdoorsdoors but doorsdoorsdoors opening up a corridor stretching before his eyes so confusingly that he is suddenly not sure what careerdors leideroff from where and which cardoors leider off from what. Do corrigos corrigible off thep or chorijaws corrijabble off thee? Confuzzing; and no sign of Alyce.

He waits and listens. Wets. And begins to list. Then something sounds off to the right, as though a sound was made. He frows himself at the door hurlingly, hell's-bells!, hurls burlingly, and ought have even taken the door off its hinges had it not been so pantomime opened that very instant. Aye, with Jelfo pummelling in lookout coming on through into a darkened room. All dark, save upon a wall a film projection which Jelf would certainly not like projected too far, like the type oft seen with coughdrops at Driveins after the restaurant has ended, or running to recorded audiences in the artyparts of town where

(the dog leapt for joy. Poor Joy)

life is just one gay flimsy prom in a flammy pram factory. Even Jeff's grrrs are grinding to a halt before it. And, Gob the Duke, if it isn't a plot We All Know reconstrued by that callous silveroxide beam sparking in the dark. Starring, yes, Alyce as the nubile and bountibeaut wife all bounce up and spring down atop bedpit shouting 'Iwon Iwon Iwon', and. Yes, Kenny (Ratshit) Griffley, made-up as the abounding cuckolded Quilty Sewell, who is at that moment of real live action grabbing for a make of the lottery telegram. And, to put it mildly, Griffley (as Quilty alias our Jeff) is acting atrociously, even for one bounded by that clown's make-up and those flappy flowing feet that flop from under those plaffy panti-fluff'd-out trousers, braces and Chaplin all. Yes, this is true.

61

On film before our very pupils. And students. And not only is Alyce not only not Alyce, but a young and beauteous Yoni stand-in for Alyce. Which is a bit rich for someone who could only get a stand-in if she laid down on a parade ground with her mouth open for a hobnailed hoof clomp in. Also

(bitch seeks butch for home pursuits at homo)

since the wrottenly ritten script is obviously out of the hand of someone who thinks reality is but a finely-tampered steal, the whole thing stinks of the handwork, which always stinks, of that wryta Kenny (Ratshit) Griffley himself. Yet with each criminal alteration of reelity presented on that silver screen, there gorth forth gushes of mobmass hilarity, especially every time there is a focus on Griffley as Jelfclown as Jelf, who. In reality is having to satan there on his hardy laurel and watch this despicturability from Alyce. Some samples freely follow the following:

Alyce: (stand-in): You can't know the depths some people can go to, lacker.

Quilty (Kenny, the clatshit rown): Fair's flair, Alyce. Not all of us borneo'd with pluperfact teeth manners intelligenocide and outright beauty of forme like licking you, Alyce. Oo, say, Alyce, what is that telegram saying first prize etcetera that you are hoving to y'self by your own hand Eheheh Alyce (stand-ing): You've got so much nothing, lacker.

Quilty: Alyce, I'll do anything!

Alyce: Anything, hu? Y'wanna start crawling?

Quilty: Eversomuch, A.

Alyce: Y'wanna lick my feet, too, lacker?

Quilty: Pant-pant, panty pants.

Alyce: Y'wanna roll over on your back, too, lacker?

(pet like to meet well-heeled lady to follow in footsteps of ex-master)

'*ALYCE*!' Realifer Jelf that, with his goggles reflecting a flashback of the end-of-the-reel-numbers (like a flashgordon countdown, cheers and whistles!) across his video amplifiers. It's as though the whole chawfing sidesplitting auditorium has become a laser s.f.ing out of control. Hee haw, so some age-old donkeys there too.

Then, soddenly, the room is swatched all agloe with electri-sight and, yes, there. Is 'Art' Munro somehow there and, yes, there. Are, somehow, the same yoniyonker weirdoes and weirdstags who were charcoaling his formal self in doggone poses in the arstudio back there. And, too, 'Art' Munrowit clapping his pads yfere similar to a kindiegarden TV kiddie bear, going: 'Dear boy, how timely spoofing this be of thou! Kiddies, low, therebe the star o' our small cinematograph, worthy product of our Alyce Academy...' But before that morbid mobego can even finish with him, Jelf has throe'n himself threw a side door, by a series of lungeful and lunging stumbles sideways. While behind him, this: massive mass Cap'n Marvel applause more more bis ness you murine you! Proving what a slap in the eye it is, when you contract the Clap.

(poised bitch, no lady-in-waiting)

What a chase still:
Jelf has trussled himself out into the same corridor again. What a way to find yourself! But now there is echoing a vox full of ribnudging nurgatories implyings softsounds whistperings about him all about him. Once again some dirty dog must be lying doggo and daschounding the truth about him to pieces. 'You cut that whispring outand show yourself, Alyce!'

63

and making scornfully along the corridor aslike asif he knew which of the doors he would tear from its fashionplates, uproot from its jamb up, jabblewok frum its jeepers. If only there were not seven or eight more than one of them. His ringing voice still straining to get heard above the herd. Meanwhile,

(Grace, you can return; the dog has fallen from another)

mindless to the drama melpomenading upstairs away, Amos has finally agone amock it looks like. Even so, it is jolting upright to find him flawed on all fours and growling grrrrandpa-to-u-too from the floor at one of the Dobermann pincers there, itself getting up a steamy grrr grrr back at Amos. The two trails of after-dinner mints straiting along in stretch lines, one from the smozzlc of Amos and th'other from the arsmeller of the Doberdog, have something to do with it. For Amos is winning hindsomely over hand at who can chomp the most post-prandials in the foxiest and trottiest quicktime, and. The Dobermann caninity is getting all huff puffity about losing to some old goat when at stake is the reputation of der german master-race. Anyway, it is embarrassing for a hunting dog to be beaten by his own game, yes.

(the dog Toby does his Judy for dog supremacy)

The Alyce chase still:
during which witch time, Jelf has locussed the door behind which is located the whisperings against his Jelfperson and thinking to himself: *unthinkable*. And also wondering what kind of locusts could do this overheating overthearing locotalk. And here we switch on a snatch of it:

1st Voice: (female) Sssh. He might come in.

2nd Voice: (female) Oooo. Do you think he would?

1st voice: (female) Nar. He lacks too much.

Distincturely, yes. Jelfhimself can feel his cheeks burning: oo this
has gone too fer alyce. He bellows in a forge imitation (what's the
onamatter, pia?) of a bull on Belle, 's true, and flings open that
door in a passing imitation of a riptearing hurry not waiting for
leeway. He does; and, is gleeted by

(dogs find tough old master a bit hard to take)

darking and heaveness breathing. Dimly-lantern'd in a room
where the air has got foul of itself loitering in every corner of what
shape room it is, too dark to be ascurtained by Jelf as yet. All he
can make out is a fustian row of blinding footlight, plus the stout
outline of a four-poster, not to mention, even as we do, the two
fcmalish shapes on it, making in the murk like two climbing vines
engaging in an interesting entressellated vignette of rubbing
royals, one against thother. One, being from the befuming
perfume, Alyce, and the other being, being so approximo to Alyce,
surely with a heavy cold, which, if you are near Alyce is a v. wise
condition to haveat or covet. Caveat. And fat, this other one, talk
about. Saying the Lord's Prayer on the run wouldn't even get your
tongue around it. It is of such huge dimensions such that one half
of the woman looks like a crowd of people waiting to see the other
half roll-up to roll-up half of her. She's even got two names by
repute out of desire. One half of her is called Nanette; the other
half is called by megaphone, but only upwind so that your voice
can travel far enough, y'know? And,

now Alyce can be heard to be the shusher who had buzzarded
around Jelf's ear out in the corridor. He is trying to adjust his
sights. But no rifle and the footlighting effects affects. The heavy
breathing of those two occuponents bed-pronant there, makes him
want to cough to clear his scrotum. It's all v. vixeny difficult.

'You're in here, Alyce,' now trying to cry out above Alyce's
wallows in the gulpy shallows of Nanette, incredibly enwrap-tured
by nothing much more than a mini-loinlapper, nothing more and
nothing less, so that one, even as close up as Jelf, can't tell where
one leg leaves off and the other leg clefts in. Staged dialog fans the
flames:

Alyce: Ooo, I think hubby's arrived homey.

Nanette: Oo, what will he do, pant-pant?

Alyce: He might come in and lack at us.

Nanette: Giggle-ooo.

Alyce: He might just have to come and lack at us, whatsui say, sexooey

Nanette: Nice. Roll over, et eat etna etcetera. Nice?

Alyce: Yummy.

Nanette: Jam roll?

Alyce: Yumjammy.

(The Hounds Hunt Ball --packed-out relic of good Old Timms)

'WHEN YOU'RE BLEADY ROODY, ALYCE!' Yes, Jelf from under a highly raised voice straight to his pointed finger shaking oliver you're twisted Alyce and if i ain't a man u're manure u are Alyce. But yes, again!, even before

(Dogod raised Cain first of all)

he can spflutter even more than a further thin veneer of an ensuing anger melting into rage, somebody switches on the lights allover. And this time Jelf finds himself in a theatre up on a stage in the wing in the poop again affronted by them same yonis 'n' yonkers, yes!,

(dogooder relieves dog famine single-handed)

including (aye) 'Art' Munro, who is now doing his nanna with a final gulp. Nfact it is he who has his manumitt on the light switch nearly blowing a fuse, i.e., 'nonononono... NO!' Then gushing artianguish, all fickle and foppy, like every theatre director ever born a theoretical manchild put into practice, 'Dear boy, really! Thoust canna persist in these 'orrible interrhuptions o' artists' rehearsals in like manner, fie on, no. Hie thee a bugger off thence and mayst next time the timing of thy entrance be more upshot correct in't.' Then turning back to Alyce and Nanette in that birdoir seenoir with about the same grace as if he was a baby Billy Bunter with fru-fru pirouetting on a music box and, 'Thus, drats, retake, sweet ladies! And more *theatre de cruel*, more...'

'YOU STUFF IT, ALYCE, CHEQUIE-WECKIE AND ALL!'

(theatrical dog extracts the core of playwright's outporings)

Egads gooksooks! Did th'thing named Lacker, alias Mr Lacker, in the play give birth to a litter in a lather of sweat (c.f. Dot the Hot Dog) Zooks, ye gods, gad flies! Even 'Art' Munro, yes, is deflated by such flatulence. At their Alyce! Unprecedented? So unprecedented that even the Precedent of the Master Rapists Association once declined her, sending along a rasp in's place. He did. Yet it is the Alyce-she who is first to recroup her voice.

'Is that lacker flashing some sort of golden dental morse code at me?'

'I don't caries about my cares anymore, Alyce.'

'Does someone here read morse gold'

'Just leave i lone to my poverty-striked misery, Alyce. I've dashed my last to-do for-u Alyce so negotiate your chequie-weckies right up your yawing vault. Here i huff and i mean to huff off for good, so huff yours for the rent, Alyce!'

'O, lacker, wow. You crazy? Who else is going to steak you so you can suet me for divorce?' Then the dying hen clucking:

'The lacker can't even afford to get rid of me. Can-can but can't can-tata.'

(dog so gland to see you)

To such a background, Jelf wheels bravo away in a spinoff onceandforall, heading over the brow of his beaten as he unhinges himself from the stage door and flits along and down a flighty twosteps atatime going a cross the mosaic floor aflee frudoor, now reclothed and closed, out into the open of off-putting fresh air. Are greens. Yes, Jelf, astriding out of that scene over the frontal lawn to passby the front gaters, ali oops. Yes, he is, with regiment in's boots and regimen in's jawline, set solid.

Quilty appurtenanced again as Scotty to throw up Jelf. Feet of clay? Well, still a bit half-baked.

(big fat lump in the throat of dog)

Still it was a chase, and:
synchronic chronic Alyce, regalling in her statehood as The Grandame of Lingam on that theatrical bed upstages the Jelfrustoff exit by opening her abyssmal legs to their cavernous extent (beware of small bitey animals) and magnumly invites all the yonis and the yonkers into the snake-pit with a hoot-your-horn of, 'Who's gonna come in and *cup*?'

(dog sees two skint deadbeats, does double take)

At which time of which, Jelf just happens to be trying to outrun two very dog-tired Herr Dobers trying to hun him down and receding around the herrline before his arterioclosure. Yes, and he hacking around the hackles, going: *heil see you in my drams.*

(dog on a long stalk seeks long tall streak)

68

Enow, the wheel has turned full circle full circle full circle, ratitty-tat ratitty-tat ratitty-tat. Yes. Our Jelf back on the train, going blissedly back to blessed Sydney to be anon just another nong among a lot of other anonymouses.

(Jap dogs come in all sizes of Nip)

Trains to the countryside, honestly, are enough to give people agrophobia. They are. And how comforting come-forward to see once again all those Sydney roadside adv. boards shoutshatting out at you type of: 'Welcome home, you misera-bald bastard, you; wipe that smog grin off your kitscher.' Oh yes, back to Citysyd where lossof self is a warming thing of glory lorications unto Dogod. Yea yea.

(dogging the human body: police hound disarmed it; dog with gall bladder got stoned)

Jelf not to know it just then, but back in Sydney, Constable Wilkinson is still around, around. Though bepuzzlements are beginning to show on the brunched-up brow of Constable W's proto-scowler. Meaning, what's happened to the doggie dung-faker outside lottery vendories? Just lying low or, and here Constable Wilkie's boil bloods, constipated by some other constable's attention? Meaning there's been nix for nichts. Nothing piled onto the pathways or bygoes. And nobody, least of all our missed and steerious Mr Fido Bigs has even slipped up. On. No.

(draw a bead on the artist's dog)

Dogodammit, and there was our procinct pro of the precinct, hot on the steaming trail too! He had thought, getting hot. Unless the foul doggy sausager has escaped to the Nullispoor Plain or someats thereabouts. Cusses; a thought, that! Constable Wilkinson's in danger of getting a splitting headache so his brow quickly knits up again. He curses and cruises. Around, around.

69

(dog with only one ear lacking full human attributes)

Jelf now rolling one of his hugely handsome eyeball'd lens out of the window which is travelling as fast if not as full pelt as the train

(man running at full pelt still got a hide-away from dog)

and yawning with his divine curls vinecurling divanly around in and throughout of the gurly fingers of another girlie, call'd this time Cealy Misslainy, all painted and panting out of their pores in's hair. Her and her fingers. This is quite true, no bull or knobs. A bit warty, though. Nfact she is so wrapped up in and around him, we can say our Jelf is all dolled up. Not half. B'wigged again to vantage gain; and orbitals sparkling like heavenly Hindi bodies over Azure Minor (starring Cornea and her See-throughs); yes, and his pearlies so white and even that it makes you wonder whether God in fact was a graduate engineer and not just the backward dog he spells it out as. Aye, and all this embodiment falling upon the shoulders of poor blissuffering Cealy Misslainy there, who was never really made of the stuff to be a caryatid bearing up such a classical architectured form as his, but who

(Cassanova, all's clear; the dog's unearthed another rake)

is bravely stroking The Jelfessence with her libido absolutely starkers, would you beliege. And even veiling her eyes with a purple desire so the world can't see her inner lacklustre. Things are so hard! And Jelf himself? A free man for the first time. No tie no alyce no lucre no more alyce boodle boohoo no nothing holding him back now cept perhaps this Cealy M.'s leg vice. Still, he continues the conversation:

'So this phlegm fatal she did say to me, "I'm sorry, sir, i know it's your world famous play and i know you've come all the way from Horsetraylia to see it, and with openings in New Yorkers and Gay Paree next week, but unless you relent and share the Royal Box we can't find a free seat for you for the next six month solid, dad.'

70

(zeroing dog; Spot on)

At which Cealy Misslainy dares to indempt an interjaculation, yes!, with, 'Gee, i bet you could be a famous male model, too, if you half tried. Try me.' Which goes to show that a female's mouth is all man-edibles, jaw jaw jaw. Shocked and interruptured, Jelf opes his blinkers (o that she should ever ope to see the like again) to admonish her when he sees, stuck like a manphagous fly upon the compartment door, the hands nose mouthylips chin forehead and all of, yes, Amos. All flattened into fat fleshy pads against the glass panel and going at him, 'Ch-ch-chuu-toot-toot...' by worde of mallf and rolling stock. O, the pane of it all! A sight that even a fertile creative writer could not conjure up a template for, not even Edgar A. Poe. Nor does it take much bran work for Jelf to work out that since

(sorry dog with man-sized hangover)

carl Amos is on the train now, he must have been on the train all the way to Alyce's and back and. Therefore croneAmos must have been in wit of what passed there, where our Jelf was not able to pass for anything but what he basically in summation is. That is, Jelf minus Scotty equals Quilty! Crust o bloody mighty!

'YOU FILDY OLTH STOOLIE!'

Yes, our Jelf now up on his best feetures and railing to blow off steam astern of Amos amoving off for his old but still lively vitalvite. And just think! Poor little Cealy Misslainy is supposing that Jelf's sudden burst is just a portion of his potable passion and is trying as forcefully as virtue and her karate classes modestly allow to get the tweed-dees off of Jclfdumb while he endeavours to get past her hot crutch-clampers to Amos. Anyway, too late now. Amos has gone off longoa. Phfew relief.

[hungry dog like to strip female entertainer)

Pari passu, passepieding Jelf has managed to passover Cealy Misslainy, in the midprocess of dropping all pretence of a cover-

71

up, and leaps out after sennett-scent stool-pijin Amos for to murder not muvver him, and who. Should be pasearing along the corridor at the same time as Jelf Jettisonself. But, instead, there is only the same hairy bulldog of a guard, advancing down from the Amos end of the corridor, with the same Great Dane that, on the journey outward, tried for a gratuitous grate on Jelf's leg of bacon.

(Great Dane, King of all Dent marks)

Bugger that. Jelf retreats back to Cealy M. She sighs. Must be her lucky day for a ducky lay, aye. She says, too: Oo ate vous?; my turn? Nothing for it, but to hide behind her and shake it.

(party dog does a lot of treks for different people)

Then again, siriusly again:
the very wise man looks at his dog along the muzzle. Then again, he who misses his dog should adjust his sights. Then again agag, tiny dog like to meet tall dark stranger for a bit of high life. Thus again: dog leash, life span. The dog is a lifelong friend but a short acquaintance. Then against that, blind dog has no peer. Again, fancy dog with nosegay for your bouquet. Then again, dog that runs you right into the ground likes its blood boiled. Then again, country dog came down over manmade gorge. Thus agen, successful local hunting dog gluts the home market, yes, and, when dogging the human frame... healthy dog got the sanity; hangdog got the hand out; the whole pack, the piles; last dog couldn't get a good grippe; sweet-toothed dog got hold of a gumboil; unwelcome dog got thrown gout; old dog got arthritic joint. Yes, and then again a hungry sea dog needs more salts. Also seen on TV in an ad. was: pet dog food company needs more manpower; rejects and social dropouts welcome. Just goes to show that, pup gruesome into dog. Yes, so fire a broadside at the gun dog, otherwise it's in the bag that your goose will be cooked.

O, lift your leg for Grrreat Dogod and Its bitch of a Dogma. *Ohm.*

HENRY

That illsprung winter sprang into a following spring, almost as a sidereal sideline, and did so less than three months later. Wherenow, as a syntonic to a pick-us-up, usurped, we are timewise. Spotwise, whence where but no wherce for wear, we are weftly weaving through a Sydney intersection.

(dog lover living only for her pet)

On this corner in question, there is a building along side of which is an alleyway that runs by our building on the right side. There, too, is a door, a way into the building or into the alleyway, whichever. Yes, and the door also lops off stairs leading to a landing on whose landing is another door on whose hinges much of this story ajars, if it hasn't jarred too much already. Bugger you, anyway, as the dog would say to your sidekick. You're all plural arseholes. But getting back to the building as a whole

(red setter sees the son go down)

is often a bit dicey in this neighbourhood, being one of those neighbourhoods in which, it is rumoured, there is still in't one or two blacks domesticated into docile domicile, which is enough said. Isn't it, you white sum of a piebald bitch.

One such blackman, mama-named Henry, is now bringing us blackbirding back down the said alley, into thathere building to upstairs us into an arrival in front of the said door up on said landing. Behind which Jelf (yes, old whoja himself, who elf?) somnols nicely enough in his bedsit so as to seem positively at home, which he is, half sat up as he is, in his bed amongst all that brown rusty furnishings gestalting away around him, which is. And his waking

(groovy dog wishes to nose up to a D.J. on a platter)

Jelfinstinct moving his hand immediately straight upto his wig to insure that it is still in place up there on its dome. That done, our

73

Jelf rolls his molastic bo-peepers round his Womborld even though he can see furg all since everything is a myopic blur, which he can't even see as a myopic blur, and then sighs with an udderly cow-like content to a world that has held the Dog at bay for another notch of nightime. Here being where our Henry, full blood abo but part of our story nevertheless, has brought us. Just as now,

(gay dog camp follower of men)

Jelf flops his arm across the shape on the other side of the bed (being the deb side) to Adonis his pearlies through a yawning grapey great gap, going: 'Where'd why'd woe'd i leave off, huh huh, honey?'

T'be answered by Henry, who is the shape on the other side of the bed and has remained as full blooded, topp'd up, since the die-earnal day he was squirted up against a back fence and hatched out of incubation by the sun. (That's why darkies live vas deferens from we willywinklys whities, and wouldn't you hatchet them all like that, you doglegs to the Right). Only when Henry tries to claim he is only half to a quarter Abo does he change his tone. But no hope. He is so melan, he's more than a bit fruity. Oh yes, it's Henry through a glaze darkly! Going:

'Leave off? You didn't even get odds on.'

'Out.' Jelf in groan, growing, and shrinkier.

'Met her huffing off down the stairs, when she said to me, "well plurry bye bye to him." You unflipped flop u.' Henry, as he rolls over and curls into the mattress with a luxurimoan that a masochist would give if he had just been kneed in the knockers.

'Out, you dog!' Jelf arf-arfing, iffily gone off.

'Jelf, you tell me what's a mattress on that basement floor.'

'Your own pit, so pitter, you pate, and outskee ski,' Jelf puts in. Fart be it for him to say that something now stynk.

'Who was she anyway?' Henry sniffing something awful.

'If she told you not, how am i to know?'

'She knew you.' Henry.

'One night of bliss and they claim the world.' Jelf.

'She called you just a dead prick.' Henry, but already oozing snoozing along with snooring snuggles and snores loud enough to flaw you, just like as all good Abos do when steeped in sleep, slap in the Dreamtime Dept of your local department store. Slurping it off. Aye, and,

(come back, Honeybun; the dog's finished off sweetie pie)

all so intrusively impertinent that the Jelf gets up to his full paisley silkened sleekness (with built-in secret cubbies for hunchback, gyney genitals and all) and bat-rays his way to the door. He does, even though he is still feeling a bit braille for the world yet. And, as if he hasn't already started off on the wrong foot, his next step takes him out onto the landing where Che, the yip-toothing and yipe-frothing rotten little chehuahua from upstairs, is just waiting to work off a vengeful and faultfanging grievance against the first of the Jelflegs pyjama'd, now pugjammed by it (*leggo leggo*). What a drag.

(fighting Fido big-mouths boxer before climbing into the ring)

Not only that, but there, too, crashed out with one eye a manhole of unplumbed depths and the other eye a sight rarely seen by the naked human eye and both fixated on the Jelf-sumness unashamedly, is Amos, bum-to-splinter and scrapping himself towards our Jelf, like the original Gent who went 'fee fie fumb eye smell the bloody man'. So that there is both chehuahua and Amos (i.e. dog and beast) with uvulae where their mouths muth be and gobs going gliblubbery like they would never cease up and die: 'Bloody poof bloody flowers on's bloody jarmas...!' and 'Arf arf arf arf...' Y'know how it goes.

75

(lonesome pet willing to share common humanity; own joint)

And Jelf during this Pro poorgressing. One leg in dragchain and the other, a Amoss rolling stone gathered. Nor will the crone be stubbed off nor the puppydog punted cither, until columbined together they bring our Jelf to rest agitated. 'S true. He counts standing to ten from a standing state. Ensnagged amongst the crumbling masonry of the misery of *me 'ere*, pleading to the dear Dogod o bleeding heart whyfore every bleeding day does i have to suffer this bowbow moment before every first bowel movement. Before he callows upstairs: 'Maggie!' Who is new to our story (toss up a nu Miss Matic). Aye, Maggie. But our new nee Maggie is all bustle and backside one floor up going like the clappers presumably grilling her brats and grrring at the toast for grissakes and getting her hubby Ray done. Nfact, amongst her own domestible blunder-bust, the woman is no erfly good to our Jelf.

So we don't meet her just yet. No. But soon, too soon.

(whippet out and wipe it)

Instead, to recarp:
Jelf, ajama'd, is jammed up piebald by a dog (Che the chihuahua), holding one of his pieds in its gnashers, out on the landing in the appartment block of Ages; and with a rot of ague (Amos) on his other walker (pyjamb'd), while there is one djerk darkie (Henry) abed in his cot coshed out on his cosine cote. Aye, and Maggie (the lendlady upstairs) incapable of stopping her dog Che from doing scherzando to the death with the Jelf cuff, nor even to tell the bloody little thing to cuff, then fa cuff off. There! Henryamosmaggie and Chehuahua the chi. Dramatis personics (asdic, tomtom and harry).

(dropout been through the dog system)

76

And all this time Jelf still stands with his still small sounds of zounds! here gamjammed and pynned down going muttering above the mutt:

Again again the day breaks between the beast and the bestial old bastard endeavouring t'lower my upwrought length into the murky gloopygoo of ordinary mankind. Once more i am in the Old Nick and Cerberus shakedown, whobut? Dear Dogod have petty on them! Life might be short, but just how long-suffering canst it get? That's the rubbing. Further, when life is a stormy sea, brines in your head is all what counts. In that i cadge you not or i am a dirty dog ditty. *Ohm*.

(dog dies of food poisoning; master ill-treated)

Enough of this, says Jelf, giving himself the runs? After all, he has stood on that spot trussleggedly so silent for so long without thresh or thrust that even Amos'n'animal paws in their hoe-down attempts to hew down our man. Even they. Until, so fido'd up to the teeth with it all,

(dog gives swaggie the bum's rush)

Jelf pows into actions which causes Che to nearly lucene its gripe and leaves Amos behind in a flood of streaming blood-eddyings rosin from the creeky mouth of that old wash-out, aye. How did he do it? Well, he draked and dropped his daks and then took himself off on the nob. Not now nobbled but for certain now knobble-kneed, and bristling all over like a pig's trotter in a gig, naked from the nudger down. Going as he goes:

(young bitch swollen with child had quite sufficient, thanks)

'Maggie, i'll kill this dog!'

'Good.' From upstairs coming downstairs, Maggie's little Surly Echo.

'I will so too, Maggie. And your father here too, Maggie, and gee, Maggie, do i need coffee, oh. You there?'

But Maggie with no chance to answer in a way that would give him no change, for even now our Jelf has slambanged into the bathroom across the landing there, where, as on every other other morning, he has to go to lav off a dirty mood. All over.

(husky gets sore throat dressing down sloppy skier)

In the bathroom in the mirror. And all its furry rondels of blurrtones opoptical and mypopsical, Jelf tries to see if his wig still adheres. Yes, adhe'd still! And his choppers? Still capped cosmetically, the very haulmarks of Jelfself! There is, reaffirmed, such a thing as unnatural selection. And,

(dog with two heads, a glutton)

gaining satisfaction that thereis still a little bit of camelflage left in the ole Cosmosetic (handed to him by curtsy Dogod on two palates, dentured abit but crashed repaired, aye). But, really, no wonder his face flushes twice or wince a day. Even his eyes look like two incarnadined seas, lapping bloody bodily against the sandyreefy sore of two eyelands passing for his dual eyebulls, with the green one turned red and the red one going to gangreen and both feeling like it too. (It's just his optic nerves going to pieces.) He shuddrates upon himself at the sight of himself. For some reason, our man doesn't seem to be able to facet his surfacing at all today, nay. Though, for

(dogging the human corpse: stuck-up dog bung on the side)

why is curious. For this day ought to promise not so much mulch as yesterday or all the other yesterns all back in a row of boredowndom. As a fatter of mact, Jelf may now be broke, but he still has a pocket of resistance subsisting within he somewhere. 'I

78

subsist, therefore i am.' Who did say that before he ex-spired ex-cathedra?

Anyway, not so long ago it was all Alyce cette and Alyce ca. But he has since shewed that shrew. Oh yes, hasn't he indeedy. And now no Alyce and he's still alyve. And whassmore, another diurn has turned. Another day, another day break! So, a-shower you shower, Jelf! Soap suds lather up laughther, gig a gle, glug a glug, and plug on with your big bootiful lughole. Go sponged down between the legs of your massive talent, you bigbad buttible man u.

(fat full-bellied pack weight-watching their near-human bodies)

Jelf now entering the shower alcove with a razed high step that will soon find relief in realife but first finds dog's shit. Yes! Dog's dags, a dagged nuisance? In let and hindrance by the drain hole and the Jelf kakkikicker getting it right in the pooh again. And why not? Haven't we already said that there is no acre sacred from Dogod's Lit Acre And as though to add ensuite to insult, Che, that beasthuahua, arrives back on the scene with a dash through the lavaroom door, without even so much as knocking, to embark upon a doggy-glott that seems to say, getcha being outa my doings you human dung-heel you. Aarf aardwolf, fair dingo. And where's Jelf but hopping on one foot with the chihuahua grrr-nipping at his dripping toes. So can it be

(give a dog a better life and it will only nip it in the blud)

only Jelf's fault that the faucet he turns is the hotscaldstim-minger tap and not the cold top so that he is screamily steam-heated by soakshaken head and foot? What a crying shame, and what a scream! With Maggie's vox over all, going over coming down: 'You leave my dog alone down there.'

(solitary dog alone liked the man)

O, if he only could he would! It got hold of him enough to send him stark rabies mad, more so that the beast has swaggered off with a grin o'er its beastly head, leaving our man with all the scalding. From Maggie and the shower, both. Yep, Jelf done dog-done down again. He sits afloored, having already this day become a nervous reek down-gust of himself. Dog left. Tumulch over. How does the saying go? Is it: that he may be all a-turd but beneath there be a real man frying to get out? Which?

(bolshy dog caught Red-handed)

brings back Constable Wilkinson to our minds. Who is at this fnoment still around, around, a mobile case of mutter over greymatter. (Don't try any sharp angle; Constable Wilkinson is around, around.) And who is even more puzzled than three months ago when we last heard of him. For none of the doorways of the lottery ticket offices around, around town have been fertilyced by that dirty lice Mr Fido Bigs, operating on the back of a dog's disguise for three months now. Quite frankly, it all stinks. But he for one is not fouled. He's been too good a copro for too long to be fooled so easily. Already he has vowed that if he ever gets a lead, he will collar the animal. Which is but by passing reference to tell you Constable Wilkinson is not only still in brown study of the brown stuff (CWWCing), but that he is stall around, around. A-whirly djiggy-djig, almost.

(starving dog fell into the hands of the law with relish)

Here is Jelf feeling once more. Feeling does not make it better. Still, feeling is better than a felling; requires filling, too. So he razzles up his voice, going: 'Start getting my breakfast, Maggie,' to the tune of Mother Dear Don't Wait For The Bringing Home Of The Bacon For Father's Just A Pig, when the bathroom door is thrown open again. We have to think Jelf thinks it's another chihuahuan sorty to sully his persil-white with composture anew, otherwise why does he shout out, 'Piss off, you bloody little animal!'?

'Ohfuc King yeah?' A voice comes back strung as an ox, for it is acid oxide Raymond, Maggie's hubby, her better hoof, whom we haven't met in the haven yet, no. But will again, once more. (Walk on, part.)

'Ray did i think it was your shitting dog not shitting you,' before Jelfshouting out again to Maggie beyond the pale of Ray, e.g.: 'Eggs and lots of ham, Maggie. Important day today, so pile it on, go girl go!'

'Who the hell's wife is she, anyway?' This is the Ray ex all-in wrestler, now a self made man mane mad.

'G'arn, you know Maggie and me, Ray.' Jelf.

'Yeah. You'll be buried together.' Which is a barely concealed threat of bringing a lump to the Jelf throat, yes, before he, that Ray there, always ogre to pleas, withdraws. Whereupon (no peace for the wick) also Henry enters so primitively that Dogod Itself must be atramental in making it happen. Henry, too, castingly herethere for Jelf's toothpaste with that icky extra stripe of attention when it comes to toothbrushes in a bumrush. And finds it.

'New fang brush an'bout time.' Henry, bristling up.

'Leave down dirty getorf!' Jelf bristling down, but now so knotted up with anger, he is a macrame wonder. And taut... even a formal education wouldn't help, uhuh. Even this darkie has the in front of him effrontery to to and fro frothing free at the mouth full of his dental flumpy foamflow and having the raw nerve (rear molar right bottom) to flubber at Jelf him:

'Nooffer portaant ay, eh? noshaa shooz loooosh-shout innavue, huuu?' ('Another important interview, eh? Another of those lose-out job attempts, huh?' adding chortle refrain to the

81

uninterpretable vowels of an archaic caucasoid born with the defect of a mouthful of O.P.s. toothpaste propensity.)

'Would you kindly reslither outside, my good migrain, you?' (Puta blackmana backapace aday.) To which Henry: 'O pull this; it's a real hum donger,' and 'You white bugger, you really run out of money mournay?' and the atrabilious autochthon b'henry b'jesus b'coming cantankerous also with: 'Where did all that boodle i let you lend me come from then?'

'Shut your black trap on the way out, Henry.'

(happy is the dog puffed up with Joy. Rest in peace, Joy)

Alas, what we have here is a lost and thurber opportunity for black and white to palaver over gum lather in the lavey up a gumtree. But now door shut. Henry huffed at last. Alone, Jelf. He bolts over to run the door, then

(effeminate dog hangs around camps)

ruckles around in his pocket, pulls out his pyx box, sharries to the mirror shillying there, throws left corneal right contact lens into this eye, that eye (tele and visor), blinks up and blunks down two or free times and sees once again all that is around the brims of his orbs. Though if he knew what is to be dished up later on, he would surely put his own eyes out again. Quite liberally.

(long life to the dog who lives by Prudence!)

Thirty minutes later finds, not before half that time, Jelf shirtfronting his bed roomed mirror, reflexing on the Jelfre-fiection, now all decked out in's got-up interview gear, top. This is so classic a case of overkill that he surely must slay all who interview him. Going oh fagtastic oesophagal scrumptious me. Creases attired and barely panting. When:

'You lug like an oversucked lollipop.' This is Henry from behind him, all decked out himself on the Jelf pit. 'Jesus, what would anybody hire you for?'

'Intelligents. Good looks massivity. Expanding personality unexplored horizon', Jelf re-iterating and now re-itinerating towards the door sweeping all before him including the Henry tribefella by virtue of a swift two-handed hold on thatabo one fellah's handle as he continues, 'plus years of uncluttered unscuttled experience and fly-applyability slaphappy. You poor ignorabo, you may tooth your pick, but after you with the boot. Move.'

(hunting dog chases athletic man in high pressure blood sport)

But on the mauve is not necessarily in the pink, ono. For out on the landing again, what else but the usual ambushade by Che the chic chihuahua all full of yipey at the resighting on Jelf as mucho to say in Mexhuahua 'I just amore your leg, amigo'. Also Amos trying again to attach him/it self by the gums to the other Jelf gam (a singular silly gambit), not giving a hoot or caring the boot as his crass incising peckers sink into the indecented Jelfcalf and, 'Bloody know whereya bloody goin' gawd's bloody teeth, why bloody dontcha bloody lie bloody down'n'bloody die. Need we say amore

And Jelf? He is mindracing onto: O Dogod if finally i be pulled quagdown into the mire too, let not my appetising appearance be soiled spoiled oiled or slopped-on even my tamper'd temper may it keep its place. Before he makes an unbroken, but out of breath, break for

(fastest dog achieves fullest pelt)

the milkpond of smooth creamy humanity and kindness, out where the streets run with good things to drink for ulcer-bearing bods who keep getting it right in the guts. Friesdom and flesh air! He has made it, uncluttered and unattached! And This Day Blue and still with not even a whisp against thee. This dayturn sunswong swaining. So let so! So, sollustros! So little lethereal disturbance that even a wig feels secure, yes.

It must be some day. Not arf. Not so fresh now, but at least going off for an interview, which. Makes it all worth will. *Ohm.*

(adventurer had to shoot Rapids to survive, now seeks new hound to be Rapids II)

We interject. Pausing for a scratch or two to pick at circumstances to reintroduct our author, Kny (Kenny) Rat (shit) Griffley who is going along a Melbourne way plotting up quick and easy ways of wheel-dealering prosey rosaries to them what's catholic in literature and partial to a lick of any Cath who's capaciously pram solvent to give him fame 'n' fortune cheap. In other words, even these three months after, ole (Ratshit) Griffley is still doing writey things that very few people in this world would do, fortunately. Or could afford to. But now re-entering into. The story. Okay?

(witch hunt over; the dog got over familiar)

Plus, too, by way of mnemone (remember one me, mm?), Constable Wilkinson is going around and around like the thoughts in his head. And heisting still. Oh, yes. Around and what's around more rhotating by rote, his mind in sausage circles, all sizzling skullduggery. Sheer drudgery, tis, too. But by how much we are not at lipberty to say.

So now you been tolled, we can all get back on the merry gore round.

(inscribed on tombstone: Jack Frost, Bitten)

One hour later, which is another ticked off, a gander is in fact influx faring throughly dap by dapper, step by stepney, dainty and undented along the thoroughlyfared city street, with. All the ladies gandering this fab and baffling luke (look, look!) going by. Who be? Who else could it but Jelf? This is a marchpast that, even in lifesaver cycles, would make them put an ooo in the centre. Yes, The Jelf abroad; poor broads. All down this Sydneyside street, previous happily hitched darlings all go loose at the scythought of him. Yes, seen and serene and sirened and partoots sigh-Irened. Goodnight!

(gutless man disembowwowelled)

What he is doing is sartyrorial for the interview for the job that's to reward Everyman with Easymoney by Job! This is not what he is limping for; it is what he is hopping for, ever since he dashed out of Alyce's art studious life. Plus her chequie-weckie butts, but. No social service he can benefit by others either. And,

(seductive dog will chomp anyone's bone)

so armed, doubly, for the coming interview and so done up like Dogod's dinner, that he has failed to notice the two chipwrecks off the block awash in the tide of his doings. Yes, he hasn't. Henramosy and Amoshenry, them. The one, the two. The onetwothree. Again: shiffly shooft in shiftee slip-streaming shafts of shoof-shoof-shuffle and shoeshoo softly behind him. And it's even almost too facent to redraw your attention to Amos in sumpsimus of, 'bloody bloody bloody bloody bloody' gutterals, fit to make Sydney-sighed. Now,

(plump dog big with Fats)

it was on a sharpish corner that it did happen momentarily (a hairpin moment hairily) that Jelf turned right and stunned, yes, to stone, a virtuous femme (and fortune!) by the name of Eclya M. Isslainy, who at that time was busy watching the heavy clouds of a bad climacteric coming over to unclot her complications. Poor anonymouth Eclya M., where once ladies college, now coagulated in lock-on and lostful lust and even legging up to bandy her bandies at this Jelf him, full farce fool fuss. Folly! She must be

85

(unhappy dog reduces to skin and bones)

forty as the wind goes out to pasture. Still, Jelf's seen worse on a
farm, so gives a mere hint of a smile, but enough to hint the poor
dear over the head with it. O, beambearer of all suckholes, pure
thaumaturgyro. Eclya sheerly cliff hangs, cleft in midair, while our
Jelf passes having now papaled *Nostrum, pickit*, and

(sausage dog like to meet saucey lady for a roll)

leaving her with stun-of-a-gun papaltating heart. And even before
she can even scream blue movie, Henry has caught up to her and is
doing an iago in her shellike, just loud enough for to embaraharass
Jelf huppitying it up ahead going: 'Lady, ain't that cat up front
one big hunky-dorey?   But, lay off, laydy, cos if that most
beautiful hunk of afterbirth doesn't get that job, this poorold man
here and me, we don't eat. Nup, duped.'

Thus ruddily and rudely awaken back to sorbent reality, Eclya M.
Isslainy, tries to shrug off this black buggerlugs assalting her ear
by tossing her pudenda in the way she was intending it should go
but. Only to find Amos all gumming her up by leering into her
poppers from a tissue paper half thinness away. Plus, too, Henry
getting a bit too nippy by rhynchopulling her right tit nagging
'naughty naughty' to her very riff-raffishly aloud.

(leaping wolfhound, beast of the earth and foul of the air)

And if this is abreast of poor Eclya, it is even more broadside to
Jelf. He cannons off with such unreportables portagassing from his
sensous lips that if he had run into a naked match then and there he
would have fumed. Yet not nearly quick enough. No, for
Amos'n'Henry have teased Eclya M. Isslainy where it was
kneaded and have slipped back into the Jelf stream whoo-
whoolfwhistling the Jelfself as the thrice of them furrow on. Jelf
stops suddenly quivering. Amos and black-Enery quiver to a stop.
Jelf upstarts. Amos and the boong upthrottle. But to no effect at all
at all. He re-revs; they rev up. Revelations for each time he starts

up again, red around the chops, all he getting, too, is woof woof you burly wolfine u.

(bitch, promiscuous for men, drops 'em)

As he motors on with thosetwo's werewolf whistfull thinking trying to penetrate his rillrealm, Jelf ponders on The Seven Ages Of Man. We Litz in on him, going:

Well, thou'st can stuff this for an ornery horny ornitholog lark, fuck it, all. Why should all blessed life be unwinding bandages on my blesses? Here is the seven band-ages of bondaged manacle. The twinkle in pappy's eye is all booze; the tingle in mammy's eye is all bounce. What's more, it is just puerile to get born. Pubescence only takes you by the shorten curlies. You sprog progenies and you'll eventually get seed off. Pimply youth is all puss and no pussy. Middleage is all panting downhillt. Senility is all out of breath and no pants-downing. That's seven bands around your stained Bonds for a fart-off. No hard feelings. Droop dry shirks. Lingam to legume. Ain't it *ohm*.

(Death dogs your heels)

Really, though, the situation is too much for day broadlight. Humiliated, pitched-up to a work, his knob in a gordian twist, Jelf seems to lose all uncontrol. As he turns into the new-feat, nuely-feted office blox, he suddenly pounces himself into the ceremonial pond in its court-yard (this being justice!), wherefrom does he commence to pelt (what a hide) the Hen-Amosry persondium with agates imigate out of the pool's aggregation of potential stoney aggressions, each. Going to them: *getorffjaggedlost and go hence etc.* And who should come running out of that office block doing his own blox but, he whom we haven't met before, Commissionaire Watchit-Whereschit, mugging his rockjaw hard at Jelf: 'Get outa there, ya idiot!'

(grrrist, Dogod, it's only me, the lump in Thy Throat!)

87

Jaysez! Peeble Jelf instantly drops the pebble like it was a red-hot brick which it probably was once part of a bit of any-piece, then tries to smooth out his guilt to make the pool look like it always was. But his foot knows when it is in a real scrap and only further disturbs the people-to-pebble harmony (don't rock the boat) of the once-neat pool now a litholunatic's nightmare v. moreish. And all the time, huge Commissionaire Hugo Watchit-Whereschit shows the stern stuff of forwhy the company has commissionaired him in the first place. Yes, C.P.O. o' Co., so p.o.q.! Raising the question: how can one pass the ram rod when all ewe can muster is sheepishness?

'Juvenile delinquent,' Commissionaire W-W aloud a-Jelf.

'Do you be talking to me, my good fellow?' Jelf, telling him. You yokel, no yoke. Type of thing. But:

'Bloody oath i am, mug.' Charming. This man's world outlook is all lest we forget. Who he's done over. Incredible how some prog noses can put the boot in from out of a juttish jaw.

Never mind, Jelf sails serenely on on surly edges past Commissionaire W-W, like asif to say *serene goodnight siren sigh'n'ara seeyou in my novel's reams* right up to the foyer by the foie gras where slida doors, one 'in', the other 'out', are there automatically. Yes, both ways. Which means you-bloody-well-wait-until. Which means Jelf has to wait'n'weight watch no go. No wonder, either, since he is attending the 'in' slida door for them who want to enter the street from in there but not for them who want to winter in there from out of the street out here. No. So slida door and Jelf atropheye each other. Man and machine machinations. While,

(Shag, you dog, get off Rocky)

Commissionaire W-Wearschit shakes his nodding noodle contemptuously at J. before he himself glides free as a let-in breeze thru' the other slida door that Jelf is not getting impatient in front of. Compris? And moves over to his desk that is as oppressing huge as that which the World Court might have tried Kafka from behind. (While Jelf, of cours, remains teleluxing the sheer tectony of doorish automata, going: *if these doors so smart why aren't they in an auto where it really mata?)*

(tombstone inscription: Cur Runt Turned Off Him)

Finally inside the foyer. Yes. Amongst all thathere flinty scintillashine seemingly cast in the same mound of a plasticoat paint tin containing the grey matter of the architect's mind. All wax and wand. Nfact it seems the only thinking ever put into that foyer fou is the thinker of Commissionaire Watchit-W and that's as oldunique as a stone-age woodadze and about as sharp:

'You!' (Jelf starts.) '*You.*' (His heart stops.)

'*You* ain't after that job, are you, juvenile delinquent?'

And Jelf: 'Actually, sir, i was standing here figuring, sir, which Armed Force of the World i have seen you in.'

O, a wit withal and withit ha hee, but a bit hitlerious, no?

'Military Police. Ten wars, including two Worlds. You saw mean' a possible third, ya must've been the only delinquent that ever got away.'

'Hee hee.'

'Don't he he me, pansy pitwis. Third floor muster quick, move!'

There! Inevitably, it comes. That once-upon-atom (or twice every twosome) crude and uncouth crunch, that suit of the inearth on your peace-person, which. Just goes to show that sure as shit a stranger will sooner or later confirm what you first thackeray of him. Makepeace, but Shake speare!

(mountain dog last seen on Hill side. Hill now a missing person)

Third floor, still unthawed, Jelf is trying to find his own happy level where happenstance The Big Interview will take place, yes, but. Right now, he is busy trying to get out of the lift under the scrutiny of four snatches, ex of Miss Caley Lain's Secretarial School for Short Handed Girls. And each of them gazing at him mute as tits on a bull staring at a ball-tickler unctious to make their acquaintances. Not even bothering neither to come to his rescue, and he a visitor, as he struggles to close the bloody lift doors that are now buzzing with a buzzer that wont shut up only shout rape to all the world in buzzstard liftlip. Hjelfp! Just as if it were in a fit of emerging machine-reasoning. Hjelpf! Hjelfp! An alarm belle in the loft! And alljelf can do, stuck half way in or out, which?, is shout at the top of his vox over the din.

'DOORS DONWANNA SEEMTO...'

But as soon as our Jelf belts out thus, those doors shut (no buzz, buzzing off) returning all the biosurrounds to a sexless silence, conducive but not condomive, to the spouting of vegetable'd secretaries. Whencehappens, these secretary hens reput their uninvited heads down again and refuse to look up at the jelf now, self-ful but unselfishly, standing before first secretary Snatch, going:

'Good afternoon, me name be J...'

But what happens then is this: the first Snatch waves gogo you to next Snatch along, who go you go passalong to third Snatch next along, who waves our Jelf to goget gone guy to next Snatch next door along, who too waves vaguely gogogo please pass go and get back to number One Snatch. Aye; until Jelf has completed a fool circle back to first secretary Snatch, who then deigns him an I-eye ysmuch to say lookee who's here, whose wood did you scratch out of, plus:

90

'Have you completed one of our application forms? Please complete one of our application forms.'

'I wrote in.' Jelf elfishly to her. But she:

'Here is one of our application forms. Please fill in one of our application forms, starting with your name in BLOCK LETTERS where it says write down your name in BLOCK LETTERS.' Blocking his further passage by far, too.

(cold dog on Ice; stiff, Mr Ice)

Jelf now with application in hand and form seated on a chair there, with each Snatch gone back to staring at him with eyes of sheer moot points. Yet now, Dogodammit, he has sat down without a pen with which to write his scrawl and so has to upend his butt again to approach first Snatch (woe being begotten) for to Oliver for a pen-or-summat, with her there having a biro already outstretched impatiently you-bloodyman. With a sickly grinning, too, of course, and a: 'Please fill out one of our application forms starting with your name in BLOCK LETTERS.'

(dog thinks.it can do what it leaks to a tree)

Returned to that chair, Jelfathomed is again in deep whattery. He would like, for example but silently going, someone-anyone to tell him how an intelligent block of mahogany, namely himself, can write out his monicker in blocks, especially when above him there is a very loud electric clock ratchet racket going gong gong and on. Also, you Snatches of converse, he can hear you whispering about him yesyes out of the corner of your foible moinds. Aye, him, your future boss, you buttsure fats you. Haven't you ever seen a bloke have a letter block over his name in this arcade of bemusements? Ho ho ho. Name him dotty en bloc... But

(dog returns young mother home with stretch marks)

he gets no further in defiance. For through the air there loud and lunkish comes:

'Bloody bloody lift whassat bloody lift bloody...'

With those lift doors all otiose ajar and bluzzingly alarming allover the aerispace in another machine-fit of pique-ing on a human. But this is no human. This is Amos; and nestling sweetly within the gorilla armpits of kindly Commissionaire W-W, who is carrying the Amos like a baby to the four Snatches there in awe and aw and ah and oohah kitchy-kitchy koo isn't he just a little ole Amos living dole? Isn't he ever.

(the world is Dogod's oyster)

Whilst Jelf, with hoddled head hid between his fivestems attempting to disguise heself as HMAS Hymns in a deguassing situation, going to up heaven: *O Dogod, Thy help in wages past.* And hurrying to finish filling out that application form in order to complete the write-off job totally. By which time, Commissionaire Whatsthis-Watchit has arrived at the four Snatches in line with l'il ole Amos, going:

'Wants to wait with his boy. Wouldya believe it Even caught the mug throwin' my rocks at the poor old bugger outside. His own father.'

'Charming.' Sn.

'Grim chin.' Snat.

'Arch Ming.' Snatch.

'Crim Hang.' Snatches in snippets. Apt.

(outlawed pack on Lam, poor lamb)

'Thought to meself,' Commissionaire W-W, an ex-digger now-daggering at Jelf adding, 'a bleeding nerve, what? Coming up here, broad as daylight. Applying for the job. Felt like giving him a job in the moosh.'

'No doubt you did.' Snatch one.

'Deedy you did, poor dad.' Snatch two.

'You'd think he'd give the poor old dullfyce a bath.' Snatch three.

'No tub, dob.' Snatch four. Snap!

'He really isn't my father you know.' Jelf trying to make himself heard over the crying shame of thanetose thatAmos being dusted down, but only succeeding in marking himself hurt. Not only that now, but now not only surrounded by our hirsute commissionaire but sir-rounded by three new sirs on the scene in Herr-suits, all being heinus to Jelf in their hertz!

'Have you come for an interview? If you have come for an interview, please fill out one of our application forms.'

'I told him to fill out one of our application forms,' first Snatch snatchurally natty, 'but he won't tell us his name in BLOCK LETTERS. No, he willnt.'

'Because if you have by Some Chance come for the interview,' goes one Herr suit, 'then we will have to ask you to pardon this darling dog...' meaning that dalmatian leashed out by his side and which seems to be having some sort of trouble with its Jelf-hating tendentals deep down inside its throat, grrrrr-owl-wise, very wise, '... Because we find a dog is such a wheedling-out help at interviews. Such good judges of character. Nein? Oh, and did you say you had feldt out one of our application forms'

'He's trying to sneak past that application form of ours and get in for an interview, sir.' Snatch snappy againo.

'I said have you come for the interview?' Herr suits becoming a bit bellycose now. Rollypollies, the three. Not to mention Commissionaire Whatchit-Thatchit who bibs his poke into our Jelf's ribs and frights away, 'Answer, punk pansy juvenile delinquent!'

93

'No!' Jelf, going notjelf oh no not me never me no.

'Pardon?' Herr suits in uniform similarity.

'I mean,' Jelfglot, 'just pret ending. Call me fin.'

'Pretending to have come for the interview? What vat? Vine for?'

'Let the dog go,' the Commissionaire urging too, with the dalmation on cord in accord. All waiting for Jelf's answer, but he not thinking as clearly as he might, going:

'Only did come so i could pretend i wasn't home in cosy, chosen beddibyes. Bye.' But really meaning: fuxfuchsfuscfucs-fuk all-facts-are-flukes and all i want to do is find my Neitchze in life, so how come me always at mealways anyway? And he even might have said it had he not been going so fast, at a rate of four downstairs at a time (going down, sinking fast) which is far too veloce to throw your voice back over your shoulder, unless you're just bent. Yes. And how about all those stares, following him? Crazy!

(a dog is always trying to make an impression on you)

Finally Jelf crashes out of the foyer and runs foyever'n'ever headlong straight into the street. All thatoutside sunglo and, oh, it is enough just to partake, like all the other inhobbits of Sydneytown, of the vapours. After which he will prom priddily and grow a good much better. Lost interview? Lost horizon, too. Too fictionally far away anyway.

(dog with a lot of food laid in larder has much more than any one single human being)

94

Here we pause for a minimoment for a quick cameo of Jelf waiting outside there with both feet well and truly astood within that ceremonial pool. He is and they are. He has, too, the most polished the most beautina the most avoir-by-weight the most killingvicious automatic seekout'n'destroy stone in the whole of that ceremonial pool in his hand. He has and it is. And it is aimed in raised slingshot armed at the 'out' slidadoor so as to zoastrally royal prawn that old bastard A. when he pokes his glooper out. Jelf and the agate out on a limb. But

(always some dog trying to follow in your footsteps)

when Amos does emerges from that building, he is all hagi-hairily airborne up by a hand-in-hand of Commissionaire Where's-Whatsit, sucking a sugarlump sweetmeet as though he wouldn't flick at a fly getting flirty. Yes, Amos in protective custody of the irk-some, sick-em-all commissionaire whose jaundiced eye turns on Jelf just a splitting second before he adjusts his karate black belt in a way not conducive to injuicing in harmony in man, no. Oh, Jelf Droopstun Drop-stone. Jelf Flyaway. Jelf Jetset'n'go. Dead giveaway, fading fastways. And that startled a few passersby too. They didn't think he was a pop art statue in the ceremonial pool for a moment but did thought he was pseudo just the same. Goos to show.

(Spot got a beauty)

This 'ere be a bus. It rumbratts lelelelelele, so much that it makes people shudder just to think on it. It does and they do, quite rattled both confused. Cept those who think they be hooked upon a kidney machine and probably will need to be.

Whereon assumed bus is Jelf now loholding briefly one of those three million ads; this one saying that if you are extreme bald then rub thisthatthing (Ma Trixie's Matrichsk) into your sheeny head for four and twenty hours each day for twenty four days of the lune, Looney, and, by crinkley or crikey, which?, thoust shalt have

95

the hairiest fingertips of the pud-pull. Right at thine fingertips, too. Service, an ace! Jelf's hopes rise, but he's had too many yeasterdays for him to be tomorrow rosen, aye. So he, our wag under wig under stress, resumes his adding to and fro (he is trying to add up and down, but this bus doesn't allow that; even eyes are rolling) of his sum piggy bank wealth left in his life. Not now a thing to be v. bankrapt in. Nope. Life is all take-away from a small whole to a big black hole; how can he conkentrate with all this subtraction going on Aye,

(feed, fido, thumb of an Englishman)

now Jelf is occupied in adding up in the only seat not taken up with crippled old ladies (Australia has some) or over-inbulged preggy peggies (Australia has smums), four or five of which are standing over Jelf passing pointedly between them the time of history when chivalry hadn't gone the way of all cavalry. Gallup pools say so, too.

But then they cannot cop how many cents this man's life's fortune runs into. Headlong. And, to be franc, no man in heistory has ever summed up microdots so quickly.

(four men eating make a quorum; four dogs eating make a bloody mess of quorum)

Now at a certain busstop:
Some opt for life and jump off; others take their lives in their hands and get on. Thus it somehow happens from this that there appears next to Jelf a woman in a Black Floppy Hat. Yes, and so closing in on him as to be in ectosaturation of our Jelf's aur, a, bit of a cheek, sort of thing. Nor can he say getorf and stop pressing what would be promising for a heavyweight wrestler's thigh against my inviolable. He just feels too blue in the red. Anyway,

(dog tackles Fire; Mr Fire's flame put out)

all bodies therein begin shuddering like they have taken en masse a messy emetic or suck thing, which means that the bus is come to

96

next stop, or. Broken down, which? Black Floppy Hat, too, flops all over our already bustled Jelf as she pretends to be trying to alight but really in order to lop a lap drop of a note onto the Jelfsum totalness making little cents. Any of it. He picks up this deliverance. Manna? Cheque from the Great Gutted Guilden Eagle? Funds from the Good Ole Joker God Hesame? Here's the expected two cool million i've been expecting althatime yeah yea. Then reads what Floppy Black Hat has dropped on his clanger. He does; isn't it startling? and. Re-reads but it still re-adds like it first read, and reads, if you haven't already read it:

'Mate, he who knows you wear FALSIES, needs no lottery to guess who be THE dirty footfoul pathing dog, Mr. F*d* B*gs, uhuh.'

(O, Dogod over-Lord)

Yes! And when our Jelf finally tumbles to the note, it is as though his body was tumbrelling on account of a note, vocal. He screams and raves. The bus moved, too. Such a young man and in dementia 2. It makes you thick, donnut? Until, movement everywhere, finally the Jelfhead is fisted out of the bus window tinkling all over. So violently that it, the Jelfhead, doesn't seem to think it of thought that it is out-thrust on the wrong side of the bus, with its face pointed the other way to that which Black Floppy Hat had hitherward hightail'n'opped it through the throng of that pfoofpathed maenadding crowd. The Jelfmouth for all the world to listen in any direction going:

'THAT'S A LUCKING FIE!'

(dog over Ere Long. No longer 'ere)

For fie. No fee. For b'now Black Floppy Hat has hasta'd la vista off into the maidening crowds. Beside Jelf is now only a small fading coughing boofhead who people think might be just another public servant being a little more de-filed. Nothing unusual to turn a head anyway. Who doesn't know that Sydney buses are built so as to only carry madmen anyway

(Dogging the human corpse: pie-dog stuck in throat; sausage dog hit snag; frenzied dog got glandular fever; and the dog Em with its first love Ernia)

When his time came, Jelf managed to throw himsjelf off the bus in one piece, then. He quickly followed. Bruised? Well, let's just say he's now a bit brushed with use, the old scrubber he. Causing him to have a wandering and maudling re-spurtal of the thought process in times past when life was all rosella and tit. Bits. Retrostepping back into the Time of Then when:

in the city Melbourne with wife (a lyce) and a jazzy chez he and some childred kin (carp happy little kiths, give's a kith) and a hot dinner waiting for him piping like muzac from the transisters. Four of them. And out of a can. And not more than a few days old. Open. Yes, twas tangytrue. One thing about that Alyce then was she did know how to reheat. And hygienicsnot init! (Not talking of cans now, though hygienic snot in those too.) But that Alyce then, she was so hyenic that she absolutely refused to reheat up food more than seven times a week. And ne'er on the wok. And he, thatQuiltythen, now our Jelfself, eagerly re-homing his pigeon toes every night, once a wik y wok, to chez his own. Aye; and now just look at him now.

(fed-up dog had skin pulled over his eyes)

Thus standing on the paved cement, peeved and mental, and stylus very much of a write-off, Jelf, almost not knowing what daze it is. He must be the only crepitude in living amoeba memory who was left behind by a Sydney bus. And just to think that

(Fast dog. Quick, and the dead)

a few houris ago, he was full of shirpy not twirpy. He went out whither and has come back whattle. If the world doesn't whittle-whattle a man down to nix, it reckons he's just whet. You tell him how a man can win unless it's by a shortened head. His poor bleeding own. Aye, meaning that thereheis now paralysed, when therehewas a few hours ago a wizard of whatwoz. Broke, perhaps, but not his cover. Ups. Standing on his own two built-ups, too. Going:

(Oliver, all's clear; the dog's got it in a Twist)

it must have been that bloodybloody Amos telling what he found out about Alyce and herplace and herchequies and herwheckies and bloody Art Munro and his charcoalagulatings of my soft parts, and i gotta do something more desprate than just kill the old dirtystoolie swine before he TELLS MORE OF IT.

(sausage dog got worked up over skin)

And, dear drearied reader, that's where clarity began stopping for our Jelf. For at that time in motion he upbeamed from the ground beneath his pigeons and clocked onto, straight ahead, a construction wall on which was a poster posited there by some bastard posterpaster nameof Bill, displaying our Jelf as he was as Scotty as posed at Alyce's arstudio and in charcoal allover the place! Aee ayes! Himjelf! Imposter! On poster! And not only that, but a caption reading: 'THIS DOG DOESN'T DO HIS OWN DOINGS. WATCH YR TREAD'.

(dog over Joy and end-Joyed it)

And that's only describing one poster, not the dozen like it there, too, in charcoalings that would do butter in a blacksmith's forge, George. And no matter how you look at them... all golden auriglitter of awryglasses, teeth in golden sunset specstacular, dome wasteland, concavity of chest, hump hopped to it, saveloy wickywok etc... it's enough to make (it does) a groan man go beserck, even unto tearing at a fully grown wall with his own pare of fingernails. Enough, too, to make

(fleet-footed dog has whole naval company at its feet)

Constable Wilkinson who indubitably is around, around climb out of his beaut machine to stop this shocking display of pathological anachronistic anacreonism, or, to be more exact, such fucking round, as is attracting a crowd again left ri-centre-ght. Plus it's embarrassingly unAustralian to see a screaming man cry in full grown public. With the good constable going:

'Yud better not be sticking those ugly picture things up on that wall there, pal.'

So that, where before he was going up the wall, Jelf is now all overcome with a crippling feeling of being bricked in by the sight of both caption and cop ('shun!) and what the two coming together could bring to bear on recent doggish crimes against the state footpaths. He gulps down a quick gulch then takes up the part of a deaf post in a deep gully.

'Say,' Constable W peering closer, 'ain't i seenya ming before'

'Whomewhome whom me, sir?' Jelf, this, but fast Jelfading fey'd away, voxbox stripling of bark fast, and now disappearing, as he did, into the next door of the next door pub rather

(police dog chewed over last clue)

anaerobically, or so thinks Constable W. in a fleeting moment in which a flashflood of education, so unOzstralian too, tries to mount him indecently.

Will Wilkie go after fink or wilco after thought? Trussup or trouce on? Tossup. Trounce on. So he shrugs his shoulders after Jelf-now-scarpa'd and goes to continue on his around, around about way. But not before he stabs his jabberwaddy at the poster face of Jelfscottyquilty at Alyce's arstudio to order any action local citizen taking unction there: 'Get charcoal and put a mo on this moosh or i get the vice squad in to wipe out the whole neighbourhood. Kay?'

And he was pointing to the one amongst all those posters there on which was a straighout photograph of Jelf. Art of the impossible. Quite probably crafty, too.

100

(dog down in mouth; bearing arms)

'A sorry comment on the world when a man's not safe out on the streets anymoro, all morons.'

Guess who. Yes, our Jelf. Sat lingering longer in a lounge along with Henry. Lounge, pub, not lounge, comfy. No, for this here is a Sydney pub. Even the signwriter who scripted in 'Lounge' on the doors of this Sydpub, wore a WWI gas mask so he looked deadly funny. Truestruth, tis. That's the only time they take you seriously in a Sydpub, when you swank into onewearing a gasser of a WWone mugmask so they think you must be a signwriter. No piss. You crash a gorby onto the floor in a Sydney pub and they thank you for keeping down the flies. (They have bluebottles on their shelves, too.)

(dog on the blink. One more eye still to go)

Anyhow, Jelf with Henry, and adding: 'State of tatters of the gut garters when man gets abused all along the snail's outrails outside. A real trial.'

'Change beers. Mine's got more in.' Henry, changing them by slight of hand.

'Henry, tears in my eyes for that gesture. True friend, you are, the only true one.'

But Henry, shrugging back a bit, while knocking back a little bit more; going, too: 'Blowfly. Big yellow pussy arse. In mine. Now in yours. Thanks, mate.' And this is Henry on his best behaviour, too, since he's getting his beer free. Honestly! A boong's nothing more than a blackman. If that was all, then it might have been all. But of course it isn't. No day finishes with Jelf until night fells. The only working out he'll do in life is incontinence. For even as fly blows (there she bots!) into the Jelf beer, a blind black dog, with blind and black eyes in oggle of its ughers at Jelf, sits staring

101

(fat dog a burden on mankind)

extensively at our hero, though it cannot see through nothing, no. And aye, a veritable muttlike mull it is, too, plus its brindled eyes almost touching. In the way they promise to show no pate on him. True, and:

'Bugger dogs, all. Are.' Jelforsworn or worn or swoon't on't, either/or.

'Don't get nasty just because some Big Floppy Black Hat drops you a bus note.' Henry heehoo raising cane again.

'It wasn't what she said, it was what she said.' Jelf.

'What she say?' Henry enruptured.

'It wasn't what she wrote, it was what she wrote. Passing indecent notes. Not to mench filthy posters upon public walls.'

'I asked what she said.'

'Have your fling. Never mind the mud. All i am saying is there's only one way to live. Upright. Another way, you're flat on y'small. So's a corpse. I may be quoted.' Jelf oldselfjelf we know. Who doesn't? Starting to get some hops back in his feet.

'Don't give me that.' Henry, in wry.

'I just have. Twas titled your last beer.' J. elfishly, the imp, but now suddenly trying to catch his breath caught up on a real sock-in-the-eye sight so shocking it could dot your eyes and teetotal your sighs. It manifests itself in the form of

(dogs find most of humans get gruel to them)

some dreadful old indescribbable floozy, no longer a fairy flooz, no, seated across the Lounge so forte fruity that he could almost smell her from here and so deFunct a fungoid as to have seemedly things that look like haemorroids all over her legs, especially on the gooseflesh above those winding sheafs supposedly stockings. Is a fact. This is a stocking sight even in a big leagured city like Sydney, and Jelf shuds. He does. Fancy having those twin shockers legging over you in a vericot! And though he cannot see its head, it takes no imagination (although it would be some imagination!) to figure it as the most fucused-out face ever. Jelf shakes his unbeliever and returns Henryway, going:

'God they get some shockers in this joint.'

'Dogs sure hate your guts.' Henry spanning his fanner at that blind and black and dog thing growling lowly at the Jelfeet so patently waiting patiently to put the bite on, and. 'That dog's so old, man, it can't even see or hear you. Yet it still hates your gutstrings, sure does.'

'A dog is no heart and all fascist pig.' Jelf.

'All i notice is that you've dried up on the booze forthcomings.' Henry.

'Observant friend buddy etcetera.' Jelf.

'So this man got to go, Tojo.'

'Don't leave me, Henry!' A Jelfscreech to pin you up the wall.

'What ghost into you all offa sudden?'

'Dangerous, Henry, oo yes, for the likes of us there outside outsize. You being black. Me being beautiful. Don't leave me no noway of oonot. Dig? Bread, here, look, for booze. Get yourself sloshed on me, buckette.' Certainly Jelf, but not Jelf as his usual sjelf, as he is now, with Henry's hand to his smooching hotlips ('kissme chocy roll caked') and fumblebumming in his pockets for lotsa loot also all besotting alot. Yes, but Henry now pulling his fingfeelers out from under the jellylipfs of Jelf and himself lispouting:

103

'No, must; got to meet this new Diva of mine. Jelfy, she's got a head like a dragon, but she's white. A bloke smokeblack like me can't have ebrytink. Bysee. Do stop polluting your beer with that there tear. Oh, also, you using your service pit this arvo? Here's hoping you ain't hopping in.'

'Sorry, lotsanlotsof postshock convalescing to do.' Jelf, too, true, too.

'You can do that on mine. I'll do my Diva on yours.'

'Tell you what, 'Enery. You go ruffle all the fleas upon yours with what thoust to do. I'll rumple up my nice clean black satins on mine with what i ist going to do. And i hope you get bye. Bye.' Brush off or brash out, Jelfwhich?

(dog claws dig in; Doug out)

Alone, what does Jelf gleam? He glims that Functy Flo again, is what, o'er there and this time she-it (o shit) is peering around that protective pillar between he and she (sheet!) and is, yes!, gamwinking at he! Aye, leggily. He was right too; it is the most fucus'd out face he ever did give adamn not to see. But there it is. What'ere it is. And she/it giving Jelf a dreadful prospective come-on u hunk u, with one of her scabpickers around a pint and th'other draped round the ropey neck of such an old alcoholic that the poor bugger is trying to imbooze his bibe from beneath the nether region of she/it's titless wonders. And the sight of this is, quite frankly, all too much for our Jelf. Tis. So,

(dog meets past master, opens old wounds)

he heaves himsjelf up and out of that dfoggy djew and scapes himself off the landscape of Funct's gordogodonic stare. Where is he going? For lulu loo to put it in olent ology, that's where. Keeping his blinkers portcullis'd so as to avoid eye of Funct Floozy who is mascaraing purple passages at him as he passes her by. Then entering the john, going: *Hello, John, what a relief to be around to rejohnyou again; u'n'i, what a splash we make. Johntil, now. Ah!*

(dog has one last brainwave, then leaves the table)

Now if y'ever been in a Sydneypub, you know all toilets are really shithouse. Y'might go in to P, but you will come out Xing yourself. Confusion, he say: for man who go to john in a Sydney pub, writing on the wall. Even the water comes out flushed. Jelf himself is so ashamed of these sordid surroundings that he hangs his head. Out. And weely wees. Quite extra-vertively, too, until his poor libelled eyebles, indelibly defamed by an indelible pencil, hit on the demural that shows out its largescrawl macroscript:

'i PHONEY FALSIE FEEBLIE; 1/2 FETISH FIDOFAECE. MR FIDO BIGS IS A REAL DOG STARTING WITH JAY'

Even deep down in his throat of throats, Jelf knows that he has been rattled. As roth and eager rage take hold of him, his thoughts are dogged with Amos Amos Amos Amos Amos most be Amus a rolling stone to gather Amos will i throw myself right down his slope Amosamosamos i shall stone you out of your amindose... and finds hisown self

back in his seat even before he knows it himself with his piss in hand at his mouth and drafting his drink quoff by quoff; this is after all the quoff that drams are made of.

Yes, stunned even unto a coming sozzledness. Blissful forgetfulness on way? Nuhuh; for no longer stunned into that intention by which to see the horrors of the world in a cooling breeze than does he notice --most horribly without being given notice --that the old Funct Flo overway is grummeting her crump (pet it, petit!) at him by concertining her leggams in his direction lewdly, dogamn her. Rolling too her purple tongue around her vermillion lips. If that's its intake what must its outlet be like? And so horrendous looking at both ends that Jelf has to lug his fascination closer towards her or it, which? His eyes fuzzball, then

105

squizz, then squinze. It cannot be? Surely not a lewd so luridly lewd? *O Dogod Thy help in ages piss't...* For he has seen enfucus'd clearly now, that fucused-out old Flooze, to be

Amos! Amock in drag of hag rags! And our Jelf suddenly in ejaculatio praevox, every bit of him a killer, going:

'YOU'LL BLEED GUILTY FORE I'M YOU FINISHED!'

Just as, though, in the right outside corner of his lefteye, a fleck of dust gets stuck into scoring quarries in the surface beneath his corneal lens. Going, him and it: Ochristophercit o bifurcit o christcystchrist alsighty, for something that has to look at the world all the time an eye hasn't got hardened to it. Trying to hang on the edge of his opfeelmic nerves. Not in tears but being torn. Yes. Our Jelf. And going to grit pains not to show it.

(run if a dog makes an inquarry after you)

Nor is it until he is hooked up into hawkeye anew does the Jelf throw himself back onto the Amos-plunge. Only to find that Amos has shot through in as minute a time as it would take a fleck of minute dust to get under an eye-lid. Aye. Gone!

Jelf casts himself from one roll to another roll. But only the dreg left where it Amos was Functing it up, and that dreg is the old alco who was so far gone that he was trying to pick up the Amosfunct, when he'd do better up on an operating table to have the urge cut out. And now looking oops at Jelf honourbound like one joss jostling against another for fair Functzy Flo's Favour.

'WHERE IS HE?!' Jelf beside heself, as he shirtfronts that old dregs there besides.

'Yer fly's open.' Dreg, with his lake level rising, as he raises his eyes up from his flat feet on a firm rival's statement.

(dog shook hands with a shake of its head)

106

Now Jelf has plunged outside where the air itself is trying to catch its own breath. His eyes like the windows of a poker machine, with one blank one, ball-bearing around in his head for to search out AmosFunct, if only fate be kind instead of feinting on him like it most always does. But this time it smiles. What a fate! There he goes, does Amos, swadding on the other footpath on high heels and swinging a sequin'd bag like a prostitute on the run; and accosting acumen and aghastmen alike by codfishing its lupsticked cods-suckers at them. So ugly he might even be the real thing. Attempting, too, a lesbian word-on on a passing nun at the very time that Jelf dollops out a drop in on him. Like a bombshell. They both explode into

(the dog thinks; therefore i am not)

pantomime fragments fragging here and going frag there for two seconds flat of bloodcurdles of Jelfiend and Amoscream; murderhelphere! before suddenly passes out colduck as though he had been goosed in so an attension-getting manner that Jelf suddenly feels a bit silly gandered at. Plustoo the shock loss of Amo's action-and-reaction causes Jelf to topple backwards spine arse over tit spinningly, milling and peglegging back onto the bus street where, in Sydney, only fools rush in. (Even Hell's Angels fear to tread on an onrushing road in Sydney. You make it across a busy road three times running, fast, they call you King Cross Lindberg in Sydney, true.) Anyway, Jelf flails back helplessly onto that road and stumbles, yes! inevitably!, right into the path of the mobhensile Constable Wilkinson who just happens to be around, around here at that same honk of time, during one of his off-duty prowl-arounds for Mr. Fido Bigs, puppy poop personator, that he frequently does, even though it has made him the joke of all psycho dogcologists around town. Yessir, Constable Wilkinson trying to brake but cannot avoid

(jealous pet took the new baby badly)

angrily running over Jelf's foot, if greater evidence is needed of how displeased he is to find Jelfeet lying all over the Quean's Hiway, no. But even before he gets to the stage of booking

107

(binding in the mash, much) jyelpfing Jelf for impedimenting a Sydney pliceman's pogromess, he cops (he really is a good cop) sight of theAmos deposited upon its back on the pavement on the broad of its broad's-drag and looking every itch like the only Sabine woman who didn't manage to score eventho she has waited like that for hundreds of years with her legs uncrossed for here's-hoping, so hop-in. Well! poor Constable Wilkinson is tracked in his stops, going. Chime hells bells, a chimera! And,

while all this writing is going on incessantly, Jelf is careering from one hop pity on one ft to the other, but getting phftt all pity from any of the gathering citydenizens there. No way known, so need you ask the way possible. Sickening, tis, or sicked upon, which?, especially

(if the dog has sicked you, at least you've gone through the bugger like Epsom Salts)

when, seeing a member of our plice force, he surges to attention by roping his ropey feeling sjelf up Constable Wilkinson's serge, Blue, going in gluckenspiel of onkonkaparingaga:

'Gee, donno why i left my foot infrontof polscar like that. Do beg for you not to take me away, sir, meaning SIR.'

'Don't try hopping away, you,' this to Jelf; oh, and the injunction of it all intersecting!, 'I've got my beadies on that good leg'.

At which Jelf turns to granite, intending to demon strate and straight to Constable W. that be he rock, he is not litho to eroad himself away, no. So Constable Wilkinson inspects the Functamos cadaver fouling away right in the rightofway, thinking as he does so that it is hard to tell whether It (Amos) is new dead or just too long living. Brother, if one wants to be a lotacop, one has to copalot. Truthismic, that, too. Then reverses himself back towards the rigidjelf, saying from out of his identikit training which kants that all men are criminal until proving t'be guilty 'ngoing: 'Tell me not what line-up i've seen you picked out in, pal. Just shadding up and pud no lip. One, deliberately trying to get a police-driven vehicle involved in a bodily accident, no accident. Two, causing grievous buckety to a harmless little old lady...'

'That ain't no lady...'

'Mooshutup! 'S better. Little old lady. Three, you got desire to tamper with that, sure as i'm a dog-lover you gotta be a pervert. And keep it buttoned cept to say yes to all that.' 'Yesth, osthifser.' He doeth lipth! At rigid digit and so plump rock bottom that even his own cleft gives lisp to an ossifer oth the kwoun in fwont othal thwez peepwul. With some smart alec at the back of the crowd making it wovenly worse with, 'Say, it's a comedian, too.' A northsoutheastwest span-of that Constable Wilkinson has already taken a compass on, anyway. Encompassing all, too, both spectators there and the Jelfhead. With it, now the Jelf loaf, falling like a leafleaving within the wicked basket of the Wilkinson mastiff developed arm. Triceps even. And the Constable divvying unto the fans there, going nod-nod and:

'Being a suicidal sexrampist you can understand about the little old lady and throwing himself under a police wagon, but a funny haha joker too...' And proceeds to haul, as though he was a killer in heat, Jelf towards the plice car, if not towards a mark for life at some unremarkable police station where lifers begin at an early agent. (Early jailbirds get a slug.) Yes, in truth. Njelf in noway keen to achieve distingashing marks nor cut his teeth on the custodians of sockiety. No, he isn't.

(dog gets plenty of lip from fat accident victim)

So he Jelf-strughs and stirups and strains ughly, but none of it matas, no, for the arm of the law is unbending, yes. For the arm of the law is lubberlocked. For the arm of the whitlow is painful. For the ammo of the law is vice. For if the law waits for neume, you will soon be dancing at the end of a rope. No man. Nor any use. All this entering a head while Constable Wilkinson is carrying him off like Jelf was no more a mere human being since he is not a member of the police force. Piece of piss. And the Jelfbody doing elliptical paths while his melon be squozed unto splitting pips.

109

Spitting headache, too. Goes to show you just try to smile and the world smites with you. And, if this wasn't

(better the dog work at your feet than nibble away at your manhood)

embarrassing enough, he is hauled past, yes!, Henry and Maggie there in the crowd, splatting their sides enough to be foaming at the mouths. HenMaggyrie! He shouts. He pleads. He wriggles his heft-up body at them. He spluts and suds, 'MAGGIE...!'

Haw haw, generally. Did we hear a hawser neigh?, and Maggie going:

'O i say isay i say, is that criminal talking to me?'

'HENRY!'

'Did somebody call Henry? Do tell.' Henry so jocular (black comedy) that if he were subject like Jelf to the crowding mads, they would surely crown him. So that now about a thousand and one people there are laughing through the tears in their eyes, there being a thousand and two present. Jelf last but least. Even Constable Wilkinson laughing laudly and playing to the gallery in a loudchaffing voice that goes, 'First up, we're gonna do this mother-fucker over ha ha.'

Unnoted, unheard, under rated, Jelf screelms eyebocks upleashing a plea of, 'Not your police horror hounds, *please*. Ask her! Ask him!'

'Whome or you?' Maggie to Henry.

'Whomu om me? Henry to Maggie. Oh, that rolls them all in the aisles, rolling eyes, tearing hurrays and so on, so that, weak and speechless from too much bellylaughing and in danger of losing this backward arched over criminal, Constable Wilkinson has to bring his pistol up to the Jelf temple just to poke him towards the back seat of the Wilkiewagon. Insmuch to say that an adam's

110

apple a damnday keeps the dock awash. Damn that! Jelf is now
screaming himself up into a blue. Round the gills, going:

'Before i die, sir, just want to say, finestpoliceforceintheworld
alwaysadmiredjob done and if frowned on by those who don't
know never have loved those fine bodies of dogtrackers 'n dogs 'n
other snarlers if we were alllikeyou sir your majesty then there
might be a little common decency let live sort of. Thing. Your
honour. I maynt act with the best wilt in the world but i could be
livingwurst.'

(never get into scraps over dogs)

And, just as the whole world began pressing nigher to see better
this mindbending display of pustulewhupping, even as the Jelf is
kissing the hand that is going to bleed him, Pother-ingay the Postie
(the dog's delight) squeezes by on his bonny but boney way to
some place that probably needed the letter he is delivering weeks
ago. And as he pothers poofpoof on bye, he ducts a derrydiction
into back seat of the Wilkie-wagon:

'How's it, Jelf?'

Well, what a rip off!

'Tellim it's me!' scrabbles Jelf, incidentally coinciding the top of
his voice with the azimuth of Constable Wilkinson's first play of
whiphand. And, too, when the Constable Wilkinson hears this, he
pauses in his downswing (he was only joking with a shaking hand
anyway) and perts in sheer pissotery. He does. For even he is not
too fuzzy a fuzz to know that sometimes it is not only the san-pan
man who takes the piss, no.

'Kay. What's going on here?', he scowls as quick as an ungiven
pistol whipping, and at Our Jelf, and so scowling that makes a
suspicion as good as a line-up.

(dog pepper Pop's corns)

Yet who places himself then upon events but bloody Amos. Yes! Who pongs to his one foot and foots it to the high heel on the other phfoot with a sodden burp of speed, spreading disbelief and disarray on all gaggled there; and now vox boxd by staggering towards a bill-board nearby on which is an advertisement for Cockette foundations for gays'n'gulls in androjeans. Where he, Amok gone Amos, paws at the picture of a Cockette jockstrap around where a young man's model hairies would be and spruking:

'Come t'good ole bloody horny orya never bloody know what bliss issss...'

With his floozie wig (a wig to keep indian warn) aflopping like one of the Duke of York's men playing silly buggers up and down the hill; and his lipstick everywhere save gashing along that gash of a mouth of his that looks like it's been subject to fifty stitches none of which will come out or die up; and one of his falsies slipped right around to give him one no-mean tit right in the middle of his back; and one of his stockings around his ankle like a sock, even socks, without elastic; if the sight itself isn't floccinaucinihilipilification itself then it must mean something, no shit. For even

(better a bitchy dog than one on your back)

now an ambulance has arrived to a rambling halt there. Its two ambulance men amble out with all that Sydney urgency of two men regretting getting out of a Sydney ambulance, as in ambulance men, two of. That is, taking all the pains in the world about it. They start out for Amos but soon start back agasping when they see what they're here for. They turn, each, together and separate Popeyes upon Constable Wilkinson (who's still around, around but by Dogod on Amosight wishing he was aroundabout, aroundabout) as much as to silently say we didn't know such catastrophes could still stalk up on us. Plus too: if you are a gordian of the law this is knot nice.

'Yeah, *that*. Get to it.' Wilkinson high and a bit flutin' hoarsey.

112

'I ain't touching that thing with these bare hands!' This is the younger and more screamquish of the two ambulance men. He tries to turn in his badge there and then before he is admitted into the incurable disease ward on return, but is held back, forcibly, by the older stretcher-bearer, going: 'Lettus remember our oath of Flit On Cheering Angel which we all know is an anagram for Florence Nightingale. We all have to start learning somewhere, so why not at the rock bottom?' as he bears the youngest man bodily over to the body of Amos, who is now digit dildoeing, the silly dill. There, they hump Amos off to the ambulance with as much care as is possible with such fingertip control. With Amos, shedding layers flying pins ali kazam kazoo kiss my kedgeree tingle your tongue on my unmentionables etcetera, bloodying them and bloodying thisthat and just waiting to get his hands on their private parts. And this came, once, clair de lune off the top of his nut: 'Hands offa bloody merchand-bloody-ise if yain't buyin'!' before the door is flung shut on him before the ambulance men take off, the cowardly custards! (The ambulance was later found abandoned.)

(Dog tired? Then don't move a muscle or you'll whiff you didn't)

Leaving even all the flibbertigibbets flabberagasping gastric. Yes, it's true; it took Constable Wilkinson to burst the bubble. 'Kay,' auctioneering Jelf by the scurfy nape of his scruffy, 'who knows this sickscxest psychosissiest assault merchant who's one of the hardest cases i've ever run across still at large?'

But the crowd is now dispersing, up purses and all, dispriting distal spiriting pharma dispensing off, when one Anon lady (by name of Lycea Misslainy, a spinster of laines and wool-sheds and a woman of some good parts) gurgled a giggle that passed an answer to Constable Wilkinson as she passed an arm over her brow passing him by, and, 'Know him. Who doesn't?'

Ha ha. What a laugh. As a breeze it has been luffed out. So much so that even Constable Wilkinson, against his batter nature, dumps our Jelf upon the roadside dump where he first didn't make a very good job of running right over him.

113

'Very funny, commedia d'artist, but next time don't count on help from your friends.' C.W. to Jelf.

' *Friends*?'

'And dowanna have to run over you again, 'kay?' Thus said, a warning well given always warming to the cockles of his heart, he recomposes his face into that famous tourist attraction of an expression, that Austhentic posture known around the world as 'mugs leather urn',

(mad dog gets Englishman out in the noonday sun)

before reclumping his tonnage back into his rusty steed and citigrading away out of that shemozzle there. Around around-about. And a goad time was had by all. Too. Jelf got it real good.

(*woof woof hope you choke*)

Still on the street, there are now only three people in gutter-snap there now, twain standing (Henry'n'Maggie) and one stood-on (Jelf, stuffitall). They are in their cups, but in all truth Jelf does feel a bit of a mug. For a moment his sassy eyes read out to them othertwo left behind here to drain quietly away. But then Henry sprinkles a few ashes over our Jelf dog-face and intones some songcycle that sounds very much like 'May The Holy Spirit Nettle Onya, You Weed', while Maggie herself rhymes the time with her ribald hahas and heehees syncopating. All ways, but. At least this spurs on our Jelf to think and stop, going: *o dogod i am come to fruition only as a funure of a fig fie upon life fig-lief* And

(eat up your own Chow)

now Henry going: 'Yes, osthiffer. No, othfisser. You kill me, mate.'

'Just a little matter of my barethreading hands around your stringy black abo throat. Tell me you volunteer before you die.' Showing that our boy Jelf can still figuratively kill 'em in the Isle of Aisle.

'Can't stay, sorry, Jelfie. Still haven't made date alonga me new Diva yet.' If Jelf Hooks could keel!, but no matter for Henry has suddenly departed, leaving only Maggie chokethrottl-able within her chortling there. Left, we might add, with a man with a fire to fan and a foible to boot and a pecking order to pick at, both all three. And do here remember that famous Australian good oil that goes: if yer can't argue with a man, shellac a sheila. So what chance has she got when thisjelf jumps to his feet?

'Put 'em up, mug!' Jelf ole J. L. Sullen himself barefistedly sparring around Maggie and barely saving her from a thrashing, or, watch this fast footrot. She is and she isn't. After all, a good thrashing she might just enjoy, and certainly willing to enjoy finding out if or yep. Anyway, there she is, the centre of his circling, sprucing her nails o hum and spruking:

'Gawd, one hand tied behind me back and it wouldn't be a fair fight. If I'm three stone weakling what does that make you? Peter Pan under the bed, i.e. little pisspot?' Then does she feint one of her kneecaps to his groin, which causes our Jelf to stumble backwards crying for quoiter and for Balzac sakes maggie a knee can be a madcap in upset ballast. She merely snapping her snippertips in his smacker and now enters quite unhindered into the shafty of their appartment block hinterland. Too much of it, all of it.

(look out for the hen dog that bit you)

'World?' Jelf shouting outrage, open mouthed and openly, quite, 'You hear me, World? Y'think y'can shove me around every minute of laughlong day? Uhuh and nope, World! Y'hear?' and whipping off his tie and throwing it down to the ground at his toes with a defiant jesture. 'Just one of any of you mugs try to take this away!'

You must guess it how ever, however. Aye, even before the dust around the deserted tie has settled, there comes in thun-derosa three little boys (three little turds meaning i laugh you) ploughing along the footpath playing or plagueing, whichever side you're on, chasey. Indeed, and before you could have committed juvenilicide on even the smallest of them, they have already done three dodgem car turns around a pole that turns and turns and turns out to be our Jelf and ended both it-jelf and it-tie in the slush of the gutter. More. For no sooner they have beetled off when Maggie's dog, Che the Chidehuahua, yea, the same huamaster as has bordelled on our story before, comes bowhounding out of the appartment blox, bowounces onto that tie, then dog-does a daytime flit with its booty back into that hole from which it did re-cur from. No time for Jelf to put the booty in, either, and. Telling you,

(dogs won't spare a tear of you)

the man has really arrived back on the short and narrow pathic to see. Spoken sadly but trued ruefully, going: *i am ergo i echo iambic.* He cries out. He does. First a soursob, then a full and mellow slobber, then finally like a wounded in animal.

(there's not a dog that won't get the wind up from you)

Who cares who caries? Not one yet all. The World isn't even ready to let him get off its giddy. No. For now, across the intersection, Henry waving 'toodles' to him and looking like he is enjoying a rich joke about his retching, wretched mate.

And if that wasn't bad enough, standing with an arm lock on him is, yes!, that Black Floppy Hat. True, and what's more obviously this is Henry's new Diva. But equally obvious also the Black Floppy Hat of the bus-slipped-note-infame, and, now horsing at Jelf like Henry is. If Jelf was a cowled mock, he couldn't be more publically monked. Not only that, in truth. There is some totemic about that Henry's new Diva, that makes our Jelf start. To run. From the gutter upwards. Frentic frenziful frowing himself into the teeth of the block wherein is his own appartment placebo. And just as well that those djoors are not real djaws. Eh? *Ohm.*

(smart alec dog gets mouthy for the licks of you and me)

Jelf,
fleshing up the stairs, diving up as though droven by gadarene, twostep at a ticky time to give you some idea how his gristle was mindracing, hogtied to the tied of human arffairs, (paw me more swine, winsome), is our Jelf, hounded out of torn in turn, fearful that Dogod is having meaty ideas about him, and in danger of a run down coming on. Yes, and not even his disguise as Blin D. Panick is covering up his confusion and blind panic. Broncobustling and rhynchorunning for his besitting bedwomb, in whichwhere (even) everything has gone so much to the dogs lately that toutes de suite seems to be all in one tearing great husky. All going to prove, too, that if

(only a stoned dog can pelt you on the run)

you try to expan into the world, you are just spicked off. It's true. Try to weave your way through the world outside and you're spun off. We are not knot-picking; this is for reel. You cotton? Aye. A man can barely ford to fjord his djoor anymore.

Throuwhich hejelf now forges; a wrot iron will still; wrought by routing; brought by routeing by bedlam to bcd'o'lam; his own feathery fathery fartery lazy field (he is fielding better already) of bed steady. Aye, the Jelf retreet from the streat, now entering himsjelf into his big blissack yawning his gap oh hum you big beautiful humdinger. Oh well, forty fathoms sleep snip-snap-snorum. zzz *ohm* zombie.

(once the dog catches on it never foregoes)

117

Just to give some idea of what the Jelf world thought means: Since the world is spinning on its axle, it must be in a car-een. Makes sense, doesn't it? We mention this, because, at the same momsical mument that our Jelf was bound up for his bedwomb bolting, a number of things were happening in the voisinity there arab-bouts. (Oh Dogma, Mother of Dogged Ones and of Ass All!). For instance a young mother, a yonthy Mrs. Eycla Misslainy who was always ready to do one allways, has her li'l children put down at the vets and takes her dog to the kindergarten. Not only she, no, for

also another mother in moth bawls is dropping off her littl'uns at grannies from the London flight overhead. What a crowded landing pattern there was, too! Theregoes, too, A. N. Other yummy mum (mum's the ward) who is waving her kidiwinks off to school (schoo! schoo!) across Highway One against the redlights (a district of illfemme, no joke), and

(better a dog in batter than a dog on Fry)

if those weren't notably notorious enough, there were one or two other goings-on worthy of note, like:

heregoes a funsical mumsy, giving baby a lick of mummy's icecream by shoving cone'n'icle down its throat (poor Baby Blunted on a Shove Tuesday!). And heregoes migrain'd motorist who is waving skoolchilds (with the sckids on) across with a flourish and curtsy before he runs them over; therego a daddy who did apply a brick to the accelerator of his car before waving 'urry-òme and drive safely y'all hear to his kiddi-kidles in the back seat; herego tram fro on a to-line; therego lights green all ways; herego a smash'n'giveback raid; therego dog kissing dog on the lips instead of the labias (the end!); herego the young lovers knecking each other with hacksaws; therego a man who did decide to cut his clean shaven neck on the sui side at the tenth strop stroke, shouting 'El Cid' on the side; herego blind truckie; therego a bubblecar hearse causing an internal jam; herego huzzwife who wanted a slash so badly she lived on a razor's edge; therego three bibs in arms who were dropped down a drain entrain to the

118

supermarket to cut down on the food bill; herecome bus without brakes (T brake, the driver's gone!); therego real bomb bowling along street; herego man who goes by the name of James Joist and who is blowing up his tyres from behind that bomb shelter; therego a ton tonne crane ending its days as a shopping trolley; herego the genius, Bilious Bill, who first suggested that

the dog has gone on the meat waggin'.

Aye, all this and evenmore. Chaos. Chaostic and caustic! Causting all sorts of thingoes here and theregoes! Just going to show that Dogod is gluttoning up our main streets. It's a Dogod's life, tis so. Too tooth rue if not in fract. Nor is it the mended that counts, but the breaking up. Not the thaw but the phfaw. Unless it be thaw but satisfied, dog fashion. And we have been deleterious selective in our examples, too. No wonder Jelf hast cot to the got taken, by jamas! The zzz zoot suit.

(Killer dog keen on homey-side)

He cries to sleep in, does our Jelf, but it is hard to get off the wheel of life when you are tied astride it for the Commonweal welter. Going Jelfishly: *dire Dogod dear deus and halloa allah, they are digging my grave, that gravelly dug-out, before i even get in a giggle let alone a groove. At least this bed foetus me like a glove i love.* O yes, and,

(the dog loves you best offal)

yes, our Jelf pupa'd like as if tucked into mammary (Mama Mary, titular, pray for the loss of his mammory. Swads his name? Yes!). And abed and so plumb tuckered in there that the wind might well been taken out of his sheets, which do in fact need a bit less wind put-in and more airing hung-outo. When then comes a knockturnal noc apun the Jelfdoor. Audibly ordible, too.

(Knock, knock, who's there? Dog. Dog who? Dog 'ere. Dog ear what? Dog ear got you bolted down.)

A knock? Knock, knock! Damp't it, Hugh's there? Corps esprit or corpse aspree? Undoings or undies? Tap-tap tiptop! Grow a weigh! To open the door is to open your flycatcher and that is a bit mouche, ayeszzzzz.

(the dog loves you in spice of yourself)

But Maggie has her own key and now swings into the Jelfroom with a sauntly walk about her mopbrushbloom and broom-sticks, making like some Austracian (oyster to the yardarm!) piece of Ozzie muliebrity in all its ass-idity. Busylizzie, going about her busty bustliness about our joculess jokeduress Jelf cleaning his room, careful only not to fall into his pit, and. He is, too, so used to such interruptions that he doesn't even have to glim his swimmers up to partalk of her, going:

'Next time do not knock, Maggie. You don't want me to think you recognise such things as common decency privacy, etc. Might bring on an excitation.'

'Get you.' Maggie being as quirk as she can even unto lifting up the floorboards if she must. Or smells it, the must in there.

'A sorry thinks, Maggie, when a man's bedroom is an open book.'

'If this crabcrawl was a book, if wouldn't be allowed in the country and they let anything in.'

'I might have had someone in here, Maggie. *Please.*'

'I've got to get this room straightened up. But ask me nicely. A gal loves to be cravened to.'

'Maggie, i plead i please i lift up my pleaders to be in Pleiad, Maggie and. For the millionth time, stop that bloodless thing called Amos who is your father from following me all day

120

everywhere. He's trying to character assassin me, too, in cahoots with a Floppy Black Hat.' Jelf, getting so agitated that he is now in emidanger of breaking his covers. And, going also: 'Whatever that father of yours has got may be catching, Maggie. I'm too young to end my days with a rare incurable mental disease.'

'Who'd want to give a scarecrow like you something personal like a germ?'

Thus peaked, she slopes off, out of the Jelfroom muttering beneath the breath about her Amospapa while her dog, door left dangerously open to let Things Out There In, runs yappingful laps around the Jelfroom like a muttish mullethead floating around brontosaurous waters of the world. It does, unhinged and unhindered, both seemingly, with the Jelfthroat going: 'Don't forget thy boggiedoggie, dear Maggie ha ha!' But it has, funnily, followed her out on its own cord. Then, oh,

(see the dog about a man)

silence. Sense lent. Prayers be to Dogod for Its benefidoence! Even safety itself settles beside him, all warm and cozen, and: *O Dogod you let them have a key to your door and they think they can turn you out. Pick your turnpikes. I have no dogsire to have applied to me the swing of a pick, no. Nor the turn of a pack. Nor the lack of a lock. The trouble is in this world, there is so many people in it that any old fleabitten dog can pick you up for next to nothing.* Yes. But,

when you're frying the only thing to do is zzzzizzle, and now Jelfalling off after one or two brinks. He is one of the few men in the world who can slink into sleep. Sleepy thyme. Spicy!

(Knock, knock. Who's there? Mutt. Mutt who? Me, Mutt on head!)

Jelf zonked out, for how long? Some time, aye. And during it, he also jerks in image like as if he was hounded in's dreaming mists.

121

Dreams of 'must-you', must be. As if, too, instead of embarking upon his soft downy head-down, he has been barked upon, all over. He sweats. Tosses. What dreams these are we cannot say. Perhaps of police horrounds reigning down from out of the air, hellbending their razor-sharps for to give the Jelf a pain in his rectitude. The skies around his sleepery doze worse for wearwulfs. Perhaps trials of brute strength over him. Perhaps strips of bark did felon him. Who can know for sure, except Dogod, O Great Ensconcer. Only that,

(for a dog there is no plaice like homo)

Jelf, our man, awakes again with a start almost as soon as he slept off to slip. He finds, too, reality just as morbid but not so morphid as he thought. He need not avert his eyes further than they are, even when the door opens. Again. So soon back, Maggie. Oh, just in time! As she (as it must be she just as it must be she) pads her angel self up to the Jelfoamy altar to bring surely soothings forsooth and unguents urgently urged for to oil his palms and cool his creased brow and to take him within her embracing charms. One touch of your paw, Maggie, and he wilt be Rex Scued whiff. Him going, nearly so:

(the dog has a bloody hide)

O, Maggie, figure of figleaf, flimoiselle, in figureline beside him now! Staymoiselle in his desmesne and demand anything of him, demain or any other day. Daymoiselle, day do! And let him, patstroke of your booty and carecrest ye, ye lovely nightingale who has come fortwise into fort of foam fame, fane of all foughties where thane is he, the Jelf. Yes, the Maggie vision lying beside bedside just out of hisjelf vision.

And him now getting up out of the Jelfmouth froggoing: 'Maggie... you've come back, Maggie. Good dear dogod kind Maggie. Good jump too. Say that cause i know you are thinking to yourself why has that big strong heft of a man, me, got his eyes weeping? Because Maggie i am in shock with all those rudeshocking shockingrude lies lies lies lying in weight in That

122

World Out There. This morning. And your rotting father and that rotten Floppy Black Hat and now. Now, Maggie, i've just had a nightmare that you have rarely heard me suffer when a normal man would have done away with himself by now because of it, yes, and you will need all the come-alongness you can sidle up to me, snuggle, to help me snap out of it, i can tell you, you little hot dog diggedy, you'.

(grizzly dog like to indulge in a good bit of a gristle)

And with all that free female flesh oozing pith and prithee on the roll-over next to you, who needs provocation more, so Jelf just gussets on: 'Ah, Maggie, my hand to your smouchy smoothness. Your arms to go around me. Soft murmurings in me shell-like now do make, my little pollywolly. And the answer going:

'Wish you wouldn't do that, mug.' In a grubbily, strike-a-light-izzyoudere aboway kind of tonsiltone. Henry, yes! Not at all, or any part of, Maggie, and quite unlike Maggie could ever dream of being. It's true, plus:

'I want Maggie!' Jelf.

'Stiff that.' Henry going, 'I came in to find out how soon you can tumble out. Mate.'

'Nevereverno will i uprise again, no.' Out of mouth of Jelf, believe it, motheaten and nearly going up the wall of his wail.

'Wanna put in a quickie reservation for this arvo, mate.' Henry, in quick.

'Abotawns have too much reserve already. Consult a map. So no.' Jelf, nuhuhking that on the head, got in quick.

'Tomorrow?'

'No.'

123

'Next day. Day after. Try to say aye.' Henry, all mouth, but starting to mooch.

'Ayeeiiieee. And no.'

'I'll lend you my camera.' Henry, moping.

'*My* camera.' A minor J. lends correction.

'You could go up north, shoot a few outofcontrol bushfires. They bring up the sunsets beaut on colour slides. C'arn mate pal long lost buddy old oppo. Go walkabout do. Meknow two three longway blackfella dey longa real tribe. Dey lick whitefellah.'

'No.'

'Listen, mate, i can't take my Diva down to that bull pit of mine, can i? Itchy on the back.' Henry mopping up.

'So scratch its every hairy.'

'Do us a favour, mate,' Henry doing his bast, and: 'don't call it it.'

'You off your head?' Jelf with a Jelf look.

'My new Diva's different, Jelf. Head like a halfbaked month old pie but classy. Meaning belooted. Loots of lot. Nkidnot. Nfierce. Nfiery. A furnace and hot. She's also out of her fuck-wits like all you whities, but unless i get her into the snakepit soon, Diva's gonna blow her stack before i can blow mine. Lost loot too. Dig? And i wish you wouldn't put in by myself while i am sitting alongside you. So there, and out, you louse. Get.' But

(the dog should not be let louse on the world)

he has only given the sic (sick) Jelfthought time to thunk, going:

'Rested now, i shall not comment on the shock coincidence of Big Floppy Hat and this new Diva of yours, no, except to say that if

124

her name is penny then do shovepenny on some other board. Oh, and is she broad?'

'That your last word?', Henry angry and engine going.

'No, "toodlebye" is my last word.'

'Well then, sweet nightmares, big white farter.'

'And malnutrients to you, Abo.'

Parting now not as mates, but like two men possessed by the beast of company, splitting up when each is like the lonely dog that only wants a little chunk of humanity given it and so have you wholly to itself. Aye, leaving off where the dog would have to be shot off, each thinking like the dog that thinks that the other man is tripe yummy yum. Stupidity! But neither of them even thinking with their common scents that impasses like this are precisely why: a bitch will play with every menses she comes across; the dog is such a good swimmer, being so paw-poised; the mongrel has such a mean temper, he is so crossed.

No. Instead, Henry decamps. Only pausing on the landing to momentarily trip over a drag in torn dreg; a dragonheaded fireblown blueflyed crappitude in crepe bag of bones; a decrap't messpot of pot puree, a

(dog with appetite for life make a whole mess of jours, old bean)

poor thing done-in crump-pelted, shagged out in rags of a now really fucused-out hag. Yes, Amos! Half himself, half seemingly sane, having escaped from the ambulance but only out of sheer shock. To the two ambulance men. Nor until after a struggle, in which both of them thought they wouldn't get out before the sheer power of Amos's armpits overcame them.

But our jelfselfhood does not even have to put the boot in to Amos now, no. Only boots to the door of the pad, and. He merely flaunts his high-falutin' flautistic voice, going:

'Listen you ancient ruin, you. Shan't pick bones, not i. No. As a thing-near-death, you are quite incapable of making me, a vital essence of jelflife itself, think that things have happened that could not ever happened. No note from under some Floppy Black Hat, no filthy writing on crudhausen walls, no posters, no country house train trip posing no dog crudding trying to crucify me no posing artclasses slanderings. All nothings. No such things. So signing off, and shut down.'

Thereupon Jelf retraces back to his cocoon (o chrisalis almighty) so immersed in its coming comfort that he does not notice that Amos has slivvered, snakes alive!, in behind him and is even now licking and liking his wounds and runes underneath the Jelfartsack. Which bears out the fact, as the de factotum said, that

if you have a pit, there be probable site of old pock. Great pitty. *Ohm.*

(Fire dogs ingrate)

Siriusly though, again:
dog flying through the air must have been only an air's breath away from you. German shepherds all jerry built. Then again, too: puppies growl up quickly. Then again: dog makes an issue of foetus by chewing on the existing facts. Some dogs say abortion must be a crime because you can't take life too early. Other dogs make a living on abortion by just being around at the time. Then again: choosy dog throws back early miscarriage in disgust. Then again: there have been some dogs that breached healthy infants. To all dogs, too, maternity is just lamb seasoning. Though a starving hound will think there's nothing much at all to childbirth. Afterbirth's no picnic either. As to death, the dog considers it can be shared by all or enjoyed by one. And euthanasia? Well, ask a dog and it'll think that's only being lb. foolish, puny wise. Old age, too, is only the Waste of Time. What does a dog feel about all such things? What do you want it to do, drool you a picture? It has strong gut feelings about things like those. Thoughts? Aren't they

the things that make the human twitch and so give the dog indigestion?

So just remember that it's no good saying, 'Ne mangy moi, you dog,' because if a dog hates your guts it's just had enough of you for the time being, that's all. Nor answering personal adverts that go like this: 'Starving dog needs hypnotherapist to cure lose of appetite'. So here's a hint:

give yourself, not your wordly goods, that Dogod may save you for a mouthwatering day. *Ohm.*

DIVA

Henry's new Diva she saythis saythat dothis dothat. E.g., to some shlopping woman, with name of Ms Layce Islainy to her credit, and who, full of credit, is just now hurrahying after more credit got at that time along the street minding her own budinose. Where Henry's new Diva, she say to her, 'Him black' meaning Henry, 'Me white' meaning herself, Diva, 'We go djiggy-djig him-me so put in on that, you fat old racist fart.' Shopping femme, too, was only glancing past them at a shop window dressed out in, wonder that, signright or wrong, to read 'Credit for anyone named Ms Layce Islainy! PLUS: Hack the Horrold Angel Sings the whining slogg'em for today --"Lemme Laybuy Lammington's Lemming"'

(beggars can't be chewed)

We mention this only to demonstrate straight off how Henry's new Diva of Henry's, that she ought to be an abattoir aid. Henry imply to Jelf she was fierce? That's a fierce ha ha. She's only not fierce when she's astunning; and when she's not astunning, she is sitting. Nfact, she is so stunning, this new Diva of Henry's, that she ought to be an abattoir aid. It's true.

(dogs like beefy men primely, but stock men in the soup'll do)

And then there was another time along the street when Henry's new Diva shesay this to a pack of hefty dog-faced labourers up a scaffold when they whistled at her from across the roadway thisaway:

'Watcha looking at, you hogs? Fraid i'm gonna sprog little tawns by this aboboy and pollute your big whiteland? Shove off!' And they say: 'You shove off, lady.' And Diva shesay, 'You fat hogs, he'll do you.' Meaning peraspirant Henry taking a shortcut route to suredeath, sure as shooting, and pushing him forwards, and they, the dog-faced labourers, saying, 'We'll do him' and Diva she saying this: 'He'll do the whole lot of you hogs,' and they saying that 'We'll do the whole lot of him' and

128

the pack of them, each and all, then deftly descaffolding themselves like a family of marauding baboons out for a murder. And not hogs at all. And Diva only knuckling a wave at them on her clenched hand. And H. very badly in need of coaxing or axeing her adgzeways off to prevent a grave situation from the site developing on him, and not succeeding very well at all, except his feet dancing little dances, somehow. Each labourer, too, is heaving over two huge biceps to each manjack heavily loaded for to say a few sentences of deathdealing prose into Henry's earlug about to be lugged off to nearest abo final resting ground. Sort of thing. All all his new Diva saying is that (oh, loud myth!) she refuses to pack 'em on count of them cunts. Plus she shouting to them to comeon you cunts 'cause he (Henry) has done over bigger cunts than any of them anytime sametime inbed or imbedded. Yes, and then what? Well,

(beggars, canine choses!)

Henry's new Diva commits a new booboo, by now removing her titcups quicker than a quack can qucatch it, a squirt can squint it or a quaf could quoif it in. That's the truth. Brassiere right off; a bit high; and now she is flauting those mamamelons at those manjacks, almost jerking to overcome the road b'now and bullmad, they, at this cupculpable if not palpitating jibe brassairily flapped at them. Plus too new Diva yellingthis gogettwatted i am a darkie's piece of arse cos hebetterman than the whole lotta youse louses bugger off. And if new Diva hadn't caused so much traffic chaos (the wricks of those wrists!) on account of all those headlights jammed on to new Diva's boob-bolster flagging there, the heftuge abo bouncers would have scaled Henry's smaller height by now. For sure. And allon account only for that his

new Diva shesay thisthat dosay thissaythat all the time, yes. Enough to riddle you ree.

(dog skins derilict already skint)

And if you think that was all, you have not read on. E.g., egged-on nowise, Henry's new Diva now continues in stroll, dragging

129

Henry alug behide her, with her titcups slung over her shoulder and boobs bouncing titbits for all to think (so she thinks) how loose can a white girl get, going out with a blackabo and allowing him to fiddle around withtit? Aye. And it being rush hour again for houris everywhere there so that the atmosphere around them is so chilly that all the stores did shut up shop in case it was the cold blast of reality looking at their prices.

(Knock, knock. Who's there? Collie. Collie who? Collie your dog of quick!)

Henry's new Diva's not even content with that, either. Now she has bought two grapefruits to put one to each titcover. In. And is whirling the whole contraption above her head as they walk along, and. Diva sayingthis loudthat this is my abo's slingshot this is my bull abo's bullroarer this is my abo's extra bit of sourgrapes old fruity abo darkie bong boob bouncer of mine here. She does and is.

Still Henry goes along with her, not struggling so much against the ghenghis stranglehold she has on him as from preventing his feet from wanting to fleet it to the other side of the road quick bloody smart. Trouble is, it is difficult for an abo to hold up his head since abos loafs never rise, no. The thing is, too, his new Diva may look and act like she's recently been part of a fatal road accident but she is crash-hot in lash-out cash. She is. Henry's never known an abo nonsportsman so oodled with boodle as he is now. Beside, he doesn't feel too black beside this white cheek of arse, because she just makes him blanche all over. Which is so peculiar, she gives him goose pimples, like now when she puts her bra back on broad, openly; but back to front. Yes. So that she now perambulates with her two squashed fruits squeezily in front and those two titcupped begrapefruits plugging lusciously out of her back. And wailing melon-dramatic in and out of what ever comes and goes, 'I have been cupuled from behind by this blackfellah!' and 'Return my service, behind my back!' and 'Broken in by backing back blackfetishist' and 'He has turned me black to frantic' and 'Baa bra black slip'd, have you any other way?' and 'I'll Always Be Trod To You In My Fashion' and 'Back home in

130

two beauties where God gave me top titters and my blackpappy got me top tips' and 'I been melon-collied by this black dog behind!' etcetera; thisthat yakyak.

(the old sea dog gets his legs)

What we are saying here is that every time that Henry walks out with his new Diva there is never a dull moment that might not be a duff moment. Each moment is a monument of time. Duffed up and donedown; thrown and frowned on fro and hither; told to get stuffed, stiffed, rimmed and hornjagged from goebals to woeballs. Nor does he know what New Diva really wants; won't wanky, no willn't; nor winkle his willic, no, nor turn on anything, really, except maybe a mob gainst him. If she come across, it's when he meets her over street. 'Strue.

(some bitches have their men-struaight regular as pie)

All Diva seems to do is saythis saythat. Most often Henry does not even twig what she is saying (not smuch as a twig off the ole femmily tree), how she is saying it, when she is doing whatever it is he is not sure or snore of. And talk? Torque's not in it! Talkish delight? Daylight's notin it! Talck powder? Like a canonade, that canine aid! Talk telly? Talkie talkie tal korder. A troika to end all tall khers. Talk about talk talk's not in it all talk No play.

(dog overlay carpetbagger)

This is how they met, Henry and his new Diva:
Henry was emerging from the depths of despair, which is the same stratum as his basement room. Now even a cavilized abo as our Henry must feel beneath people's contempt since he lives beneath their pathpaving shoe leather, as he steps out into the septic steppes of the whitedazzling world (where the abo son's blacked out!) and. Dogod it!, runs into this white stuff Diva, read real dog,

131

who ups and starts yellmelling pelmets as if he was bound for her throat, rather than the boozer. She did, descending

(the dog bound to eat you flat out)

upon him with all the queandeemdom of the big white farter. (And when the big white farter puts in a personal appearance, man, you blow, y'ear?) Anyhow, this whitlow whitey of a Diva suddenly tries to get him by the dick and is crying out black muder or something. Truly. All Henry can do is call up the witness of Uncle Tom from inside him, too, viz; T's didna loak at missie, no ma'am uhuh,' with her sayingthis:

'You arsehole, you were looking at my arse,' with Henry saying, 'Noaa whoaa moamma. I's be a good nigger blackboy darkie dung Abo about thishere tawn, i is, uh huh. Police help don't no do, please missey.'

Suddenly she laughs as though she was being carried unnaturally away on a horse and bray. Henry, too, gigs with a bit of a giggle. They have, as well, looked well into each other's eyes. Even they are dancing twinlights. She takes his arm below the white cuff; she saysthis therethen:

'You kept me waiting out here. Now we room moor. Let we berth, you blackamoor you!'

And that is a fact of irenic fate. Henry's new Diva clutches him to herself and lags him off back down to his room, a base lone and lonelybin; aye, apparently knowing full well where it was from the very first. At his door she merely dived, did Diva, into her own pocket for the key. Did Henry mind?, being thrust in and quite thrown over, by new Diva divine (but that head!) No. Nor care a fig off a fern tree either, for somehow she was a key that keystone copse'd his black corner. What we must remember is aborigines never have the right shade. They just meet for the sandwitch. Anyway, a man has to vir off the strait gnaw row, now and again. No?

132

(arty dog takes its dramatis personnae in stages)

Berthing, Henry's new Diva saythis: 'Christ' shesay on open sesame of Henry's door. She saythat. Crabbing her eyes around what in effect looks like the subterranean boiler room beneath the Black Hole of Calcutta. Fable, yes, but still looks whole lot like it; and so small that it would be a bad ballad for a swinging cat. Diva shakes her Medussa'd locks in stony silence and sayingthis that if this is the way our black brethren have to live then no wonder they look so down caste.

(Tex, the homosexual range rover, pulls on his chaps on backwards)

Yes, she did. She took a step back still shaking her looks. Henry tried to grope for her lower band with two fingers erect in estimation of the size of the situation. 'Why don't you wait until you've got the feel of the place?' Henry. 'Nope, uhuh, baby abo. I dig perversions but they have to be comfortable come-fors. Yep.' And looking like she might be able to take the plunge. The wrong way. He throws up desperately, 'Something else might be arranged later' and Diva shesay 'Oh?' cocking her eyebrow much closer to our H.'s cocked finger so that he geths husky with thwick pwassion. 'Upstwairs. Mate owf mineth's place', at which shesaythis: 'Try arranging it, lover. Yes?' At the same time suddenly waving a wad at him in her nit-pickers. Whole dollars and upward denominations, many. It, too, is a real wad, not a mere waddy waved over an Abo. No wonder Henry was thinking whatever the abo equivalent to 'Call me Ynn, Flynn.' Is. From the moment of Henry's promise of the upstairs Jelfpit to her then, his new Diva became brawn spanking new.

(tricky dog deals with card)

Then they saidthis saidthat to each other, going: don'tu dare koshish me, you ignaceous charrley you! Kiss off! Smack yr'own kisser! Kith yr own Kinsey! Please, prattly pleas; do i not please you, mi one only onew Diva in my mia mia? Gun ya! Hold your tongue! Your tong makes me hot'n' coal! Your tangyerating tongue wants to make me spit! Wop! Swop your own spit, toon, and come. Yes, u duckie darkieyu; just keep yo'r dicky daks on deck and comey. Be led, blessed, by yr new Diva what i am, whater to your parch, higher whatter will i be to your what-for, hiawather to your indjun ink choler, hot whater bottle for to this dreaded flea pit of a awfoal bed. We will have patience and whait until something better upstairs comes along, do. This taint a bed of vice; this is a bed of lice, a hoppit floppit. This is not a hotbed but a hopbed. Y'get in there, y'start from scratch. Yet here will we lay down our deeds of white virgo and black verso. For the time being until upstairs comes good.

'Jelf's 'sname, me mate, no problems.'

... Yes, in that bed and 1 am sure we will be on then. Jelf's, isit yusay?

What a promise she put him on! He thinks she's a probe probably (Beth, Sheba, geth Semeny!) of such pro portions that straight away he goes to overthrow his new Diva off valence onto his bey'd. When all of a sudden she tries to twist off his hands. With a torchturous Chinese burn. He turns to ashen, there and then. Then does

(better to cry for whelp than wolf)

new Diva saythis to Henry that he must go very careful how he do touch (tch!) her torch. Tuttut, King, tetchy; she says. Perhaps one dark night of reverie, but first he must be born anew, must be recreated. First he must be recreched. Yes. She did saythat. Pluss: recreched kinder than afore, in socks and gartens. Redone afore he can she-do. For she is his New Diva and he is her Chosen One. Yes. Her horny aboHenry. Wilt thou, or wilt thou wilt, O Abohenry, be the new Abo-manable Bennelong who ben a long time in recoming? Heh? Eh? Hen? Nwry not? For blessed are they two who raise themselves to the bed upstairs eventually.

134

(dog got Nick in time)

Then did Henry's new Diva lift him up, lug'im across, and lay him down as gently as a newt borne babye upon that beddy byes there. She did. As though he was a swad in (dingdong) lingland. As though he was a twiny twerp in the twilet, nor hindrance, of his toylight. Abed, placed. Laid to wrest. Swiddled in swarth, the inphant swart star turfed in sward, tufted in warts'n'all, nail'd, toff'd in babybyes. Tucked up. Tuckered out. The infant'd Henry by Diva put on's infantee-side. Not in fun nor in fawn nor in fain, neither in profane nor in phone nor phonaemic nor phoney fooey nor neither philofict or vilefact nor sycophant nor sick inphancy. Nor fancy fpants on the nappy of his nack. Nor twas Henry baby put to bysie by Diva Daisy by feint or the fee fie of de foe. Noe! But by all that's wholly water, by fount. Yes. By foetus foundt! By the sheer relief to get off his foetus at last. Now embryon, soon'i'm Byron. Yes, for then does new Diva get into bed with him too and does, yes!, she

(the dog only kills for humanity)

gather Henryhimfant between her loins. She does. Lying over him in truth, with leg pinning this arm leg pinning that arm and the Henry head encased by box. Pewbic hairs, hers, that fruity fphew ensconcing his sconce. To Adam with the belly button, she gives her fig leaf for his loaf. In wraptures, he! Evevaginated, he, ever and Eve'd. Oh, listen, Adam Abo, to the Evesdroppings ponst thy crown!

And that's a fact. In the cool of the afternounce, they lay in bedding there. Eva and Adam. Ave and Man. The Abo man, the Diva Eve, the eve'nsong in the cul of the eve'rglade. *Ohm.*

God diva iva hard on, lady godiva.

Diva say notdothis don'tdothat

whenst ever Henry tried to tickle or lickspittle begging: please the peace of your piece of tail (tale me more!) eve'n if thee are as high as one of my Abo forefathers just out of the grippe of the grave. But Diva humming only:

'Ni fimble ni fumble but nimbly nibble':

Diva saythat do that, yes:
'nibble nibble Henry pup little Henry listen Henry new borning new morning the sun to my son uprisen uprising patina asigh and pastel sad as your ayes.'

Oh, trapped Henry twin and tween Diva's legs in bearing brace, man born of woman now Diva borne to man child, give to me this one of his nether mother ever eve'd more, to curl beneath the fig leaf tweet sweetly dew adieu eremore to the tip of his waglong tongue, and a tymphony of tamponade to wipe away the stains on the brow of his pore passing strange, Henry frozen in new born, the oh-so-light and the very, very early. Henry unwoken, Henry as Could. And:

New Diva say Sybil say sibil say sisal siz:
that Henry now this Henry Chosen One grubbed on the vine curl atoes lapping Diva's tears (o crust of christ) upon the vineleafig Eve mama mine mime my o my. And Diva wiping his eyes wiping his mouth wiping his nose dry up those. Old weepings dead skins yester skuttles tinged and tawn on hither you. Wiping away, new Diva is, with her pussy pads as white as snow and every where that her

Hairy went, lament was sure to go.

(If you're lucky the dog will at least keep out of your hair)

There and thereabouts and aboutbyways they stayed for forty days or about that and about this. Henry papoosed and Henry's new

Diva feeding pap man arise the dawn of time. And this was the go-spell that Diva did him according to her gobspiel:

(humans can become too fondue of dogs)

The godpelt according to Diva

1 The beginning of the gobspoil of Diva mother of all things, queen of the first man:

2 She that *is* as she *was* as it is written in the name of the prophets and the elders. Behold, I shall set my Chosen One above thee which shall prepare the way before thee.

3 Diva, one that is known as Kun'a'pi'pi which is known as Earth Mother which is known as Woman Goddess which is known as Young Woman, lo, even as Old Bag.

4 And Kun'a'pi'pi begat Wed'ar'rag'am'a which is known as the Rainbow Serpent which is known as the Roadmaker and Wed'ar'rag'am'a brought forth all the tribes of the Aborigines and there were many:

5 Ti'wi and Ma'ung'Jam'bar'boing'u and Gob'ab'oing'u

6 Jab'u Gom'aid Bur'er'a and Man'ing'ri'da

7 And the sons of the tribes I'wa'id'ja Lar'aki'a Gun'wing'gu Bal'am'um'u Ma'ia'li Wa'ga'it Ma'lak Ma'lak Bri'nk'in and Wa'gam'an and all their suburbs.

8 And all the sons and women and children of the tribes Dja'van Rem'barr'nga And'il'ya'ug'wa Ngu'lkpun.

9 And the sons of Nun'gu'bu'yu and the sons of Al'a'wa and the sons of Mur'in'ba'da and the sons of Wa'dam'an and the sons of Man'gar'ai and the sons of An'u'lu.

10   And the people of Jam'in'ju'ng *were*, and the people of Mud'bra *were*, and the people of Ga'wa'ra *were*, and the people Dji'nga'li *were*, and the people of Gu'rind'ji *were*.

11 And these are the tribes of the Aborigines according to what *is* of their fathers in the sight of Diva.

12 The sons of Wam'ba'ja and the sons of Wa'il'bri and the sons of Pin'tu'bi and the sons of the War'ra'mun'ga.

13 And the sons of the tribes of Pid'jan'dja'ra Ar'and'a Ko'ko'ta An'ting'ar'i Man'jin'dji Lor'it'ja Nga'li'a Wan' ei'ga.

14 And these were of the Diva mother of the tribes Tan'gan'i Jar'al'di Ram'ind'jer'i Di'er'i Mam'ar'ind'jer'i Man'ang'ki Pil'tind'jer'i and the sons thereof and the women and children thereof generations without number thereof.

15   Wir'ang'u and Band'ja'lang and Gum'ba'ing'ar and Nan'gi'o'mer'i and the people of the tribes known as the Nar'rin'yer'i.

16 And these written by name came in the days when the sun was new upon the earth and the stars were not so far ofF and many, but playeth live and in concert.

17 And the tribes increased greatly and they went to the entrance of the sea to the south, even unto the east and west sides of the land, to find hunting grounds and they found the land was wide and quiet and peaceable, for they o'Diva were to dwelleth there of old.

18 For the Diva is a jealous Goddess; and she hast kept all the sons of the tribes as the apples in her frequently black eye.

19 Even as she gaveth them plenty wherein they were happy; and she made them eat of the honey out of the rock and the oil out of the flinty hewns;

20 the fat of kangaroo, and the flesh of owl, and the sweetness of the insects with the cakes from the roots and flour from the seed, and the fruit of the cherry and the plum and the wild fig;

21 And of the fish and the birds and the eggs and the mammals in that land which were plenteous did *She* lead all the tribes of the Aborigines.

22 Now she hath returned in the naked flesh to demand of them her covenants;

23 that they *should* receive her words; yea, blessed *is* the black man that enlargeths her belly in all things.

24 Thus was the first lesson of Diva unto Henry, Her Chosen One.

The Lamentations of Henry:

1 How is this man come so low down! How I hath fallen within thee, O Diva, wherefore have I uttered mentions of things between thy skirt. I blasphemeth covered with unmentionables.

2 Therefore, I abhor myself, and repent in your sack and ashes. What shall I answer thee? I shall lay mine hand over mine own and mouth it.

3 O Diva, I am unworthy to be held in thy clutch as a suckling that maketh to be a hog.

4 Thou hath bared thy bow legs and maketh me quiver; thou hath hedged me round with thy stronghold and mine taboonakkers tumblest down.

5 Shall I eat of thine fruit?; as thou hath exposed thyself, showeth mercy on mine ridiculous.

6 Diva, Mine Covering, Mine Tampon, Mine Sheaf Unto Life, thou hath woven mine shortcomings into linen wads of stunt cunning work.

7 For I didst come out of the waste howling wilderness into mine enemies' cities and I dost dossed down.

8 And verily did I followeth the false propheteers of white Baalies down the path of the most Evile St., saying, 'Baalies to Thee'.

9 Thus I know I am the Ancient Man who pisseth against the wall; I beateth my meat and hath hearkened unto the white Baalies and their false Tenuous Commandments:
(1) He is the Lord, *their* God.
(2) I hath made of myself a cravin' image.
(3) In vain, hath I taken his name.
(4) I hath rested on the seventh day and got the sack.
(5) Honour the great white father and mother;
(6) they shout, neat kill.
(7) I hath been committed adulterated.
(8) I am a real-deal steal.
(9) False witness must I bear with.
(10) I hath not coveted any of mine neighbours' things and where hath it got me?

10 And then did I take unto myself permacrease coverings to my body and all manner of puppy hushness unto mine feet and for the colour of mine skin seeketh I redress.

11 I hath left mine tribal land go to the dogs, who really dig it.

12 I threweth my spear from me; I casteth thy conveyants off; I laid bare, my Heart.

13 Then did I lodge with the harlots of the streets and the beggars and the thieves and the robbers of the towns and the suburbs of Baalies.

14 And the soldiers and the officers thereof banished me from the streets, crying that I was unclean in the sight of Baalies and the townspeople thereof spat on me saying I had diverse fleabites disgraceful to the sight of Baalies.

15 Until one of the Baalies priests brought me forth from the heap and endureth me unto prison for the hell of it, saying:

16 Thy colour is all darkness; and thy choler is blackhearted; thy Diva naked is a real goer; and thy manhood hath lain its head in the dust; and all the people of the tribes shalt be put to the edge of the sordid.

17 Wilt thou, O Diva, put me to the grind now?

18 Then have mercy; let me grind thee.

19 Am I yet a man? then cast me not away as a mentruous cloth, but let me home in on thine bleeding heart of messy.

20 Hardk I trumpet, sblast! For home is where the heat is.

21 So endeth the lamming tonements of Henry.

(save a worthwhile dog's hide for curing)

Forty days and for farty nights, too,
stayed Jelf in his own hive (hive a dive, too!) buzzing then and now but mostly upstaring wall-eyed at the blank wall. Really only moving to scritchy-scratch himself on his crotchish lowlyings. But does move, as well, to yawn out of the other side of his mouth stuck on the pillow. Pillow of society, he. The Wise Man of the Eased. Pano Rama himself. See the Pano under the bed, ram'd! See Pan O Rama's Wise eyes run themselves down to earth on the wet, blank wailing wall, Iris!

Ah yes, Jelf, all that time, apot in his bed, a pit in his spot, a pat in his cowering, safe and as sound as a smug on the mug of a bugger in a bearhug, even if his eyes have fallen out to make one sheaf of corneals ajelf to one sheaf of corneals ashelf. Len's. But not asheaf like a baby, no, but still awake. He's really still in so zappy an electron-uptight that were he in sure-fire therapy he could not be in greater shock. (Going: *erg, o! it Hertz!*) What he really needs is a voltjolt back to a higher resistance of extance. *Ohm.*

(moulting dog goes after Bigwig)

There was, too, during the same forty days, an amorphined Amos at the foot of the Jelfself pit. And as rotten a sight as one could wish to smell. One prurience fadist, that is. Nor is he a case of a rose by any other name, but a smell rose high. The poor old bugger, he's just a bit stiff; even his own body ordeals odour. That's true, too.

Yes, there he is, bedecked and a wretched wreck with not a carl in place on's head, nor much cloth on his b.o.died. Never mind! He's managed to creep in to crash out there, so as far as he is concerned, which he is not, he is back home where he be pongs.

(bulldog took part of the mascot)

And, too,
for frothily fro'd and forthcoming days that numbered forty foulish nights, Constable Wilkinson was revolving still around, around. Sir Conference! Sir Cuit! Sir, come inspect! Shy Locke in a ronde bout mood with his glass eye to, too. Circumstantial evidences; spherey strange. Enough to make a man semi wary, hemiweary of a rondomondo in which a crude crudder like Mr Fido Bigs can remain at Largs, and freehold. Yes, around, aye, runed, it is prole officer Constable Wilkinson (as circular'd on the roster coaster, off the rocka) on prloe and prade! On's pride semperever tt»o. Tis Dizzy Wilky, Con's son on the table turntable, turntable! So a round of paws plauding, please, a round

of chase'n'toemartyr on one round of white bread! Let's record it for our circling Circe Cecil of the Flimsy Circle. Icing eyes, la and no l'after at all. How hoopless can ye get? Spere's sphfair, give him a globe! Can't you just orb it? That is (o vale, diction!) our Constable Wilkinson around, around, so that he is nearly going round the twist, watch! Oh, timing! Nervy tic never toe, no, indeed, and

grinding his snarlers in round terms, and girdling up his lyon's loyns, yes. For when he will, by sheer fuss of will, come that full circule and arrest, arrestingly, that escarpa'd filthy depositor of doguana on the footpoohs by Lottery Oriffices. Oh you may well trill hee hee like

his fellow law enforcers, but our Constable Wilkinson knows that next time Mister Bigs, that master of mastifmessy mischief, strikes offal up again, it will surely be a most dirty B's-nest, aye. And when it commas, as it surely sull, who will turn off the fans Eh Eh And, since nobody but Constable Wilkinson is volunteering, you can't spoke wheeler talk. No. Meanwheel, the clocks

go around around go C. Wilkinson clock in clock off like clockwork, clockwise retracing his stepstipstepstip. On the look out for a dial. Dogsdates!

(punter races, but goes to the dogs)

Forty days, forty nights, yes, and:
For every dog grown forty days older, there have been dogs that in those forty nights have taken the part of a man and hammed it up. Kyddu not. For every day of those nites (the gnats! that's nit funny!), there were men pack racked to the bowwow-spit and tongue lashed. Aye, lashings of it! For every dog grown forty days older, there was a master'd man who died the wiser. In each of those forty days and fierty nights, there has been a master Mortimer mortified by what his dog has done. At the end of those forty daze and fourty noughts there exist alive dogs that have

143

brought brilliant gangrenes and blues into the world. A man has even

(poor watchdog got bad spring)

bequeathed his body to his dog for medial recherche. A boy has given his heart to a pup. A woman has been found skewered whiff. After much digging, a dog saw his mistress in her grave. After much scratching, around, too, an arty dog discovered a genius after his death. A poor man was a dead loss to his dog. A young lass was found waisted away: but the dog was just ribbing. A piece of skirt was said to have been real dogdish. A baby a day carried the whole pack along.

And they were but a few of the eye events which did not even make the evening yockal papers during those phfawty days and thoughtie nights, doggone! Darn it! Greyhounds walking around with hare lips all over the place.

(Killer dog takes up its post humorously)

Even so, the worsted was yet to come, what was worse. For, during those same forty days and nights, the time for the publication of a Forthcoming Book, gall'd forth and quill'd by a His Nibs, was drawing near and dark upon the horrorizon dawning. It was:

A book? Aye, a book warm! Coming out in hard colours!

Yes, and by Someone We All Know!

Who about?

Only about Somesap We All Knowed Railroad!

Of fructish fiction? Of a fruct diction! Traction? Truncheon! Facts? Factions, Totum! About who b'whom, i.e., who is Horn We All Know?

He who is wombed innocently in his bed at this v. moment the mome! Will he be calling for Moma? Mummified! Mneme me, meaning...

A man in misery even now, whjo elf!

Not J..f?

Yes.el. !

Who's the author, someone novel?

Not very much thankye!

Authored

A third!

Old Hats?

Yes! Packed down, all!

Is it then Patric the Yt?

X!

Issit Moe Woest?   A Lax Buzz? Shaver Herb? Bay Oak? Day Whim? Mi Body? Pete Canary? Martian Flyin' Agen?

XX**ft@@!

Be it Ha Potty? German Gear? J. M. Cutesy? Bee Ree?

No!

Ezzit then Tonk Nearly at all atall et al and ales all 'ellsbells?

Nearly!

Cagey!

Wigwarmy!

KGE cagey?

XX!

KGB, rushian into print

No, non! Tis KRG, Ratshit ratchetting into print!

Not Kenny (ratshit) Griffley?

Unkennily!

Kenny Uncannily?

Tinny stuff, aye!

Then say Y on, that for Y issit that KR Griffley, latched-on litry
lecher, has a new book coming out that will give the Jelf We All
Know a little rue Roue

For the X on him in it, that's metaphor Y! For the Y affronts! For
the persnl C through, that witt Y! For the dark zide of Z in what's
zed!

Go on; goonly?

'Armful by the armfuls, not arf!

Doog dog!

And only featuring Alyce spilt with a 'Y' abed crutching at Tier
last strayw with her sagging gut just got out of a rut, that's all!
And a broken and broke J..f We Alknow, her lawful he in an awful
het! And then even throe'n out of his own haus by that frauhussy!

146

And all the time, the Ratshit KG instigging at the gate for this Subject Mater!

For the ill-feted book?!

'Tis not the book but the broach! Not the coven but the cover! Cover? Sadistic or sadisfying?

Both on it! That cover only carries a fobbish pfotogriff.graphly taken of a prejelface We Know To Be without precedence or preface! And that faece is publicly adorning, if i may take on an expression, a million or so publicity posters o'er the metropolis!

No?!

Baldly!

Baldly, then, who issit?

Warm!

My opus, too?

Warmer! My eye!, most myopic!

B'wig'd b'dog'down b'golden'd teeth? B'goggle'd?

Warmst, swarmst! Swarmi!

Is't so call'd?

No, still warm!

Cold?

Cauldron'd!

Jelf?

Sssh, elfishly! Name no gnomes to no men!

147

Nomen innated?

Sush! Must leave that questchinning the shjelf!

(Peter and the wolf; peter'd out)

The Second Gaspiel of Diva:
(cant in nude, but can be addressed):

Chapter 1
Thus it hath been recorded of the Generation of Hen'ry, he who was chosen by Diva, Mother of all tribes:

1 Insomuch as Diva went by way of Bal'ma'in and saweth Hen'ry toiling with his nose to the grindstone in the land called thereof by the white Baalies the land of milk and honey.

2 And Diva didst approach Hen'ry and casteth her tail upon him and dreweth him up and in, saying Follow Me, Folly Nut.

3 But Hen'ry thus spake unto Diva saying, Let me first returneth one time more to the Ars of my Baalies white masters that thereto may I kiss them there before I followeth thee.

4 For I am beHolden to them much, and am behind mine payments and the thing that *was* now *is* all rusty.

5 But Diva was angry and chideth Hen'ry saying, O ye of little thrust; let pigs poke pigs until they suffer a Caesure. Thus was Hen'ry smitten with Her Coming and tryeth to Come with Her.

6 And when they Came in Hen'ry's lodgement that was like unto a lowly stable set underground, Diva was filled with wrath;

7 And Diva rose up and leadeth him upstairs saying, Therein this place is a lodging fit for Diva and Hen'ry, Chosen of all the tribes; therefore do thou this and smote this door down;

148

8 Even though he who dwelleth within that *were* called Jelf, a Baalies but *was* the friend of Hen'ry, still Hen'ry raised his arm against the door to smote it down.

9 But Diva said, Mine come is not yet timed; and drew Hen'ry whence saying, Remember thou this place when our come is better timed.

Chapter 2
1 Thereafter did Hen'ry lay his head between Diva's loins for forty days and fruity nights; and was sorely tempted though finding his peni'tense not hard enough. And in those days, he gotteth at nothing he wanted to eat.

2 For Diva sayeth unto him, Thou must be born again; and berthed up a new man; so wake up.

3 Now there *were* in a large church that was in that neighbourhood certain scribes and high priests and falsies of white Baalies; and they preached the word of Baalies to the Aborigines there-abouts which *were* impoverished and gullible as shit.

4 And Diva entered therein that church of false witnesses of Baaliescorn; and didst she make eyes at the whore-shippers of Baalies therein, saying,

5 O ye, full of all poop, wilt thou not cease thy perversions unto our black brethren?

6 O ye vipers and wind screening vipers! verily does Diva say unto you, that the hand of Hen'ry, the Chosen One of all the tribes by Mine reckoning, is upon thee and thou shalt be blind, not seeing the lightuntil morning cometh!

7 Then did there fall on that Baalies host a Flash of Lightning and a Terrible Darkness; and they went about seeking someone to lead them.

149

8 And Hen'ry, when he saw what he was caused to do, marveled and believed, proclaiming to all the people of the tribes the power of Diva to maketh him the Chosen One.

9 And they departed from that place; and Hen'ry thereafter *was* full of wonder at how a fuse came to be in his pocket slipped.

Chapter 3
1 And it came to pass that Diva and Hen'ry came to the uttermost of the city of Pa'rram'att'a; and did there see a multitude of Aborigines that had come to lodge together within the house of a real joke called Jack'ie Ja'ck'ie, being in number many men and women of many tribes and many children of many tries.

2 Now Hcn'ry sayeth to Diva to come in whence and see the multitude bunked there that was even unto the Baalies as a leper colony that is unclean.

3 And Diva beheld and sayeth unto Hen'ry, Verily I say unto you that this night you shalt see how thy Diva can pass the night with brothers without number, even on the outskirts of town uplifted.

4 Then Diva entered into that place, and when they had gathered her skirt up in a corner, she spake unto them:

5 Suffer even the deprived, the hopeless, the maimed, the poor, the blind, the weak, the bombed-out to enter within my tent; and she spake also unto them:

6 Receive my body for it is worth bread; this is mine blood which raceth for thee.

7 Ask not of Diva whether thou mayest Come Across, but whether thoust man enough.

8 And did She thrust forth her cavity to all who couldst at the time, saying, This is my body; Eat me.

9 For verily I say unto thee again that I am Diva; and unless thee eat of mine body thou shalt never know a warm shack up.

10 Then did Diva also say unto them, Behold, I *am* Diva; I am The Way big enough for all; likewise behold there Hen'ry who *art* my Chosen One and on whose right hand I sitteth.

11 And Hen'ry thereupon didst he hold up his right hand so that all should seethe that indeed had the Holy Gust entered upon him, the chosen out of all darkies.

Chapter 4
1 Thus the first time had come to pass that Diva sheweth Herself and Hen'ry, Her Chosen One on whose right hand she kept sitting, to the people of the tribes throughout the foul breaths and depths of the poor in urban.

2 Now there came also a multitude out of the four quarters thereabout in the place called Wa'rrin'gal (meaning, Town of the Town Bike) as Diva passed out.

3 And a large crowd gathered around Diva and Her Chosen One, Hen'ry, bringing forth many people of the tribes sick in the head for trying to live there.

4 Even were there also some afflicted with an unclean spirit, known as christ'al meths, and others of them stricken with tar brushes.

5 Then did Diva fling out her arms, saying, Give thanks for what ye are about to be handed out.

6 So saying the Hea'ens didst seem to opt and poured forth upon them shekels and peanuts and pennies, yea, even cents and mites and all manna of small denominations for parking meters.

7 When they that were there received this, they marvelled and did cureth themselves therefrom with clean and good proofed spirits and were less sick until the following morning.

151

8 And even that was the first miracle that was performed by Diva as was written up in 'The Star'.

9 And when they heard these things, many of that place brought to Diva and Her Chosen One their infants that they would acknowledge them; but when they saw the infants they denieth everything.

Chapter 5
1 Now it came to pass that when they were abroad during the Festival of Spending, a large crowd of pedlars came out to meet them at so and so a place within the walls of such and such a city.

2 And amongst that throng was a Yahoo of Jewish Scottish Roman White Russian part Abo descent, a blind man whose name thereof was Zac'for'a'bob, son of Con, who was a tailor for chrissakes.

3 And Diva stopped on her way through the crowds, saying, Who is this that dost pointeth his bone at me?

4 Whereupon Zac'for'a'Bob falleth on his knee before her and cryeth out, O Thou son of a bitch goddess, What wilt thou that I should do to receive back mine sight so that I mayest receive thee in my fashion?

5 Then didst Hen'ry rise up to chastise Zac'for'a'Bob saying, Thou art better off staying sightless.

6 But Diva stood before Zac'for'a'Bob and raiseth him up, saying, Give ye praise unto Diva, for this day thou shalt make unto Hen'ry the Chosen One fine raiments to cover his back if thou wouldst cover mine.

7 And the garments will be vestments and underp's and coverings for his feet; but to minister unto Me shalt thou make unto my Chosen One an embroidered coat of gold and blue and purple and scarlet and fine twined linen, with cunning work.

152

8 And a cods-piece thereof shall be of the same, according to the work thereof.

9 And thou shalt take two onyx stones and cover his onyx stones with the same; and on one onyx stone shalt thou graven my name Diva; and on the other onyx stone shalt thou graven Nuts, which means Berries From Heaven.

10 And thereafter did Hen'ry put upon his coveted garments of gold and blue and purple and scarlet and fine twined linen with cunning work; and he was a Big Man in the land. Big deal.

11 And Hen'ry was strong in that he representeth all the people of the tribes. Diva's Chosen, that he became truly known as the Abo Pounce; and he saith unto them:

12 That ye may all suck.

Chapter 6
1 Then did Hen'ry go down unto the corner, and preached of Diva unto them that were passing.

2 Then came one out of Baalies unto the High Priest of the Baalies, saying, Behold, why suffereth thee the tribal boong, he that dareth to speak openly upon teaching the black buggers

3 Then went down a captain with his officers sent by the High Priest to lay hands on Hen'ry; but they did not because they feared the people and because

4 They were stoned out of their minds.

Chapter 7
1 And the lesson that Hen'ry preached unto the gathering crowd was this:

2 That the Baalies do not heed our church, but deny us from the least to the greatest.

3 But I say unto all my black brethren: Enter into Diva and find each other, even those fallen in or lost in thought.

4 And tell those who crave unto the white God Baalies to shove over.

Chapter 8
1 Now it came to pass that the Baalies Prime Minister Yahoo of the land came unto that place to speak to the people thereof of love and charity for the lame and the weak.

2 Oh, yes, and Abos, too. I forgot.

3 When there arose from one side a great commotion.

4 And Diva appeareth, borne aloft by four sons of the tribes, and She was without covering on Her body except bruises of joy.

5 Then was She lain wherein the spot that the Prime Minister Yahoo was preaching from, and then did She spreadeth apart Her legs, proclaiming to all the viewing nation of Baalies, I Am Come to spread love and infection amongst Ye all.

6 For the Erection of the Second Coming of the Clans was at hand.

7 And believers were the more added to Diva, multitudes of both men and boys, even many inches unto her there, according unto Hen'ry.

8 Then the Prime Minister Yahoo rose up but was he found wanting before Diva and was he mocked before the whole viewing public.

9 And when this had come to pass the Prime Minister Yahoo made a public gesture towards one Aboriginal at least.

10 And the guards laid their hands on Her and Her Chosen One and put them in the common prison.

154

11 But in the morning when it was that the officers came to bring them before the magistrates, they found them not in prison and doubted of them whereunto this would happen.

12 But one of the officers of the guard by night openeth the prison doors; and for this did he receive the Absolute from Diva. As it was poked so it was wridden.

Chapter 9
1 Now did it come to pass wherein Diva and Her Chosen One Hen'ry departed to a place called Ca'nbe'rra (or Sent Out To Pasture) to maketh a tabernacle before the parliament of the rulers of Baalies.

2 Wherefore would every one of the sons of the tribes be therein welcomed unto the whoreship of Diva before the eyes of the rulers of Baalies that they might see the Aborigines putting the hard word on.

3 And as they travelled through the streets of that place, many cameth near them as they passed and didst mock them and calleth them names.

4 Now on the first one minute of their journey, they came across a cordon of a herd of Pigs that didst prevent them from journeying further.

5 Then did Hen'ry cry out to the Pigs, saying wherefor art thou?

6 And the leader of the Pigs answered him, saying, The name is Legion, for we are many.

7 Then was Diva transfigured before them; and Her face did shine as the sun; and her railings *were* as white hot as the loads she *is* spreading around.

8 And She cried out upon the Pigs, calling them devils; and saying that they were unclean of spirit the greasy mugs.

9 And She calleth them filthy swine that they may enter into themselves.

10 And hearing this, the herd of Pigs verily were choked and ran violently upon them as though it were that they would dash all to pieces.

11 Therein that place there was Bed'laam, whereupon all of the people of the tribes there were put to the edge of the sored, even the women with child were told to get ripped.

12 And in the midst of all was Hen'ry, even him that was Her Chosen One and now born anew.

13 But Hen'ry was a new man unto Diva and his way could not be diverted, yet even so much as his waters passeth away as the Pigs swined on.

14 And all those of the tribes who boreth witness of his deeds hollowed out his name, for he was Diva's Chosen One, on whose head she was sitting right or wrong.

15 And Hen'ry knew thereof that it was that he was Body Beautiful Himself and begancth to shout it unto the world when amidst the pitch of the battle he was struck dumb, crying for himself.

Chapter 10
1 And this is the last parable that spake Diva unto the sons of all the tribes:

2 If men be born of Baalies they art sons of bitches.

3 But if a man be born of the tribes, he is a son of gin, and a dog to boot. With hobnails. Little squeaks lubracated.

4 Therefore hearken unto my commandments, which I givest unto ye for the bettering of thy sins:

5 Try to tribe harder.

6 Tribe to believe in the Father Almighty, Master of heaven and earth, and see how far you get.

7 Tribe as hard as anybody could to believe in Jesus.

8 Tribe very hard to conceive of such a thing as a virgin.

9 Tribe to deny number 8 at all times.

10 Tribe hard to believe that ye shalt be uprisen on the third day, and then tribe not to be too disappointed when you're not.

11 Tribe sitting on the right hand of the Father Almighty ha ha;

12 Just tribe it and you'll be judged the dead, and quick.

13 Tribe to believe in the Holy Ghost just for a laugh.

14 Tribe to believe in the holy Catholic Church, for anything's possible.

15 Tribe to live in the manner of the Communion of the Saints and they'll get you for insanitary overcrowding.

16 Tribe out the forgiveness of sins and you'll be better man than Gunga Din, mate.

17 Tribe to believe in the resurrection of the body when they've sunk your feet in a slab of wet cement.

18 Tribe to tell 'life everlasting' to your baby living above the acceptable infant mortality rate and see how comforted he'll be.

19 A bloody ha men.

Chapter 11
1 Then drew unto Hen'ry all of frantic Diva for to lead him up the stairways straight and narrow.

2 Whereunto lived Je'lf, an unbelievable son of Baalies, and Known to Hen'ry, the Chosen One.

3 And didst they stand before the door of Je'lf of the Baalies; and Diva tooketh Hen'ry by his secrets and said unto his uprighteousness that even then was making itself upright:

4 Hen'ry, there art a bed in thereof of which that I hath spoken unto thee;

5 Hen'ry, mine time and thy turn hath almost come, yea yea.

6 And how they both got it will be told by the author.

7 Yet there are many other things also which Diva did, the which, if they should be written every one, even the obscene world itself could not contain the books that should be written.

(shadow of former self in the dog house)

Psalm of Hen'ry
(As pants the arise for thee, where once lowly now swinging in the breeze)

To the Heads musician, the flauntist; with tonsils atwivver.

1 I shalt love thee, O my Diva, unto thy very core-us of my song, Yea;

2 And when hath I listened to thee that I hath not hummed to thine lips luting mine heart?

3 I am black and I swoonsweep and I am black and doth we swain and I am black yet do we swarthswarm.

4 I am black, yet can I still man humm. O my Diva;

5 In all mine days I have met none that giveth me such joy and light and scintle where prisms of colour had abound me.

6 When they have seen me with my white Diva, they have shat up shops shut in piles bled in tiers oozed in tears.

7 And O turned away when she loved me for laughing and nobbled me a nib and tickled my pinks.

8 Diva, my goddess my chomp my lovelie, I am an.

9 I am an, yea, and passing enwondropassim strange, by Diva by jove i love i hove unto.

10 How shalt I say Ye have saved my sumness, and I fuck thee for it, when you have gived me life itself and I love thee unto all of it.

11 Diva dive-a driver dyned
    All formed of word and loved of kind.

12 O I do glebe for thee. Glebe glebe glebe glebe,

13 And do so thank thee for the first time of thanking in my black life. Thank you. And thank you. Diva!

(there is more of man in a dog than what he will cough up to)

Intromittent of all that has been going on between Diva and her Henry, the world has turned, not only on its axis, but also quite crazy, even after centuries of physics books. Take, do, for example, what was happening simultaneously all around them. One brief scan of your radars around a mild number of Sydney streets would have scened for you the following screenario for real and not reel, viz vizually:

the mountaineer who chugged his grind up all way to the top of the tallest storied in town, planted a tree in the shape of a wreathe there, then threw himself off the edge to his eternal.

Aaaaaaaaaaaasp lat. Then the nong who was sent to hose the mountaineer's remains off the packed footpath decided to hose down the bystarers and leave the splattered remains in peace, many pieces. True, and one of the bystanding got so wet that she picked herself up tossed herself into the decorative pool where there wasn't one lifesaver with a hole on duty there. So she was taken by a shark. She did that quite quietly on porpoise too. The same woman left behind her two or three babbles in arms babyishly goo-ing up the footpath there, so that the bystarers were driven to thread, smash and pulverise the sweet little things into the footpath and into dusty goo to put them out of all that orphan misery coming up from the water wail. The man with the nozzle hosed the babies okay, but only up against the mountaineer's goo, over which he stood guard. Meanwhile another man he toppled out of top window when trying to get better butchers of what was going on below, and he then came pummelling aaaaeeeeee and plop with the wet mob below urging him on with, 'Go go go go, man!' Whereupon the man with the hosehold went into a rage and slapped-'n'back-handed the remains of the head of new goo rival for goofacturing an unwanted mess on his footpath, the goon. When the Fire Brigade settled on the scene, all put out that there was gooing to be no fire. So they set alight to the shark that was pooped anyway trying to keep down all that female frenzy before they took their smoke-o there'n'then.

(dog defaced all that expressed human kindness towards it)

All of which Constable Wilkinson merely passes his yawning eyes over, before they narrow his range of vision horribly by lamping onto

a publicity poster bleating (but silently in taste) out the new best seller of (aye) Kenny (Ratshit) Griffley's new book, which, if the cover mugshot thereon is an indication, must be as obscenely porno as it is all balls. And that noodle upon that poster is

160

nunuther than that Someone We All Know As J..f, but naming no names. No. And it really, even as we see it for the trillionth time, is so shruddreadful that even Constable W. moves on around, around it quicksmart. Aren't those bystarers just mentioned in for a shock if they turn and see it?! Slander chance of that and what an ugly way to tell the tome.

(don't let your dog get under your skin rashly)

Meanwhile back in *The Haven*:
Forty days and forty nichts after plunging himself onto the ole horsehaired, our doughty Jelf suddenly uproutarouses himself and is ontop of his feet still anchored to the jaded edges of his legs, aye. But now, booted and spurred, bewigged and repowdered, recapped and retrode, relensed and reviewed. He is. The Specimen again. In fact the itman is back built up to a heman for the first time since his breakdown forty days ago.

(pick the fleas off a dog with a single shot cannon)

Indeed, in front of himself in front of the mirror he even smiles with a mile's wide from here to there and hock to sock, in the renewed comfort that the big wide world out there is still divided into two divisions --them what's ropeable and them what's rapable. All the rest ain't worth an assay, even in the belch of a bitch. So there.

(the dog will swallow your pride manfully)

Meanwile of that man-will:
Henry still chiming in on his Diva between her legs with this running down his chin:

In seance skeins of curlquites quite curling spiritum spirituum tuumult moulten chumberance cherubim serafin softly soft oftly

161

my love sophomoss mossy intercurliculcult comely home-line nee homity holiation humadoration thee me theme in ulmust ullulation ove ave ovary ovation trolley tree lala thee; and me kyrie eleison sumus sanus anus to nous u no uno one of omniallevery holi-thing in pride in fall in butterflight and trance, dance, traceance steep by steeple steeple worshape worth shipshapeye eye i iris you;

Diva, i loveulate unto thee.

Then did Henry raise himself. Brought up. Into the world for the second time. Yes. This time Henry, I cap I, him, hymn hymen, hmmmm. Humming, Henry rising highrise and all his eyes lofting. Our Henry. From Diva's feedbag; nosegay; from Diva's tufteta. With all the scales of ancient life shredding from him like morphostic confetti made from dandruff. And his smiling cerulean eyes now into his Diva sweat and brow. She, too, silky sleek in their silken floss cubbyniche, aye, for from her chrysalis has the imago upurged surpassant Henry. New Henry. On the fortieth dayo. Yes; it was

the first real day of his new short life lurch. We are not joking.

(wither thou wither, there goes the dog)

Diva! He says her namane, hard Iovent longent sparkling spuma, for he lovenges her when she saythis saythat. And from the pupatula, does Diva smile mamilla mater returned with plus-echo, dear choice child. For Diva sees from out of the pangs of manbirth, not him ago, but him imago. Hers, and. It is good and weakly enbeautigloric, yes. The uvular uvathrob unto his vrumming voice. Diva! now! look! yes! He and thee himu hupped from your two lovely lipias, your painted labias. Inelectably ta. And him an Abo. This is the true Native-ity? Oh, yes, that's right; the

divan comedy may now recomma once again.

(come home, Lassie; they've got a whole new leading man for you)

162

Diva, we would clapp thee if you were not so clapped out with the clap so much already yet. Just look at Henry's eyes as they intake the basement he shards with sharing cockroaches, beatles an' other mania in the mind's eye. He sees only it around his Diva, going 'Splash a bit, colour up, de-grease, blast buggies all to hell. Could be worst. Might come good.' That was her or him saying.

And now he haply bursts for the door. Makes.

'Where go unto?' Diva.

'Dunno. Pull a few pieces, knock a few white heads together, do a bank, uprise abo with ammo.' Henry, aglee in glow.

'Have a cool cool frescade, luvver.' Diva contentaroll with what she glims there. 'I am your Diva.'

'You are a white peace of arse. Love you.'

'Not until we get upstairs. A bed to occasion a big one on, so thoust did say.'

'I'm working on it, like he's a stubborn white arse, that Jelf.'

'Time we were going, too. Together. Yes.'

She slowly unwebs herself of the pupa, freshful as the sweet dew on her new mother's flesh, wetencrusted sweatensweetened, happy and sleek, and goes to him at the door. Henry takes her in his armo amats. Henry nestles urtica-eating sweetly her; it has been a long lungful fromenade all in all.

'Kay, my hart.' Henry he saythis.

'Time for us to see a certain rutting good art exhibition, my stag.' Diva she saythat. Swiles and go outes. Leaving him, her Chosen One, to follow. He watches her arse jilling, then does. Swallow after, going:

'Thought's staggering, my Diva, my... Alyce.'

Alyce? Yes! Did you Hear That? Should have. It was as hired as we could make it.

(young pup was only teething)

Sirius being what serious should be:
lithoed on a gravestone: He Was Doggo Even In Death. Engraved on another was: Bit, Now Pieces. Then again, line-chipped on another was: Scent To The Dogs. Then again, get your own back; run on Spot. Gay dog appears in fairy tails, too. Like, the dog Prince lent over Sleeping Beauty who never again woke up to the fact. Little Dopey dog took Snow White by the core by the apple tree; poisonous! The Wolf showed itself a dirty dog when it jumped into bed with old granny. Never fear, though: the dog got Mother Hubbard's last bone. French poodles are like all dogs: piddling little things that can never say no to a family tree oui.

Then again, a hors d'oeuvre is when the dog bites the hand that's feeding it. A meal had, too, when it licks its master's chops. Fat dog lover tried to escape quick, only made it chop-chop. But then the dog does so like a bod of pudge for breakie. And then again, you have relations with a dog and you could easily pick up funereal disease. O, throe your life to the wolves! Then one more: the dirty dog is all smutt. Do, too, call a spayed a spayed. Then again, a dog won't take no for an answer; it will drag you along anywhere for dinner. So don't command your dog to lie down if you don't want him to suffer indigestion just on account of you. The dog is likely to get indigestion over just about any part of the body. But it will enjoy a hot-blooded race for you. One wouldn't think, either, that at first dogs come in little packettes. Or the only good dog is a hungdog. Though it all depends on whether you are accepted into an upper set of canines or a lower set. Anyhow, just take heart; whatever you do, at least Dogod thinks you're a good liver worth saving.

164

And that's why Dogod makes God look so backward. As It Is Writ. And ever shall be. Who ain't born under the Dogod Stare?

Oh, all those coming salad and dog days, and the manmade meats in the sandwiches! Ah, men. *Ohm*.

REALYCE

And how clerkishly clever of you to have seen right through from the start that Henry's new Diva is Alyce. Aye. And not only that, but to cotton onto that Alyce *is* Diva that *was* Alyce and *shall* be Diva *was* you having a real mind on it not half. Intellectual of you, veryso everymuch. After all, life is so full of bunk for every blink. Or, as the card-playing cheat said, if in double, doubthomas.

(dog with tangled nerves, chokes)

Just like Jelf was Scotty was Quilty wasis evershallbe. And just as Constable Wilkinson iswas, asitwere, sailing around, around trying to find out who *is* Mr Fido Bigs. Not forgetting all the others, like Kenny (Ratshit) Griffley, all trying to slow down the inexorable March of Time. Berth, living, dearth... to each manjack, the jack. Aye.

(a running dog has got the wind up of you)

Jelf. The sjelfsame. Has excursed briefly down out into the rariesphere called the Old Wield Outside and immediately plucked out of the thinnish air (like consomme is to soup) a Cunx, who was noshing on onan One Man Pie one moment then gnashing on a Jelform the next moment as he bears her away and whose name is Ylace Mislainy of no fixed forebode. And being of no uncertain menner, neither. Anyway he culled Cunx by merely jelking out his Jerf arm out of his appartment bloxsdoor and grabbing the first thing that came to hand. Her. Who was out on the footpath right outside the side alley door, without him even having to expose to the Without his delectablessence to a madmaneatingworld. No.

(nothing else mutters)

Anyway, that was the upshot that has led to Jelf being now in the sack a-Cunx, who is showing herself up by being full frontal nerved with all her shoos off. Yes, her shoes shied shot right

166

underbed. The only thing that has kept her slightly decent is the kipping on her raincoat, hood'n'all, intact and without it. Even now she is

(dog with plain features of an ordinary girl)

nibbling mad keen to get at Jelf's golfballs perchance. One never knows with Cunxs of obscure histories. Knobbling away with Her Nibs trying to snib off the old bloke and ankle-inching her lower inclinations across those black satin sheets towards our man. He going:

'You wanta nibble, go ahead and nibble. Who am i All i ask you is to keep calm eyes open and do not suck in over-passion. Shucks, nothing shocks me anymore.'

But still It (Cunx) inches footily closer and closer (gibber an inch and it gobbles a mule) while one of her man-maulers underhandly undoes whatever are the mainstays about her own personage. (Age Miss Ylace Lainy's age is such that she ought to nono better. Yes, yes.) And underscoring her over emphasis with red gnashers that talk with an Australian broad's accent, eg ug:

'Why? Doin't cha lie-kit, laaaaaaa-ver?'

'Please do keep on nibbling, miss. Being hopeful that you art a miss, oh yes in deed, else it would be impertinent of you to be here, eh heh Though going on with the story you interrupted on me... With the curtain just about to go up, so I cast my shiners round the Concert Hall...'

'Thorcha seidit waz a whorled Premyair?'

'World Premiere, o too true of you. Y'see the Concert Hall was the only larger nough hall in the country. Just. Interest, crowds, bookings, publicity, you know. Worldwide. Creates all sorts of jams across the ways and by waves. But never have i let it go to my head. Have not. Always craved humility before superstar status. Anyway...'

167

'Seyay...'

Now Cunx has the impertinacity to be sniffling the air while Jelf is talking. She is and has. Bloody furfux! Was a man ever hastled so much by so a hustler? No laugh being laned with a woolly bull of a femme dog.

(dog appreciates sheer guts)

Now Cunx (cunt it) even doing it again right in midst of his thought meaning: 'Seay... Pheyuw, geeesz...' like as if something had gone off ofal, something awful and screwing up its (Cunx's) snout (keep screwing; ywanna driver?) in such bad taste that one might think Jelfhimsjelf is not whiff a fart! She is. Nnot only that. Now she's knee crawling knee trembling along the Jelflea pit on all fourpaws like Davee Crocket with some skunk capping him off, and:

'Lis-ser-n!'

'Listen no, tell me not. What are you, one of lipped Libs flipping off the top of the loop?'

By now with her arse over tit ('Cunx's) looking over the end of the Jelfeathery where she spots Amos almost amort before her old eyes getting a little bit older for the sight of him.

'Aaagh!'

'You said that with perfect BBC English, did too. And bet you thought the pong was me. Now if i may go on with my story.'

'Ifya think eye am a sort wattle leap inta the snayke pit with sum blowke oar rothar just cawz heze got somethin at tha footoff the cot...! Geez kreyest, 'ear eyes draaaws tha' liene ...' Cunx erxy unctious and Telp papal:

'Finished'

'Far cough eyes am! Eyes ain't goan throuuu eny motions with a waft at tha enda tha blaoody drivewaay, thenk ewe. Vee march. Mate.'

And out of the expressway she doth trundle. She does. Huff way out, huff way in. Huffing'n'phffooing, upping then hoofing it out of Jelfhaven with one foot on and one shoe off, when whodo enter none other herself but the esse of Maggie, in all her enteriety and not one jot missing 'cept all manners. 'Must've forgotten to put the knocker back on that dooro, Maggie. Am very sorry you have been made rude, to appear.' Jelf grilling gist of gggrrrist at the interim between Maggie jerking her thumb at jabberwok'd Cunxiform and Cunx being struck dumb, also near speechless, which?

'What's this one then?' Maggie, still thumbing her think. 'I do not know, Maggie, but It talks.'

'Do-w-ewe m-eye-nd?'

'Say, it really does talk.' Mag mag at him all the time.

'Even the beast of us can catch onto a bad swatchtwat, Maggie. Sap most times rises, too. I shrug, see Meaning, i'm too sad to let you see how delighted i am at you leaving off so soon so goodbye Maggie.'

(give a dog a run for its mournay)

Whereupon, Maggie gone again. One wonders. Why, if so many women hoods herethere make beed lines on a man, there ain't more honey on the bed lains? Women always lie back at you.

'Eyes s'pose eyes s'pozzzdta think thet waz tha blaoodie maid.' 'Inaccurate. The homemade. But do tell if any of your sisters talk less. If not, then do feel free to wheel around your mother sometime.'

'Ya punce!'

169

Typical of Austraylian wombriety. All bellycosy. Skin burns come from their gravel. Voices. It's not a womb, it's a dungeon with wall metres think at the head, no bull. But bull needed. Like bye bye call me bey.

(dog shows lack of form of mutton dressed as lamb)

But the door is no sooner slammed shut hinging on the hurtful exit by a madly unhinged Cunx than there is yet another knock. Knock. On a door on which somebods are forever tiptapping. Must be, the Jelfmind goes to polishing its own fingernails, the Cunx (It) return. She to plead with i for a recunx, going cunx i come in or not? No you manx. Yes, caustic you can. Which? Yet the knuckling of wood cunxtinues so much that Jelf has to bearly pad up (bier peet, cold feet) to open the door right across the other side of his room, a farflung wrrummway away and manages to make it without smouch as a pant (o spiritus lenis i am without pants) where he opals that pothole not on re Cunx turned repantant, no.

But boy, that is, male child, budding homo, one of, a newspaper whelp of Sydney lolling innocently enough on the landing, which either means an ambushade or thiskid has left his stilettos dumdumshells icepix radiodehomoing vices at the door. Or else his horn is still green, like. Y'don't tip newspaper boys in Sydney, you just keep your fingers crossed. (Buy a newspaper in Sydney, make sure they don't sell you a pup; be content with pap.)

'YAH?' Jelfortissimo. Being of necessity in order to shout above the hystericapers of Che the Chihuahua wrecking and re-echoing the ecosparse with images of Jeff-renderings down.

(hose down the dog; then turn on the water)

'Boy, i bet you beat this dog real bad, huh' Boy.

'No, no. I just feed it slow doses of poison. Thank you for calling sonnyjim.'

'Hey!'

170

'Little boys should seek out bedrooms, never. Get behind me, you ungulate you; keep your cloved on.'

Jelf tries to retract nana from lethal zone of dog intent but this newsboy has his dear tiny little boot putters-in jambed in opporto, for in Sydney they have to learn quick how to put the boot in, that's a fact, and is now mouthing out of the side of his juvenile gangster:

'Ya don't look like Him. Who else ya got in there, huh?'

'Would you believe leftovers of shitty little boys by charnel?'

'Guess ya're Him. Somebody said forta give ya this. Somebody said forta say look at a great ugly mug on page three and... *run*.'

Which he does. Oh, he really does burst into a run, the little squirt, raising Cainine phrenitis to phever phitch (amazing the heists that some small dogs will go to). Having thrust at our Jelf Vitals a newspaper containing page three between two and four. And our unbeknowing Jelf in noscentily opening it there where

(dirty dog after Glamourpus)

lugger than life and larger than luff-up bygad bygod bygone byodsbod by Dogod ichabod is. For all to see. Adv. Yes, adv., hugebloodygreatfucking, one of. Vertigris by greengills in photogravure of Quilty/Scotty/Jelf as He Really Is, in alias of Mr Fido Bigs. Yes, to repeat: that re-pat jobber, Fido Bigs, the great depositor! (Who Knows what his mind's like in that void?) And all splendoglory at his Quiltyform Tojo the Jap best. With caption collering in 120 point bold condensed upper and lower case Times Roman centred updown left right aligned leftnright and justified, never: REWARD: DUNGEROUS MANURER IN FALSIES BASE RELIEF

(get the vet to fix up your dog for good)

An infanticry? Or some little Kitty in bad straits? Which? Except that we can tell from the brutish swine of a smile that appears across the Chihuahua's Che-chewing dreadfuls; and, in any case, Jelf has gurgled his full flighted fling full length over his flop pit and has secured Amos by means of hands round that old necro neck. He has. And is heaving that bag of borns in part drag (vestiges of vestments, dragrags dollying) and full drag of those born bones (for the hounds; sent, laid), going:

'Filthyspy-doubleagentstooleytellingratrottendealer...'

And Amos all the bumrushwhile all sweetness and charm warmly oozing benedictum vobis my yob, 'Lift me bloody arm. All bloody man bloody power n' c'arn scratchy scratchy give's bit of bloody tickle eheheh?...' before being floored on all fours out alongsidcof Che, the slap yappy hua, on four-point landing outside. By Jelf, who finally loses his temper once and for foulmouth all, going: 'Pseudoanthropomorph!' Well!, if that ain't the most

pure lipfilpth! Could even be enough to give you an icy pshaw below the belt. It is. Even Amos has frozened within a moment of time, the dog even. Thrown out of his mind, the dog too. Left stranding on the landed while the slur is doored shut on him, the cur also!

(the dog will you tuck in deliciously)

Now rebarricaded, re-enscounced, pupa papa'd, poxy epitted once amore in bed, he. Jelf. Having just taken another ten pounding hammer ringing in his ear, feeling fire welted and wrotting fast, going for his own paella of mind, so that it could be called a babble out of the side of the Jelfspiller were it not for the straight up dribble in it:

(dog keeps a trained eye on your achilles)

'Young i wert then, so i said i'll give it a burl all my,' this be Jelf kanticling his eyes blank walled, 'mates money in their world on me and i get first break,' (*breath*), 'let fly at the diamond and three

172

fall down plop plop plop,' (*inhalairo*) 'next shot a softie into top left pocket then coupla delicate back cuts into the centre pockets,' (*pneugulp*) 'coupla double-ups and,' (*huffpf*), 'suddenly left on the black without a miss other buggers against us no,' (*puffhf*), 'chance in this world mates cheering me the big hero etcetera,' (*aspirantspire*) 'money gimme in the bag and black set up over the top pocket line it up. I do. Up. No. Sweat,' (*asweat out'n'in*) 'Here go. Es i. Miscue. Forgotten-tochalkmycue.' (*weep in weep out*) 'Listen, Maggie...' (*for tis Maggie agit adoor during this*):

'I heard you assault my Aged Parent.' Maggie. See?, toldye she had.

'Listen... who can say what damage that miscue did for my future well-being, Maggie?'

'Why is my poor old father lying out there in a heap'

'What's that got to do with how i've been bruised trussed doggened in life?'

'My Aged P. shouldn't be subjected to what goes on in this room at his time of life.'

'If you can still think that can be a father, where is your self-respect, Maggie?'

'To think he looks up to you. *You*. The dirty old bugger.'

'Yain't no Rose Marie thyself, Maggie.'

'Oh well, pardon me for being born beautiful...'

'Maggie, don't gooo ooh leave all me not, Maggie, i am a saint without sanct or sanety. I whine i misero over all. Come to bed, Maggie.'

'Naw, i've seen it all.'

173

'Want to whisper filths to flip by, Maggie.'

'I've heard it all.'

'MaggieMaggieMaggiePink.'

'Naw. I've got this rash in an Embarrassing Position.'

Which information passed on with infectious comunicability passed over her shoulder as she shuffs unto the window to jeeper her creepies out onto the road, out and down from there, both. Where there is

(the dog'll eat you straight off the face of the earth)

Alyce (O Diva!) striding along mitt in mitt with Henry swatting flies flying talk and both swatwalking towards the art exhibition promised by her, the duo frowned ondownpon by Maggie up there in recce recognition:

'Do i pity Henry. Do i.'

'Never mind Henry. Pity the poorly, Maggie. Who said: unto me is the porridge, o great oats of England?'

'Talk,' Maggie not even pausing to inhale when Jelf ex-ed, 'talk aboutalk, gawd, can she ever, that bitch of Henry's. Didn't she ever collar me the other day and chinwag to the daggy dozen. She even asked smutty questions about you and nobody can get smuttier than ask questions about you. Say, you know those,' Maggie's nicotine pickpocking the air entwards those wall posters over yonder of Jelf as Quilty as We All Know Who still upsetting the construction people whose temporary wall it is, and, 'sticker things showing mug-shots of that zombie stuck up over there...'

'Stickers? No no i'm sure i do not, Maggie, no no.' Jelf-innocence.

'Y'know the ones that cop copped you trying to claw off wall by the pub, you puritan you. Anyway, that talking bitch of Henry's says she knows that shocker on them real well, on account of...'

(O Dogod, open Sesame, not me)

'... the church forced her to shack up with him for years ago or something. And wouldya believe, he's a real con. She says he actually looks like that when he's out on His Jobs. Cops after him allover. Wears falsies, even clip-on toenails. But those who know call him Mr Fido Bigs on account...'

Maggie never heard, look you, his jelflung soursob pinched between expanding bloodvessels in his head. All she registered on the gist scale was that it had connotings of a human scream-out enough to preform nausie noises, before whatever it was was itself drubbedly drowned out (lying in the guttural) by the grandslamming of a door putting a banging on the sound effects. Indicating somebody on the lam. Having strewn black satin stainers of sheetmessic from pillow to post, door. And now sounding screw-loose and rudder-adrift as he trails his voice (piper chase!) through

(dog has the sour look of a poetaster)

the open Jelfdoor, via the oped and fallen gyape of Che-mex the Hua-mix, down the flight of stairs and out into the street below in tangential circles and other curlicles supersonic. Super *ohm*, has to be. A glocken stuck in the glottisspiel.

(dog disfigures mathematician)

Two bloxs away oethenwise, brunt onto the sidewalk of a real ruin of a block of flats and staremazing up at what is afore them, are Alyce and Henry with pause for gaspin' in pall of and gaspout. Pridelioned, she; a bit purloined, he. Looking, both.

175

For on the wall before them is progressing quite well ta a community action portrait of 'Whom We Weep For, Whjo Elfse?'. Aye, and it is a civic sightsome too! This is a thing to behood. A human head gone to its most auriful lensgth of rawbone exposition.

(dog with loss of beauty of former beauty queen)

As a smatter of fact, in order to gain the local council's permission to paint-on, Alyce was under ordinance of local bylaw to offlimit the area to all children under the age of twenty-one or, if perchance one foredoomed himheritself by chancing to cop an eyeful of the painted moosh (or part thereof), then certifiable officers must shoot himherit on sight. Truly.

Not only that but the ten-storey high painting has been divided into numbered squares, slightly off, for the expression-istic purpose of an invitation to members of the adult public already adulterated to colour here, tube-on there by numbers, whenceupon each is rewarded by half dollars of specified species. Yes. And all under the superating-on-the-op

(many fatal accidents cur at home)

slobbervision of, aye, those eyes!, 'Art' Munro. Yes, he of the earlier chapter and now wailing whaleishly against the wall act-statically, with all the yonis and yonkers of Alyce's Arstudio in minor supervisory roles. And a queque of general public half a kilometre long not by half!

'He sure does...!' Henry, finally, with voice croaked with humantones of pathy.

'Lack, like it says.' Alyce in leer, and Learish.

'Yep. Lacks, the word. Who is he?' Henri, ryght out withit. 'All will be revealed.' Alyce, promysing a slyce of lyfe.

(revealing yourself to the dog is just breaking cover)

'Poor white sob ain't got much left to reveal. We tribal fellahs ain't gonna need a revolution if that's what we're up against. Give us a fleet of ambulances, is all.' Nosocomial Henry, as en wry.

As 'Art' Munro puts his lumberance into some sort of action traction spouting puff and wind, jellying from a gelled mind, coming towards them grampus like a blubbermange in breakingwater surf-you-right and halycon-been-lately All body and no mindover mend; the Moby Dick of Arstrailya's Art world which is itself the Mopey Dick of the Sth Seas; and megawatting in megalophonics of:

'Lovelacey lady! Thou mincing piece of artyarse! This 'ere be thine exemplar of all thine Pro creations! Th'academe's finefeatheriest hour! Sockin' it to de popul t'daub itself of Nature's mostrest wondrest "Boohoo, Wall Know Who And Now The Wall Does Too"!' And wiping his cow's eyes on a virgin pair of pared-down gorgeous gussies, 'If were but happyhappen our Dear Boy wast here to see him heself so divined combined in a Poe art. This is indeedo a Quiltysquizzy pop-eyes epoch larger than a shithouse wall. He wouldst be heckstatic!'

'Henry, this is 'Art' Munro.'

'Marvellous scrump, He-enny. And love that abo tinge; it do so tingle.' Limped enpudged rouged enjewelled with his porgy pokers running over Henry like as if each finger was a worm out for a Saturday night's gigglewriggle. And the next time that Henry looks, the Munro is being scened arioso as Moses at the foot of Mount Sinai on the Hollywood Estate, shouting, going:

'Disciples! Me boys'n' goylasses! Daub thee! Aye, daubdraw ye! Yes, daubdrawcrash upon! Touch up for Hoi Art, half dollarbitties a dabble! Oo do rollupsies puppies!!!'

And, oh, curtains, too. For who now wheels around the corner on one weal, his shoulders drooping like drapes on the vine, but

(dog carries around his mouth the twisted look of a bemused man)

177

Jelf. Whjo bleeding elfse? In bolt in nick of hey nonny no no no right on the noggin of the spur of cog flywheel of a clockspring. Copping a gander of all this right between the limpid pools, and. Backpedalling even before his gastropeds are heaving themselves up, mouth high. Groundhaltered and disbelieving that it is the hejelfself who is there in blazon brazen out for all the homogenes and homelilasses of Sydney to ughle at. And Henry going, 'Jelf!' and 'Art' Munro gobbledy gooking, 'Aha, Deah Boy!' blethering wobbles towards him and Alyce at clap hands (it's even starting to show in your hands, Alyce, you gonorr), and Jelf gawdfish bowling, as he tries to execute the hoky-poky and turnaround freewheel on those jellyroll legs before he

shocketted off like a son out of a goner, squealing high velo-shatty. Yes, off, buggered. Jelf.

(dog trot, survival course on the ballroom floor)

All of which deliriums has Constable Wilkinson orbied as, as coincidence would have it, he happenbyed while cruising around, around the aroundparts thereof. Ullo ullo ullolujah quod d'eye vide?, qothinks he. Something stinkish for a pitter-pate for a starters. So he steelwheels around, around to go after our Jelf with his 'plice horn blaaaring and his fumicul-car blazing hot in persoot. Yes, he does, while behindermost:

(dog collar'd human neck)

'That was my mate i was telling you about.' Henry, pointing to where Jelf was is not, both.

'I know.' Alyce.

'The one with the bed upstairs.' Henry, with his former intention showing.

'Oh, i do so know.' Alyce, showing her formermost.

(shocked human got the dog shakes)

Meanwhile, on the shoot-through. Jelf pelt thought to be peeling somethingviz: i'm not thinking i'm not to think i donvvanna think be unallowed to think moving legs movement in the rectum stand eructing o pain in the arse go go vive go live go surloin no streak brown kakki no i live long on coming on vile i am io in the ion shit it all gogogogo doggo doggo o dogod don't go on i am coming in bowel wow movement cross my i and shi my t, gonna blast...

(opening your heart to a dog is just suicide)

Is he, runoozingly blind and flatus out. Fate is a fart. That is taking our running and getting-runny Jelf forwards (for-what?) towards the nearest bookseller cum lottery ticket vendor. Yes. Jekyll and Hide's got nothing on it. Or to do with it. And now, yes, before yr latenight reading reds, are none other than the leg wraps coming off Mr Fido Bigs coming up! Yes, strue, and fast, on both counts of pants! *Ohm* is for Omo is for a coming hose down. Execrable behaviour!

(sunk teeth in deep Walter)

Alyce, ameantime, licentious:

'And what are we waiting for? Is issor not my time come, my Chosen One?'

'Rutting, my Alyce?'

'A-rutting we go, my Henry.'

'Diva!' Y'know what he's saying and whotis he's saying it unto.

(gummy old dog jaws ten to a dozen)

179

Now, in front of that nearest bookseller cum lootery tick't vendory there happens t'be a poster in wiremesh besides which runs a reaired carpet doortodoor shoptoRolls unto the Kenny (Rodshitent) Griffley's Leisure Rolls there and och. Aye, that poster is displaying something shockingly displaced in nature itself in the very nature of the Jelf muggins, who and which (both) is the subject martyr of the Kenny (ratted R with urns and Rs) Griffley's hot new outnow book. Plus, banner which rings the world's attention to the news that Author K (Ratty) Griffley, in permawave and always cheery with a hand one, is inside in personable person. At This Very Moment In History Time. So Hurrah and Hurry In & Handout. And autografting his ratscratcht squiggle onto any of hisnewbook soldnow. Dust jackets that are throwing dirt on Jelf's coffin already. Aye.

And of course it has to be that Jelfleeing in zoomic Jelflight, with Constable Wilkinson in purrzoot, turns a rtangle at top revvvverie and ploughs into that poster-carpet setup in one fell swoop of oops. A daisy! No prank either but prang. Ending? As promised by such a poster, ending in a foot stuck in it. And right through his own head in print what's outnow in Griffley novel print about it. Yes, and

in sight of mind, both open, to see what he has stepped right into, Jelf suddenly clutches his lower abdomen going claxon, him and it, for all to fuccough quicksmart u-hear: (I'M IN PAIN! I'M IN PAIN...' and dragging at his final daks for to drain away what is near to becoming ickily irksome within. Shitty fate. And now, fully exposed as the real aliaslad of Mr Fido Bigs, that skunk in whiff's clothing. Plot and plop, both. Poe and The Po, which? Whatever, its got to be moving, if not at least bowel rending stuff. It is, and

(bitch shows yet another face to its young ones)

here swhere coin gets its sidence of the Jelf and Griffley (R) and Constable Wilkinson, the theo'd trio, Dogod down troddened. For, in the midst of Jelf showing his immense relief, comes at That Time (of course!) Kenny Ratshit (G), riding himself high on the curl of his own permanent wave through the spumata of I-blown highego. Oh sure, and not looking where he's guying until he billows (he bellows!) right into the bogway of Mr Fido Big's archedover aitchbone, slips slurpily, and makes a pan of his coiffured handle. And all three going:

(police riot dog deforms student ranks)

Shit, Jelf saintencing himself to the service of Dogod. *Shit*, K G (Ratty o'er tit) dunnied on and just about dun in; ground down and bemoaning the one sausage spinctered on's temple, a skived coma to his comatose, aye and

shit, Constable Wilkinson *thar she blows* and *at last Fido Bigsie in patson* and *whacka fucking diddlyo* as he offlights on his apprehending right on cue on the left hand down trajectory *comereyu c'm'here!*

(dog, high on grass, fell down on Gay Blade)

Well, one can imagine the sudden hurdle-gurdle hurly-burlies allover there with Mr Fido Bigs (Jelf-the-Wereweoulf) berling off beslobbring and Constable Wilkinson berling after, Grimm face and all besmutt, and K. Griffley bestuck like a pat of ratshat in the let-fly ointment, stif-fly. What stuff! Really jammed in.

(a dog's bach is wurlitger then its bite)

The chase:
Round robbin' Sydney went The Chase, therafter known as The Great Chastity. And the cause of Constable Wilkinson's being thenforth nighted, darkly back pounding his meat afterdark. Never mind that now; The Chase, what a chastey titbit of a

(more police ought to be back pounding the beast)

181

chase, all over Sydney! Through thorough and thru fare by ways aside streets par king up lanes pass ages en trances ex trances uphill and dole up Dale and Dill. And even though the good and virtuous Officer Wilkinson had all the dogs in Sydney on the alert for him, Jelf beat him to The Last. Meaning the best shoeing won the shoo. Yes,

(dog has fading Beauty going fast)

Jelf beat him to the last gap in the crowd crudwatching Fido Bigs outside the shop there Jelf beat him to the last corner of the earth's next street Jelf beat him to the last place in a certain restaurant queque Jelf beat him to the last cream bun Jelf beat him to the last chocolate flavoured glace Jelf beat him to the last seat by the window Jelf beat him to the last efficient waitress Jelf beat him to the last bowl of sugar Jelf beat him to the last cubicle in the Mens can there Jelf beat him out of there at last Jelf beat him to the last green light change Jelf beat him to the last parking place Jelf beat him to the last supermarket trolley Jelf beat him to the last place in the shortest wayout queque Jelf beat him to the last free sample Jelf beat him to the last Special Offer Jelf beat him to the last free stamps Jelf beat him to the last one through the door Jelf beat him to the last bar stool Jelf beat him to the last piece of ice in the bar Jelf beat him to the last free round on the house Jelf beat him to the last free peanuts for customers of the bar Jelf beat him to the last dashout to make the last afternoon show Jelf beat him to the last ticket back stalls Jelf beat him to the last back row seat Jelf beat him to the last Pass Out Jelf beat him to the last thing they both thought of Jelf beat him to the last look back Jelf beat him to the last doubletake Jelf beat him to the last joke disguise Jelf beat him to the last bus that went past Jelf beat him to the last seat facing the engine going the other way to the last passing bus that Constable Wilkinson was last seen on trying to last out and last heard shouting through the last side window that he swears that Jelf is going to beat him to the last round-up in the sky. Too. Jelf beat him to the last laugh. But the last and bittermost straw of all, Jelf beat him but

only just.

(the dog loves you just the way you tastefully are)

Jelf must have beaten Constable Wilkinson to the last park bench in the last park latilandia in all of Sydneyside too. Saying that there has to be a park bench existing somewhere in Sydncytown, because Jelf is parked on ring ringed by parkland upon such a bench now.

With his boko closed and his eyes clawed, which?, and his lipstite. All behind his hands are all the unintegrated parts of his face threatening at last to go to pieces. Museumwise. And he sits dumbfolded in plain view of a blindfounded world that seems only to want to touch him up now that it has drawn him pale. Aye, it's true. Jelf in the twilight of Mr Fido Bigs fading fast. Where once a werewolf, now a was-dog. And going into his palms:

Ooo dogod pleas do let me enter a please in the curs that events are taking, for i am onlie a rover who has j ust over crossed; if this is my earth i am just another earthen ware-wolf with the bite put on every day and o even if i was a sweet thing i would only be sucked out to linger-longer, strue, and i noway wanna dissolve into all smiles belonging to some other rude buggah, the beast no negative nix nout bloody zero.

(dog has the wrinkles of an old lady all over its face)

Though something wafts up against him with a sickening pffhcw even before he can think up the devastation to the tendon of his flexor digitorum sublimis that the Wilkinson handcuffs might have wreaked. Something reeking now. For real. He efforts a digit opening to see through eyeball plus eye... dog, terrier, one of, and sniffing joyfully as it edges upon his boot, to boot. Just in time to cock its leg before it piddles on it, as if the boot, as part of Jelf, had not taken enough piss already. This does happen.

(dogs gout on a limb)

183

Fuch koff futzing pfooch, you. With a kick enough to krink and a doggy yipe enough to yelp for hyelp. Stricken, a blow for mere mortality. Ha ha; bout time; put up your paws. But no sooner has Jelf enclosed down his shopworn visage to envisaging his poor lifestate again than but the

(dog can't see for the dim eyes of a blind man)

dog's boy is in headhigh of hoist with a stick above Jelf's head stave-size just going into an ecstasy of apogee of down swing on the man. In the manner it is written or wridden, which?, across the sky of circumstanks: From Factotum to Wearer-Wolf Dogdirect. But our man has this time lashed out with his shitkicker in time to kick the little shit. And connected, which is a change for the jetself, except that the upshot is an upshout resulting in an earful of an airful of dog's boy going whaa mummy and daddy heavyweight champ &ce.

(child-loving dog plays with its food)

Even after Jelf has recovered the haunted hutch within his own hands, all thingers and fumbs, his fanny ticklers are being bent back with a first rate prise by the dog's boy's great boxing figure of a fatherfigure in a certain stormy manner as if to say, 'come out whore weather you are' with pestulant homicidal undertones undertaken. Safact that, and you can

(boxer raises the vanquished's arm)

imagine Jelf, now a greatly prised trophy within the grasp of boxerlike fatherfigure, going, 'Sir, the dog procreates so that all of our goose can be cooked. But, though i may not be down yet, i have now given in. Sir. So do feel free to do your worse, but do beg you not to make it lasting.'

Whereupon dog's boy's fatherfigure is so disgusted that he lets the Jelfingers fall snap shut down again around the portcullis side of the Jelf embitterments and mutters dog-rashmaking things that would make a mockery of Jelf being our hero. If we had not heard

184

worse already. And, too, takes his son (now rising risibly) and the bloody dog (now larfarfing fit to beast) and moves distant in a distant manner. He does.

But still something pongoes near at syphillitic hand. Until, finally, the Jelfingers open fatally again to take in the inevitable whatmorenext. Whothefux? whowhowhowho goes air? And looks up with a snarl at the top of his voice to voluntarily see what he never figured he would. It only being Old Nick Himself. Dead true. And so shocking the Jelfself that, before we can recover our observer status, Jelf has already nicked off. He has. Screaming made and scramming mad, which? Yet, if

(snooty dog snaps at any poor old bum that comes near it)

only he could have seen beyond the facing effront he might have clicked on to fact that (Clue Klucking Clan) it was not Old Death Nickself but. Yorik Amos, amok and uncommitted amore and only, with his nithead hodden in a KKK hood, which, when pulled back unreveil'd a skull that really was Death Warmed Up, spoofing it up as Deadeye Nick. Yes.

And in so a gnatural way that now, with the J. in elflight, he cackles, cavities and all, from out of those dead parchy lip-spittles and turns those shrunken and fiery furnaces onto the dog's boy, rehoods his hideossity and advances. Adios, kid.

(little dogs make terrible bruits)

Meanwhist of which, Jelf is slowing down slightly everso now that the panic in this Panlandia is bating with loss of breath batting his brave heart and settling down to a mere hopping for some respit from the roasting in spite of a fate turning him rotisserie wise by its rough handling, when, Grreating Dogod, lairikinising over the other side of the park, did feel fit to pluck four manstarved and crazed greyhounds from the hand of their stunn'd human and to point (Dogod, the Great Pointer To) their tearing hurries straight at a mouthwatering Jelfeast who

185

(St Bernard takes lost skier by the hand, helps himself)

revives his viability in a minute of furrious flurry by imitating, emits and all, an emu with knobs on, and knobbled, trying to get air between a mirey quagmudpool and itself, and only jelfacturing some insufficient progress tupwards the exit gate. With that zuppy crew of greyhounds clawsing in fast and positively drooling in their exertions to head him off, perhaps with only one snap of the jaws between the winner by a head (Jelf's) and second, third and fourth, meaning that if

the dog is at your heel, blood will drain from your face.

(wolf whistle means love to have your all)

 Bleeding well and bleeding-well torn, hard to see for that he is flying clothing rags like bunting, no bunkum, and barely able to hug himself, Jelf finally at last drags himself's jelfness up the stairs staring down at him towards his own have-rent-haven-room, with his vital pieces only held together because he is b'now so highly strung.

(dog hung drawn quarter)

Even Mean Mex, the Chihua to end all huamans, waits up on the landing for the approaching Jelfness with a sneer. Yes, a sneer afixed to a lobing slower, not to slather him with kisses but to cosh him for a strip of that cloth that, prior to him being greyhun'd and grave hounded, once passed for one leg. 'S true! And the trouser attached to the bunting that was once the other cuff is

(prostitute's dog lives off its mistress's body)

Amos himself bloodydoody bleeding and (bloodybloody) torn from the boxing given to him by heavy dog's boy's father figure in parkland, hanging on to the Jelfbeing by his only two teethy Amos dentals not removable. And Jelf flighting his spittlesibilant painful vox just once to a Dogod that really is a dog of a god, going:

'Goana finish the job off i am lizard licked anyway'.

Piteous. Even showing under the arms. Nothing left to happen to him. Yet home at last, against all odds all dogod devices all god aim or goddam, against toute and tots and toots and out-tos, against ageing and daggydawgs and agrrregates afar and aggressions not fur off and the agony of a goner; against all of these, Jelfulgence has won through to be back at his elemental source, his own hive bedsitting pittance, going: endimmed but end i'm amid.

And, shaking for the shack key to intern: am starting to feel bit more bedsteady already. But then: soft oddyssey odd i see can it be... there being in view in there in his veryown room, Henry enriching himself in the Jelfartsack and shooting up and out a disarming smile with a snake arm charming his neck belonging to a thing coiled on the other (outer) titside of the pitside. Head of whomwhich now peers round Henry yoohooing with an outward tit tittering and inward tch tittle-tattling. Alyce!

(give the dog a born)

Alyce, yes! Realyce alyve and for real! Does Jelf rattle or rictus? No death rattle left to rat on with, let alone rick left to let fly a ricochet of wreck. No. Just a little hupoops ups perhaps, too, just a little poop out as a squeak might from a squawk of a half hawk, now

(the dog cleans up a little Grubby Fingers)

flown forlorn fowled and feather-tipped in flight off. Indeed, whatever the pidgeon was a moment ago, he must have been only at an embryonic stage of possible development, for did not we all hear a shell crumble... *Ohm*. And so *ohm* and so *ohm*; whatever it is, it goes *ohm* reverberating back down the stairs from where the

187

Jelfigure had just come up. Getting higher as it goes away further. A real scream, isn't it?

(astrologer died under the sign of the Dog)

Then again almost siriously:
if the dog stays with you it's only protecting the food it's laid down. And again: all dogs are lousy buggers. That's why a mongrel dog is something got from nothing over not much. If it's growing a nuisance, ringbark a dog roundly. And then strip the bark off. Beware, too, of a stray that flings itself at you with more than what it could ever say. And never give the dog a hand to cherish. No. Just nourish the goodness in yourself, for the dog will come to appreciate it. Also, say, if the dog throws itself at you: knock him back gammon. And certainly don't egg it on or it'll break down your outer shell. Then again: Dog Juan was caught liver loving. So never let the dog scoff at you. It'll always run you down in front of your friends. It will. Like he who had inscribed on his tombstone: He Was Bolted Down. And on another tombstone: Collar'd. Nearly was gravely engravened: Went To The Dogs Early In Life. Which reminds of the epithet: Flea'd But Caught On the Hop. Just goes to show you should avoid at all costs being put through a Lupe-the-Lupe. The dog on high to overcome you. And remember that a mongrel is just a crass between. After all, Dogod lets you fatten yourself today so you can live for to marrow. Remember that the irregular shape to a dog's mouth might have a mother somewhere. But remember most of all

that the Son of Dogod is canine again soon.

O Almitey Dogod, Lord of Rex, swallow up the Abominable and spare rib the Abundants; yea, open up thy Dogob and I will full fill it. *Ohm.*

BOB

Jelf, he goes
'e goes ego seeking
eco ekeing

esse, this is the
                      yes, i am!

(Snoopy into your private parts)

Here we have close up of Jelf close by, three seats behind the bus driver and back sighted cinecally by window left hand down port side. Seat D even. Seeing him now with a smattering of a smugile on his Jelflug.

We, too, ingredient up theme music of Jelfolktones (oh, that muse emetic!) proprogating throughout the land all the strains of beauty tunes which have done so muck to make country life worth leaving to the untransistorized kangaroo. Unsophisticated, too. Both. And

the land beyond the window in constant stretch once is old Aurozzie, land of hope and glowery, passiming bye, wish it wood, and promising proms. It does.

Shadows on this cushy side of the bus call for the shoofty techniques of lightupping, no More tone, tone being lowered everywhere already, and. Extras in the bus there are average middleaged Oz Strayan mums and dads out for a hodiurnal howdovvn in the ole torn tonite. They are, and looking like they each are on ways variose from varicose operating tables travelling alongside of our Jelfessence who be at this mmmment riding high having ridden himself of Sydneycity where

(the dog is a wolf in Shep's clothing)

he was ridden into a sunken cheekiness by that slimey slug Alyce. However, that was then as then was that. Hours ago are years

189

hence begun, you son of a. No, and. Forgetfulness is the ticking by that goes with a clock on the head. But let us forego that and forge on fornow for Jelf is being driven by a bus in urge going into this faraway hinterland hither where they say exists the best chance for the survivence of the fretened species. Hejelf, specifically. Plustoo:

the camera never lies. Down, and. Though these be early kilometres yet, the Jelfurtherance is definitely on the up and up. Instead of definitely on the upper, spread. Nor is this a make-ape job that has given him that new set and baseline to his lower jaw, oh no. Rather some Jelfsighting of all that freesome country passing by his window, but at least not passing him ex anus by means of a bum's rush out through the cloaca door by some arsehole called Alyce. So,

let's hear a good ten microsecs of that themeswept music to heart feel by. Canned for all those at home canned into watching this crap which always moves sideways. Then cut musicle, music so tendon, to fade off fad dead, and catch those here-there airy halations streaming sunploughs through the bus sunroof in lens-blinding actinoplosions stars and faerytales coming true, large as a 23 inch metric equivalent screen. Switchromatic filters exchange fags; take it Camera Two, for

Jelf is feeling the twinge of hope enticing him to get set on a photogenic glimmer of hope.

(dog shows up the bad form of a rotten deadbeat)

Remembering that the angle of dangle incidence is equal to the heat of the meat's refraction, and that this Jelface (a bonnyface and boneyfarce, both, too) might even light up a teeVee critic with its scene of mountaining contentment. And fading Jelfro to launchforth into the next scene for some. But

(you might have to hackle your way through the pack)

do please keep note that we are running on footage over a delicate case-essence here. We need to enscrumbulate real sleuthessence to bring our subject up to his bast advantage. Jelf vintage, aye. Betattered still by recent alround greyhound treatment; enforced perfalse from top to tie and far below; enwigged (real jazzy jazy, too); sussed and picious of all who approach in case their cause is an end to Jelfextancy. We must thus disguys ourselves as common outback muscidae (flies to you, you pest) without raising the slightest suspecta-tions of Jelfear, y'hear? No mean task either for us mob of Telelitists, normally only fly-by-nights, plus four humping great cameras and x number of contingency girls worth humping. Eh, what's that? *Ohm*? Right *ohm* the track, you are, too!

(who turned the dog's courant ohm)

Jelf spatial partial
self spectrum
light shaft unheavy
                        speakpeepsee ping through
jetsam same
                mesa gong going goy
Jelfree flesh sol
sole fou soul foolsomelight and solar shleen
coming whoo-air to dweft on, and
each track avi-aired,
a far, far Thoreau fare

Jelf are   he is
on the roe'd

(affronted dog takes a front)

We have a long shot of yon mountains topped with all that photographical peaks'n'animals nbirds ncows steering n'all other types of animal free-booters bar none. Bringing near tears to all the dearies' eyes at home so we must quickly zoom back middle

191

distance to get a loaded can's eye view of all that scrub spearing along in a real bush outback hundred kilometres or even more outside of Sydney. Yes, and

then to handheld telefotozoom, with musical surge and ever higher stilt, to pick up, godfa chrissakes:

trashstuff wasterefuse mullocks dregdroppings beercans aluminium revoltution excremental bumpaper newsprint blowflown chunda the sun foiled foibles tin toybles cratescan cokescan tinnedmeatscans sweetscan shitcans tincans beerscan wrecks-car bombedoutscar abandonnedcars carscan canscar tinscar tincars. All a canker scanner bot blot on the earth of the camera face gummed in. Lypt-reading our eucalips and spoiling the TVitality of our Summer skives.

(Put your dog down; you don't know where it's being-ed)

this
    is scrocket to green slandia
soft li thsome all blueties
land of Infanta
               go some summer white and gossamer
swhite swarm
queen bee
long swarm to thee
          and o
i feel swarm here so
mmmmmmm

Are, fading from outside, bush flowers flowerless for years, out of fucis and back into fucose! Zeroing now in onto the flocculus halo'd by heck and hclios on the Jelforehead there and then. Pan back to draw a bead on the beads of happillary sweat on that Jelface, swarmed and smarmed in this warm country now. With a dead panning across the Jelfrontal profile for to take in the mid-adaged Australian (listing to the right of the passenger list as

192

Acyle Misslainy of Alice Prangs, or a Town Like) Splitbum who is staked out looking satiated alugside of him. Sat, and she

all set to prop up our reverso shot of that poor aged frump (name of Isa Frump) who is sitting, looking sizzled, directly behind Jelf seated before her. And she clucking her reptilean with great disagreeability, both and which, as she goes casting side-askances of distress at a fruity manifestered seated next to her whose. Head, adropped on her poor frumpish drooping shoulder, quite sincerely, looks like the head of an Eoanthropus man straight of the offcentre of a palaeontologist's nightmare snoring away there, and

broadcasting B.O. in waves of media competition. Like, if he didn't mean it, he should mint it. On the nose no better, exactly in fact, than Amos would. Which he is precisely is who. Yes! And isn't that Amos all over? Foul called.

(ill-tempered dog snaps the children's heads off)

No wonder then that poor aged Frump looks in danger of passing out overcome by exhaustions exerting exhaust fumes (a gasser among others) from her shoulder. Curious, too, how, unlike everyone else there on whose eyes the Amospherics are beginning to show films, our Jelf imprints no bromide at all, nor prostrates no irritated gland. Nup. Not even a twitch on the Jelflughole for our mass audiosentinels at home nor any such antic of amos misanthropettifoggery, even forged. When it was not so ere long ago, clean air or throatickle, that he would have attempted to do a bloodily harm to the bodily Amoself. No, no such sub images for the subeditor's subintelligence, sub it!; nothing except perhaps a

slight overall relaxation of the Jelform, before he openly flips out thisside cornealens, then flaps out thatside cornealens, then doth let both cornealens flop unto the floor at his feet going at no less than the speed of our sound. Slightly faster than the bus, perhaps or for sure, which?. He does!, and we are panning to his right to

(dog thinks death mask is just outer crust)

193

take one quick take of Splitbum sat next to our boyo with herself staggering (a bit stagey) sideways in amazement that the man next to her is plucking out his own damn eyes, ayes. And quite frankly recoiling from the recall that the man must have done something so unimaginable to want to do a thing like that that it probably serves him right. Plustoo, some people have a nerve! But then with her dominion girlguide's dominant tendecencies foreing to the come. She throws herself bodily to the floor to scrabble after the blind creature's orbs in danger of curtains for them and him, both. And would they ever squash so messily so!

But b'now the Jelfatherlykind hand is upon her crinkly head as prelate to relating into a gentle and humble piece of the soundtrack:

'No no, please bother yourself not.' He.

'Think of your poor eyes.' Her.

'Merely shedding graft tissue, dear lady. After the operation... oh woe for future woos, bit of a shoddy job by the surgeon. But nothing, really, no.' He.

'Oh.' Her.

'Have to look these things in the dead eye, dear lady. Just grin, bear and continue to shed three a day from my right eye and two a day from the left. Give or take.'

'Oh!'

'Get used to it. Truly. Merely sweep them up with the toenail shavings these days.'

'Oh,' catching her throat catching her looking up when she catches sight of even more. Like take a double take. For the Jelfperson is now wearing glasses, but not glasses surely. Stage props more likely. Reams of lighted rims around the two little Jelfisheyes. Surely an eye equivalent to a hoof shod. No man can

194

be so blind as to think that mere glass can help him, and. As they say: once common man, now made to peer. Well!,

poor Acylc M. Splitbum could not have ever gazed into someone's eyes and seen only her own. Reflected back collide-oscopic in a hundred places. We can imagine even marginally how she looked confronted by her first smiling genuine freak. But let us not attach further reflection on this, but fade off, anyway, into:

This
bus, this
Cerebus of the cerebrum
brummmm

(dog takes on the grim face of a hounded man)

But flashing back to our tee Vee images where the Jelfoureyes are flashing semaphor'd danger across this sunbent country that has to breed 'em dumb since a single bright spark from even one original thought could set anything off, aye. Hasn't yet, touch tinder.

(hammer away at a husky with a sledge)

Like the sun in comparison to the Jelf reflectors, Acyle Miss-lainy ('Splitbum') has wisely palled into pale insignificance too. Poor dear, she would ne'er have been in the crux of the mater anyway. And anyway there is still behind her our commiserable Frump who, in her own tiny spfear, is bravely staying conscious in the breathing face of Amos. On her shoulder still, and. Who now undams his damned-up eyes and lets the goodlight shine through. He does. And it is touch and go whether at that moment the sun itself would give up the ghost. Ing of your teleaerials. And shut down, even on peak progrom time. Yes,

rhadamanthine Amos owls into light consciousness to judge Frump's shoulder bolsterness harshly with an overpowering growl. Before falling off to sleep again at the sight of all that Motheaten

195

Gnature out there, but not falling off commiserable Frump. As afore said. No, and she cursing herself that for the first time in all her mammy years, she is not wearing a shoulder holster for to bolster herself when today she could have done with one, either or.

(the dog gains, you're loss)

Remembering also that:
we are using here whitelight filters on the Jelfittingness to heighten any actinic action, if any. Need you ask. We strain, being good Striners for sensitized reflex work. We gauze for an impression; do sift'n'pan for an answer. Tired of reading between the lines?, then just watch. What is before the camera, comes before the lens. Oubliez that not, if you can't remember it. After all, if we place the camera in front of what is in front of the camera, what comes after when we are on the spot before?

Well, the camera cannot lie because the bloody thing is too dumbcluck to know how to talk to lie, and besides, if you insist on an answer an' all, here is an answer from the off side: we have as much Right to an answer as we have answer Left. Centaur spread. So just go

back to sucking your succubus and on with the tail, Ma Supial. *Ohm.*

(death trap wide open on the port bow, wow!)

Here we are now outside of beyond where yonder the original black stump (dead) is with an original late afternoon (dying). From a vintage point from which, from over the Jelformed shoulder, we have a long shot pinning down the back of the bus in pan as it carries on as straight as a die, very dicey, towards the rim of an unspeckably isolated part of the inland like Flynn where you could far-fling yourself and nobody would know, no.

196

And the bus is doing this without him, happily waving it cheerio, woosh me good luck as you wrath me goodbye. Moving off, the both of them, the it and the Jelfhimself. (Soundtrack a Jelf hymn on the back track.) He does. Fowards the flarfung horizon. A veritable horror zone, it is, too.

(ugly jags on the starboard bow, wow!)

And we see, in doggish close up, now, those beads of fresh alfresco sweat (pores for refresco) on the Jelfocalspecs from his ear-to-ear grin radiating against all photometers, both. Plus, the Jelf swaggering along with that swagger of his pointed for nowhere that the telezoomic bino-occulated camera can scene. No. For there isn't anything up a-head that would turn one, unless it is to look back longingly, though not his. A bushtrack to end all. There's not even a duststorm to hang a test card on, nor a zoon to make a zoom by. Yes, this is the Dead Hart of gorzy Orzetralia, bleeding shame. Never mind; Jelf is in

(the dog thinks you such a dear hart)

freeform freefrom. Freedomed, bouncing his lightglobes against kodachrome looking, too, strangely ortho-from-the-shoulder out towards some omega site. And dusty hue'd and tawn, even tattered. But not forgetting either the outback flies flight plan which goes: when you're on a good thing, stack to it. But then he has already forgotten it anyway, going:

Jelfro
scarecrow
       scar-crowned
              star crown now and
this is the land of Oz zee land of
this is the
          upturn soar terns
and in the shell of the Great Turtle
thee shall swalk laurelled

197

lorrikeet paraclete

by the aloe aloed and the
lowant sun sumptious for
thee assumptioned and
Ariel avi-flown, for

this is the land of the Aurora
adawning
adoring   adorning

(Dogod, It says: carri-on walking, travelling man)

So Jelfreed, he cannot be flypested enough to even cast backwards for a shudder over his shoulder. So he cannot see from our reverse angle shot over the Jelframe to telezrummm back a couple of flagging hundred of metres if not thousands to where

Amos is staggering to keep his mandarin shuffle adapted to these outback conditions. Hardly adeptly either. The poor old bugger. All pooped and not very prowed of it, either. And now grunting to a haltered and, unless there is a rival camera crew attached to him, crowded from skull to corns with all-Australian flies without kidding. They obviously thinking Amos to be their greatest boon (swinging!) ever and going out of their tiny little minds, even comparatively. With Amos bearing up, at least, that old Bush saying that goes going: 'When joeblow starts to blow hard, look out for the fly blown'. A bit highflyuting! Yes, yet hark! What muffled cry? Someone one can't see for all the fly life getting tsetse about it, or something for the TV repair man, which? Yes. The cry from the Amosenescence. Dulcetry to the fly animals' ears, if they did have any. And then, both he and them, suckers all, now grounding their backsides downonto a trackside eucalypstump where are domicile

not very docile green tree ants after a little relish for coming meals sitting down amongst them and themselves, both. That is, Amos now really in the rear. And getting it in the neck.

198

(dog likes to relish his acquired manhood)

At the same time, or similar, dotty as a spot on the horizon, which he is beginning to correspond to, and beyond all bounds of imaginative leapfrog, Jelf is now far off and. Stands and turns and waves the talons of his tunny hand to distal Amos going byebye old croney see you in the hereafter since you ain't Never-Never going to make it nohow. With a Jelflourish and then does he scow to scarper off shikkedly, an iota of a scintilla burst into Jelflames o going O:

this is the land yslandia
                    Epeiros
i do thee makenstance forever;
land of my Yes-Yes
                    my isthmus of
my never-never my
                    landfall and leap my
my o my

i lodge
in spirit
in places unlogged   i am
inun dated

this is the land of my Never-Never
                              ever again

(blast the dog!)

Has the man gone all Agfacolour gaa-gaa? This be for teeVee belt, not for some artyqualtic sjelf alone. Negative. He's supposed in viewing pose to be the paysan what the mass-savs at home want to chewcud their choccies on over on, not the person to knit their browsings. Artrick cyclist'd, a dirty phrase. Poe tasting poetry indeed! Paltry! The man must be sub versive. Anyhow, do try to buzz on not off. As we do. *Ohm*. Quite electric, isn't it?

(hang dog. Do.)

Later. If not in twilight then surely crepuscules in the blood. No? And a quite extreme set. Almost outlandish, in fact, really. Where we have now a close up of Jelf on lam on the land, a little less stridant, a little more stringent, perhaps, but stroppy hoppy happy hippy strinefreaky he still be. For cert. And noticeably with his wig (yes! for the good camera never cambers, no)

only half on his dang head as it goes flipflopping each time he reaches one of his feet towards yeta nother yeti step. Leaving bald a number of wiggy adhesive patches now doubling up as fly paper for the thousand and one fly-stuck on him out to get their last kicks from snuff'd glue. What a wig wag the man is. He is even smiling just as though heno now where hedo be going to. And

doing so on a bushtrack that is going to where no soundtracks have real gone. Bakelite sun, even. What be called the mallee country from 'honi sweat qui mallee pense', a common mal-leedy. That, and. As the old Bush saying goes. It's got, in fact, so facking fur out of Fat town that even the sheep complain like real swine. Even the bolshy flies are beginning to fly the other way. 'Strue. And everybuddy knows that flies can't tell ponent from oethen, not like all you folks Tviewing out there. With Jelf wooshing them flies (blow'em a kiss!) a fondle goodbye, going:

i am Friar Tuck
i am Genghis Khan
i am Little John
i am the man from the East son of the West father in the North
    brother to the South
i am Hiawatha
i am King Billy
i am the Aztec
i am
    iambic
words don't bother me-o

200

(life is a cur ate egg)

Exteriori in posteriori and ten minutes later. Jeepers, is this a Willys or a willy-willy, this willy-nilly cloud of dusted coming up fast? And our Jelf is jerking into action with a staff of walking life held upright in his hand behind his back in the middle of the track making like he is White Scout staked out for burning at the stake. Cut lot steak. With his wig like that already looking half scalped by pesky redskinners. With, too, the drawing of the car to a halt, quickly etched in by a sharp break in transmission for the following:

Car? Fourwheel thereunderof. Family? Fiveweal thereinof. Sanity? Questionable to be so way outback here --black out? Names? Pater familiar, namely Al Yce and his Misslainy Yces all staring glacier eyed at this Jelforeigner staked out beneath their front wheel. Distribution? One maledad (Al) and one femalemumsy (Aly) frontjammed, and three babes aux armes (smart Alycks One, Two, Three) in rear. Types? Can tell by maledad's cloths that he is bit of a cocky bastard, now winding down window going like whadya wanta give us the wind-up for?, and jawjutting somehow all his jutey nausal Austral-words in together going:

'Yeah?' unamicably amigo, si.

'If you are, sir, going trippies around Austrackia, just drop me short of anywhere or by place and very grateful shall i be too.' Jelf, a deep bowline to his backbone.

Well! Even the little smart Alycks are now window wondering whether what they see is an err or, a stray. Yet before any one of these cold Yces can scream 'hold it, hold up' Jelf himself looks to the top of his head (a feat on the ground itself!) to where their disbelievers have alighted upon his wayward sidewayed-on wig and croons, going:

201

'Do not mind this don't. For tis to keep the sun off my old bald head as a coot, sir madam and kiddiwinks.'

Well againo! laugh about the talks doing the Yce rounds! Not only that. Now that Jelfingers are going as papillant points on his specs and:

'Don't mind either the gogs. They be there for to keep me humble, kids.'

At which the little smart Alycks flip, slapping their ickly flippers together goodiegoodie a real idiot at last, scum in scum in. Which he does with Jelfittingness. Now all settled and settling back and:

'Guerdonin, mate.' added after. Maledad malaprop? Not bad, though, you've got to emit.

(train a dog, then report the accident to the station master)

Whereupon the Jelf entry commences a three prong little smart Alyck attack on the Jelfactuality, viz: Iddlebiddy girlie stares blinking well unblinkingly at the Jelface with her cheeks a bulge with half masticated grub in her cakehole half grown but chockablock enough, ta. From the shovelfull of it on her poked out tongue. While younger boy buggerlugs is rolling its smart Alyck zonkhead round the Jelfneck to be vis-a-vis eyeball-to-ataboy going: 'I got the pressure pak on. I got the pressure pak on' etc. Plus while, lust but not leased, third littered kiddicunt starts a beginning to pound a way through the Jelfortress with a murdrous rubber machete. Over a poundings weight, too. Killo grim. And if the Jelface, despite all this is not a smiling, imbecilic, all-forgiving picture for your amazed tele-veyes only, then vide the Epilogue, do. Pods of sweat, too, hearing the Jelfspool spieling poesy for all you camera camarades, going:

i am all
that there is to know;
there is to know such
a lot

202

i am imago
        going i am
come up butterburst
imagene that

(Superman --super dogsbody)

Really outback now, and
notably almost mute, if not dumb too, are these silences
throughout the duco'd decor, despite the Jelfpun punning
runningly all the timex.

But then all wayfarers in Awestraylia know that it is a creepy
thing to worm your way into the bosom of an Australian family
since they first off think you a snake. They do. They be so
bellycosy, the Australian tough guys, that they don't really travel
around by car, o no; they just ride their country into the fucking
ground.

Yet still the Jelfestivity abounds, but he is getting not a crack in
their suntanned crackling in responser. He is not. Only first
kiddicuddles still staring at the Jelfascia with her mechanical
scoop stalled full of that same caking food. Still gob stable too.
And second kiddipoke still coiled around his Jelframe with
breathtaking proximity of his li'l aniseed wagger tongueing: 'I got
the pressure pak on, I got the pressure pak on'. Plustoo, third
kiddiecaper is still pulverising the Jelfountainhcad with the steely
edge of that rubber machete causing non-tickling trickles already.
But still the Jelf maintains a firm third thumb on his all
angelessence. So that

(man alive, must be a blind dog!)

we must ask here what has normed in on upon to change the man?
Mum's your uncle, indeed! Back home watching. So here's the
prefab perview unprogrammed: This

upfruct of Jelfextancy, it is all agleaming corona the sun the austernity the soundtwang the mountwings podes and anti-podestinies. Somehow. Yes, and the rhythm sticks when the sun beats a repetition on your neck and whence the opal is forming. And your body making noises *i am i am i am*, but the colours, the torquoises and the tangerines and the aquamarines, the colours still coming on. Oh, yes. And the grey nurses still slipping through the dark shades and the sandstones still inching along all our treadpaths and the webspider still hanging from the hunch on all our backs like us because it's lost the thread, and. Yes, the numbat the echidna the cockatoo the dingo the wedge of the eagle the emu the. Hear the eucalypt lisp. The galah the goannananna the jacarandaroo kangajacca the koala the lyebird imit imit imit the muttonbird and the mopoke and the play-at platypus. The waratah and oh *ohm* om the wombat. Yes, listen you people, listen to the austral sound bubblings of your blood. Listen to your Auz infanta land and when you close your eyes, the last of the great golden eagles has just been butchered and is swanning onto the marrowless bones of allourown. Tis. And on the

Jelflambeau is a fulge all around his inselfj such that you might swarm your hands by. Light intensity. So that the man Jelf cannot stop the tears swelling in his eyes talking. In love and the world. Together?

(seen on a tombstone: Pants, Undone)

And yet, through these Jelf exhortations, femalemumsy Ayl keeps casting little sidelong fluffs of longsuffering eyelids at her maleman Al uneasy that a bald blind stranger is verbally exposing heself in front of her family. Even maledad Al has trice as many times yawned and piggyeyed Jelf rearvirsionwise. Not forgetting first little piggie in food rasberrial ooze at the Jelfhim. Still. Her and the adverb, both. And still second little piggie breathing his rotted first set all over the Jelfput-on going still: 'I got the pressure pak on' and third little piggie going aaaeeeeyyaa with his machete on the Jelf vine trunk all the way homo. Still, yes. It's not everything; there must be far maul to life. No?

204

(man walking dog... madman and manmad)

To teleo the truth, the images are fading fast in low relief. We zoom on and still

the same car carryon goodyear for carbunkles, since it is the only car so outfar flung that overhead a satellite yanks its crank to report car's position for indecent exposure outback. It did and is, both. Meanwhile, on the soundtrack, moving statics of laughter. Yes, even through the laughter coming through laud and queer. Perhaps tis cruel and inimicable laughing Fate? Or Dogod lurking around the next shoulder of Hill the First?

(dog walks around with its tongue hanging out between its pants)

Tis neither, no. Merely the Jelflexibility. Is true. Tis the warbles of mewtones. For somehow or other he has all the Yces thaw'd and chawfing thaw awl the world to Teevee. Psstting themselves laughing in fact, as he is now vaudevilling (alive in concert too!) funnies with his wigwarm. Nfact they are positively clawing at him bis bis bis u funstuff like tivi bissy showbiz bee Busbybear. While, here, the Jelfoolish is making a bird's nest with wiggie; there Jelfoolish fabricating hairy monster out of awful wiggie; here Jelfoolsy jelfacturing a mushroom out of woopsy wiggie; there Jelfolly is conjuring up boxing gloves out of that silly old wiggie; here Jelfrolic is pattercake pattercake bakersman with that funny old wiggie; there Jelfossick (enough to make you) powderpuffing away with party wiggie; there here and here there, too the Jelfun-head as Ruskha peasant fussy zulu fuzzy Lady Muck Henny Penny crabby Fanny Hill... need we go on even visually? Except to say that the fun-thinginess of all that Jelfunniness is when

he places old wiggie back on his own head where it used to belong. The living end!

(Unbeliever tells Dogod, go take a running jump at Itself)

205

So that even smart Alyck girlie is now laughing so dancer with its eyes that it nearly swallows a particle of its gobfood. True! Amassingly. And other Alyck boy is shaking so much that it is missing the Jelfhead whole machete beats at a time. All that was bottled up has gone from the pressure pak kid, too. With the final touche of the Jelf adding these Jelfphonemes in addition:

i am as old as
this oldest land
i am oldest in this
isolandia
i am
       The Dreaming
                    i am of
the don of ages
time present
        past tensed
              future perfruct
dawning on me
          onoma mine
i am Ooion, Ooion am i
and
it is still early day
the egg and the it-i
we are close
        palaeos
we mate one

(apres moi, the dog, off course)

Dusk and a few darkies coming up.

But first the Jelf confession, believe what you see or discharge it from your ears. It is, Jelf confessing. Verbally in terms that you can see from the centre of your living rims at home. 'Strue. The car humming into coming nightstretch. Little Yces, getting smart, evangelized in sleep entwined around the Jelfperson. Even the

206

flies not more fatally attracted to the metallic glintlight of his goggles and have buzzed off by gad and dragon their heels. Off. They have, and

now the Jelfreality is telling itself to Al and Aly like his story wartishly wert, warts and Alyce and all. How he was had by all, in ways We All Know. And femalemummy Aly so got used to the idea of a total exposure that she is necking cosily against maledad Al, himself grinningly nodding circularly at Jelf with each embonpoint he is choccy making, chewing it all over, and silently going like: doggammit by the left gam, this is better than yatching TV to hear; this silly eejit telling it all off his concave chest. And

Jelfhimselfj coming into moonglow, coming to know that there is no need to distillate the there-and-back. No. For by the time he has finished, he has only just started. With himself. Dark and womb and warmthumming of what he can be. Behemoth, be he might. Yes, and. In ooion, in egg, in hmmm.

Tis the end. Al and Aly nodding sagely goodonyer go and goodonyer try and girliekid's mouth horrozoontly open like a gummed up postnucleated foodmilling scoop, aye, and one boy somnispieling about the application of pressure pak to private parts, aye, and the other kiddie dreaming of machete'd slices of the stranger parts of lifeforce. They are, all, when:

(It's not a lick, it's a tasting)

'Just here thanksalot,' with the Jelforefinger fletching frowards a creek bed ahead, if not outspan of any TVcoverage.

'Yermine hear?' Al amazing out between the twin gaps in his mouthfuls. Amazing.

'Iremine here yep.' Jelflourish meaning he means here. And before the Yces, Al and Aly, can even look back regretfully, the man has eased himself out from beneath the kiddiecoots and is already a ta-ta and many tas fast dissolving image into the next sceen here screamed for the first time.

(Lassie drains blood from Dracula's face)

We seeing from the simpering view of our video vantage point the Jelfringe edging upon a dried-up billabong. Under a distinctly unpithy coolibah tree, lone humpy and a few for lone and lorn darkish figures of ginwine natives. For real as well, and

behind that humpy is a big cleftmouth mossferny cliff. On past that humpy is a sandyrock desert, okay ochre enough to thrill photolens and lasses and even to frill sleeping lizards. Let lie. Where, too, each rock could be a ham'n'eggs coming-right-up. Meanwhile, back at the humpy, there is mongrrrel so mangy that even a Frenchman wouldn't touch it except perhaps with a knife and fork. No and perhaps, both. And that abodog has got up so furious that even its champion chompers look like they've got all snarled up with the fur on them, tis true.

(act absolutely repellant to all smelly dogs)

But Jelf still plugs on into the jaws of doggie death where once he would have laid down jugged at the prospect of teeth being set on edge. Against him. No longer, neither, that lost and hungdog last look on his profile about to be perdue. Instead, only a twinking gleam in his concentrated eye as he performs the great Oozstaylian swatalk (being that you walk with that leg as you swat with this arm et ubique, even in umbrage) into the very teeth of this abocamp. Appalling things, both.

(anthropophagous is a real dog jaw buster)

Resulting in the abodog having to prove itself not above advancing its animal appetites on any old whiteman by laying a charge, right there and then, against our Jelframe. And it does. And even a lightning reverse angle of the camera cannot catch the flash of those passing canines intending to nip him off in the bud. Some buddy!

Yet when we next train our sights, the Jelform is not only in tact but is down on his knockers patting that befanged beast down where it most whimpers and best wags its willytail. A real wag, and. Both doing a mandogman act likeasif they were in the wrong shooting script. Yes! And even when we

back train on the abocamp to the humped-up and hunched-over Aboman and his aboro-gyne, they too are in sharp contrast with the usual sticks and stuns that Abo-beings make for TViewing. They are, because usually you've scene one and you've seen'em all. Isafact. But here as we zoom we are thrown aback. For the abomanbeing there is

Bob. Aye, the Bob we've met before. That Abo from Dubbo dubbed Bob who Alyce bucked. On her and in Quilty's/ Scotty's/Jelf's home on that fatal

(TV compere got taken off the airedale)

day so many farcical pages ago (a farce that you've got so far!) the day of the Lottery Loss-out for a Lacker We All Know. Yes! but now Bob no more a gigolo than any other Abo-ing. Being that Abo originals are so always down'n'out that they don't even bother to count them to ten. Except at muster time. Old Bush saying adheres here, going: let the boongs stay where they are; they keep the flies out of town. Says a lot about the sorry condition of flies in this country. No buzzagain.

(dog makes his man stretch out at full lick)

Aye, Bob. Extreme exterior shot of extreme conditions of living. Colour. Bobnative humping a log outside of native humpy. As it is now and was no more. And the fact that if a squall isn't imminent, then this place is just squallid.

209

Yes, Bob and his missus-abo standing cautiously in front of their humpy there in case Jelf is a new local john come to introduce himself before he tells them to piss off on. And

their abomutt prancing along side of Jelf with its very demanding flea bites, both ways, and then settling back on sky high dogyawns at our roll of as yet unedited film between each lick of its own arse and of the camera, both in that order. By now of which time, Jelf is at Bob's side and on about abo abode:

'Mind if I share with you, sir?' Jelf v. iffishly.

'Ain't got much, bud.' Bob, being short of a bob. Not half. Even.

'I've got bugger all to give you, sir.' Jelflung out hands high in peace person.

'First time I ever seen that dog ain't gone right through a bloke, bud.'

'Being because, sir, never had a bad thought about a dog in my life just newly started. Freely and fleas admitted. Wondering whether sharing with me is going to be too much for you?'

And swivelling his point of view around this rude place called home sweat home, where so many Australian abo-beings have to walkabout when at home. Because you'd be off your facking head to want to sit down in it, aye. For, for an abo, home is where your heart is. Poured out in. Your Austrayin abo-beingbody, all he can do is try to humpy it all over this dog-graven country. Next time you come across an abobody's dwelling, you look close because it might be the one you yourself have thrown out with the garbage can. Or sue the map maker that got you there. Because that, in troth, is where the saying came from which goes something like abo-beings are just trash. It is.

(Squeeze a dog off the road)

Anyway back to Bob who is speaking with a passable imitation of whiteman's Engleash without spieling a drop, going:

'If it's all right with that mutt, it's okay by me, bud,' before whiteman, doggie and Bob go off to worm themselves by the fire. They do. They sit; they are sitting aglom. Whereupon aboBob and abomissus and abobabes invite Jelf to sit closer to the warmth to take whatever he can get of whatever they can get. They do. And here we dissolvol into:

quiet o the merry go
spin spanning a circle o
fire circle
        chalk crom
        chalice ohm
churinga

my soul is in yr embers
what will our ash
jointly be
        so sing me now
a song of your father now
for he
     might be he
or her   the quidam who
i am to embrace

           fire & glow
i can see mine own eyes
now   o   yes

(greyhounds coursing havoc among the people)

Camp comfy humpy fire! Believe it or get knotted. The meal is mess of, having been made. Jelfed-up, having been fooded, and leaning back against the lean-to, he having been learned something, too. All round contactment. Yes, with abomutt

211

mooching on his one hand and boyabo peekaboo out of reach of his other, and. A burp is as good as a huck out, yep, going:

'Grrreat, sir Bob. What was it?'

'Rat, bud.'

'Did you say rat, as in Kenny (Ratshit) Griffley?'

'A real rat, right.' Bob, his boof bobbing.

'Hmm, much smacking of the old labia lappers and may i say, sir, that as soon as i bring it up i shall definitely think of nibbling it back down. Yes.'

Abomissus giggles in passable imitation of white missionary lady burping like a nun in a mission of taking a holiday from the mission, aye, and Bob goingon:

'Missus ere sez thanks, bud.'

'Just want to ask, sir, why you don't go and buy big steaks'n' things from that general store back along there I saw, somewhere?'

'Where'd you think I got the rat from, bud?'

'Oh.'

'You got it, bud.'

'You want me to say I'm sorry for all this? I will, sir Bob.'

'You're alright, bud. Have some rum. Keeps the rats down.'

'Civil of you, sir. I cavil not. Here's good yuks to thee and thine.'

'Wanna sleep with me missus, bud?'

'In return, sir?'

'In return for what, bud?'

'In return for you webbing with my thing called Alyce longa time back. Do not want to be indiscreet, but you might bring to mind the shattering effect that had on me.'

'Great run, that was, bud. Cock ups all over three states, bud. Bone breaking, yup. Yer missus, but, gave me a piece of her tongue right where it tickles, bud, give y'that.'

'Thank you.'

'She still carrying that head of hers around?'

'Under her arm, sir.'

'Uhuh. Figures. All me missus wants to know is what it'd be like to bed down with an even uglier bugger than me.'

'She really thinks i am, eh?' Jelfattened up with pride of. 'Bloody sure of it, bud.'

'Take that as a great compliment, sir.'

'Know you do, yer mad bugger, bud.'

And so they firegloaminged so that even the little aboboyo feels no need to perform for whiteman and can pass the rum flagon by before refusing it in the non-existant refuse bin.

Of course. Goingjelf:

i am come in shareance
but have i drought to spare
will you, then,
                brother
share
all that i can sparse?
 u will find me patchworthy

213

i am spareparts   i am
Ooion   one with you
fittingly
egg shoal'd

(Simple Simon met a pied dog, now going to fare)

Gorge, now, in gorgeous lunalux; and, now, after dusk and darkies, the

Jelforefront. With the middle and long focal lengths taken up with this moonlit sky (lit all over on the TVstudio flaw) for Jelfolliage is elfessence now. Meaning that if there is a pansy silhouette against the mixed lunaluce lighting, there is a Jelf silhouette against the moonlight skylit. Aye, and yes,

the Jelfantomessence up upon gorge top Phoebely, but not now feebly. No. But we do angle in for a different angle, just in case or cause a white man squatting like a dingo at howl against moonbeam is only an illusion of a smear on the whole human race. But it is he, Jelf, alright. In a dingoform against the full moon which is appropriate, and appropriate for this full time of monthly cycle, both, going djingowise:

'Aaaaaoooo-oooowwwwwwww!'

Yes! This is fact not fantasy. The camera never lieus. And we must say here that from across the star matinee that canopies this yslandia of pastels past and pastels austral and pastels in grace and wonderwine, yes, and from the skating-fold skim't across sumness of all of thine inheritance nestling tremelo as a titling within our scan, came, then, the audio primary on the horizone of your watching answering mind:

'Aoooo-ooooooooooowwwwwww...'

of a real dingo dinkum somewhere fair off, ululator to the great conscious light that Dogod made in image of the One Tiviglow. Thereby mating with our Jelfang, initiant of the great Fangternity of Dogingo, in mating kind. 'Aoooo-oooowww!' again the Jelferine record'd live answers the howl with an animated verisimiltude that even Baden Powell would have been proud of, oh yes; and, too:

'Aooooo-oooooowwww...'

From the lair afar off (fair's far!).

'Aooooo-oooooowwwwww...!'

Echoes oyes yslandia oz by jelf b'jove. The Jelframe in Jesusblithe surrounded by crepuscular light going in inner wonder and

(you scaredy cat humans!)

that was the last time our hero become dog was telescoped or shot at. Very few even scenario'd him for sure. Hereafter and herethere, reports, sometimes flashes, sometimes knock backs from teletelestics came in of a Jelf deepening image. Including etchings off the old block. At Oionawhoopwhoop, he was an Imperial six feet. At Coonagimblegabble, he was shaven foot seven feet. Ametric extreme! At Korangulambeerglugger, he was reported ate foot, eight footed, too. In Muddled, the report of him was too mudgee to be jelfful to anybody. In Nitspickskullduggery (NSW in dungarees) he was scene on local sets nine phft tall by none foot video, and taped. In Whackadidlio he was reported as tentacles high and ten folds in girth. But

one common feature of all these hereafter rapports was that the Jelframe was all alight going so inner wonder that all was mixed up to hear this of the airwaves:

215

through the shade, the everglade
the sun never shines but on my
rock   *ulura ulura*
and no rain but
                        in my nostrils
the sweet smell of damp on a
dusky season

phantomland
the coolibah the mallee the red river gum
the riverlet's in Sturt's blind eyes
the distance in my own
howling
              and
                        dancing in the saltlight atolls
where did i meet the ab-original
in all the kaleidopyro
starspurts
of his fire   shook hands
shookhands shookhands shook oh

my land
lended of
the gauze transluceries
where
              i met my
              black metaman no better
but better off dead

Plus, too, these Jelfurtherutterances of scrip scimped there-
wherever, but now script'd herenigh, both, going:

Yslandia mylanta ystraliaust, yes, i would suage thee as thou hast
insaged me where the gibbet trails where the ochre brews where
the gum gauzes as sad as, where the furnaces of your fernsomes,
where sandstuns of granstones, where the mallee instooms the
hold-on grip'dfast knottworned. Did i transmear did i criss into did
i cross within did i myself over and above. Did i message me

216

suaged of rootcore yslandia Ozepeiros australaurora. My fabeulandia, unrolling from my head in front of the eyescreens of my soul set, there and there, where: i deeped in wintry gulley vintnry'd valley of Loxton of Wentworth of Flinders and Sturt;

where the forests novae'd all the light temmingsenses vague on the rainy season;

where the ore in adze and the iron in awed, auriportunate, there did i ant on the didgeridoo idle of the mechanical meconic, and there did my land Ys throb. Fata Morgana. And did i carry me precious as a land piece humming, a Be;

and the parrots pinkproem'd the riverulets rinn and the roverlads ran and the rainsimpers scorings brawn bruns of the euleaves my lypts did i speak of, all the swirlpools of my eye, all the agitosump of me, all the essextancy of i and;

eyes rolling grown as i come out of the dormacy of my long summer parchment, Yslandia aerated, bubblebuhls of i, a coming wideness.

Ohm.

(pet food --canned Bach)

Then again, almost as siriusly:
when the dog Bachs, you're going to dance a Gallop alright. Like the hiker who had to leave suddenly with the pack on his back. Against that there is the fact that inside each and every one of us is the dog waiting to get out again. Like the top dog that was the Fastest Jaw in the Wrest. Even if you try to run, you just get flee-bitten. No consolation either that a dog with a fine coat will probably fleace you gnattily. For no one is safed; the dog likes to eat its meat a bit on the turn. Even pensioners are hung around by dogs until they give up and become more tender. No wonder they say: dog your heels --they like to keep the prospect just ahead.

On the other hand, two dog coats are quite enough to keep you covered for a little while. Just as old dogs do not dye; they just distemper. But then religious Jews respect their rabies. Like it said on the tombstone, going: 'He Proved To Be A Real Tearaway'. And on another tombstone: 'They Wouldn't Get Off His Back'. Next stone down, too, said going: 'Didn't Even Last Out The Dog Watch'.

Which brings to mind how the dog greeted his human guest at the dinner table, going: how nice to shank your other hand; how nice to meat you; how nice to hold trunk with you; how nice to rumpstake you out; great to have season'd the opportunity to quarter you in my house; you must last out for supper, too.

Still, never mind for
all dogs go man-ic some time or other. Arfter all, the Son of Dogod is puprisen on Day the Third. So watch out Day Jnr. Yes? So look up to the one Dogod; your trials and tribulations are over!

NUMBSK

One month later up pops the question. Who be The Numbsk? We have not met The Numbsk. If you had come across The Numbsk, twould have been a coming across by The Numbsk. Aye. The Numbsk would have no doubt thumped your pumpkin a few powerdrives. Then sunk hess boots in once or twice for the bruising you might have done to his knuckles when he laid you out for it. That's The Numbsk. Numbsk, he ain't bad; he just fucking insane. Numbskie ain't on the loose; he just not locked up. You see The Numbsk in Sydney-town and you'll say to yourself there but for the grace of god go you. Or there but for the disgrace of you go god. Ja. You see, The Numbsk is a fylfot. Fylfot Numbsk, naziest of all the Nazty Party of Australia of Streins. Nfact, stretches beyond a joke does The Numbsk. About fifteen centimetres beyond a joke. Wide, that is. Tall, he must be about twenty centimetres or so beyond a joke, so much so that he has become a national identikat around, in and out of Austreichlia as he goes on his merry insane fucking way punching heads. You got a nana, Numbsk'll punchit, blowit or kickittin for yerr. No focking wurries. If you be a Semite, or a bit of liquorice or shaggy like one who's hairdogged,

(go get hairdogged the morning after)

or like up in front of a U-F-Off demmo or some such anti-patreeotic shin ding, just don't skulk around cause The Numbsk sure to be around, you poor numbskull. For Numbsk is the king Kleiner bonkbouncer of all weakpiss Curlilocks out of woodwork-crawl. Unis Unitarians united c of es shit-heads included. The Numbsk, he no Curlilocks. The Numbsk has his melon shaved like a melon that's lost all its herr. But not bald, like our Jelfount, but bald clean as a pip in a squeak of a stuck pig and busting to boast about it. In other words, to put it baldlybland, The Numbsk throws himself around very Nordic, the nordy boy. Being why they call him The Numbsk (Numbsk, ullo!). Frightenstein, frankly freightening.

(the dog, the monster, the Jackal in Hide)

You should know too that The Numbsk is Der Stormtrooper
Numbsker 1 of Der Party's unit no. sweine and chief scourge of all
unAustralian achtungivities whether they be from out of majority
rights or not. Not for nothing is The Numbsk der blitzkreiger of
der noodle here und der jewsqueal't noodle there across all of
Ozlandof wherever der swines do gather in groups to shout und
rave against der Fatterland's politik. Ja, The Numbsk, more than
der Feuhrer herrself, is off his rocker complexschen; that is why he
so badly wants

to get Alyce. Again. For he has put the boot in upon Alyce three
times already on account of this Alyce has an open public thing
going with some blackcoon who calls her Diva or some zing. Und
she don't noway learn from the bruising of The Numbsk's toe
through his steelycaps, no. So The Numbsk, for this while in the
modern histamine of Ozlandof Nazi politics, feels beholden to turn
his monster back on der major human tides to and froth the
hospitals and devote all his dutiful energs to straightening out this
whitey fraulina Alyce filthwhoredirtybitchcunt who ploughs round
with that black aboliquorice little jerk called 'Enery Heinrich or
Einery, Vitch?

(dog gives live wire a real shock)

Thus it is that the otherwise pokesman of der Die Party has turned
all his attenshun to abo Ridgydidgy Affairs. Being that each time
The Numbsk has copped sight of this Alyce, as he has strolled
along the rampage in the course of his duty scouring der
Ozlandolf of Curlilocks und blackmonkeys and been made to give
her boof an inner view with the steelies of his hobnails just to cap
off their day, both, this Alyce has toppled over in his path where
he, The Numbsk, happens to be shaking a couple of flies off his
hobnails   onto   her   curlies,   going: heil   stones,
bitchwhorecuntboxmolldirtystinkingfilthy-harlotjustlikemother,
bitch of rutten batch. And she tackling pink about it with a curious
trompe bone in her quaver voice going in mascho tonophones,

220

'The Numbsk! The Numbsk! The Numbsk!' And always mit his foot in her mooscha. Holding.

(dog with wet nose; take lab smear)

Even though The Numbsk and Alyce have got this thing going, zieg for zag, we should correct the impression that The Numbsk ain't a genuine political animal. He's human motion put in; and, sure as shit, he's an animal. Besides, The Numbsk isn't as sick as he makes like. He's never had one sickie off work. Because he has never worked in his life. Infact, The Numbsk livers a reich and full life in his tiny little cum-stained room down in der nether region uv der worlygig. Neither is The Numbsk as sadistic as made out. Even when he be called on by his Fatterland to smash der nongs heretherr everybody can see that The Numbsk gets sad before the istic. Arfter all, his homelife did only last for a few months of his heart beat. Ja, tis sad ubst true that The Numbsk, he was oberlieged, ja, to wreck up his own homelifeschen mitt his bare mitts when he became disgusted with all that mural depravity on his bedroom wall, caused by the dirty nacht-time behaviour, spilling over into his innocent ears, of those crooks, Mama and Papa, five times removed. Bang bang.

Like that sheila twatmoll called Alycebitchcuntfucking-whore, legs apart to that blackabo jungle treemonkey while she shitwhorebitchcuntess allows herrself to haf der relationings mitt his, The Numbskie's, steelycaps. Grunt ja und jungle jangle. Dirty filthyscummyallcuntholeshafttunnelhawkfork-tress... Jas himself to think about her.

(Wagger und der Ring of Nibblelunge)

Now The Numbsk endeavours to carry on with his i-witless account of last Saturday afternoon's demmo for to go into print in the forthcoming issue of 'Stormtrooper' official broadside ammo magazine organ d'vice.

(Man, dog's mouthpiece)

Now The Numbskie's composition in der current issue goes likedis herr: 'I saw all these black monkeys, like, jabbering all over where they weren't ought to be grouped outside the zoo. They looked just like a pack of apes and the police. Gosh the police, they were just wonderful. Them wallopers round about trying to keep them black hyenas in their place and getting things like bottles and bricks and things thrown at them and abused. I thought I'd go and help them and got a few hits in and a young copper winked at me and told me to be moving on. I moved on and got a few hits in some other place. One young copper was getting insulted and I went to help him and I got to hitting a few creeps. The coppers told the black poofs and Curlilocks to take off and leave and they wouldn't go, like, and they kept insulting all that is decent about Australia. They said all whites were dirtyfilthyrotten scum and I heard them and I saw one of them doing something with our national flag and I stoved his mug in a bit and then I moved around to the other side of this bunch of monkeys. This Alyce white trash what goes around with a nigger monkey called Henry or something, she was there. And this Alyce dirty harlot saw me and she started yelling 'The Numbsk! The Numbsk! The Numbsk!' like I was after her. She does that every time. I Wonder Why!!! Then she fell down and there were a few blues going on. She was just lying there waiting to be carried off like she was begging me to and I gave her a good kicking. I remember getting my boots all dirty and I had just polished them. I kicked her as hard as I could in the head and things and I believe that white dirtyfilthyharlots should not go round soiling this country and all it stands for with a bunch of black Corns that want to shoot decent Australians and insult all them decent Aussie coppers. I moved back and gave her one in the stomach and then I pinched their flag and then I took off. This little black monkey called Henry took after me and said for me to give back the flag and I said, 'Do you want it then, you poor black monkey runt?' and he said he did and I let him have it across the head. Ha Ha! heil, rain or shine. I remember it jarred the hand I'd just got out of plaster hitting one of those Corns two weeks ago. Then I took off again, but this little black pig and this Alyce I keep having to kick

222

when she gets in my way all the time, they come after me with the police and complained that I'd tried to rape her or something. The police took me down to the station and I managed to get a boot into that dirtywhore named Alyce as I was going. She'll keep. Anyway, down at the station, I swapped names with one of the young coppers down there and he said 'I don't blame you!' and they let me off with a few backhanders and remarks and when I said I'd kicked a dirty harlot white sheila shacking up with a black monkey, they let me go. When I was walking past the window outside and the young copper he leant out of the window and he said that next time I whaled into black monkeys make sure I didn't get caught. Anyway, they know me down at the station and them and I are mates a lot. What I want to say is we all got to clear these black animales off our decent streets before they start having their lusts out on all of us, women and children too. They are getting a lot of them down out of the trees into the streets. And I know where it is starting from a place that is where that Alyce Whatshername lives with that little black monkey called Henry that I took a bite out of the ear of. What I say is we have to deal with the problem right now. Alright, I will. Heil Hitler and cheerio to the Presidente of the United States!'

(fall for the dog, and Cuspid will spear you through the heart)

Now The Numbsk has lowered his public mantle and started with scissors and glue to stick down letters from a newspaper fur to make up a mirky note to Alyce in order to put der feuhrer of God into her, ja.

At same moment, does The Numbsk start in on to bash his meat (*mein hair her hen hen mein her hair her hess mein got*). Biffbashbiff with a coming concentration cramp whilst he sticks up der very messy message (*messcr schsmut*) for that Alyce whoremolldirtyfilthycunt person, to read the new order, reading:

'Boots straps spurs you halort white trash. If you are sceen around with that black monkey again, you will come in for STRICT

ATTENSHUN, You had better no go to tomurrows' dirty black abo demmo OR ELSE. My whip and/or jackboots what I am even now polishing my pod. Yours sincerly, singed THE NUMBSK.'

Now The Numbsk finishes off bashen his meat *heilheilheil*. Ja bers be.

(on tombstone: Spoilt Child Pelted By Too Many Fetching Things)

Now The Numbsk en rooted way to deliver, for bitter for wurst, the warning note personally to Alyce that hangs out with a black rangatang with his hanging out (dirtyslutwhore-cunt oxscrew). But, curiously, The Numbsk is feeling all warm and warthog happy for no natural reason that any medecine maester could findclinikline the matter with him, nein. Nein-theless, The Numbsk feels so human that he is a fairly benign disease right at this memo; even his nonexistent blondefair hairs are beginning to stand upwards towards the glory of Valhalla mitt die joys ov Spring, growing. So much so that he gets further than halfway on this journey across Sydneyside before he skins his knuckles on a passing moosh; and tis more than twothirds of the way before he gets pieces of human earole stuck between his teeth;

(sunk teeth, claimed savage rights on capsized hulk)

and tis more than nine twelfths of the way before he feels the need to wipe new haemo sappyens stains off his fingers; and he is almost at his destination before he has to use his famous Numbskull butt right on a buttin. And not one time did our Numbsk need to abuse anybody personal like, no. For this nacht be a nacht when alder coons commies seem to him to be well and truly in their place. Tonight is this nacht, the nacht before tomorrow. And tomorrow is the day when he, The Numbsk, will hopefully again kick in the beauteous bonker of Alyce Bitchwhorecuntniggerfucktress. But in the meantime this nicht have funnies. Ha ha ho ho; enough drole funnies und what funsk icht wast, too.

(the dog called off; what a waste!)

Unknown to himself, The Numbsk was really affected by the lynching light over that Sydney evening. As he did walk through the rays of ascending crisplumen. The lux light that aeriaurioles the auster ocean there, that dwells in jewell beside the cityside known as Sydney. Shimping the waters of that purlent harbourmath, twinning embroidance of silver threads, guilden gushes, toccatina tittup tittup of the lappswish lappswoon, now ensuft insoft hushvibes stullswornly ssh. For this is the Sydney of the nightingale swong. This esse be Sydney of the breastheard. Where gulls gullop unto the seabird estuasanctua calling thee *here-it here-it here-it* below the their-besoaring now. Thy Sydsent, thy swainswept, thy hope-hept, thy sweetessence of trustrance, thou hast held crushed to thy bosom, crushed precious enprayed. Thy Sydney dying this soirsong, this e'entithe, this purple rond, this risen sadown, rimmed by thine pacifix sea.

Not a heave heave'd heaveninvented across the rotula above thee, wherest will flow all this night the universes odic to come incanto and descent unto you. Oh, for Sydney now is encreped in the twirls of its sea within the curlicles of seaspray, avis avifauna, within the cups of overflow and neap and gantry tang tango tangibit herethere with brindle and brine and saltish svelte. Twill trilluna trance, tri lastern lattern-glance, chrism cloth and child... this is twilaureate, this is the lorimerate, this is the lucarneous nacre that sworn unto thee, mer of Sydney. Evehummed eveswish't evephosphor'd upsuaded unto thee of Sydney. This be thy praedial proudly given unto thee by our pater-Patina. His loriot, whenst you all, in maunderstance, do gleen it twilight twilook twilent in thy Lipsburie pinfold. This is Sydney penfold all stop't. Thou all rosemarined.

(mon cur blesse)

Meanwhile, back at the wrench of Henry's basement:

The Numbsk's euphoria ceases such neinsense before it seeds itself seedy. As he stands before the abodoor of Henry towit hence came he, The Numbsk. And garners up his lionlike loins for to be the full manly Numbsk again, scourge of all yidcooncom and etcets of Sydney town. The beauty of Sydney-cidal at its dusktidal has inspired the artist in The Numbsk so that he aitches in's bones to put the bootiful beaut in again with the delicatessence picadillo of a fine pocket dill, which he is, for the correction of the bitchwhoreharlotnigger facke-doutcunt Alyce. Who needs all his, The Numbsk's, attenshun.

He reads, slowly but surely, the signrot thing on der door derr, which goes: 'ABO-RINAL ACTION GROPE. Come in. Piss in our pockets.'

Decadent heehaws too, no doubt. It brings a lump to the throat of The Numbsk to think of inner reidings on the wall inside, graf and titter. Anyway The Numbsk, he pauses to lurch around with his fizzy fritzle orangeaids drinking in the seen around in case of traps for boobies. But only the finely tuned vehicle of plumbing pipes' gurgles are sent back to try him. Hee hee, he goes, ist going to be kiddiekliner stuff, ist icht. Und so he, The Numbsk

(dog not funny, send you into stitches)

takes the rap. Rap-rap, acht Numbsk, yer own rapscallion and rapacious T'Nsk! Yer little RIPper! And sounding like Frankenstein knocking at the castle creaker. Which is precisely what Henry, relishing right then the left tittyvat of his Diva's Alycecrypt for to gain strength from her for tomorrow's demmo, thinks it is. Making him even hiccup. Struth! nozzle to nipple both nearly nibbled!

Rapraprap yerr rats! go those giantose mugmiffers of The Numbsk as polite as he can, for a coon's home is his concentration cramp, ja.

(the bitch riding high on a heat wave)

226

Henry opens the padblockade. Whereupon The Numbsk introduces himself by grindesbung a few hits into Henry's smackeroo, then measuring him for a gouge after applying his admirably-executing kreiger klunk klinker klang blitz upon the black monkey toppo krinkly. And whilst all this is going on, Alyce, abed, is a badly bent and corner-hutched woman screaming, 'The Numbsk! The Numbsk! The Numbsk!' As if Henry didn't know. Now that The Numbsk is executely effecting his celebrated Ball-Tearer with a finely fraught double pirouette in time with a certain Wagnerian air of the true artist at it. Right before Henry's own eye, can he believe it. Followed by that virtuosity of a coupe de grass, his V2 Klinderklundergozzungck with der hobnails, spat on and polished and applied to the prostrate glade of the coon Henry's neck. Just to stretch it all out a bit by way of saying tis he, The Numbsk, just paying a little flying visit. 'Ullo.

(dog trot; dog must have a man's confidence)

As his host Henry slides down the wall, The Numbsk now extracts his note for der Alyce whorebitchsuckcockslut who is still in high scale cantissimo, going, 'The Numbsk! The Numbsk! The Numbsk!' and. Making even The Numbsk feel a bit embarrassed. True. So much so that he blushes demure before sticking his message for her onto the collar of collar'd Henry. Almost, too, spieling all his pant milk, going to her:

'Yerr orta be ashamed of yerrself, yerrort.' Then swings sway and away. He does, The Numbsk. Thunders across the suspended bridge of Henry, bombed out, towards the clear light of temptless day, shouting back over his Rightist shoulder an addendum, going: 'Yerr orta be ashamed of yer pudendum muliebre!' or something of the sort. The man has schnapped'd in two, must have. For not eince has his orangeaids been swung onto the madscreaming Alyce, just as though he has been too shy to look her in the dentable.

Ja, ohm Jaohm, Jaw hole.

(savage dog to make you go all to pieces)

Now The Numbsk, on that same night, is pacing in a crisp pace updown therrback, jackbootiful on the heil-clicking of the walnut floor of der Sydney Town Hall at der annual meetings ov der Nazinationalist Party ov Austraylia. Yes, streich a light, it is the infant corps! There being preshunt there fifty-two reactive members of der Party, meaning that there was a fool turnout of little feuhrers present or prior sent off their heads. Plus one or two others who would also like to feuhrer mein gott. Mind haven't got. And,

all standing uprigid, even The Numbsk, for the appearance on stage to the marshalled bands of the LP world of the Commander, the bigot feuhrer of them all.

(the dog is a feuhry animal)

Nfact the most rigiddigid of them all is The Numbsk. He so click his heels that he, The Numbsk, sounds like the Kraut in the pantomime called 'Sauerpuss in Boots'. Now The Numbsk fronts his hooter up upon the plateform to platelay it on straightline to the Nation As A Jawhole and to his Komrades with arms pulling their legs, each and every one admiring bloody subordonors of The Numbsk. And what he was meant to say was:

'If you've read Mein Kampf and fed up with the rat race, if you like the feel of boots, if you're alone and bashed around in a city of million, become a stormtrooper!...'

Or so it went on paper, given a bad spelling here or there, even as it was written phonetically. But for the mushmoosh of The Numbsk it went ratroaring around the echo chambers of the Town Hall, modulating itself so myriadly it finally demodulated itself by itself to become perfectly clear, as: 'If yerr mind's camp and fido on the ratfaces, if yerr like the boot-ins, bashing millions around on yerr lone.'

228

But that was all The Numbsk got out before his Numskill'd orangeaids fizzed onto a human thing silted at the rear of the Val Halla there. He stoppered short. He did. The Dumb, stukkered numbsk, yes, at what or whom he wast seeingschen. Managing only to stammer with hisjabberwoked digit pumping towards the lone figure back there and to gulp up a gloopy guttural of die mensions teutonic:

'Jjjjew. *That*!' In danger, now, of choking. He, the figure, and The Numbsk, the finger, both. Plus three Special Branch detectives and two Jewry undercovet agents cringing. But not for them.

This time his, The Numbsk's, message is quite cleartoned upon the pathetically ragged little figure straight out of the Patriarch's Sartorial Handbook who sits beadle-eyed at the terminal terminus of The Numbsk's digitpointer to a thousand items of jewmerchandt eyes. It is, going, vot is that degen rat doing being allowed loose in here, ein swine Who was snoring while he, The Numbsk, spat speaking getting narco'd ras-berries blown at him, bye gott. From behind that huge red beard so chin hung that its

(dog with wet nose, needs wiping out)

hairs down in long plaited reams of biblical prop portions. A wierdoe's beard to end all baddies' beards, indeed. A bear'd to bug you. An auberginous curtaincloth embroidered with entassled strands that resemble rope ladders. Each enough festooned with lianas that in there might be carried Tarzan's last call. Faintly swinging, and. Of such overgrown luxuri-furriance compared to that windswept scalp on which nothing grows anymore that, if it is not Moses himself, it is not Moses. Yet some Mosaic! A man, this, obviously

returned from pilgrimage, step by step, mind over body, stag by ger, having soulsearched and now in somesuch like it. In robe in beard in goggles tacky with stickytape in. Essence of. Jelf. Aye, Jelf. Yemember rejelf? Having returned from the Nulla-Nulla broke and bleeding yet oozing prophets even as his snores are heard to be fit. Having sheltered in there for a little kip before the final stage of his journey. The Jelfoliage jelfollicumulate jelfungus jelforest jelfleabed father-figure, now, latterdei Wildman of Borneo to be Free.

Whom The Numbsk, though, is now thinking to be some Richard the Zionhearted trying to make him even more parannoyed. Yes, and The Numbsk bells like the bullow he is. He does. At which our nascent Jelfasleep and Jelfthinkings had come to wakeup quixsmart and are immediately trying to slither himself and his rags, which?, silentandissimo out through the side exit. With The Numbsk splintering the eaglectern with his naked but angryred meathammer be-feuhriously before letting himself loose after the Jelfpreciousness. Und like all gudde sturm troupers, der other swatzkiddies luftewaft out after The Numbsk after the poor prophet Jelfigure fleeing. To the side alley there.

(were wolf, there dog)

Now The Numbsk, giantian within the ripplent unifolds of his browniform swatzstickered and all, is outside in the sidetrack of the Sydney Town Hall and, in the murk'd light there, he, The Numbsk, is heil hitlering with one arm jolting upright ramrod straight at the end of which is the Jelfegg shining twirplight with feet off the ground. By a metre or so, at least, above hop hope. Neither, at this particular moment, is this a great relief for his torn, bloody and naked feet which began to come about after he had lost his sole in a Centralian mission chapel. More concerned about his life right now.

The Numbsk grrrrin fit to grind on the Jelfnerve cystem on account that he, The Numbsk, has got hold of realive Jew Elder caught with his eider down. Overdue too. At long last, now The Numbsk can really turn Nazi, heh heh.

(hold on; the beast is yet to come)

Yet something stays The Numbsk's hand from turning to vice. Perhaps it was the cheering audience of the other storptroomers, Grimmslike shadowlikes splashed against the walls around them with swatztikas. Or The Numbsk's sporting of the spoorting stinctk. No matter now, for

The Numbsk suddenly begins to quire questions that will either bone or fido this jewgreasymug. I.e., mortal twist or ironical? Listen to the spraken of the doubledeutsch, do, going:

(Old Tellah got jaundiced over fast-running yellow streak)

Oh, The Numbsk jars and the Jelf jas back nodding and knowing.

On violence, Jelf goes ja, und:
viols strain vibrous waves and nirvana tensions. Out where Aust strum't its stromb to your ear twas there a fathingale in emit emulsions within my earsight. Did i hear and almost die; yea yet a honey hum eater did entuned my head to waterupts waterows watercrestings waterflows and thenst did i altar my breast fed. Violence, no, but yes Oh yes O too much yearning to sing unto death.

Of nationalia, Jelflauts ja und:
i amst all gone went and arrivuletted now amst enback again. But once, by heliosot besought, did i seeped ontothe blastograss green as fern warm and firm inlaid where i looked by pineal over the coolgladed wateredge to stare at humantide upcoming and downswarding. Tithe. What did i eye? It said: look gobbulanting man up man pup manning round the episcopallyptic world; it said unto me: rise rousten rise rem-bulent rise uprident strident and rise. Yea, for the swelch vive the swelch via the fluviatile reas you waiting, why? Nationalism, all hail brim. Stone first thrown.

Of civilization, Jelfoxed ja ja noodle noddit, und:
This one sapling did i see in ysalline yslandia. Did they wine it yes did they lakelet it yes did they tricklet it yes did they rigate rivulet it yes did they serein it yes did they dibblescade it yes did they infuss exfuse intraflow extratend vine cultivine ululavine

231

vineleave it yes did they tears of christ it yes did they chrisma-chant over it yes did they call it on yes did they swan for it yes did they swoonrond for it yes did they threnurge on it yes did they drippfeed it yes did they philofern on it yes did they sophisoftly over it yes did they doxovox for it yes did they hymnascent for it yes did they linguaqua on it yes did they lavalavish their aspires on it yes did they dote epidotals annexedotals their ainedotes their innurectomies icing splodge it yes their langurruages yes their dead langrudges yes their yes languettes roseatted yes on it

did they call it, the sampling, civilization. Yes and crystals christotears fauceta leaves yes bellbirds at its feetree its lapwings its waders at its given pool yes. Water libation, water lobestrobes, water lifeformance, water grapesvined, water in bottloids, water as botryroses yes but. But this did i see yes it the yewtree it the yangylangylangtree it the eutree it the scentfilled tree it the lifeofolliaged it the yslaked tree it the little lemongum little lemoon resinrose tree it did not rise up no did not blossome blue flows any blosflum flowerblues any warmlight warmlapping warmluxured warmyslandia flowerets flowing no but did i see despite how they did hove their haveance to it it bruin'd and drydying and storporended little lemoon scented little it scentred at; all paravailled for nothing did this i see

from across the track truck grooves rivulanding road running liquiddities across this yslandia distillands. Pity or piety? Yes.

Of the Enemy the jews the boongs the chocolate frogs the coloured apes the yellow hordes the corns the coons the bolshies the wogs scum vermin people people the etcets, Jelflannels ja, und:
of augury, yes, augury day and nightienycht, i am the i-am-of. Of soulace solsaved solesalvaged; of divines of divintners and port and negus; of orfree freedrumming of gladsmancy and joymachy in the great marquee of all the people, thence there-are-we; of nekton of planktowns of fish wish of flushcords of the seabreeze of winterkelps; of all the bios'd of all the life-tide, of all the exzootic and allto gathered gether; of innexus of apoplexus of the pyroselexus. i am the Spanish flywn i am cantaflush canthar ideas, i am the colorfluorescence of reign-bows. Sir, i am ROY G. BIV.

Of faith, felfencedja, und:
none enuncio; mayst i gleet unto the erratica lapwing? Shrined
blueswage corded sergeways they ply of the spinet spun black
lanalamb, evenso i have stammer'd havenso that they stammell'd
hocks and hanks. But i am The Dreaming i am bolden ingrace i am
enjoyed with sumness summit emissions from the rock at Ayers,
aye.

Of The New Day Coming, Jelfluvialt ja, und:
supernova novae nous and drenchange for to comet transva the
skyreen, yes, there itwere the Magus Pragma of my Milky Way
via lactea tactically speaking; my luminal liftupping there; my
planetotal pleni-all coruscated pointescintillate being. And the
moon lunnapted so newly and brog eyed that i'd crescento there.
Of The Day the phenoday the showntime the ploughshared
starwinnows in our minds, all, wherce stoletoed did i refill
refulgent and novae'd over the omega top of the prime night of
That New Day Coming, the firstiary primer of i am. Zen ith'd.

Of The Cause, Jelforcedja, und:
on every back it was. Where i went wast waste. Whatwas it thusby
i know not. But extra-ooned, they all seemed in larvae and roe life
and sploding tryouts beCause of it. Yes. Causes of myrrh and
mirendurance during daydrop dawnflence nightset mightnoon
midnadir middaired pmam mamp It the Cause, always evolvting.
Equiquatic aquaquixotic epeirote land where i was and saw and
rare'd back. Rote on rote on rotatory on right aright on legs that
flew that ran that leaplept that scritscratched that beggarburrowed
that plead fledged that cryptcrawled that spun in spinningspun that
livedife because of it. Breathed ate lived loved longshort-mediloci
nomen men fenomen masculated minisculed slimmed and
enslimed. All entities omnoses hologryphs totallytes
alphagametes, all allways in ode to it and. It was the cause of their
ways of manyman; vitae of lifelobs; vias oionslobes; thoughts in
plurapaths, vitae and via viaducted, sir. The Cause and whey, aye.
So much for.

Of Race, Jelforthed a ja, und:

233

Of the baramundi errata deus and python, yes, and enshore the epanospawned did i episeeit did i oerwing it did i stand and watch't henceforthards when did the Omnius ensurf, mocked and turpterned and gullibelled and crustcraveaceous. Meaning the turtles.

The turtles, sir,

themockedturtle theturnturtle theturtledishimmer the turtle droved dived dovedowned and the turtlediva and the turtle epopee and, sir. The turtle youngflaunts the turtle babymergs the yontherings the infantails, they scrabbed they screeled they entirailled boundared by the seasyght, enbloodied by the seizeside, imbondaged by the seaslantseascape, murdered by the see thousillions the seen oons by the sawed nature striped and bare in thread and torned by their blood squealspiralling, yes. Natures seeways and byways and butchereverence. Saw i eyesoabsorbed, sir. Oh sir, a sorry actino to see and ah. Sir, invie'd theretime was a Race indeed to re-mer themselves and no races shone with gods good grade as they did't.

Of the Feuhrer, Jelfalsely to ja, und:
heard tell of one or two, wherever dry bones parchmented with my yslandia Oz. Aye thine Yslandia on those enbaked-days when Zephyr and Favonius and Aeolus rend out of the cave on biers of hot dustcoals; a fly time; a drydam day of the north whined whirl; the dust euchre. And, sir, roundon those dayust bowls therewent not a bowerbird from's dustbowl and all the sangly singing is sup'd up to drygrain secdrained and pithedout; they dudhanged their heads. All and any thingone alive. Without will unto that dyinglad day, all withering fewer and fewer. Land piccolo'd to by some feuhrer selfmade for to follow the hard dayless soul of the thenandthere. Yet snuzzle into pasteur like a doeroo that kangacame and whenst did the perichange come again it lifcbreathed the dynamoes of eachandevery. Feuhrer? Ja, feuhrer follow him now than lastime, sir.

Of Democracy, Jelflowed. jas, und:

234

a craven idol did i see overall, sir. Prowed and spired and rammst enspired, all alumalloyed all colours of the chromed cromlech chromosomes some that wilst zoon some that wilst not zoom; spickspanned across the maternial yslandia on zroomm and throttles and plastoblasts moulded and unmournedfor. Power, sir, in puffled muffs pulpit tufts proselyte toughs demo doings and demon dungings and demodic demosthenes hermesset for to brighten up the glintertinselbriums of the all acrylic acalledfors, acriedfor To-Haves. Power, sir, in sporan mouths and woollen glooves and beefy powerpresses corruscant grooved with stereotweetdual-quadrophonemevisivisedaudiants, with crayons of the potbow and glitglower radio irradescent irrevox and boxrocaded boidered anbowed. Demotion, sir, of the noos-oons-ens-urs-eco-oes-etios-sols-es-is-ontos-idios-autospheres incepted, excerpts of quoted dialective analectuals and papphorisms of the advertising men, those myrmecoids of inventitruths infravoted. Tallismen, sir, armubandits, sir, armbandulets, sir, politicians, sir, parasuiters, sir, misters errmania, sir, chromed and shiningonnew'd and pinnedpon, sir, telestic elastoplasts sir. The policlerics, sir, of all mencould. Democracy? Oh, sir, the power breaks!

Of Dirty Dogs All'n Every, Jelfenced with ja jaja, und:
dogs without wonder, dogs without mysteriums in their compostures, dogswithout doubtquakes, dogs without quailtraces at all, dogs without fresh orbs, dogs without new thorned thoughts, dogs without querrule, dogs without evolvus, dogs unevolvafluxing. Dogs the-Alrightios, jack, yesyesyesyesyesyes threshing in packs of enpicked negawonder into the pack level mean moiety of.
dogs packs of dogs
without a quod damn
without idionecessities.

Dogs of group delicatessence. Dogs without questhummings. Dogs without a quidwhatessence. Dogs without an altered word friable paragraphical; dogs with their altared word-applies; dogs without querests; dogs without questeemings; dogs without new sightings new soulings newances nu no question about it.

Dogs without question and dogs everywere and way, *x* and *n* numberoses of dogs dogs in wateruns dogs in gutterushes dogs in reedbeds dogs in claver-hutches dogs in hayshines dogs in sunroofs dogs on beachuntings dogs in rayinishings dogs in dekko magazines dogs in funish-ments dogs in flannelations dogs in silkniceties dogs in mod-gearalls dogs in fact dogs in fickeriction dogs in royal prawns dogs in pastels dogs in merino dogs in the seadogs in the mer dogs in the merde bushwacked motorcaded putdown pittance and muttuels. Dogs high and dogs low and everywhere *No Men Allowed, We Are Not Dogs Yet.* And ja

men allover
as negroman dogs whitest as jews as dogs as doggish as savage as dogs as bloodaenemies as inter sameas likeas similaras asthelike asthesame asvery simul to, as hard to individe a dividual amongst, yes;

all men dogs animal dogs higher animalower men lesser dog greater or lesser grated; spotted manity and indognity sanewise difficult difficult difficult to tell apart. Very isn't it jarring dirty dogs, ja, jamming, All.

Of Women, Jelforms a ja, und:
epigene and paraclete and rhizogyne rosewined and buzzingly fed to supplice, i didst trope to see her gyning scross this yslandia. Freewild wheeledfree with her sunburnt bronzekiss introfolded rendoarms shrimped and her hairess easyeyes for all her emcumbeauty devined to thee; fluent in heritance to be here bemine. Of women, sir, didst eve drop from a botticelli, a particle of pastel of all the skies i enthrapped mine bodyce in; of all sibilsybes didst i soundunto, she hushered me to sigileep weeping for mine allman entwined; of all the iso-eyes didst i spree, she drew the percussives of immanent gloryheight shortlasting be but glaggladglad bittersweet she was; of all the tiptouches didst i run my cale fingers over, twas she who instrokt'd me with perseity quickling tit quiver-alive, with the rapepidity of Lifeunto, with touch and stive, with the me-she-we weanity. I am weened, Sir, of women, for that i didst cryall her Woman, didst she cry stall me Man.

Her Name Quickquick, Jelforestalled ja, und:
her name is spunlight silk like all the weftsoft flamingoes
enwreathened within the rose fructoseary of your deemest mating
callover callavish callife callaudamus calibean ventlates.

Her name!

Jezerel jezebel, she doth sing for the piccaninny, she doth regale
for the mardiman the maddened me the middenmantle the caliban
the hebe-man the laughloved the loftedlove the lovelaughing.

Her name!!

Jezerel jezabel zoe-on zoe-ne zoe-sounds be all and everyion of a
zwitter, she, yours, his, thine, theirs omnimine omnimien
omniman's.

Mine? Does she flugle around with her roundelling fanny?!

She doth rosulate in petalbloom; she doth heliote in ver millions;
she is the wandering dew the manna the torrentes-sential the
plumbline the harbourheap't; she is the wreckers the junkyardage
the solelorn the cutgrass the sheeply nibble nightly shribbled; she
is thmine sentientence to life thmine spurton thmine emotorary.

Does she knock?!

Betweezen't of her legs, she hath the androcrib and the
sarcophargus, the cradle and the tower of eternmental silence, the
priapism and the prison, the one track and the retract, the
insulmath after; where she ist thoust be manchild, where she
filialates not, thou art manchurl.

Her name!!!

Her name manent from wonder yslandia; her name emanant all
suck and succour; her name heraldemania from canticled yslandias
of Oz of fez of fuzz of fair of fir of Ur and Ut and Usa; her name
napes Misslainyies of Accyl Acyle Lycea Ylace Caely Ceyla

237

Lycea misses slains swainswans all etceteraes settle-eyed, or perhaps Lacey or Layce or Yacle or Yclea or Calye or Cayle or Aecly or...

Her real name!!!!

her emane is Alyce. Sir.

(the dog Patch gives you the eye)

When the zound of that name had mainsay gained on him, The Numbsk went so weakened at the noch knees that he threatened to go all broken up at the kneading. Of Jelf's larynglottis between his, The Numbsk's, thirdigit and lidigittle of his Extreme Right hand. One would have to have been fucking insane to try to Pasiphae this mental bull, so Jelf did but a bunk very bloody bunderstaghorn out of It and performed a zippy exodus out of the o deus reach of the ex-odius, ja. While all der little nazis there were occupied in going one-twothree heilp him, The Numbsk, up. From his knee trembler.

(man of refined taste doesn't dishonour his dog at the table)

At the same time a little earlier:
Henry is trying to up himself and plant his feet on the floor there rather than wall here. Difficult enough, though, to stopper up his bungole from another bemoaning. Going, oh what hitler me?

All he can remember is The Numbsk's feet, thousands of feet up in the air, having a thundering good time. Fuck that. Before the bombhead started to drop a leaflet. That flapped once from his, Henry's, collar but not now. He does know, however, that he has been heaped where it is very silly to have been heaped and that is on your own doorstep. The only way one could get over that is to step over yourself which isn't very convincing even to a casual

238

observer. Either. Or to Diva. Diva? Diva Diva wherefore art thou, rident rigagigalow'd Diva? Oh, what a rusk we took taking on That Big Baby Numbskull'd, eheheheh?

(mummy dog rocking baby tooth and fro, towards froth)

But his Alyceodiva is well within as she might be pushing up against the far corner so as to force her way out. Still, and. In the same crumbled position upon their scrumbling bed, palpably palpitating and quail'd. She, yes, Diva, a little bird now slowly emerging out of its shell with all the shock of what it has had to see within that selfsame shell, going twitwit: 'TheNumbsk TheNumbsk   TheNumbskTheNum-numb-numbsk...'   Flying sounds; with

one of her dukes absently picking at her Alyce cunny and the other lives limply holding The Numbsk's note against her left tit, a little to the left of her heart and quite a way down from her lumped throat, which? She doesn't even centipede an eyeball Henry's way when he crawls up to her from a height of two centimetres above the groundswelling, where, against the bed, he levels himself rightside if not brightsoapyside up, foaming and rubbery, until

(dashed, bad luck)

his reds are eye-to-eye with her crazed pinkies. Diva? in husky, husks of their former selves, both. And, weeping for what he is seeing in her id-wretched greens, he manages something in indirect speech, going: Alyce his oleaster his own whiteruption his Diva his Alyce his miserere his holy gust his sucknoll his napsack his moollen will his blackwhiteyellow-tawncolouredalbinosioso melange. His. Diva! What?! Wrong? Spurt thee, punctured holed-out unstuck untackied unad-herr'd? Diva, talk, for tomorrow we got organized our own demmo upon the rotten white streets. You remember? Diva, a note, that theriomemo from that theomaniac Numbsk, The, not going to blow that up, surely. I am bleeding but i can bleed some more. He can, can Henry. His jaw in set, his bust in plaster or bust, yes.

239

Slugly, Alyce reptiles a recall to the noosday sum, until her retinals are mooring once more on Henryside, until her spirit is right in wordingwright:

'Of course we're gunna have our bash tomorrah!'

'Diva!'

'Yes.'

'Diva...?'

'Yes, all right; suckseed thee now, rego...' reopening her legs for him. Lay egg.

(you lip-smack the dog if you're so desirous)

Then again getting even more sirius:
a lapdog is the one that drains up the last of you. Beware of walks, too; the dog runs on to use his ahead. Then again: sheepish dog turned wolfish. On the other hand: a wolf whistle, a howling success. Like the young adult male dog savouring the first taste of his man hood. As the coffin is to us so the meat safe is to the dog. Which can be blamed against dog trials --too many judges and not enough jury. Where, once, at the opening ceremony, a bloodthirsty dog that sang hym froidly. Then again: dogs lap it hole up. They do. You can be sure that a dreadful fate dogs our heels. Yes, and that the cunning dog is waiting for you at home. Like the city dog doesn't like country hies. Or the lazy sheepdog that prefers to wait for its master's last roundup. Like the killer dog that stretches good men's tenderness to the breaking point, then goes beyond a joke. Even walking along a public street is becoming a bitch of a thing to do. Then again: first prise dog, wouldn't prise open. So second prise dog got Jemmy. Then again: third prise dog left the left over. Fourth prise dog left behind. Fifth prise dog wasn't in the runny. Like it said on the tombstone: Called A Halt But Wasn't

Obeyed. So prepare thyself; for it is recorded that the Dog finally overruns Man. And

through all, remember to splay to the Son of Dogod. For the Son of Dogod is canined off the cushy. *Ohm.*

MAGGIE

Our homo sapiens is rising again and the Jelfsap now enters encore (encore, encore!), but not, no, on the sly breeze. Balded as before, even extra on the boot, he is so unwashed that, even as a marshmellow of a mashed fellow, he now pongates on and in the nose, both. But nothermind, for our Jelfriend is our Jelfothingale and the man is our man, he and himself, yes.

We thus do thrust contempt at the street kerbing (and bent) constable who, on the Jelf way between The Numbsk's hammermilling and the Jelfhome, into which our Jelflint-hearted be now entering, attempted to take out Jelfjesu in on a charged-upped trump for exposing skin up top. True! But then someone like that, constable or no, is quirk enough to be quirk simply beneath our Venetians. Godsbods!, our Jelfinite may be indecently bald, but he is nowaywise balderdash nor flesh flasher, nononot. No matter how badly he needs a laver up, the soppy.

(starving dog seeks well-heeled man)

Swishing en aura in en trance Jelf sucks in great wafts of that badly needed and badly kneaded air there. Which need arises out of his o'erlivedlong fatigue and also out of his being so gland to be back chaise lui without too much of a chase; his clodhoppers all bleediness and reddytawny like as if they have only been nailed below him to stop his bleedingorey legs from fraying at the ankles, aye; and clothes tittatterswinging from this Jelfleckinetic that they seem to be near being quite put off by his body. What they could be, of course, is ultra-ragmodgear for mad moguls. They aren't. Not in the plural sense. Scents perhaps. And, too, that beard is now better seen as

(the uppercrust dog collects Old Masters)

so crinose in its crinky that it could easily strand up on its own as an article of clotting, yeayea. But then, affected though he mite be with cakes of everything but soap, there is that same particular inner light verily varilighting him up inside on the stairs there.

242

And it is noway the usual flair from his lenspecs, but something arising out of his new eyes newborn'd on new sightings now returned to roost. Even his hunked back is now no more than a lump in back of his throat. Somewhere. 'Smiracalled; all stops, out!

(pack working on a hunch)

However, as a sirius intermission and while Jelf climbs his stairs, a few brickblocks away uptown, some Happyas Larry nearly stepped into the centre of the intersection and proceeded onpast all discretion by driving seven sevinch nails into his now-sievedhead with a fourpound blacksmythie's hammer. Which wasn't quite enough to turn the trafficking into a bottle of nerveneck, but did in fact get in the right-of-way of one baker van backing in advance. Driver of whichvan got so uptight screwydriven, especially when Happyas Larry bloody-well poked out his bloody tongue at him, that he did his loaf and immediately fell into blows with the mashed and mess'd potatoes that was exHappyas L's head. Causing a newfledgeling copper, who was coming around the coin to see what was the musher here, to throw up his arms in surprise which. Went off for a couple of rounds, capping it all. And putting a bullet right through the major part of a Seventh Day Adventist whose seventh day advented quicksmart because, being one of Nature's obedient childs, she did hapfully choke back on her own nausea on account of her mummsy once saying for her to keep her bleeding moosh shut at all times. Strue. And her colleagues, ever true to The Goal, immediately garnered up tickets for the Act of God Appeal for those many willing to pay for a squiz at her having been squeezed out.

(doggone, grief!)

Now at that present time, too, one or two strange things did up and happen: one was that all tarnal, infernal, carnal laughter from all those who paid their admissions to see her threw a nearby rooftop sniper into a jealous rage of not getting his proper attention and so

243

he shrugged and got on with telescoopingly doing his rounds (work, work, work; pick off there, pick up here). Another thing was that

the bakervan driver, now gorn beserk, anvilled the hammer so well upon the sevinchnailed-corpsing-out that an errant union official awarded him his Mastersmithies certificate there'n'then over his dead body (the sevinch nailed man). Who wasn't dead anyway, yet?

The third strangessence was worst in that the novice copper proved noviscained and was now yelling 'Blue murder' and thereby blew the lid off of police brutalities (a lot of bruit over such small bruises). He did. And the

(pregnant lady thought to have dog biscuit in the oven)

fourth occurence manifested itself in the form of a coming past Ambulance onto the scene which kept coming and coming and coming because its brakes had just rather failed badly as physical entities, until it became an amblurr, and nothing more, that lanced on the largest section of the maiding crowd onlooking over their lollies. All toll'd a lot of lolling, too.

And the only survivors of all in that vicinage was one man who walked into the Routpatients Department of the General Horsepittle one hour latter to have seven nailholes in's head plugged up, and one newly-mad, nuely-made Master Blacksmith seen hammerdriving off in a bakersvan in a puff of smirk. All true, too.

(Tombstone cut: Past Master Dog Mastered)

Still our Jelf flights himself up the dragging stairs and still so bedraggled that he looks like a tapestry trying to turn itself into a higher art form. If at all possible. Unkemp'd, feeling ropey, he could be Lear, too. And inexorably moving up towards Che, our bushwacking Mexican chihuahua waiting on the topflight to dogflight itself onto its long-missed pushover who is, thank Dogod, deigning an appearance to put in once more. Little saliving grrs, waifing in wait. And all sorts of chilly con carnals going through its mexmutt mind when the Jelfessence

(dog takes two leaps for Joy)

viaz con dogios into its furyfur'd view. And just when Che was beginning to let loose one of those chiheehaw grins like all dogs do at an impending leap snarl tear, accompanied by a fang fare well worth the moneysworth, then, lohold and be!, it hangs its tail, hinges up its head, hodges its podge and commences to whimper sonata. It does! Not leaping but lipping, not snarling but snazzing up, not tearing but in tears. And, miracles of all mirrorculleds, blow us if the Jel-francisassissi doesn't actually handle the mutt with his bare hagiohands! Yes! Knuckles, fingertips and all, seeming not to care about the fact that: if ye one dog pat, tis enough to give thyself a stroke, aye.

(Tombstone chiselled: Throed On The Dog Heap)

During the exact moontime the same as that, an ophiologist unknown to us, unless you know an ophiologist who is a smart arse on fat snakes, came helter sweltering in out of the craggy midsummer sun away Outback, and sat he down on a scrunt petrockified boulder of some peculiar lithomorphic structure resembling a screwed-up homunculus. He does so weary in body and with his thought for today, which goes something like that here he is

(out of puff, short on dogdays)

so waybackout wackedabout that if by some remote chance he does come across a snake specimen doing snakey sneakings out here, then he will have to analyse its mind and not its morph. Such a creepy slimey would need a couch not a lab. bench. It would command a full page of 'Lancet' medical journal as the Marco Polo of the snakes' world.

(Scratched on a tombstone: A Cross Over'd)

What we are trying to say is that this be so far inland even a bushfire would go to blazes. And hot?! Ophiolly hot, actually. So our snake man opens his packed lunch of saltablets on the ageless stone on which he is sitting and is just about to add condiments when he espies that the stoneystool has a v. peculiar smellodorious and rugous scale of a tail on a time scale unknown to man. Going, as his heart thumps with excitement, oo, oons, an original unoosal zoon perhaps oorinat-ing! He makes a rumbustical grab for this rarething and heaves. Causing the whole rock to collapse into a state resembling some poor jerrybuilt geriatric. Which it is since it is

(a little nibble just to tetanus you out first)

Amos. Yes, again! At the height of a new low in health, and heatstruck, that he is now only a ophidilogical mistake for a slatherishsnakey Marco Polo reduced to a slither, even though his appearance is enough to ruin the reptiliation of asps in general. And all the old boy can odd gob out is:

'Bbbbbbbbbbbblllllllllllllllooooo...' Stoppered right there. A bit steep!

(next door is tombston'd: Victim of Double Cross, Not Half!)

Roundabout the same murmur of the old bamboo spring we are backwith Jelfrancisassissi afront of his door at the end of his pilgrim (but still pilus grim), having endured throughout the whole breath of Ozyslandia the hickways and bierways and wendways and weighouts and weirdins and waylaids and laidbyes and onceways and newfrees and rendroads and randyroadsters and parkdrives and forrestthrus and coastalongs and countrylearners

246

and bushlanes and bushwracks and mountrains and highplanes and lowliars and valleyways and crosscuts and throughroughs and cutruts and tyretroughs and blacktracks and peterouts and sandstonkers and limewashes and riverforges and tablelandforks and hinterlandintersections and coolsacks and walkswelters and shoeshrinkers and sea-loffs and sealsonrocks and trudgeridges and swaglights and swagheavies and semitrails and lorryleadoffs and parkingbays and ribbonruneast and ribbonrunwest and nostoppings and motormacadams and caravances and caravines and cargo-holdups and traffickerbs and drivercurbs and skidrows and cattleroutes and expressways and onandonandons and tramlines and railroads and networks and menatworks and die-directions and bushwalks and hitchikes and longhikes and overhauls and underpasses and throughtraffic and stopgobacks and turnrightturnleftturnherenoturnthereturnwithcautions and turnoffs and switchons and lightups and dipdowns and gear-grinders and hogroads and footpaths and softverges and loose-gravers and downgraders and uphillings and riledcrossings and railversings and highspots and parks and guerdons and flowislands and safteyzones and petrolpumpedoff and petrel-shotups and pedistrains and hotrodhouses and rudehouses and roastcafes and shortcuts longwayroundabouts and winding-accesses and twistandturns and deviouscorners and detourists and switchbacks and rollovers and turnstilts and exhaustions and fumings and carpasses and carapaces and member-shipasses and flypasses and takingtolls and roadtolls and morguetells and spurtonarterials and backpassages and driver-drones and overlandrives and fordferries and holdenups and lifespans and footbridges and frogmarch and rundowns and fastruns and backlanes and sidepaths and freeways and wherenofeethavetrods and dcathcauseways and flaggingsdown and

beginning to flag at the end finally, yes, now, Jelfootweary but Jelferriedacross. He stands befloppy in front up to his own jelf door, seeing this time the Endoftheroad. Yep.

(man first coursed, first served; dogberry happy)

247

'... lllloooooooooooooooooodddd...' ! Goings on!

Whieh was getting a bit unnerving, even for our nerveless snake expert; ophidiologists are all slippery customers; also this Amos doesn't resemble any creepycrawly that he's ever seen on a time plate at any tome, but much more like an overagedead manmorph. It even seems that this rarething is trying to tell our ophidian something. If not actually to talk. And, since our ophiologist isn't all that ophen-minded, he entrusts, perfectly happily, his Amospecimen into the hands of a passing Flying Doctor, who, a wonder there to behold, almost drops his kite. A rarething not even preserved in a jar, either. And is just about to minister his kite some air with flaps when the rarething completes an audible phonetic in upshout, going:

'... ooddddyyyybloodybloody!' Full stop with exclamation mark, both. Followed by a torrent of bloody words comprising bloodies, not at all like a creepycrawly. Which bears out what the snake expert prognosticated. That being that this is not so much snake but possibly an age old toad that had been frogmarched out beyond the boyangs by mistake and finally Rana'd out of steam, yes.

(You are the wag that tales the dog)

At the nearest arresting bush town, which refused to be stunned back into life even by such a medical scientific joke, they did, in conjunction with the local God's Gifts to Doglives Society, contact the fabled Constable Wilkinson of El Sydney CID for to hand over Amos to someone who couldn't officially refuse.

Why our good Constable Wilkinson Simply because, throughout the whizbang hills and dales of this wizardbeaut yslandia of Oz, there was none better known as the sleuth self-sleweth for loused souls. After his whirlygiddy and famous pooper-chase of Mr Fido Bigs. The dill must have been pickled at the time. When he accepted their phone call.

(on your knees while the dog preys)

Jelfetchingly lowering Che the mexicanimal to a genteel landing, on it, and then intergoes within his room at last wherein is his cherished sleepy downy feathery fluffy cozicushee gorgeoso mattress, oo yes. But on it is

(Welsh tombstone: Die Bark)

Henry, alone this time, and waiting to greet his teeth at him, with his head even more swarthy with The Numbsk's ridden bandages than it is abo-usually swarthy natural. And so here they both are face to fixture again; the bow restrung, the tension retaut, the lesson retaught, the coin metering the cidence once more. Abo to abominable. Abohenry to Jelformid-able. Each in a true trussed-up state of world wariness, but calm weary and calm wary and carmelite lit upped from all those intwixted and betweened calamities. Mates. Even matey. And for this first instant regarding one the other deeply with a longprior inluxing of their liking eyes. Each a nod, for thee a brieforever nod of i dearly know thee; and thenandthere, for each, a quiet, quick squintdown, no more than winksize, yet tis of thee i can close my eyeseers and fear none. A small moment, but enough for us to have to wait upon, before:

(dogs are homo bent)

Jelfrowning now crosses over to the bedside of his room where he tippy-toes upon Henry. Right up the flue with the one toe cap he has left to put in. Insinuation enough, though, to energ Henry into the wide open spaces to land on the floor where he could land no further had he been trying to injure himself. No sooner done than the Jelformerproprietor is once again in residence of that satinsmoothcaressing sheetshaped fourposter minus four, with a usufractive sigh of longdeep-highwide polydimensionship as though he was, as he really is, a man who hasn't sunk his shaftbury much lately at all on any foldown foldup enfolding bed.

249

'I forgive you, Henry,' of high i-am because i've been every-touts and have max sennet everything there is to see.

'Boy, Jelf, you're really ugly rough, you poor white bastard pig fink you. No wonder we blacks've got that bigdick fertility thing going for us.' Henry now, bandages got up rightio again and, 'And that head, man, half eaten pastie-ish.'

'A monkish head, o monkey.' Jelf.

'Those froggy goggles.' Henry right on.

'Beneath I am the prince.' J.

'Man, that beard.' H.

'I thank you.' J.

'Long spun? Do tell.'

'Nuhuh. Too long a yarn.'

'Been sleeping rough, huh?'

'Huhuhmmmmm,' Jelfirmative meaning huhuhmmmmm to Henry and above all hmmm to bed below, going, 'I hardly care if mybed mylife myproperty myinnersanctosanctarium has been tainted. By you and the it-her. No.'

'So what could some throwback like you possibly been doing?' Henry the black, slouch hated.

'Hi 'ave been communicating with the lost Ozstraylian soul, my man.' J.

'Couldn't stand the flies meself.'

'My good abomanic, there are no flies on the flirty Aurora-raysland lost soul. Nor can close up inspection reveil where they

250

might have TiVi been, even snapshot off. But then, an abo-urban, how could you comprehend beyond limited mental powers?'

'Giggle giggle, you albino dreg. But my Alyce said you're invited along to our demmo today, you gutless wonder.' H.

Whereupon, abraising but hardly appraising, did they jabber simulsubterraneously at each other in synchrones of counter-tunes. The vocal parts of their voices intwinned for the very last time of all. With Jelf

rolling one of his two-balled eyes onto Henry with phlegmantic and going that:

dear abo unintelligible, i have returned from the soul source a wholeity of man in essence in fact i have just boiled up from primal mud like booze in froth i have been reberthed and reborn, sir, into an alround Auroraysian Ozman, sir, thus having no idea of what the fuck thou gibberish. With Henry making an unwholesome fingeroosting gesture towards our Jelfulsomeity, going:

Yeah Alyce said you wouldn't relate you white turd. With Jelf yawning an intimacy to the ceiling, going that she fuckingwell would have, wouldn't she? With Henry, upon his soul, going: *issues* bloody *issues*, you white bugger, you don't connect you're shit. With Jelf querying word *issues*, like The Numbsk causing blood *issues*? Like Alyce's *issue* once a month? With Henry, white with black rage, going that Jelf (he) is as useless as a waddy at the Woomera Rocket Range. With Jelfoureyes closing down fluttering semaphore, going true true ok so true. With Henry suddenly abolaughing

(the mortician picks up where the dog leaves off)

aboloving in the warmth of a thoughtie about his Alyce, going that crazy Alyce. With Jelforeknowledgable sagesaying, going again true again, she's so crazy she's homocidal. But now Henry has his

251

blood spurting on under the mental mantle of his Diva and, while Jelf dozes to the dozen, abo-he does go on so, going:

(the brown fox jumpy over the lassiedog)

about Diva sayingthis and Diva sayingthat and getting him out of suits and ties and into soulmates and stale-nevers and on the morrow, come Bumsk or Numbsk or Skunkski or CMF RAN RIFFRAF RUNNING or other faucets like themthose-there, this segment of Aboaboutness of town is going to see a street-shellacking, sheilas and all, street demmo longa all dem tribalfella belonga tribes of Diva and Her Chosen One and hailshine or variegated inclemencies like newspaper strikes lightning electric stormouts shutups and such, you name it, nothing gonna seize our walkparade by the neck. No, suh. Nazis or not, Numbsk or no, numbskullingnastynongs and all, so. There, and

(coward's heart in a dog's mouth)

Alyceanna is going to carry the banner, too. So stuff that, you white ginspiss lickspat little spluttersplatter gorbie.

Here does Jelf re-unenglue those googy eyes, first this one then that one and shillyshakes his coconut meaning no pardon i pardner i'll not dance that rigmarole nonono for

like i have said, i have been (Jelfroat in wabbly sweetsong now) in a mental sylence wayout beyond beacon or beckon for forty days and forty fitfull nights, aye, in the backyard of the Bunyip from which did i emerge upfrom the swamp as new-born as a baby foetid. Tiny foeties too. Yea, even swaddled and placed upon the fictional reed and there did i as mozes regrow out of this beardsley; and then did the wiz of Oz yslandia flit like a homopone upon i to reveal unto i alone the cosmosetic essence of the real Auzee soul.

And here did our Jelf expound unto our Henry aboboy the hieretic and higher erratic essence of what was reveiled unto himsjelf whentime he was in awander in the outyonder of Oz infantaland. Going:

The Ozmanof yslandian soul kaleiders here, clashes there but unprism no bars nor holds in reflections of. Insteemed, it furgs and fulges and gorms all mighty. It does, does the soul-Ozian, stink hiely. Of pine of nectarene rain of waratah of surfish saltOzone of euclids of essences of franksense of the myrrh of gum and fern and wattlehappenext and hey! Yes, it stongo stinks of dead leaves composting of new grass shawn shearings sheepings shardings scraggings and wild mountain tangs which tingle svelte belts of wheat sveltering under heat bars and iso silogerminatants. Even of flimsy tongues distrueing the strinkle of newrived and rivuletting rains and the strinkle of the waders chipping back to the waterhugs and the strinkle of starshroop'd and ashwashed skies Ozseen by only Essezoons, yes, and the strinkle of spuma pumata and plumeaviata and the stinking of the mudsweeps thickly asking. Yes, and the soul of Oz boils thick as the crickets cracketting we-are-here we-are-here, yes, and as the hawking of the kittys shagreened that Ozsoul is a petrolified wall-to-wall in the shade of green. And Henry, listen above all, the sol of yslandiOz, the wumming of YslandiOz, the core-current of Ozelyza sland! It strums streams churns and churmles into troughlings of all soul's veinity all soul's wanwaxity all soul's caulks encorked all sake's soulitudes. This is the Durodame of Ozslandia soul. This is staemen of bud, the stance the smell the nostril lahlah of our trials trailed here and now. Henry, earharken, nor is this only true for

(Tombstoned: A True Master Piece?)

the soulOz the wholesoulOzzified it do, too, looklike, yes, spawn of turtle; spawn of roe on roe; spawn of desert pea'd; spawn of the kelp, of the landrunning and the searuling; spawn of the marramcouchkangaroo grass and the salt-bushumbles; spawns of crystal spawnings in baubles of ormolu-ing verdigrising dyealum't colourfast pyrotechnesting colour-some chromoswatched aluminidus; and spawns of titswans in nidicolouses entwirpy and; spawn of the bluegum born of the gumnut swarm of the bossbees formed of the mango swamped by the crackasphalts spaw of

253

arteasings. Henry, it bubbloes and blowsbeloes; it is upmagnised; it *must*, Henryabo, must to the risent onned sunloved surface come unto. The Ozoon the Ozotica the Ozolesoul the Ozstreak the. With-instance inside-of-us the insidious the underlaked the source and gush. There being there, henry, black et white, the Ur of our soul, the spatchook in allour backyards, the cystoblast elasticoming, the algerminated already all attendant tooth and nail, the, Cystoblast. The kangarode. The cystoblast. The kangaroe. The cystoblast. The kangaroosting. The cystoblast. The kangar-oon.

i am oion

Henry! The cystoblast in our Ozsoul placed entrailodged in the spore poor spawn porient pouring pouch of our-all kanga-rooyal. Our highness.

(overweight dog, fat chance!)

...While Henry mere shrucks his aboegg sadly tro and fo. Poor Jelfuddydudddddddd.

(he who possesses little dog live a little longer)

Amos to the rescue:
on the train now going out of that small bush town in relief, it and him, on his way to Constable Wilkinson in Sydney. En route but not on rout. And prone upon a steerage seat, still not able to speak for the impediment he got from being a deadloss, drossed and refound out in Nowhere. He is straining his hairless, roving his scatterbrain, shooting his rolling eye dicily, flapping his chicken elbows, and. All in an effort to say something threateningly frenetic other than bloody. But still cannot. Frothing his phoof-phoof valve almost to the almost ultimate, not to mention his armpits secreting against his socks with the effort. Poorole Amos.

And the two other fellow passengers with him there mostly wish they weren't. What can these postululations possibly be? The poor

254

old soul is gapegoing bloodybloody-bloodybloodybloodybloody at them from out of an awful bit of a whole toffyappled toothless hole, but doing so in a way like he was trying to impedi something out of his imply-menta.

(pack down on the inefficiencies of the dog catcher)

Yet nothing, only bloody knots, comes out of that poresome old nut. Bloodybloodybloodybloody as he points to his reekreel-ing feet held eye high and very very high at that. Too. Just as well his fellow passengers have dripping colds of uncommon olefactory blockages so that, even if they could hear well, which they can't, being both deaf from congenital birth, they cannot catch that wrenching whiff of those famous Amoskunk glands anyway. No.

(the dog'll throw you up to re-veal your presence)

Which is also making our Amos so grrangrry that he actually shifts his bum, just like an outraged corpse would do if it wanted to put a new grave face on things, yes, and now raising, with a determined undermining action, his psoriatic feet even nostrilymphing higher. Right beneath their noses. And if those two fellow passengers could but see him trying to pick the sock stickings off from his skinny skinshrunk shanks like as if he were scrieving off unrip'd underipe scabs, then they would have surely puked into each other's pocket, but

they cannot, since they are blind also. Only staring static vatically at unamoosed Amos with sweet smiles Saul round. And stayputting. Bloodybloodybloodybloodybloodybloody, a. Bloody thing to have to say, ayes. Amos rily reeking now with fury at not being able to articulate this whatever fearful thing nagging at him nor get shot of these intruders in his appartment space. Nonetheless, he is still coming to the reeksure. He noses it, too.

(dog on collision course with its dents showing)

Jelf and Henry, back in the Jelfroom, with not a nother bene-thing to say to each other more. Henry removes some of the excess bandages given out free by freebooting Whacka Numbsk, The, then glims his eyes rather regretfully at his once friend tojojelf:

'Have you ever changed.'

'Not for a week. Nor cleaned the fangs neithergnaw.'

'Yep, i've already got a whiff of your piffle, boy.'

Henry, that, then patting his Jelfriend on the abo-liked curvaceous shoulder, in a nodding noodle sort of way meaning thatsall tosay for now and forever more. He gods to leave. 'Henry?' Henry heard, Henry held, Henryabo abouturns. 'I don't suppose you want to learn from what the Alyce it-she did to me?'

'Who's "her"? My Diva?' Cold and now and both refridged irrevocably on the other. Frig him.

'I mean that she shithouse, i do yep.'

'Then see you around some place time, European.'

'Sohlong, Australoid.'

(man-stricken dog appreciates hand given)

Jelf alone:
bepillowed or fluffed up against and pillored, matters nothing; the thing is the lielowing of the wearyhead after an absence of something like thirteen by ten to the eighth microsecs ground by. On the ground grovelled, Big Ben and he, both. Once-upon-a-time friend Henry, too, gone by. *Tempers frigit*, and the. Jelf thoughts drifting like waves of wavering sea seeds searip'd, ferns of neptune, neaps of fortune, frowards seawoebetides inwardsto backwoodsfro freethroth loveloathe lubberlandlocked, tentaclives

256

tendervined and sinking into the davit locker, just. About, that is, when

(lunatic dogs howling for the man in the moon)

the air suddenly breezyclangs with audiovibes aswould a roomful of beserked lawn mowowowowowers waiting by the dentist chair for their tune-up on his raw nerveservers. Voices kreiging blitzandos commando through the canary air with canards full of Whispers. Yes, once more, more of the Whispers about the Jelfpersonage and the Jelformed and the Jelfunda-mentals nervending

(raw nerves; the dog will suffer a lot to get them)

like sibilant voices from out of his Alyce-artstudio distillated past. But this time the new star Jelf Perfect merely swings his paddlers ofT the wallowed bedding and coolglides it to the door to go swing itjelf out onto that there landing, where. Henry is caught looking a bit doggedly sheepish and Che the mutt a bit shep'd doggish, and all else a bit winkled-out fishy. Jelfiendishly through grin going:

'Notice i am polishing my fingernails with hohum as i ask you, you abo being you, just who the shit were you whispering about me to?'

'Mickey Mouse.' Henry hove to, veto. Ho.

'Uhuh. Well, whoever it is, just tell Alyce to get the hell out of here before i do knuckle her over with my fee fie foe and fouly breath. Oh, and bye.'

On this wise, gently assisting the sissy mexomutt to leave off lovingly tongueing fan mail on his argonautical feet of argil, when anon does the Jelfigurehead retour back through the door of his room, leaving the mute blank verses spilling from H's lips abothickly. He did, and he did also. Both.

(it's the ordinary man in the street that suffices)

Amos to the rescue:
entrain'd still in one or two minutes gmt longer by longitude, yet
stillwith the wrong attitude. Amos staring aggressively at the two
fellow passengers opposite even though he has already spread
pieces of his detached self over the other vacant seats round them
and. They still be swirling smiles all over his rude attempts to
bugger them off with the unspeakabilities of his natural self.
Unbelievable. He is furious. If he

(border collie takes breakfast with landlady)

could come out with more than bloody repeated ad infinitum in
nauseum, he would gash them with gnashings of verbal lashings.
Of. At which the Mr and Mrs there might be so scandalized that
they might depart or die apart or preferably both coincidal. If not
sui. Yet Amos cannot speak. Something too unspeakable mentally
blocks him, even more than usual. Even more unbelievable. So he
gives up. He does. Settling back to amuse them with a blatter of
tricks he had to teach himself in order to survive for so long in the
extreme Outbark as a dogtype of dingo. After all,

(gummy dog like to meet tender heart)

old odiums never die, they just dingo away. So he lickets and
lappits the snot from his snout; he priggles up his ears; he
wriggulates both earflips; he flaps both earwigs; he flips both
flappers; he whimper wipes howls whines bays boys simpering
with sounds; he quoiffers his snout nostrils; he flegs hackles napes
shanks flanks with eitherightleft paw; he rolls over on his back; he
begs; he nibblenips; he snippitysnarls; he bares his bone-chipped
teeth; he nitpicks with his snatching gnashers; he engrooms
himself with a hound's tongue; he livers his chops; he slobs in
between the man's assembled and amassedly amazed toes (oooo
nice doggy); he

(sheep dog taken with a station hand)

258

snivvles and sniffs the woman's furibund legs now in exstatic retraction; he barks like an ancient ruff hawking up a kitty-cough; he hawks-up with his hackles up. It is even acceptable when he tries to smell those fellow passenger arses in a tizzy. But when he finally hitches back to tonguelush his own stenchy genitals then that is obviously enuff ruff stuff.

For all of a sudden Amos has been left wail alone. And is now cozening the door shut after his two fellow passengers have shot through. Bad reports, too. But then as we have said, Amos wrecks to the cue.

(clever dog to carry the paper boy in)

From in out from the landing, Jelf straightway crosses his womboid shaped room to the window that lets a little outside in but not too inside, where. He Jelframes himself a spectacular specs-flashing cameo of a bio-thing looking down into the street looking down at her that happens to be in this case, of asking,

(playful dog brings back the Ball, orchestra and all)

Alyce. Yes. Brought back into Jelfocus once more and doing a pose reminiscent of a middle-aged ugly bitch trying to be a nymphal swede in some yesterday's B-feature. A nymph-compoop for sure. With her legs as wide open in straight backed stance as her crack will allow without being further cranked open, and. That's a kilometre for a start. Swinging her handbag too in thrustfuls under her fanny light her woolly bullroarer her furry thrum. As she leers up

(cut the pack in two with a poker face)

at Jelfoureyes radiating powerlightfuls down at her from his glass window. In a nut-sheila, Alyce is fluting herself triumphantly up at him in a blazing flaunt meaning: 'here i am, lacker, and between my manhole there is still a nutcracker sweet, ole honeychile hubbybum old been.' Having

(healthy wet-nose running, cold shivers down your spine)

parked herself directly in front of the remainder of those scandalous posters so ughorribly still polluting the overway temporary construction walls. And engineered by her. So there, for a smallrolex of time in a timefoolish world they, the Jelfecundity and the Alycephalic, remain facet to fact once more, after so much of her waters have flowed under the bridgades. Before

(tombstoned: Went A Long Way But Far-fetched)

a slow-moving smile sloths across the Jelface, curlemooing the hairied but unharried corners of his mouthy moustache. When does he hurry back to his dormerdoor, pulls it ajar, and pulls out and in, both, a creature scribed as Jamroll while real name is Alcey (Elsie?) Somethingorother (Miss-lainy?) and who is Maggie's sister just coming down by going one high stepping heel after a high heel'd another, from Maggie's flat upaways. And now jamly rolling back with Jelf, by towrope and hook b'crook, to his window. Where together, he and she both, they leer the same leer back down at Alyce. In a manner that suggests two can spay, Alyce, now that the game is ovary. Yes, and. Without window dressing at all either, on the part of Jamroll who has already stripped from navel upwards without dropping one stitch of her leer down.

Well done by, too. And exclusively for the sake of Alyce whose lower lip by now has gone from pout to put-out. So surprised that even her legs came together. Poor Alyce:

(dog catcher sticks in the throat a bit)

output outraged outdone outsized outwhored outhoaried outworn outwon outerlimited outlugged outlooked outleered oututtutted outboobied by this Jamroll knockout and with her rhynch really put joint out of snout this time. Which causes the whole

260

framework of her answering leer to capsize from leeside to lopside, exposing the Alycephaloaf in all its great garnished gashitude of sour pickle, yes, it does. Just in time, as

(two-dog family goes its separate ways)

Henry transvaals the roadway to the side of his Diva with eyes that still shine in token of what he is still seeing from some ancient way-back. Browsy elementaries, and what ailments!, of his Divalyce. And his eyes even more love shining when she scowls at him before dragging him after like an abbot of unreason. She is going off alright. Rotten, all of a sudden.

(til vet do us part)

Still Amos recklessly to the rescue:
with b'now his sock encrusted feet spree'd over the last two vacant remaining seats vacated by the departed fellow passengers. Free to spread comfort and joy all over his self spread out. Yet. Italicised. There is still that something else nagging at him. Some thought-thing or other digging its spurs into him like a rat at rut in and around his small mind or mound, which? If he, the rock bottom of

(doggone nerves leaves man a wreck)

up-and-down evolution could but blabber a bit, he might even attempt an ideoshot at what that teasing thought in his brainoodle might be, but. He still cannot wunderbard save for a bloody here and a bloody there every livelong minute of the nonstopwatch. Doesn't even want to know, either, after such a long life of happy senescence. Things of unpleasantries might incommode one by leaping oneself onto one's perfectly happy feet where they are. Bugger that, and end of thought. Not quiet quite, though.

Just why is Amos reeking to the cue? That his thought?

(underdog bit off more than it could chew)

Back where our Jelfungus, that bug in a rag, is beelzebubbing Alyce hoisted with Henry stompeding away down the street where soon she will corner a new leaf no doubt. We are. He now turns his attention away from all that external inferno and lens onto

(musical dog jumped on the band wagon to throbbing heartbeats)

the internally encamped Jamroll who, much to his shucks, has jammed herself within the kombifines of his cornered bedroll where she is not only impressively stripped of all coverings (coeval rings and all; all chasted away) but is, yes!, holding out her bra and frenchie-type *bras* to him, the one and the other. He stumbles back, going: 'A flagrant liberty, what a fragrance.' And that's true, for in the gathering up of her loins she is propogating certain oleants. Ole! Enough to drive a man to spinach nightly and spine ache matinly. It's that windjamming of her roll upwind and casting all causerie to the wind, and, too, her pouting lips unmoving saying my lipsticks and stone may break your bone, but. As well as:

'Boy, has my sister Maggie ever told me everyallthing about you...'

Jamroll icking:

(dog to de sire you)

'... but what i reckon, see, is that nobody, but nixo, can be as bombed out and feeble as she says you are, honey. That a fact that you can only simulate with that feebly equipment you've got? Tell you, though, she didn't say how shocking ugly you really are. How 'dya get like that? Industrial accident?'

'Jamroll sister if i may call thee so, for i know ye not, but it seems you have taken comeuppance in my pitance there.' J.

262

'You really a negative phenomenum like sister Maggie says?'

This Jamroll rolling, o salad Dogod days! With cheeks like pepper corn under microphotography.

'What about your virtue, miss? Need to ask that.'

'Well, y'see God just passed me by there.' Shrugging an outward left tit that makes the right swell up with pride. All the time everything tries to get in the act.

'Anything God can do to make it up to you, miss?'

'Well, God could manifest himself but sister Maggie said that would be a bloody miracle, Jelfie Kelpiedoll.'

'Wondrous thing to behold. Dog rasp do grasp...' Wondrous in bloody deed. For there, poking out through the greater holes than trousers left to his syet unslept sole, is a very unexpurgated cods erectus of dictionary proportions. A rod a rood-beam a pole a perch a fourth of an acre. This, we might add, is not really like him. Even Jamroll finding it hard to gasp, easy to grasp. Flood the room with water and it would be a snag. Neither are we changing dickerections in midstream. This stalkessence of a Jelfat defies previous, or any other, description. For

(lap dog getting right down to it)

where prior donga scrivened as shrivened, cramp-imped in stylus, meagre in eager, grizzling as grist, now it switching in the breeze as swoll-headed as a puffed-up galoot gallivanting in a gale. It would make you trementumultuous just to be on the leeside of it, lying on yours. For comparative shame. Dickissimo! Even now Jamroll is trying to manoeuvre his oar into her rollock going: ooooo and *ohm* switch me on plug me live wire for i amp of little resistance. *Ohm*. Did she ever have a shock coming.

Thereupon, with little further to-do and much more to come, did Jelf cross himself first before proceeding onto her with his plenipenistude, and. Soon he is jammedamnearly rolled somewheres within thepluggings of any gaps left between the satinsheets, in her and them, while

(give up your wife before your dog)

she suddenly finds herself bumbasking on the deck of a yat-chet looking up the length of a conswayance of a mainmast that is rising higher and hawser above her yes and she trying to mount the mainmast but keeps slipping halfwayummyup halfwayummy down yes and now sitting on the Heads and being arsed how she likes it in her own way and yes still only barely grasping with the wonder of things to behold and hold, being an eyewitness of all that belle'd ringings with all her own gobble up gobble in gobble around gobble gooking gobble almost gobstopping and yes near to being choked with joy and yes tears in her eyes saying don't hurt me any more (could you, ooo?) and yes all her decks now becoming awashed and all her seven sees that open and shut all clogged up and sorely opened and between the two mountainous sees of her chest she holding a whole wallowing whale of a one within the likerish relishing of her licklips at the eyelet at the end of the only true block and tackle she has ever been at sea with and yes she tongueing spitfully forcefull tide of that nectarmarine which close scrotumny makes appear so and it does, not once which soaks her, not twice which spumes her, not thrice which sprays her, but four times which drenches over her cockled heart wavering for this jelforminable priaprick that has circumnavigated her currunt and cannonaded all over betwixt betits and tidings. Of joy. And it

(suffer to give your dog a stroke)

still hasn't lowered its primammary colours from behind the prow of the Jelfnoah arched. If she was an animal she might have trouble clammering up this plank fully. She goes cooka-doodledo, in case none of this is for real eyesing. *Ohm.*

(mistress --the piece of tail between the dog's legs)

264

Even before Maggie's sister was herself ready to take second soundings of these unplumbed depths, it was a oho rise and shine again. Jelfself did hoist her highdrollic into the corner of that suddenly satyrical room so that she may cram up on it more closely and did yes yanked her up and off in a position that staticised a backward somersault halfway completed that was in reality a backwards tumble that was to prove to be some assaulted back-up with her head and shudders jammed upon the floor and her fanny airing smells and his hands upon the wall feet strident of her and, yes, did he aim and spur on until she explunged her plumbed loco depths whenceupon did he screw drive her cockwise and anti-cockwise cockscrew and cockroach going, just cock a snook at this for i am the phantom cockatrice from fucking cockaigne yepyip. And all she could do was oi oi oi and oillade each time she blew gusher'd. And when she had almost come to the sad parting by coming adrift, the Jelfat did twitch with such a gushet of rushness of blood to the head that it did jerk her bodily upoutand away from that corner and flipplexed her wheedling into the rarefied heights she had never reached before so stiff as a bored on a fourbore muzzle in such suspended animation at the end of a ramwad and then

(Tombstoned: Lying Doggo'd)

barrrooomful of boom boom boom. Upshot of which was Jamroll sister of Maggie flopping over limp as if she had been shot by dead eye dick up on a greasy pole.

Still was the Jelf unflagging pole unfurled and giving to Jelface a Caesar's cheerio how are u. Better lying down?

(puppy's mamma tells of man's mama)

Amos still coming to the rescue, by train:
but disquieted and distinctly so. His brow has furrowed. It must be serious. Here he is cocooned by night and train, each plunging past the other, and closet'd safe and sound as any other piece of

skinaceous parchment in a flaming world of bad matches, with his feet up in socks that are adding even more to his ease and comfort by standing up by their stinking selves. He is even able to summon up enough farts and mothy wafts to have a positive orgy of awakening self awareness.

Yet his brow *has* become furrowed, and stayed with him. Evidence, if there ever was, of a humanoid reaction to some constunnation getting at his little prick of a conscience. If not of the existence of high-brow graffiti. Well, no mind, little matter. Whether he knows it or not, he is still *en train* to the reekscue. A fart cry from the ideal man, too.

(Scottish terrier slinks back into its laird)

Back in the gorings on in the Jelfdormer, thathere door is suddenly bust in upon to admit, omitting her angry emissions, a Maggie that is standing on no ceremony other than the ceremonial doormat, as liege as lief, and steering daggers at the Jelf with her sister. Sorore but satisfied.

'So aha i see. Not enough me and my poor old daddy, you've started on my only sister now.' Which she thinks a bit of a joke since she thinks that the Jelfink could start no such thing even if he thought himself the hero of a bit of porn. He must be, she thinks too, since he's barebumfacedly bending over the omphallus, *ohm*, of Sis where lies the path of least sisterance, and. Now buggerizing around with a flowery kiss upon Sis's sticky claw, going:

'Charmed, Maggie's jamrollsis, to meet you in my pated pit.'

'Get out of that bed, you trollope,' Maggie getting a nineteenth century author mixed up with a very literal modernday sister au lit, and, 'And you take my sister's mouth out of your filthy hand while i'm speaking so there!'

'Don't mind the nail varnish.' Jamrolling again, fluttering, still flatten'd. But letting out her clutch. Insatiable or incorrigible, which?

'My favorite flavour, ma'am.' The Jelipsf, smacking.

So that Maggie is spurred to peer closer into the gloom and is taken by. Not the gloomy sight of him. She always knew he must have been ugly deep down underneath it all, even more than she as a normal healthy person could possibly imagine. Not that, no. But the unbelievable length he has gone to with her sister. Beyond dreams.

'Oooo.'

But then, as she and her sister shrugged one to the other, what can a girl do but do Oh well, flesh from the oven...

So Maggie had no biological choice but to try out the reborn Jelfact. Too. Plunging the three of them into a situation of one ship, two captainesses and one mate, and they tried it on each other, it being more than enough, and they got the trident up here the tribender up there and they made like the tridimensional demon. Jelf in pants of her then in pants of her and in each stone throws each was throed into pantings, for more, for myturn. And when those monumental marbles got shook convulvusly loose did each feminine terminal organ pontracuntal in clammer for the foraging sac to shove them right left centre side siderally reredorsal or outofdoors. If need be. Need was. As though each had the vug gynal pulled out from under her, and allhappening while Maggie was still standing struck spasmazed upon the mat unentered. Where-upon she did finessely blow her stack.

(dog comes down to earth with a bonebreaking thud)

'What have you done to my daddy, you kidnapper?'

267

'Last time i glanced around, dear Maggie, he was drying out on a perforated sheep skull. I think it was perforated.'

'Murderer!'

'Maggie, you got a fanny like a gaslight, and honest, didn't i knee the old catastrophe crutchwise at least five times between here and the bus station but. He got no balls so it made no divident, no.'

'That's enough rest let's wrest,' unwinding Jamroll putting in a long lingam whine and to roll amore. But her elder Maggie foregoes mere gratification of once in a lifetime even though her noodle is nodding a naked yeayeayea, going:

'You think you can come back here baldblind ugly as all fuck not even having had a shave, look at yerself, having lost our poor old daddy to death, and. Think you can thrust yourself between the bosom of my family again, you got another think coming.' But then stopping with green eyes when the Jelform begins mountaining up the outcroppings of Jamroll oozing yes.

'Admirable bosom, too.'

'Her? She's a negative wonder. You just move over.' Maggie moves in. Moo.

(going under doing the dogstroke)

When Maggie did uncucumber her mummocks she sucked in Jelfair and blew out Jelfair and inthusway so inflated up her mammimelons to such a munipiezoplumpness (piezzas she wanted to gobble up) that she almost floated over to the bedrock of Jelfauna, yes, where she and Jamroll did shed whatever they could get rid of and they both did both get ridden crop'd whip'd saddlc'd spurs'n'all again and again. The Jelfat being so hugely instance of an in-satyr's insatiability that it hot-stitched with twitching irritability like a bull's balls. Which Maggie pulled while Jamroll

268

puddinged which Maggie nacked while Jamroll nibbled which Jamroll flowed on while Maggie floated on which Maggie sighcrynearlydied on and Jamroll whinedinedgutsed upon which Maggie made a beast of herself over while Jamroll made an ass of herself on which Maggie smeltered dogwise while Jamroll hatched open underside and birdsquatted onwise which Maggie hammered haunchairily while Jamroll nosewaywise got an earful while Maggie dug into her bag of umbical while Jamroll dug into her bag of 'do-me major domo prog ram me.' Yes. Pornogloss while Jelfitting all the way inaroundownsideways remained mun-ificent horny for all even when Maggie rested and Jamroll wrested both trying to reach the top of his piledriven pole glissanding shaft, for they both had already been given enough bangwhizzes to have tender membranes for many comehither times to come to last a longaiety.

Jelfat still twitching; must have an alarming tock tic.

(man and wife -- dog's main course; man, wife and child -- dog's main course served with essence of stuffing)

Really, though, Maggie is never saturnisfied, going:
'Instead of lying about here damaging me and my family you ought to be doing something about your friend Henry. That woman is ruining him. She's turning him into a Blackabo minstrel with boongmouthy overtones. You don't care.'

'Alas alack.' Jelfromage too cheesey to be worried about that, perhaps because Maggie was speaking somewhere about his vast vas deferens region, not very deferentially either. While her sister is rolling somewhere around his Jelfskull with moaning coming again to a head. Must be, surely, a chemical reaction:

'What's the use of talking to you. You've really turned out just a big prick.'

'Maggie, forty days and forty nightimes have made me penis foolish, worldly-wisened, andes fact.' Almost Jelfalling off.

'He's closing his eyes!' Jamroll suddenly jamming all circuits and possibly out to jam sis Maggie's mouth up for talking so much.

'How selfish can a prick like him get?' Now both in sororal agreement of a crisis point somewhere about Jelf's lower parts, meeting eye to eye, meaning, 'Here we are nearly buggered out with orgasm after orgasm without either of us taking a break in rhythm trying to give this big ugly meathead a blow and he's starting to go to sleep on the job; how ungrateful can you get' At which they both unison a get out and get under in mutual satisfactional agreement. Rather urgently, too.

'Please, girlettes, a little sleep less slip-in. I have been undreaming for forty nighties. You know.' And said in such a nightmorish way that sudden panic rages through the nipped breasts of Maggie and Jamroll sister scratching at the Jelf goolies groggily insane. Aye. Two furies

(came to a halt but doggedly carried on)

having-at-he yet again with Maggie titlots topless stockingly suspended blacklace blackslurking taskmistress chastising his elected member of parlavarment and withal her body of men going with its members running amock; while, yes, Jamroll becomes mistress of crerements doing necronakkerings in filly frills on a rigor mortis'd corpse as hard and rigorous as mortar unshelled; while Maggie now is a circus bigtop being ringed around the back of the alleyway where fairies floss and loins are jimmycracked into trapteasing him open or easing him shut and where clowns like her have faeces on their bums and bouncings on their faces; while Jamroll gets higher going into a nunnery where no nun gets none, non, but is being pope poked into a real lurch by each fourth former in the rugby scrummy with unsung scrotums after her guts for garters. And all to such good effort that the Jelfat is now even beginning to be drawn out to dewdrop atop its mon-stirrous seismic thrumbling disturbance, when Maggie's hubbie Ray

270

crashes hip and shoulder in through the door. Yes! Ray! Remember? Without knuckling but after a Jelf knocking for sure, on land or sea, cum hole or hell water. Aye. And all because Maggie is being fixed up down here instead of fixing up dinner up there. A real down-on intended, too. Plus for extra-marital fucking out of the marred bedlock. Going:

'Right bastard Jelfink, you're... '

But that was all the essence hubby Ray got out with. It was. You catch your spouse, largely equipped largely, and her sister, equally equipped equally, redhanded with a knob on it that makes those twolarge ladies look like two pixy pollyannas dancing around a maypole, whee, then you'll swallow all but awe, too. Guaranteed. Most especially when the Jelfat proprietor of it gradients his crane inclined towards you, with a welcoming smile going 'oo goodday, how have you vaseline?' You would, too, as does Ray, do a bunk before that bunk does you. For good, and with a relieving gulp

as he makes it back out onto the landing, with the door slammed tight behind him to keep the monster from getting out. With his head hung in comparative shame, waiting with Che the chihuahua, meek and mulling over how very very close he was to being really buggered out. Bade luck.

(deceased virgin got only a lick of a promise once)

Not long after the Jelf dormidoor opens to shed out a shagged-out Maggie and likewise (a very much wiser made all the wider!) Jamroll sister. They look like they've been thrashed, possibly because they both oh merge crawling on all fours. Their heat waves now flagged down for many a future suture; yet, to do them creditably, with as-yet unfurled flutters. So that even Rayman and Chedog regard their aspects with new admiration. And all Maggie can come out with is a rasped whisper of immense relief, going, 'He's asleep.' As she gropes to mount the stairs, not even noticing that the revitaminized Chemutt is attempting to mount her as she

271

goes, now that she is in a position of a putdown bitch without resister *ohm*.

(dog done in for a Penny, in for a pound)

Meanwhile, Jamroll sister is having it a little easier, it being downhill to the street, fullof strafes and stiffs, below. Ray watches her, then shrugs oh deep well, bugger the in laws and statute books, and. Commences, on the downslide, to drill her for any untapp'd reserves. Fat chance! She might be bawling but was balled over

at least another thirty or forty aawww nnoooo nnnotttt aaggainn times by many a slippery customer between here and Manly where she finally grovelled into bed. Silly girl, she even fell to sleep in the middle of the Quean's Highway. But then it is hardly surprising that Jamroll went on to mickey it to half of Sydneytown on her way home, for, as someone said:

you're really rooted if you're down and out in Sydney.

(on a tombstone tapped: Dog Fancier, Had Guts)

Aye, Maggie was right. Jelf was asleep, having fiddled while his roamin' burned. He has creched out; he has been too much overcome of late by sleights slights slides sluttishnesses and the scirrhuses of hands, yes. He sleeps having slipped so leadly solid into slosher. Guild for him, only it is a weeny bit sad that he will not awake a little earlier than he will, so that he might perhaps enjoy a few cloxtocks more of a dabble in the life of the plenteous horn. Than he's got left.

(mad dog ends up an inmate)

272

Amos clicketty clack clacketty click still coming to the rescue:
and all those doused embers in his uninhabited nonsupport system
of a brain are fanning warm again at the sumpthing resembling a
fighting thought which is

bloodybloodybloodybloodybloody

making him roll his lizardlike latcherson violently. Until he
catches onto the dopple image of himself reflected in the window
there watching himself watching himself spread eagling in that
compartment as all those pitchblack patches outside outslidle by.
Aye, something stirs and it's not the frightful air stalematted in
propinquity of his aurasome person. No. It is that same brainprick
that hurts so awfully he doesn't want to know about it. But is
coming to must-do. Even to articulate it beyond mere
bloodybloody words. He looks at his windowed reflection with
growing meaning behind his two films. Sights merging; vague
shapes of near focus; clickety for clackety; rock for roll. And like
bug wired into the body of blind Tiresias does he, at last, form the
words of the inner sees:

I. Me there. Yes. Nowait. Prahsnot. Summonelse? Baldcoot.
Bloody. *Him*? Jelf? Prahsnotso. Imalright. Training. Past.
Clicketty clack clicketty. But not me. Buthim! There. Hestatic.
And. Darkill. Blackness. Buggeredall. Blackart. Darkirknives. It.
Nottrain. It. Cap T. The Thing. Of All of Us. For him. For Jelf?
Oncomingcrash. Untobloody. Him. All. Thatout. Alloutness.
Allofit. Blackblanketty. Bloody. Blank. Smash-bashing. Him?
Jelf! Thatskull! Thatskin! Itis! Lookout! Jelf! Bombard! Blacklife!
Copscar! Crashyou! Comingl... Comingl'm... Coming l'mcoming
l'mcoming...!

Trying. Yes, trying. From his knees, now, straining his strudel
trying to call outo call duck call lookout call for pity for poor for a
little paltry please, for his Jelfils for his own Jelfilial sacressenced
for his Jelfadopted for his Jelfirstloved for all the horror he has
seen in that reflection. But no warning shout can he throatout yet
to his Jelflikeson. Only tears streaming down his ruts,

273

the first time in his life trying to wordstut wordstaemenise wordgrape grapplevine what his micro-pumpkin thought it had to do, even braindamage if necessary, wanting to get out. Devilish, but. Not right yet. Poor old bugger is almost having a frantic twitching off within the silencing cell confines of his body cellulost. Frantastic to vide, and mulch to smell.

Now Amos is really reeling to the reekscue. Fast going off, but coming on. *Ohm* going; but a long way from *ohm* still, though.

(classy dog has the entree of the upper crust)

Once again siriusly though:
the crippled old dog will hold you in tender regard. The young healthy dog will keep an eye on your development. The lovely young bitch will pass you by for a sugar daddy. But any old bitch who proves past it must be losing her lure. Then again: after the second spill the bloodhound began to feel the escaped convict had nothing more to give. Especially when man-oeufres were the speciality of the day during the hunt dinner. And you can tell the real hetero dog; it sleeps in dog snatches. You can tell, too, the rapine dog; it will try to curry you favour. The husky dog likes to have your nose at the grindstone. We are talking of dogmancy, of course, the study of human divisions. Seen on a tombstone, too: Run Hard But Now Dead Beat. And on another grave: Spitzed Out On The Footpath. So never get taken into a clipjoint by a poodle.

And despite what they say, dogs do not bring back balls; they eat everything. But then again, you can always leave a dog behind, because that's the part of you he relishes most anyway. After all, dogs are so dens, they're just lairrikins. So if a dog jaws on your raw nerves, try to remember that the Son of Dogod was nailed by a high-powered rifle for your salvation. When did Dogod fire the gundog on the Spot.

XXX marks yours.

DOGOD

The next day:
they have this modern mental block at the Sydney Met Office, and within it work those toothsayers called meteorologists. What meteors, for chrissakes? It's not an observatory, but an absurdity. Flashy bowties and fleshy smiles leeping out TV wise at us, going: 'Yoohoo, coming weather or not?' Twas much the same,

(toy dog stuffed up eating the child)

too, on the next day after our last day before, when the toffee-nosed secant-in-command of the Sydney Met. Office reported on the absurd ethereals of the noonsday weather. Doom, and Hailed, as large as rocks, to be the worst whether since Christ upstaged Caesar, not including Willie the Bard. Anyway the secant-in-command's report was instrumented and instrumental, whichever. Later it was to become the tale of the town, the tortilla of the table, the tort in the schools. A resort to a report to end all retorts. It was, and. Hereunder we extract from its what woe wert worse for the weather that next day. It, the report, went, going:

'Sir,
If I, thine servant, did not with mine own eyes See what I must tell thee, may the Earth Itself Cup me for its dreg[1] Whilst the soldiers[2] Yet held back the people, didst a blazing comet[3] Split the he'ens with ill illision that twas Fearful e'en to the bravest heart[4]. On its fiery Tale was a cascata of warriors, each afire,[5] Charging across the vault of the heaven-side. From the hand of a slave[6] master, did a great Flame[7] spring forth yet whenst died out Instant left the creature uninjur'd[8] Then didst a solitary specimen of avibird sweep Monstrous upon the molest'd people dispersif In terror[9] leaving bespattered and gaping Graves[10] where they had but recent stood. Now The sun tipp'd duller'd pale at high day, somuch Wast freakish nature abroad in the fullest[11] That e'en a beast did consume its own bloody heart![12]'

(1)   Reference to his own dark goings onanisms well-nonnied round the feywells of Sydney, so boy-strauss and riotous was the atmosphere becoming all over the city. The weather too!

(2)   The Salvos, so thunderous oomp bah oompbah it was getting outside. Jericho No, jerry echo building up.

(2a) deathening noise, must be a dog storming down.

(3)   Comet supersonic aircraft that did prang a postbox on its vertigo way across the city, indicating just how doomladen the air was becoming outside. Bileblack, SOS, the pilot sossed!

(4)   Starry-eyed boy who stood unflinching right in the path of said Comet SS, so dense the child was in outside form. Insides bursting, too.

(5)   Kerosened by a passing berserker with matches, showing how real violent it was getting outside of doors. Heavens, alighted!

(6)   Black Madam, better known as The Slop of the Cross (or gin Tonia) holding out five digits meaning five ten-spots for a short timer, so black as the ace of paid was it getting outside. Black banging on high!

(6a) dog takes a bit of black gin, hiccoughs, turns dark looks towards rest of the tribe.

(7)   Black Madam meeting weather beaten dick. Strike a light, how raging horned can you get, outside in the open, too? Murky; muck in!

(7a) snooty dog arched highbrow backwards.

(8)   Black Madam, or the gin Tonia, hits twitch-inflicted dick with a hammer then knob-kneed because he was a paltry old fellah, so heavy ladened was the atmosphere with gusty blows. Bopping a whopping!

(9) Fallen bird choking for breath, so turm-oiled and terned-off was the world, naturally. For the birds! It was no lark either.

(10) So spine chilling, some wore grave faces.

(10a) dog thinks of theprick on his conscience.

(11) Gale unleashed, so hideous it had got outside. She was-in bad shape all round. Lipstick gashes!

(12) Reference to a dog that missed its Mark, then tore at its own barrel of jangling nerves, so murderous it had got outside. With your heart in its mouth!

Who could begin to describe that noonsmday's weather? Horses up to their necks in mane. Unmentionable slugs taking over all the theatres. Giant gantries craning over ruins on every street corner. All were not well in the hospitals, either, nor. And,

(smart dog does quickest course to bachelor of science)

all around it had become so dark that two inhobbitants of Sydney in the habits of drinking men did collide head on, scattering piece of nerve wreckage as far as their cars were parked further down the street. Earmarked they were, too. The moon putting in a spurt on its cycle. Owls mopoking around the place owls earlier than was usual. Even the Met. officer's report was still attempting some Restoration, period, going on:

'...wherein all things Natural o'er filled with a cargo of lamentation Didst tear out the pain rending their breast as though grief itself twas too much distress'd.'

Aye, chaos totally unordered, and. Only Amos in fact still in tears in fact, being taken off the train forcibly, to the delight of the train cleaners, knew vaguely Whatfor It Was In The Air; cap I in it, too.

(Heil Dogod or It will stReich you down)

277

Bloodybloodybloodybloody
as Amos barges into Constable Wilkinson's cavity of a cubbyhole
called an office, only by him, and where he, Constable Wilkinson,
still sits to dream of champagne caviars thrown in. To him. On the
Wilkinson apprehension of Mr Fie Do Bigs, still at lurch
somewhere, not here but here and there around, around no doubt.
It's not that

atomy Amos enters so much, but that he rattles on the threshold. A
deadly silence, boneshuddering. Beckoning to Constable
Wilkinson, too, with what looks like a thirst-ridden dingo fore-
paw and in thrust. With, now, Constable Wilkinson's stunned
lapels, both, being kerfuffled with those thirst-ridden dingo fore-
paws that have turned out to be really monkey wrenches. The tips
of his and

his nose touching, both, eye-bowl to highball. It's a terrible thing
to see to have suddenly burst into your office, it going gaagaa gaa
sounding like *bloodybloodybloody*. Or spit boiling over, especially
when you're sure it's Old Dogdeath Itself come to put the final
touch to your allround personality. Now death-dealing a dance on
your fashionable lapels like as if It had.something Vitus to say to
you, other than

(dog show --another open day at the morgue)

police car rrmm rrrmmms and copsiren sounds. Like an
emergency they should be going to in. Perhaps his own funeral.
Who's his?

(humans; brutes of things to eat)

Through all the halcyon ruses and klondike rushes, outside, the
Jelf has remained a pillow'd strangely haloed in ziz by a pure and
porous white glowlight that has sleepened deeper and depoted him
for the last twenty four houris full of dreamy hours. The Slipping

278

Booty. Endosheens thurifying through that mortal core crashed out by an inner Jelf campfire. Also there,

(sweet fang after lickerish sugar daddy)

Maggie back now and fairly recovered in herself. She has snuck down secretingly, after the Jelformance on her and her Jamroll Sis's various stages of yesterday, to rebutchers if the unbelievaballed was really rooted in reality. And, even now, torn between wonderlook of that pearlywhite halo and wonder-lust about his tomthumbed dick harried. After all, when all has been dazed and done, she has been standing at his side for the last two hours enraptured by the

aurora australy irradiating up from with the Jelfzizz in flagrante delictolight caught. For only her to see. Of allthe sheenpolies of all the multidawnings of all the millipolypyroes of all the polystyrene greens and reds and blazestroamings across her sightboards; of all the lightstrophesheenlines of all the mega-ilmens and the onyxes and the living-jewelliths of the southernymphs; of all the elata latrisplurges and colour-dazzlings that Maggie has ever seen in asking dyes enriching azureallight, they were there. Upithering through the hagiohead olonga Jelfella. Medivival saint encasked and tombowled for his ladylight,

the aurora australuxuriant.

And was Maggie seeing there the whole southern skies lorming up and out from him and vaulting over her awakened and his asleepon, fixing them both with a star's breath taken on sight by to steer. Scintilla of his semble face, flashflouresce of his facefleshy, a southern-essence facefulge. Jelf's. Auroraustral aurora ozlandia aurora auroraflfiatus, for ofdeed was Maggie silent grogging in at Australia halidoming his headrenching quite. Simply. Sorrow too in her hunghead. Why?

(game dog scored the winner)

When, now, all that wuthering out whither was at its height of weathering, and getting so bile black that even the street-walkers ran circles around good men, no body even seemed to notice that other gathering of stormtroopers, wehrmarchting haupt haupt haupt swine-dry eine line, up into a real beaut ambush position that (heh heh) The Numbsk Herrsimian did think up. He did, and alone. Ja, for The

Numbsk, he wreckons, after yestern's littlegotten puschy visit (heh heh) to Alycebitchblackniggerlovingcuntwhore, that right by the coonabo Henry's own stricken door of der koop-up would be the goodie goodest place for tryst with Alycetcetera when dat der blacknigger monkeys' demonstration goes past. Und then therr (heh heh) vill be he, The Numbsk, to tryst herr arm to verbottenness. Rotten of him, and

(dog would like to get acquainted with body of white collar worker; love bites, Genuine)

on herown doorstep (here here). Maybe too he vill get a few more kicksbuttspunchspitzkreigs in on that abo monkey called Henry, i.e., trystan da coona scrawny neck, ja. This is somewhat what he, The Numbsk, is thunking as his troupe, trousers out of trousseaux and their boots out of straps but brand spanking new, clomp their uninterhaupted strides towards wherever their leader says. No question about it, either way. He, The Numbsk, in liedership (swansong, the last word in it!), having taken up the rains, of the cream of the Eagull Corpse criminals, closeknitted like their woolly thinking caps Still the dark cloud cover, komen doom low, too:
dark, dark
the sound of
having a lark

taken alive

(unlucky gambler euchred by a dog trick, taken)

Jelf still sleeps stilly illiquated into yslandiaurora, nor has. The fabuluce dimmcdatall. Now, while it be pitched-battle black outside, in here the orielled niche remains rainbowed before the living austart solsoul from within him. Even Maggie's wondrous face is all alit by the reflex alight echoloured into a maggie mahatma. For what is now sheening through the Jelface is a swatch of Oz ys landia fatima fatima... of the blackbird and the k'burra riddlelife rustlelaughter rendledition unquayd the quookaburro, the animalus the menos the yslandiaOz meansong soulrise. This uprose from the Jelfsoul. Of the Pulsensations of weanings emustridents cadencing cadenzas of aurora lightupither waves. These uprising to her from the Jelfessence. Of the sonance resonations abreacting succulant from out of the gum eubeau eucalled euphonema eusyndrous euro eufested eufolded eugreenleaf eucalypt whishwhish tinseltender roundersong. That uprose from the Jelf medium. Of the shloombrilliance of the surfed sea tiltinged with waverowed waveluxlongs of diffroe'd rainbrought sclaff smers coloursmears you-are-here down toeing the downy sandsafety of the white rosesol the omnium mmmmm that time long ago did you upmerge from, opoptic weary-eyed and watery for the sight styme of this land, this yslandia. This too roseated up from Jelfessence to her. Of the essencession of the wedged tail and wended when did you lookookaburround and in sightanger saw the greenturtled lazed upon the beach pacificoma. This, too, was in uprise to her from watching him. Him graced him chrestos him chosen him auroraided alight and alighted upon him christostolen. Yes.

When, then, was he himself wokedawake by the bursting joy of the kookaburleta choralling newdawn from within the chorograde of his own aurora lucent beard. He uplifted his eyelids, lighting up his own persuader, for to seehearfeel-smellteasingly taste and innerknow it and her and. They were, both, too asteeped in the silent gleeding of their austral greeting. Aye to aye. So sad to said to have seen, and lost. *Ohm.*

(dog with red eyes fed up with bloody people)

Meantime, too, Constable Wilkinson is mentally sinning against his in-Forced anti-euthanasia stance by thinking longingly of that tombstone writ he once did see glyphed (a sad end to a goodman's litho) out, going:

'Had A Scrape Round The Back With A Wire-Haired Terrier'.

He is. And why he is is why he is. No more musing this, nor muse merdeing, no. But in his ruff-cut way objecting to being landed with this wrung-out old washout in the back seat of his plice car. Stinking hell; CW trying to drive with a WC. Downwind of it too. Who is going like a stuck pig record, going *bloodybloody* and *bloodybloodybloodybloody*, and who surely must be boiling up a buster pretty damned soon if those frenetic twitches on that dingo's face are something to go on. While Amos

shoos shoves shoofs shaffles shpushes on the already pummelled body of our Constable Wilkinson, because his bloodamos pressure is as far up for his Jelfilson as much as it can pneumanly be. For a plumbing atrocity such as he. The poor old

(hound slobbers trouble into man's ear)

codger is in speechless tearfulls not able to cry out what he wants to, and has to prove to prod his point. *Go faster for my Jelfilial.* When, truly, Amos and Constable Wilkinson aren't gogetting on too well toothed together by their nails, no. Actually, toffee nosed at each other. In no uncertain around, around about way. How do you spell a bout?

(husky to make a real mush of you)

It was a long lung inhalatime before Jelf spoke unto Maggie, who is still magnetotally still, and, when he did, it was to break the spell within them both and to convocate, going:

dear maggie my nightmare will pass and did so and then i was standing moonlittered aghasted with a her by the hand i think of Alyce, yes, maggic dear, Alyce, and were we there englancing upon a copse, a bunch of eucliptrees and in that mooncool kiln of trees there were bits of statues of people parts there-here scattered, and. All ablazed and silent about. None moving maggie dear no just being what carvedly they were... a smile a sadfurl a quizzence a quiddine a prideful a prudence a fiercesome a fixedtight a hopesper a despairdawning a dawning light. Aye, but a woman's head in the centre of them all was with piper's pico and catching time and maggie dear she was glancing around in marvless loveloss at a farover shadow where a man's broken head halfturned was blank as stone. Yet then glade unleaf'd the shade and he came to smile sad smile quizz smile cornertipped abit atibbence, one side, the other side at me, yes and no and, i saw then Janus. Janus, i saw he was Janus twofaced biwayed thisthat therehere whereither and. Maggie dear i had seen all that i had come enlife to see,

laughing fate and gruelling fact unflinching sad, and o maggie then i kissed her.'

(gun dog shot off, recoiled)

'So' Maggie hushing a layby for him, spielling out the spell. Quietus now. This day is this die atom is this diadem dimming. Maggie now holds to tipple in his Jelface thou-art-engraced before she swives back to world darkedly through a glass window looking out. To see the HenryAlyce demonstration all goon on, as she does, acoming up the road. *O ohm hymnly.*

(big-jowled old bulldog hanging its chaps around its chops)

Constable Wilkinson has got bogged in a quandoquarry about what he ought to do with poor old loony doing the top of his Yorrick now along the front seat by him. Perhaps crashing bore

283

Point three eight barrel bore in the old nuthead of low caliber. Then call up the callipers. This old freak must be a freak. It isn't

(Marquis de Sade, you can come out; the dog's getting its kicks elsewhere)

only that this old mollusc is going to do a bivalve soon all over Constable Wilkinson's clean interior and his own body exterior. No. And it ain't only that the bloody old indescribable is going to choke himself dribbling like that out of his dobber like he was trying to say something, big deal. And it isn't only that this historical Amould keeps attempting to leap out of the vehicle to throw stones at all the red lights and then making like it was he that threw the stone that made 'em change to green. Nor that the Amos is clubfooting at the accelerator whenever the good Constable Wilkinson takes his own clodhopper off it for to brake. No, for chrissakes.

What is really goating on Constable Wilkinson's go-get is that the old stink keeps chomping his choppers onto Constable Wilkinson's bicepsionals both by way of armlock and jawlock to indicate turn left here with two bites and turn right here with one. When the dirty old dog might have rabies or something.

(jockey doggedly held on)

When allof a sudden clock on the dial, the old boy jerks to rigor stiff, like this is it, stiff coming up, and shudders and squeezes hold of the area that normans call the throat and tears for and tears at, jerkin and junketing like this was the last streamorrhoea of *bloodybloodies* he was pitting against the last throw of the dies. Yes. Causing Constable Wilkinson to flip through his mental manual on how to dispose correctly of unwanted stiffs surgically worth nix. And just when all hale, both in and ex, seems it never is going to be let loose again, the Amosystem somehow shakes itself up. To coin the It to spruke the It to out-with It at longlife last in a blood-cuddling eureka screech, painful, going:

284

'Bloody warned him! Beware the bloody ides of March beware the ideas! Beware the rotten hides that march beware the dogs while they're watching you! Beware all the killing ids marking time beware the ideomongrels beware the idea adders beware the goosesteppers on the trotter beware the noos marking your neck beware the ideomarchers beware! The idiots of smirk beware their fantales my son! My son my son beware beware.'

Then stoppering up again for all time evermore, no more to mouth even a one word more as long as he lived. Which he wasn't, after that, in too much of a mind to. Anyway. Yes, Amosilenced, a real bloody loss.

(dog with eyetooth to see where it is goring)

The HenryAlyce demonstration was of number about thirty besides Alyceanna carrying the banner and Henry. Being twenty-five or so white liblubbers and round about five or so realabos. In round figures. Rounding the corner roundabout now, all, and truly a strange bunch of belchers about the good things of demonstrable life.

The thirty or so whitestuffs each are abannered, each fluttering with a different message to the apo-abo world, since each wanted to be the star turn who knew what the real gripe of the abos was. Not that other smartarsed white bugger next-door. As this massive turn-out struggles its straggle along the street passing by the Jelfhenry appartment block, now. And marching in front is a whitey whriter who's always pushed his way up to the top, providing it was already a push over on someone else's back. Being, this one, Kenny (Ratshit) Griffley with a new hairdo which, unlike his emperor's air, has not been seen around demonstration circles before. On whose banner is the name and address of his recent publisher. And he followed by 'Art' Munro trying to get more Fellini into the whole show by filtering out any marching dearest creature there who even looks normal. But not having a pinch of success in finding anything he could even accuse of ressembling normality, not even by invoking formalism. Followed by a Whole Host of Others who have blazed their prior ways across these pages, not including

(sledge dog needs hammering to get into proper shape)

the abos somewhere in the pageant. But they don't matter. Because not one of those darkies there even knows what he, she or it is there for anyhow. Typical. That nobody told them, though might do, and. That's why they be there as a matter of fact, in case somebody might tell'em. And all being shepherded along by Alyce at the rear, last but not list, carrying her unbending banner, going: MORE BEDS FOR ABO-VIED WOMEN. She bringing up the rare obviously, too. Especially as she passes by the JelfHenry alleyway, when does The

(ex-goodygoody's dog finished with goody goody life)

Numbsk leapzig out from his cunning (heh heh) hidey hole to go 'boo to yoo' at her with a grin more like a grunt flintly given. Whenceupon suddenly Alyce rails her eyes and immediately commenstruates to go ore ore ore chick chick chickadee orchestrating round in running circlettes, clucking: 'The Numbsk! The Numbsk! The Numbsk!' to such good and loud effect that the thirty or so white crusaders immediately embark on another pilgrimage. This time for the good of their own health which improves noticeably as their involvements gather speed. In the other directions. With Ratshit (K) Griffley last scene disappearing within the least vulnerable blubbery folds of scatting 'Art' Munro pretending to be a loin of baby fat on the lam.

As for the five or so realive abobods, they just continue to swag along, like as if they were just going on a walkabo outing. The demmo had nothing to do with them anyway, quite right. Leaving

Henry, feeling enough is enos when he thinks of all The Numbsk's notches nicked into his pride; and also Alyce, going like henny-penny in doubt, rounding around in circles, screaming and shouting *TheNumbsk, TheNumbsk!*; and The Numbsk's Fylfot

286

family grinding their choppers as they ground Henry back into that alley, the other end of which is blocked by a load off their minds at last. Quite impenetrable. The Numbsk's steel caps exercising up, and. Henry steeling himself. A steal. Heh heh.

(modern Man is going to the dogs)

Alyce made a headbuzzing dash at The Numbsk and did frenazi smashereen her fists upon his knot-headed kaiser stummel mit umlout. But he, The Numbsk, only did grizz his teeth and smiled at her by way of promising afters, before he carried on with his military minded stalking of the Henry-coonabo without missing a beat. Save in Henry's heart. She reeled away from him and sought the warmth of the ground again in circles that kept repeating themselves:

'The Numbsk The Numbsk The Numbsk The...!'

Have heard it before, but never drummed out so.

(Dogod, why hast thou paw-shaken me?)

Meanwhile, up in the Jelflophouse, Maggie has already magus'd 'Hey!' when she peepered the start of the pincer movement of The Numbsk's trained troupe below the Jelf-window. Maggie whips her disbelievers back to the Jelframe, still on his back and wallowing lowing in sweet hummingness from those sleepdreams, obviously not caring what she's seen. So she flings her startled opalines back to the window, throws it open as quick as you could say sashcord, to lower her upraised screaming voice to Henry backaboing below:

'Keep out of it, Henry!'

Giving the Jelfeatherbedded such a zapoke of an electrode that he actually yawns mechanically in shock, before going:

'Those decibels, Maggie; do be tintinnabulating heartily elsewhere.'

'HENRY!'

But no Ate no eurinyes or eurinno no Fate to stop what she is englimmering below, and now swinging like a pendulum do does do does between the window and Jelf, all shrike eyes at her core, both, and:

'Jelf!'

'Here i am, Maggie, ears bruised already. But i don't blame you. Actually i was thinking about once upon a time. A young friend of mine. Mere boys were we, and he so scared of sharks...'

'They're bashing Henry!'

'... he wouldn't go in for a swim nohow at all, no, so one night we...'

'HENRY!' Maggie optimist at the optional window again. 'Sssh, Maggie. Anyway, one night we ganged up on him and threw him in off the jetty. As he hit that water there was something bordering on a crying shame and he never came up no more, no...'

'They'll kill him!'

'If they won't, Alyce will, Maggie. Anyway, a few months later they found his left shoe in the belly of a thirty-foot record-breaking shark. Funny thing was...'

'Help Henry!'

'... he'd left a note before he'd left home that night. Said saying, "Goodbye, Mum. I forgive them what they are about to do." Have i told you that before?'

Now Maggie is upon him with fury aforce, shingling him by the beard as though it was a havisham curtain for the candle bier, going:

(bad dog, eat all your Greens)

'He's your friend!' Pound pound nagga nigger eh?

'In peacetime friend he is.' Jelf as it is nodded.

'Coward!' Maggie in magnetic-eyes.

'True.' Jelf as it is Knowed.

'Zombie coward!' O true. 'Baldheaded stupid looking animal zombie dill!' Too true, yes ma'am. 'Google-eyed hunched-back monkey creep dreg animal!' Struth too, and:

'*Lacker*!' Not true ooo, ouch from wayback.

'There's no need to get abusive, Maggie.' But Jelf, now stung to the teeth, which he does lack largely, is, even at this flyspot on the clocked face, at the window enboom-alooming vocals to below:

'Run, you silly bastard, Henry!'

That done, he swings a toothy back to Maggaiety sourpuss'd and, 'Now i bet you thought i was going to go out there, maggie dear.' And makes towards taking another tumbleshine to his cot. Would have, too, only Maggie now in his way switching what is an innocent bread knife off the table, but brandishing as a dangerous dagger for anyone who has a little imagination in his loaf. She is mean for the business, too. 'You use that and you'll never again like what you see in the mirror, no, maggie...'

'I never do anyway.'

Yet her disgust at him has digressed her aggressity. Anyway his friend Henry is probably lying in a ditch like a dog after its cure-

289

all appointment with the vet b'now. She flings the steel away, only accidently narrowly missing his heart, and merely lets the tears roll down her checked uncheek'd, forming a puddle at herfeet. Which hiss ever so feathersomely as though they were cooling on the hard cobbers of cold facts. Maggie don't cry so crystal. The die is in the cast; the cast is at the stage of dying; the stage is staged; all life swings on the unhinged. Maggie! Cry not. Christo not so. Christ's lachrymal from your breasts. It fates; it's a factor.

Yet Maggie cries for what is sighed and delivered, the already souled. And our Jelf shrigs a shug at the sadsight of her. Shunt be long, a moment linger, as he takes that knife to hand, his life, in handsome, trying but to hold back for a moment longer to foment a bit warmer, going:

'Yessssh maggie i'll go i am going; for hasn't there always been an X-marks-Spot called dog on my jugular ever since Dogod did scare the horses that threw my father's coffin out of the back of the hearse? i knew that Dogod wouldst not let it remain. Please notice here that i shrug fateori. All i ask for console grief you'll have pushing me out there to the Feral Fang is that you put on my tombstone: The Sheer Nerve Of The Man Uncovered. Alsolike to say here that...'

That whichhe never did finish. No. For then painstriking the shattered aeromass came the cry of Henry getting the full repertoire of The Numbsk slow and fullstoppingly, aye. A call to the Jelfflying now, to continuum on too. And on and on.

'Henry, coming!' as he was.

(O, poor mankind, created after the liking of Dogod)

The alley the lane the backway the sideshoot the. Quick way out the. Overspill, which happens now to be the Jelf flashed down the stairs, all except the last one. The last stair of all he missed totally on account of a cat's whisker and plunged sideways headlong into the lane. Which would have been a spectacular tackle on The Numbsk and his thugsks if it hadn't missed everyone there. Where

(obese dog eager to meet toothsome dietician)

in that half ovened light, The Numbskulls' shadows grotesquely walanging all over the palling pip of little Henry enmidst them sadly overgroaned and sinking. And his sprawling Jelfriend crying out for Henry and Henry just managing to extract himself for to cry out for Jelfo and of them all only The Numbsk and Alyce with the presents of mind to

(dober man in why don't you?)

launch themselves upon that bread and throat slicer, both perfectly adequately, that has rendered itself up from its Jelfirmgrip by way of the Jelfall at the feet of The Numbsk handsomely handy. Yes. Both The Numbsk and derr whore-harlotschen Alyce vie for it, with Alyce so fizzing out of one of her cartwheeling catawauls that she is at that instance of vantage time a madeyed fuzzball easily whirlwinning the knife handkneestails and all down. And that The Numbsk so

scandalis'd that his bellow'd shock is stunsthetic on all, especially on herself on whom he now places one of his outraged bloodshots. How derr she! Very quietlike he says unto derr whorey herr, going:

'You give that to me. Yorta know better. Yorta know that ladies, even youse slaggybitchwhorelovelybig-sluttycuntedharlots and niggamonkeyblowers like you are, you dirty thing you, orta leave them dangerous things to the he men like me. Gimme, trollmollcunthead. My love, my own'.

Mit hiss hess mitt stretched out within the last frozen moment that friezed all thereabouts. And what does Alyce do? Only quivs beneath his engorged eye; quavs beneath his Iron Cross will. Ibid libido; is this idt? And meekly donors up the bread knife, handle first politely and then free of charge, unto The Numbsk, before being stumbled backwards and bleating from the knee to the breechers that The Numbsk has given her out of a very good measure. And out of the love he has for her in his heat. After which does he swing his terrible reds around onto Henry and fangs something funksomely, ere he quiet simply inserts it unhiltingly into Henry's ribs much to.

Henry's costa. Henry!

Henry, yes. Wolf pack stacked on a card. Henry, oh.

(lap dog just between-mealing)

Henry jacknifed, jacked off with living. Alyce crutching at her creamy, capped off well and good at last, smiling strangely. Jelf trying to scramble upwards towards Henry clawing with wing broken yet heart seen departing. There are crills, there are their cries. You hear? The stormtroupers

doing their bunks for this is not the time for swazticking around joints broken or not, no; even The Numbsk seemed to have been well on the bunkstrasse, doing it pronto, when something must have happened to him. For he stopped dead. He, The Numbsk, did. From full flight to flat foot, too. Perhaps it was Alyce's naked pair of hips that did whoa'd him up short. Perhaps it was the sight and thought of having her opalwinking opened nooky derr at his bootstraps. Or perhaps he, The Numbsk, had just done his dasch in this hound's life. Hoono? For he somehow

(dog picks up the butt end of old fag)

is storpor'd to stooping before Alyce's wade-open funnelway, and is cherubing at it out of his angel's asking eyes, when the Jelform, newly launched, hits him right in The Numbsk guts-of with enough force of wilful intent to knock the bugger off balance. As they say, the bugger they are, the hard they fall for. And even before The Numbsk can cry out 'never mind the soul, Save Our

Body' the Jelfiendish has The Numbsk eggshell within his nutcrackers and does

onsmack it downsmash it asphaltcrash it pound pulp thud cram klunk it pulverand powderise grind mill stunstoneboon-boon mash it beatdown beatup beatout beatbound it abracadabra it, until all that is left is pulp. Which was The Numbsk through and through anyway. The only difference being now it is not so instantly recognisable.

Then silence. Yes. Nature itself seems simply drained and notworth the cork. Only the frail throat bubblings of pirant Henry and the ecstatic whisperings of Alyce, going: 'The-NumbskTheNumbskTheNumbsk' for more maundy, perhaps. And the haemogurglorrhoea from both the murdered Numbsk and his murdator J. Too many lifetimes going psst.

(when you get there, tell 'em Cerberus sent you across)

Jelf fell off The Numbsk and hand'n'knees his abominable and bloody way back to his abo-mine Henry having to heave himjelf up to hoist himself over Alyce's outstretched underpinnings rode and rammed. And as he crawled on his all fours transgoring her two, she viced one of his ankles and did hold. Her beadies tearstruck red with jiminy afar and mating his in slowered under swimming. Twas hushomoans for the last time they spoke together from the hubbub of:

'My God, can't you do anything right?'

'That all you can say, Alyce?'

'If i was a dog, you know what i'd be doing on you?'

'The dog's already beaten you to it, Alyce.'

'But i guess i'll have you back now.'

293

'You've always been too ugly doggo for me, Alyce.'

And what was laquaceous oozing from his eyes must have loosened her grasp on all their rankling and anklings. His ball and chain unlinked. Once and feral.

(Dogod fashions bestial woman back into a rib)

'Henry?' Jelfeeling his azymouth.

'What've you done to me?' Henry feeling Jelfeeling.

'My bread knife.'

'Jesus, a bread knife.'

'It was my fan mail opener, Henry.'

'*Fan* mail opener, Jesus.'

'Lived in hope, you know that.'

'Jesus, Jelf.'

'Jesus, Henry.'

'Jesus.'

'Jesus.'

'Jesus.'

'Jesus christ, Henry.'

'Jeesus, oh jeesus o...' did then die down bent in two forevermore. Yes. Our Henry; died like he lived an abo. Pray why not? Then pray why. And the Jelfeyes, did they come to grief, sparkulent as the stymying stars of a faraway night; the Jelfessence peeling now from out of our coruscant universe growing light year *yesyesyes* away, going:

(Oyes): *toodleloo and tippitybysie all you goddam mad dogs here's where we nitpick sour gripes, yes ayes ohyes ohgod forsure yestime thisyes*

As he left Henry. Jelfrescade cascadent. Step one step over AlycepoorAlyce, accelerating step two step glebing grief glob glob, step three step, over Numbskian skullduggery in this world, step, down this lane, step four step, towards that street, step, i am strooping out, step, i am bowing off, step, stuff it, step, the staff of what, step, the stuff of comedy a joke, step, no joke, step, just stuff that for a lark, step, not worth a lark, step, damn your larks from here thee to there thousame, step, thysame theysame yousame wesame itsome itsameity all, step, he nixes you, step, he call thee prubes, step, he asks thee to close the door behind him, step, whether the passage is worth it, step, whether the room *is*, step, whether to leave is anythinging it, step, whether there is, step, whether there go, step, how flow, step, why mow, step, whence the swelling goes, step, thence are treads, step, whose the hell, step, caving within on nothing-within, stepping, going:
dogod i am step i am
one step
i am two
i am three
i am four
         rowsing cheerdrops &
one step two step i am i am
Ooion

and stepped, but did he acknow it?, altared before the altering of the Constable Wilkinson's car that did come sweetching around the corner just in time to swallow him up. One swallow, at last, reeling in the Jelfair. Aye, with

(native dogs just camp followers)

Amos coming to the wreckscue with his tragic foot upon the accelerator *hurryhurry* for my son my Jelfils my Jelfialial my Jelfolly my Jelflesh. So that the Wilkie couldn't stop entime. Anyroad it do not matter a manna anymore. Heaven hath stopped dishing it out.

(last spurt; dog on last lap)

But hipholster happiklaxon; talk about hip holster happitalk, not in it, for when the good Constable Wilkinson spearheaded his fearful head to lurch around around the bumped bar of his vehicle, he did not see our Jelf at all but, wonders!, Mr Fido Bigs in a very foetal position. And did he ever then whoop-hoops into convulvances not seen outside a sirius circuit ring for many a dogday, yapping yippees and:

'I got him! I got him! I told'em I'd get him!'

then disappeared in cerebrations unteamed. Too, was there still Amos there and he did not have to get out of the car. Too late oh too late, even for all that he had priorganza'd all.

His daughter Maggie coming to his side. But before her arrival, he has slid behind that wagonwheel and is brrm brrrmming in dirge time to the huge grits of crocodiles rolling down the ruts of his last layer of shedding skin. Age old. And, oh a crook old turn. 'Brrmmm. Brrmmm. Brrrrummmmm mmmm rrruuuzzz rrrmmmm...'

(police dog interveining)

Wasn't, no, much of a pooch, but it was a pooch alright. As a matter of fact, it was an Irish colleen by name of Colley Misslainy, and. Its eyes shone green when they came across the Jelform. Struck dumb by Dogod striking it so rich. Didn't have to sniff

296

before this Colley uplifted its cock hatch and squatted for a pleasing time pissing upon our Jelform. Now on the rode, him and it. Just demonstrating what we have been urinurging all along: that the Jelfessence, in its glory, was the very pillar of doggy benevolleyance. Now in squat *ohm* omage to him. *Ohm*age to zero ziztance at this day's end. *Ohm*.

POSTSCRAP'T

Found in a left over Appendix, siriusly:
nasty big dog, ugly great grrrilla. Dogs come up blazoning at sunrise, go down blazing mad at sunset. The dog fullmoon struck on comely sleepwalker. The dog is a daily efemoral. But a long leash is a short lifeline; short leash, a terminal disease. One thing to be swallowed up by life, but another thing to be kept down by a dog. So never let the dog licking your palm get ahead of your lifeline.

Then again: the dog, the craving idol. The dog, idyllick flesh and bones. Then again: a suicide is trying to upset the dog's scheme of things. And who is going to clean up arfter the pad made a mess of? For all dogs go man-ic some time or other; especially those that see their ambitions just up ahead of them. You start a fight with the dog and it's sure to end up licking you. Dog toothache -- homo bone hone. For the dog, homo is where the heart is. For the dog, homo is also where you hang your hate. For some dogs, homo sweet homo enough; for other dogs, homo a little bit too humeruslesss. Then again: the dog always takes some bit between its teeth. If it's the stage of life, then dog has a bitpart, yes.

Then again: mad dog gone into hydatids somewhere and they can't fido him. Had to write on a tombstone, too: Got Caught In Teeth of Gearrrs. Wrot large on another: Got Too Dead Set On His Way. And on another: Diet By Unnatural Causes.

And yet another: Victim Of The Grip. Then again: old sea dog claims savage rights on young wreck. Old sea dog runs to ground on reefer. Sea dog sights man at last; bully for him. Old sea dog slink or swim.

Then going again is: stinking man found with rotten dogs all over his body. But the dog knows human beings are scent from heaven. Maneating dog took a powder, flea'd. Then again: all that litters is not gold. All that litters is not godly. If it litters that's not good. All that litters isn't a puppet mistress. Even the puppydogs of them are forward in coming from behind.

Then again: Confusus, he say, humbled man wow-bowed low from the waist. And here's a warning: don't litter up the countryside. Then again: if the dog has broken its leashold, just be thankful it gave you no rent. If it had, perhaps your epistitch: Old Sea Dog But Embarked On Once Too Often. Or this: He Was Pack Aged Overnight. Or this: Nice Bloke But A Bit Dogma'd. Or this: Dog Catcher Sadly Missed. Or the one scribed: In Memorium To All Euphoric Dog Keepers. Or this: Taken Off While Still Tender. Or even just: Shepherd Shep Herded.

Then again: dogs prize open jaws. Even growing up is just boneing up for the dog. So sail your own barque and pad your own caninoe. For nature-loving dogs love you natural as you are; that's why you've never seen anyone garnish themselves up for a dog. No.

Then again, nature-loving dog gets bark out of its gums. Nature-loving not the word; look how it tries to step over each tree. If it wasn't for dog's piss we wouldn't need rain. And the dog hooked on nature feasts its eyes on you when it gets high on grass. Do dogs jaw on your nerves? Why? Isn't the dog man's bestial friend A dog is man's best fiend, too. And there was that tombstone going: Lain Doggo.

Then again, dogs love anusied balls. Ugh. When the dog starts pulling your leg, it's no joke. Your dog will have a lump in its throat when you've gone. Bloody cheek of the maneating dog is the very bloody chap of the old chopping bloke. Then again: it's going to miss you as its source of food when you're all gone. Like seen in a newspaper: watch dog to meet punctual lady under own pad. Though most dogs do appreciate the fact that man takes some beating in good taste.

Then again: if dogs ever have a revolution it will be because they've been whipped up. Whoever you are, rich man, poor man, beggar man, or thief... there is a dog that will find you just right. And no matter who you are there's a dog waiting just for you. And waiting. And waiting. In another newspaper; gnatty dog would like to meet gentle tailor man for fun and... a hem! In another, the ad. read: fire dog wants to be switched on by sexy electrician, own fireplace. In another it went: old sea dog would like flogging with a cat of nine tails.

Then again: the poor stray bitch was beaten to a pup. In a personal column: stray dog seeks one-track mind; meat eater. Then again: when the dog takes off with a bone, start counting the costals. Two arfs make a whole maneater. It takes a bull dozer to pack it all down tyke. So doze all sleeping dogs into the ground. Seen in an adv, too: old pederast dog to enjoy a little sniffter now and again. Dogs are no better than plain animals, no they're not. As the newspaper carried: healthy dog would like to meet worm to share the human delights of inside human sport.

Then again: seen on a tombstone: The Dog Worms Finished Him Off. Yes, the worms are waiting for each and every one of us at the end of the dog's trachea. You cry wolf and the whole pack might come down on you. Then again: the french poodle got so angry it done its La Nana. The racing greyhound ridden with fleas. Also the dog hangs onto your life ferociously by the very skin of its teeth. And who did say that dogs do not shit, they just have bowwowel movements? Then again: the dog has teeth like tombstones. Somewhere there is a dog with teeth like tombstones that have your name written all over them.

Dogs talk?; they're too busy jawing over you. When the dog wants to get something across, it mouths it right enough. So don't say caio, it's chow. And don't think the population explosion is anything but stockpiling for the dog. Cities becoming so overcrowded that they are getting beyond the wildest dreams of the dog. Then again: those chows sitting down to human flesh are at their most pecking-ease. Nor does the dog care what condition you're in as long as it's fair, wear and tear.

But then again: if you're out of puff it makes life much easier for the dog. Lone dog pulls itself, got no lead. And seen late at night: flea at a dog's home looking for a shake-down. Then again: a human being would find conditions in a dogs' home really killing.

There was the chink pug that felt jaded in there. And, too, if a dog snout is wet you can guess where it's been.

There's always been a dog sniffing around the annals of history. Then again: pet mince, Take Away Fido. Then again there are dogs that get relief just hanging out around trees. Seen in a Personal Column: busy watchdog wants to meet similar for midnight relief. Then again: there was the Dal-martian that said take me to your lead. Then again there was the dejected leader who shrugged 'take me' to the dog coming from out of space. The dog lifts its leg with each step. It's a dog's life; every little thing is vetted. Then again: very old sea dog pooping out on the deck. Life is just a debarkle really. Dear old Faithful, it remained Fido all its life.

Then again: Hiawoofer, big chief coyote. Then again: once a dog called Noah boarded two tree roots in one go, but he was pissed. Then again: Old Shep is gone where the good doggies go, so Old Shep was just a myth too. The bloodhound bitch got too gorge-ous for words. So never hightail it or the dog might think you're the party it's been sniffing around for all its life. And give you a parting gesture. The dog is just a homo sap.

Then again: dogging the human body is the hunting dog that got the hare lip; and the fat dog that got the funny glands. Honour they father's kennel. Even if a dog gets really under your skin. Gay dog fancy man. Then, too, if the dog has its dfog-lamps on you, it is in danger of losing sight of its goal. The inner lights in the dog are definitely not good noos, no. Even the blind dog will take a shine to you when you're unsighted. Incurables, too, take their dogs out for a bite to eat at night. Then again, the dog strains all your goodness through fine jawse. O, life is a merry-go-horround horround horround horround!

Being sirius for the last time:
The crisp brown fox fried over the lazer dog. Then again: jump quick; the brown dogs are foxing over-lazy. Sly fox, undercover dog. It has to be a dog's life; it certainly isn't your own. The dog is that animal that is bound to take your life. The dog pack ran all

over the little old lady who lived in a shoe; no fairy story for her either. Little Miss Moffart last seen on a tuffet; must have been curr'd away. So put two dogs in the fire tonight. Because the only time the dog will reject you is when it spits you out, Pip. As a tombstone said: Done In By Some Bounder. Another way is to prolong a dog nap eternally. Or you could put the dog to sleep before dark this very night. Then again: the dog eats grass too; you're not all it needs. When the dog *is* eating grass, the only difference in its condition from its normal condition is that your condition doesn't matter. Anyway, just what *are* the dog's conditions? Fat dog show you the most obesiance. Starving dogs show you they don't care who you are. Fed-up dogs just show you lip. Hang dog dangle you and your affections on a string. Playful dogs will tend to toy with you first. Snarling dogs want you to turn your bacon them. Skinny dogs will take any nutrition you can give. Homeless dogs will try to drag you outside. Mad dogs go around trying to break into asylums. Faithful dogs have a vested interest. Then there was the dog that went out for a romp steak. So you should have learnt by now this --never to gambol with the dog; the odds are teeth to one. O St. Bernard, prey for us. Dogod will heel even sinners. Kingdom come! it's Dogod! So

have old faithful in Dogod, the one true Gurrrru. O yipes. *Ohm.*

(bit off the old block, now after chip. Goodbye, Mr Chip).

302

www.ingramcontent.com/pod-product-compliance
Lightning Source LLC
Chambersburg PA
CBHW070224260626
47160CB00002B/677